PENGUIN MODERN CLASSICS

Selected Short Stories

GOPI CHAND NARANG (1931–2022) was a leading Urdu scholar and critic who made seminal contributions to literature, literary criticism and linguistics. He was president of Sahitya Akademi (2003–2007) and was awarded Padma Bhushan in 2004.

SURINDER DEOL is an author and a literary translator. He has published translations of Urdu poets such as Ghalib, Mir Taqi Mir, Sahir, Faiz and others.

RAJINDER SINGH BEDI

Classics of Modern Indian Literature

SELECTED SHORT STORIES

EDITED AND TRANSLATED BY
Gopi Chand Narang
Surinder Deol

PENGUIN BOOKS

An imprint of Penguin Random House

PENGUIN BOOKS

USA | Canada | UK | Ireland | Australia
New Zealand | India | South Africa | China

Penguin Books is part of the Penguin Random House group of companies
whose addresses can be found at global.penguinrandomhouse.com

Published by Penguin Random House India Pvt. Ltd
4th Floor, Capital Tower 1, MG Road,
Gurugram 122 002, Haryana, India

Penguin
Random House
India

First published in Penguin Books by Penguin Random House India 2022

Copyright © Original Urdu Text: Veena Bedi 2022
Copyright © English Translation: Gopi Chand Narang, Surinder Deol 2022

ISBN 9780143455073

Typeset in Adobe Caslon Pro by Manipal Technologies Limited, Manipal
Printed at Thomson Press India Ltd, New Delhi

www.penguin.co.in

MIX
Paper
FSC FSC® C010615

Contents

Editors' Note   vii

Part I: THE ART OF THE STORY

1. On Being Bedi's Melody Maker
   by Gopi Chand Narang   3
2. With Hands Chopped Off by Surinder Deol   16
3. A Creative Process by Rajinder Singh Bedi   32
4. In Front of the Mirror by Rajinder Singh Bedi   42

PART II: SELECTED SHORT STORIES

1. Give Me Your Sorrows   57
2. Quarantine   87
3. Lajwanti   100
4. Mangal Ashtika   116
5. Kalyani   130
6. The Woollen Coat   143
7. The Scars of Smallpox   155

8. A Father for Sale   165

9. Jogia   180

10. Rahman's Shoes   202

11. Babbal   214

12. For a Cigarette   244

13. Maithuna   275

14. The Trauma of a Lost Child   289

15. The Tall Girl   306

Editors' Note

Munshi Premchand wrote over three hundred stories and fourteen novels. Sa'dat Hasan Manto produced twenty-two collections of short stories, five series of radio plays and three collections of essays. Krishan Chander, the most prolific of all, authored thirty-four collections of stories and wrote fifty novels. Rajinder Singh Bedi penned less than eighty stories, one novelette, and two collections of plays compared to these writers. However, he achieved a venerable place for himself in the history of Indian literature because of his work: an oeuvre that covers tales of human joys and suffering in poignant prose. His artistic construct deeply touches the reader. He talks of aspirations and hidden cravings that people carry in their hearts from birth until their death. His portrayal of interpersonal relations that hang in balance by a brittle thread reminds us of the danger of losing something quickly and how hard it is to repair it, once it is broken. He is the chronicler of feelings and emotions that help people make sense of their lives. He used his mythic creativity to enter the inner psyche of women who have been deprived of their rights as human beings. Every story written by Bedi depicts a world that is unique in many respects. Although these things might be alien to our own experiences, the plot's best and worst features look familiar. His characters are always living and breathing human beings who exude a smell of the soil. They give us the feeling of acquaintanceship and closeness that is down to earth. He is the only writer among his contemporaries who can paint the colours of basic human drives through a combination of ordinary words to suggest spontaneous opposing emotions. It works like magic and leaves the reader engrossed and stunned.

When we decided to produce this anthology, it was not easy to limit the coverage to fifteen stories. While we are delighted with what we have included, we have also encountered heartache with what we had to let go. The good news is that we have stories in this volume like 'Give Me Your Sorrows', 'Lajwanti', 'Quarantine', 'Jogia', 'The Woollen Coat' and 'Rahman's Shoes'—the essential part of Bedi's oeuvre, stories for which he is best remembered. Besides, we have two essays by Bedi in which he tries to define his identity and self-reflects on the art of story-writing. In short, here is the book that can provide discerning readers hours of delightful reading and a peep into the human domain of love, aspirations and life's paradoxes that Bedi's imagination created and what he observed and encountered in his life.

A word about the translation: unlike Krishan Chander, who weaves poetry into his prose for the reader's enjoyment, Bedi keeps his poetic talent hidden and unmasks it in tiny droplets as the story unfolds and the characters confront issues that pose a challenge to their existence. We have taken care to capture and express this subtle poetic touch of the author in our translation. Also, Bedi is quick to use the earthy idiom in which his characters live and survive. The stark examples are to be found in 'Kalyani' and 'The Scars of Smallpox'. The modulations of this localized environment are hard to express in another language. We have tried our best to retain its subtle uniqueness.

We want to express our gratitude to Bedi's younger brother, Professor Harbans Singh Bedi, and his granddaughter, Ila Bedi, for providing us insights into the writer's life, who was by any measure an exceptional artist and a compassionate human being. We hope that this collection of stories will earn its rightful place as a Classic of Indian Literature.

Gopi Chand Narang
Charlotte, North Carolina

Surinder Deol
Potomac, Maryland

May 2022

Part I

THE ART OF THE STORY

1

On Being Bedi's Melody Maker

GOPI CHAND NARANG

zabaan p baar-e khudaaya y kis ka naam aaya
k mere nutq ne bose meri zabaan ke liye

I don't know whose name
crossed my tongue, O God!
The words that poured out
started to kiss my lips.

Ghalib wrote the above couplet for an enlightened friend in
one of his most scintillating ghazals. It comes to my mind
as I think of Rajinder Singh Bedi, both as a friend and as
an exceptional short-story writer. I acquired a love for Urdu
literature at an early age due to my father's influence, who
often talked about his passion for Urdu and Persian books
and his favourite authors. Before partition, I was a high
schooler and I spent most of my spare time in the library
poring over literary journals like *Adab-e Latif* and *Adabi*

Duniya. The Progressive Writers' Movement, started with
a lot of fanfare during the mid-1930s, had given rise to
a whole new class of highly gifted poets and short-story
writers. The moment was ripe, and the movement, as if
touched by a hidden spark, spread like wildfire throughout
India. Undoubtedly, the 1940s became the most exciting
time for the Urdu language as it was going through a blazing
literary renaissance.

After Munshi Premchand, three names dominated the
scene in the world of short Urdu fiction. They were like a
triumvirate—Krishan Chander, Sa'dat Hasan Manto and
Rajinder Singh Bedi. In the beginning, I liked Krishan
Chander because he wrote the most beautiful poetic prose.
He was also the most prolific producer of romantic fiction and
wrote about big subjects like the Bengal famine, poverty and
the oppressed masses' deprivation. Manto attracted me for
his depiction of unforgettable characters, especially exploited
women who lived on the margins of society, making a living by
selling themselves. Bedi was someone who was still not at the
centre of my intellectual curiosity. However, things changed
after partition when I had time to read Bedi's text attentively,
digging deeper with critical insight and understanding his
creative mystique. In this process of rediscovery of Bedi, I
must admit that two people whom I greatly admired might
have played a silent role. Professor Al-e Ahmed Suroor wrote
a short paper on 'Urdu Afsana'. He praised Bedi's style of
writing and his characterization, which was mainly focused on
rural Punjab. Second, Professor Mohammad Mujeeb, Vice-
Chancellor of Jamia Millia Islamia, who was so impressed
by Bedi's writing that he used to roam around the campus,
clutching Bedi's first book *Daana o Daam*, under his armpit,

introducing Bedi to the faculty and the postgraduate students as 'India's Anton Chekhov'.*

Let me digress a little bit and talk about the origins of what came to be known as 'Urdu Afsana'. India is a land of *Katha Sarit Sagara*, Panchatantra and the Jatakas. Our folklore is replete with tales such as *Tota Kahani, Vikram Chaalisi* and *Baitaal Pachhisi*; some of which had travelled to the Middle East and was absorbed in the *Alf Laila (A Thousand and One Nights)*, a collection of Middle Eastern folk tales told every night by the princess Scheherazade to the newly wed cruel king to save her life. The storytelling later expanded to the oral tradition of *dastan*. By the end of the nineteenth century, a sizable collection of these dastans was available in book form in Persian and then in Urdu that achieved great popularity. Some of the Urdu transcreated works that deserve a mention are *Baagh o Bahaar, Fasaana-e Ajaa'ib, Fasaana-e Azad*, and of course, the voluminous *Dastan-e Amir Hamza* and *Tilism-e Hosh Ruba*.

Later, the genre of novels started to appear in Urdu due to European influence. Deputy Nazir Ahmad and Abdul Haleem Sharar wrote novels that became popular. Still, novel writing never became a significant part of Urdu fiction, except for *Umrao Jan Ada* by Mirza Hadi Ruswa, which was published in 1899.

Munshi Premchand laid the foundation of modern novels and short-story writing both in Urdu and Hindi. His last novel *Godan*, published towards the close of his short life and

---

* Interestingly, Bedi in his presidential address at the Jamia Millia Islamia Fiction Seminar (in 1980) jokingly said that he would be more pleased if people in Russia started calling Chekhov as Rajinder Singh Bedi of Russia.

sudden death, is universally considered the first masterpiece of Hindi–Urdu fiction in the twentieth century. His stories, deeply rooted in the social and cultural milieu, reached a broad audience. As a result, many new story magazines such as *Dilgudaz* and *Zamaana* appeared, giving new writers a platform to publish their work. The real momentum was provided by the instantaneous popularity of Premchand's first short-story collection, *Soz-e Watan*, which was rendered to flames by the British authorities for its patriotic themes. His last story 'Kafan' (The Shroud) that was published posthumously in 1936—the year after he had inaugurated the Progressive Writers' Movement—is a classic of Hindi–Urdu fiction. The encouragement to write short stories also came from movement leaders like Sajjad Zaheer and Rashid Jahan. They themselves were behind the publication of an anti-imperialist and socialistic short-story collection titled *Angaare* that was published in 1933. The book was condemned and burnt down by reactionary elements. The triumvirate, which I mentioned earlier, was the fruit of the tree that was planted at the start of this movement. Though tragic in every respect, India's partition was the seed that flourished in numerous short stories that greatly touched readers' hearts and minds, especially Manto's stories such as 'Toba Tek Singh' and 'Thanda Gosht' (The Cold Flesh), and Bedi's 'Lajwanti'.

I went to the University of Wisconsin–Madison, on my first assignment in 1963. During the first year, I taught an introductory Urdu course that provided me with the opportunity to do my reading for devising new teaching materials as there was nothing available. I picked up Bedi's two books *Daana o Daam* and *Grehan* for an in-depth reading during this period. I can say that it was in Wisconsin that my romance (*i'shq*) with Bedi began. During the second year, I taught an advanced Urdu course that allowed me to teach passages from Bedi's stories as examples of good modern fiction writing. During the same year (1964), *Nuquush* magazine from Lahore published Bedi's outstanding story 'Apne Dukh Mujhe De Do' (Give Me Your Sorrows) and soon thereafter a novelette titled *Ek Chaadar Maili Si* (A Sheet, Soiled and Sullied). Reading these pieces with stories like 'Garam Kot', 'Grehan' and 'Lajwanti' shook me. I felt it opened my inner self to a new world of characterization, especially the mysterious world of a woman's passages from one role to another. I was deeply touched to write a soul-stirring article with a revealing thesis about Bedi's *afsana nigaari* (story telling) that was published in *Nuquush* in 1965 and in *Aaj Kal,* New Delhi, the following year.

The thesis that I presented in my article, which got excellent traction in later years, was that the roots of Bedi's deep structured fiction lie hidden in India's mythic folklore like Ramayana, Mahabharata and Shaivite Himalayan culture. The habit of finding the inner meaning in the outer reality gradually took Bedi into the realm of mythic suggestion, symbolism, metaphor and allusion—in other words, the highly creative use of home-grown language with a mix of dialectical small-town subaltern culture. The signs of these early stirrings can easily be discerned in his first two collections of stories, *Daana o Daam* and *Grehan.* And with time, Bedi made a more innovative and highly creative and ingenious use of these treasures in the depiction of everyday customary events. In 'Rahman's Shoes', one shoe overriding the other is a warning of a journey in the offing, maybe a journey from this world to another. Bedi thus depicts an inner meaning from a prevalent social belief or superstition. In 'Apne Dukh Mujhe De Do', the female protagonist's name (Indu) means full moon, which takes time to gradually reach its zenith—the embodiment of love and beauty. It provides the sap of life to fruits and lends colour to flowers. It invigorates the blood and makes the soul more pervasive. Indu is also called *soma*, the divine manna of old love and the elixir of life without which life cannot exist. Indu is paired off with Madan, another name of Kamadeva, the Greek Eros' counterpart, the God of Love. In one place, Bedi has also referred to Indu as Rati, an affinity with Kamadeva. In the Rig Veda, Kamadeva has been regarded as the primal micro-organism of mind, the basis of all creation. In the Greek pantheon, Eros and Cupid also have a parallel connection. It would appear as if the characters' very names in the story suggest the creative and destructive elements that restore equilibrium in the cosmos' creative process. One wonders how pervasive Bedi's reading might have been and what an avid reader he must have been right from his early years.

In 'Lajwanti', Bedi drew upon the washerman's down-to-earth episode and Janak Dulari Sita's fate from the Ramayana. In 'Jogia', he played upon a range of colours to create variegated psychological effects. In 'Babbal', the female character is associated with Draupadi of Mahabharata in yet another seminal context. Babbal himself is the naughty Krishna who saves the young Draupadi from Darbari's lustful overtures. In 'Lambi Larki' (The Tall Girl), one gets a clue to the story's meaning from the recitation of the seventeenth chapter of the Bhagavad Gita. The boat of granny's life finds its moorings immediately after the girl's marriage.

The metaphorical and mythical elements are of primary importance in Bedi's art. Quite often, his stories' inner structure is based on allusions drawn from the ancient Indian pantheon. But at the same time, it would be far from the truth to infer that Bedi consciously raised the superstructure of his stories on these foundations. There is something spontaneous about his creative process for the layered structure to evolve itself as if on its own, taking an unconscious inventive clue from these mythological allusions. Both go hand in hand, one taking its inspiration from the other. Bedi's creative process seems to be something like this: he tries to delve into the fathomless mysteries and secrets of life and a woman's inner world through his characters' psychological build-up. He does not look at the natural disposition of human beings, their instincts, the sensual demands of the body or the spiritual urges of the soul, at the superficially blank and obvious conscious level; rather his mind goes deep into the mysteries of human relationships.

Generally, he goes to their subconscious depths, which have the ring and archetypes of centuries behind them. In Bedi's writings, an event is not an isolated event but is linked in an unbroken chain of countless events, and all carried forward in one sweep. Since in this creative process, his journey is from the concrete to the abstract, from the event to the limitlessness of action, from the finite to the infinite, or from the mundane to the metaphysical, he again and again resorts to metaphor, symbolism, mythology and copious references to the Indian pantheon.

Bedi's creative process is different from Krishan Chander's and Manto's. Krishan Chander stays at the surface. His agenda is given, direct and obvious. Manto was saved by his penetrating eye to look behind the events through the filth in red-light districts.

But Bedi is different from both since his feet remain grounded, while his head soars in the sky. Bedi's style is complex and thought-provoking. His similes are not single or double but many-faceted, and his characters are multidimensional, whose one aspect is real and the other archetypal. Time and space have no bearing in the conventional sense in his creative process. In his psychology, one sees the shades of millennia of human thought. In this respect, a moment stretches itself into centuries, and a small house encompasses an entire universe. Bedi's men and women are not bound down to the present time. Still, they represent the primeval men and women who have been undergoing human suffering for aeons and simultaneously enjoying the boon provided by this earth. Due to Bedi's multitrack metaphors, his characters' problems, loves, hates, joys and sorrows are not just their own as individuals. In them, one can also see the sufferings of humanity and the feelings and emotions which have been their lot from times immemorial. These metaphysical overtones, which lend his stories a kind of universality, are his art's main characteristics.

A few words about Bedi's writing system as a context: it has become common these days to eschew direct narration and use language at a purely imaginative level. This trend can be termed as a shift towards oblique expression, which is in opposition to the traditional realist-direct styles. The styles of Premchand, Manto, and Krishan Chander can be described as forming part of direct expression tradition. Among the contemporary story writers, some favour the style of direct expression in the bulk of their writing though they have also used the oblique or the allegorical style in some of their stories. We can mention the names of Ram Lal and Joginder Paul, among others. Simile-laden prose is characteristic of Krishan Chander, which is gradually disappearing. It is in this context that the heritage of Bedi assumes greater significance. The language of the Urdu short story has now come closer to lyricism. By the language of lyricism is not meant the florid romantic language used by Krishan Chander. This language is no doubt elegant, but it lacks depth. In today's short story, poetic language implies language that uses symbolism, suggestion, metaphor, allegory and the like. It uses myths, motifs, beliefs and folklore to discover new ways of expression.

I have vivid memories of a seminar on Modernism that Professor Al-e Ahmed Suroor organized at the Aligarh Muslim University in 1967, the intervening period between my first and second assignment at Wisconson. I was invited to present a paper along with other scholars. I stayed at the University Faculty Club. To my surprise, I was joined there by a younger-looking Shamsur Rahman Faruqi, whose magazine *Shab-Khuun* had just started appearing from Allahabad. It seemed that Faruqi liked to travel like a colonial official as he brought with him his butler, who ironed his outfit, polished his shoes and prepared fresh orange juice for him in the morning. As a courtesy, he extended his butler's services to take care of my needs as well, especially as I enjoyed having a glass of fresh orange juice in the morning. The seminar was a great success. My paper on Bedi got a rousing reception. Faruqi was not pleased with my assessment of Bedi as a leading and highly innovative Urdu short-story writer. Bedi, being a native Punjabi speaker, in Faruqi's view, was not *ahl-e zabaan* (not a master of the language as a non-native speaker). We got into a lively discussion. My point was that writing is a creative process. All writers make imaginative use of language depending on the narrative's situation, creative fire and the lingual structure used by the main characters, whether the writer is an *ahl-e zabaan*. I mentioned scores of names of *ahl-e zabaan* Urdu writers whose work had not received even a single nod. On the other hand, Punjab had produced writers like Allama Iqbal, Manto, Krishan Chander, Faiz, Nasir Kazmi, Munir Niazi, and many others who spoke Punjabi as their mother tongue, yet their mastery of the Urdu language had reached Himalayan heights. Faruqi was speechless, and I did not press the point any further.

As Bedi settled in Bombay (now Mumbai) after partition and got into the movie industry in multiple roles, as a screenwriter, a dialogue writer and a film director, he got busy with his film work. He achieved great success but also faced some difficult times. Of Bedi's two closest friends (writer Baqar Mehdi and the *Times of India* editor Sham Lal), I knew Baqar well. I had to go to Bombay for some business (it was 1971 or 1972) when Baqar insisted that I should meet Bedi because the latter had often expressed his wish to meet me. I was flattered when Baqar told me that Bedi repeatedly said that 'Narang was the only literary critic who has discovered me through my work. He has looked into even those spots which I was not aware and that he was like my *naghma-nigaar* (melody maker).'

Bedi came to see me at my hotel, carrying a whiskey bottle wrapped in an old newspaper. Besides Baqar, K.A. Abbas, Majrooh and Sardar Jafri also joined this meeting. We spent a lively evening talking about a whole host of topics, including some delightful stories about people who were not present. Bedi was at his best when he told his unvarnished Punjabi jokes. Some months later, during another trip to Bombay, both Baqar and Bedi came to the airport to receive me. Bedi drove me to my hotel in his Fiat car. We had an equally delightful lunch meeting the next day. During these encounters, I came to know Bedi as a person and had a glimpse of his life story.

Bedi was born into a family of modest means, and at a very young age, he was required to assume the role of a householder after his mother's death, taking care of an ageing father and younger siblings. He had no ambition to be a writer, but the skill came naturally to him. He followed this passion while discharging other domestic responsibilities, but he never separated himself from the social, economic and cultural milieu in which he was raised. Instead of writing romance novels divorced from reality, that could have helped him financially, he centred on the best thing he could do—to keep his focus on common men and women who struggled with complex issues of life and death daily. These were the people he knew from his contacts, or he had seen them with his eyes—human beings caught up in circumstances that they neither controlled nor were able to alter substantially. Although he was published by the most prestigious literary magazines and his books remained in good demand, he never yearned to gain any academic establishment accolades. He earned fame and financial security, but he never lost his modesty, humility, simplicity, fairness and decency.

In 1974 I took over as head of the Urdu Department at Jamia Milia Islamia University. Within a short time, I wanted to have a large gathering of Urdu writers, something the university deserved to have, but it never materialized. In 1980 with a small grant of Rs 10,000 at my disposal, I launched an Indo–Pak Seminar on Fiction Writing in Urdu, to coincide with the birth centenary of Munshi Premchand. It was nothing short of a miracle that with the small amount at my disposal, I was able to gather every great living Urdu fiction writer from Lucknow, Aligarh, Bombay, Hyderabad, Ahmedabad and other places in India. With a grant support from the Pakistan's Academy of Letters, I was able to invite two distinguished writers from Pakistan—Intezar Husain and Vazir Agha. P.V. Narasimha Rao, who later became India's prime minister, inaugurated the seminar. Most attendees were unaware that Rao was a fluent Urdu and Persian speaker who had earned his bachelor's degree from the Arts College at Osmania University. He had begun his professional life not as a politician but as a short-story writer. He recited one of his stories in his address that greatly touched the audience. Although he was not in good health, Bedi travelled for the seminar from Bombay, and as a session chair, he read with comments his lively essay titled 'Haath Hamaare Qalam Hue' a title borrowed from a couplet by Ghalib, for which he received a standing ovation. After the seminar's conclusion, I invited Bedi with a group of some discerning writers like Baqar Mehdi and Waris Alvi for lunch at my residence. My wife Manorma and I have delightful memories of that day, especially Bedi's hilarious comments that made the afternoon unforgettable.

Later in the evening, when I drove Bedi to his hotel at Connaught Place, he asked me to stay for a while, and we had some drinks and dinner. We stopped the car near the Outer Circle because he wanted to have a paan from a shop that he might have visited before. I parked the car, and we walked together. Bedi gave elaborate instructions about the kind of paan he wanted to have. I told him that I was not a paan eater, but he insisted that I make a one-time exception. He got me a *meetha* (sweet) paan with kneaded rose petals. It had no intoxicating substance in it, but for a reason that I can't explain, I felt somewhat high. We sat on a nearby bench to diminish the effect of intoxication, and Bedi, as was his nature, came up with jokes and stories that made me laugh non-stop. That was our last meeting. Bedi had a habit of having zarda (tobacco)-laced paan with some substance that might have been affecting his health.

As I write this many years later, I am overcome with memories of my brief but intellectually intense encounters with Bedi, and I am reminded of a couplet of Sauda, a contemporary of Mir Taqi Mir.

saaqi hai ik tabassum-e gul fursat-e bahaar
zaalim bhare hai jaam to jaldi se bhar kahien!

Saaqi, the springtime is already here –
How fleeting and momentary!
Don't be cruel. Fill my glass quick, really quick.
The spring lasts only as a bud turns into a rose!

People like Bedi come once in a while, and their creative lives face many hurdles. Sometimes, the passion and the ecstasy of their spirit consume them. But as long as they live, they leave an indelible mark and never fail to enrich the lives they touch. His song was his own creation, and he sang it so well.

2

With Hands Chopped Off

SURINDER DEOL

likhte rahe junuun ki hikaayaat-e khuun chakaan
har chand is mein haath hamaare qalam huye

As punishment for defiance,
the oppressor chopped off my hands.
I kept on writing with blood,
raising my voice in dissent.

The imagery presented in the above couplet by Mirza Ghalib is horrifying. Blood is dripping, and the hands of the speaking voice have been chopped off. This happened because the person raised the voice against oppression and tyranny. For someone faithful to his or her creed, telling the truth is essential. This is a grand metaphor for the freedom of the human spirit. The echoes of this couplet are found in Faiz Ahmed Faiz's revolutionary poetry; he spent years in Pakistani prisons for a trumped-up conspiracy charge. The military regime continued to torment him all his life. Rajinder Singh Bedi wasn't sent to jail by the state, but he led a life that was filled with suffering. Supporting younger siblings while he was a teenager worthy of support by an elder, being uprooted during partition, working in an environment filled with lack of financial stability, heart-breaking angst caused by failed personal relationships, traumatizing events in the later part of his life and failing health because of a stroke and cancer. The oppressor in his case was probably 'luck' or some unexplainable fault in the criss-cross of his stars.

In a confessional essay titled *Haath Hamaare Qalam Hue,* published in 1974, Bedi wrote, 'I had no idea that I would be called upon to appear before my readers as someone who had sinned and that I would be required to confess sins that I had not committed. Or I had committed them because I had the ability of an artist to carry them out . . . Confession is a delicate matter. I'm an honest person. That's why whatever I say will be truth, nothing but the truth. God might be present or absent. Please don't infer that I'm an atheist. If you don't believe in God that means you don't believe in yourself . . . People believe a sin is committed first and then comes the confession. But I belong to a tribe of sinners who confess first, and then, when no one is looking, they silently write a short story.' Writing a story was the sin that he committed time and again.

About his birth, Bedi wrote satirically, 'According to Mahakavi Tagore, God was not tired of making human beings because so many were born each day. How cruel of God that he was creating so many humans that he was not tired . . . Therefore, I was born on 1 September 1915, at 3:47 a.m. to prove that the great poet Tagore was correct in his observation.'

Bedi summed up his life in a few broken words that look like separate episodes of a fragmented life: nine years in the post office, then a few years in the radio. Partition and communal bloodbath. Blood-soaked clothing. Travel to Delhi on top of a train. Jammu radio station and a political fight. Then Bombay. Good films, bad films. Occasional publication of a collection of stories. Some romantic escapades. Moments that Buddha missed probably. Lost interest in my life partner. Love died due to cynicism that comes with old age. Differences with my eldest son. What can you make of such a life? Well, we can say a lot about such a life. Let us start from the beginning.

Bedi's mother Seva Devi belonged to a Hindu Brahmin family, and his father Hira Singh was a Khatri Sikh. As reported, whether true or false, the mother eloped with the father, and both had been married in an Arya Samaj temple in Lahore. His father had a job at the post office. The home atmosphere was a mix of Hindu and Sikh cultural practices. The two great scriptures, the Bhagavad Gita and the Sri Guru Granth Sahib, were given equal reverence. His father was also interested in Sufi poetry. The family participated in all religious festivals, be it Janamashtmi, Guruprav or Eid. No religious tradition was taboo.

Bedi's mother was fluent in Urdu and Hindi, and she had some English exposure. Thus, the son had an early acquaintance with great religious leaders like Buddha and the core principles of Vedanta, as enunciated in the Bhagavad Gita. By the age of five, Bedi had acquired a full understanding of all the characters in the great mythical stories like the Ramayana and Mahabharata. Because his mother was not keeping good health, his father used to rent books and read them aloud to his wife. On such occasions, Bedi would sit close to them and listen to the reading. This is how he gained knowledge of Tod's Rajasthan chronicles and *The Adventures of Sherlock Holmes*. Although money was a constraint, the house was able to afford some magazine subscriptions. One memory that stayed with Bedi all his life was the time he spent listening to his father reading a book while all the siblings sat cross-legged around the hearth, feeling cosy and snug during winter and gaining knowledge of India's great mythic stories.

Bedi matriculated from the Khalsa High School and joined the DAV College, Lahore. He passed his intermediate examination but could not continue his studies towards a bachelor's degree. When his mother died of tuberculosis in March 1933, his father wanted Bedi to marry to become a caregiver along with his wife in the family. He left his studies, joined the postal service as a clerk, and got married the following year. His wife's maiden name was Soma Vati, which was changed to Satwant Kaur—a common Sikh name—after her marriage. Their first son Prem was born in 1935. The grandfather who was then working as a postmaster in Toba Tek Singh came to Lahore to celebrate a grandson's arrival, but he died there and never returned to his job. The entire burden of supporting the family fell on Bedi and his wife Satwant. The newly born baby Prem sadly lived only for a year. This was intolerable suffering and proved more difficult because the family had no savings for bad days. Most of the money had been spent on building a family home. To add to the misery, the family did not receive any pension from the postal department. In the coming years, Bedi became the father of two boys (Narinder and Jatinder) and two girls (Surinder and Parminder). Some people believe that the lead female

characters in Bedi's stories like 'Woollen Coat' and 'Give Me
Your Sorrows' were drawn from the selfless dedication that he
witnessed in Satwant.

Bedi's younger brother Harbans Singh, who lives in
Arlington, Virginia, remembers those challenging times:
'Mother died. Father got Rajinder married so that there was a
grown-up lady to take charge of household affairs. His bride,
I would call her Bhabhi, was sitting in the drawing room
surrounded by ladies who would lift her veil to look at her face
and offered her some coins. When I approached Bhabhi and
wanted a glimpse of her, she held my hand and said not until
I gave her a gold ring. I stood there confused, not knowing
that it was a joke. There was a custom in our community that
a male child was placed in the bride's lap as a blessing for her
to give birth to a male child. Rajinder came into the room.
He lifted me and put me in Bhabhi's lap and said, "He is your
son". They were my virtual parents all their lives.' Harbans
added, 'Our mother was terminally ill. I was very young.
I would pass by her bed without even glancing at her, not
knowing the seriousness of her illness. Once I was playing
outside when my mother called us in. Our father, brothers
Rajinder and Gurbachan, and sister Dulari gathered around
the bed. Silently, she beckoned Rajinder and then me to her.
She took my hand and closed Rajinder's over mine in a clasp.
She made Rajinder the custodian of my life, notwithstanding
our father, who was standing nearby. She had a hunch that
her husband was not going to live for long.'

Harbans remembers another incident that happened
after he got a job. 'After graduation, I got a clerical job in
the Military Accounts Department. When I received my first
salary, I dutifully laid it at Bhabhi's feet. Brother patted my

back and said, "Aaha, now you are earning! Let me teach you some ways of the world." He took me to the Kailash Hotel in Anarkali Bazaar. Those were war days, and a blackout was in force. We gingerly walked up the wooden stairs to reach the first floor. When we had settled down, Brother said that I should learn to order a beer. When we had finished our drink, Brother said one beer is generally not sufficient for two people and I should order another and learn to pay for it and leave a tip. I did all that and enjoyed my drink. Then Brother said, "You know drinking is forbidden in our society and considered even a sin. But everybody drinks secretly and has a guilty feeling about it. You must learn to drink in the company of respectable people so that you do not carry a feeling of shame.'"

Bedi started writing at an early age. He was still in school when his first story was published in the children's magazine *Phool*. While in college, he started writing for the Sunday edition of the newspaper *Paras*. He took over the editorship of a Punjabi magazine *Sarang*, which was published in Urdu script. Since the magazine was on the verge of closure for lack of finances, he contributed most of the articles and translation of poems himself. But this little adventure gave him good writing practice. Bedi initially used the pen name Mohsin Lahori for his early published work. He probably thought that his real name, Rajinder Singh Bedi, didn't have a literary ring to it. Some Indian, Western and Russian authors who greatly influenced his younger years included Tagore, Sarat Chandra Chattopadhyay, Chekhov, Gorky, Maupassant, Virginia Woolf and Jean-Paul Sartre.

Bedi's uncle, Sampooran Singh, was a manager of a printing press in Lahore, which he bought in his later years, and as a result, he acquired hundreds of unsold books. This was another windfall for Bedi as a young reader. Like an enthusiastic bookworm, he would assimilate classic English novels, crime thrillers and Indian mythical stories.

Bedi started contributing to prestigious Urdu magazines such as *Adabi Duniya* and *Adab-e Latif* when working at the post office. The job was intense. He spent long hours doing repetitive and tedious work, such as stamping letters or selling money orders. But this didn't stop the artist within Bedi from the strong urge to express himself. Some of the stories that were written during the time stolen from his job were included in the first collection that brought him acknowledgment as an exceptional short-story writer. Early recognition of his literary standing came in the form of his appointment as an honorary editor of *Adab-e Latif*. This premier literary journal didn't bring any financial reward, but it put him in the circle of Urdu's most-coveted fiction writers.

His first collection of short stories titled *Daana o Daam* was published in 1940, and received excellent reviews. The title of the book, however, raised questions. People wondered why Bedi had selected an unusual title for his first published work. Harbans takes the responsibility for this choice. In his words, 'No one knows why the book was named *Daana o Daam*. I take some credit for it. Rajinder was very particular about names. Whatever name he thought, he soon rejected. Nothing would satisfy him. Without suggesting a title, once I began to recite this verse in his presence:

gandami rang bhi ho zulf-e siyaah-faam bhi ho
murgh-e dil kiyuun n phanse daana bhi ho daam bhi ho

When the complexion is the colour of wheat
and the tresses are truly dark,
the bird-like heart is sure to be seized
when there is the bait of grain and a net for a catch.

The above verse caught my brother's attention. He jumped up and said, "Why not I name it *Daana o Daam*?'"

In his writing, Bedi aimed at perfection. If he found that a word was not to his liking, he did not correct the word. He tore the entire page and rewrote. His wife was annoyed because, in her view, he was wasting time and money. He would tell her firmly that if they were going to find any monetary success, it would come from his writing. The realism of stories also strike his readers. To a great extent, this was due to the writer's ability to carefully watch what was happening in the environment around him and then judiciously turn any significant experience into a short story that satisfied the requirements of good literary fiction.

Bedi took a significant risk in resigning from his job at the post office as there was no other job offer, but the aspiration to have a position where he could use his creative ability compelled him to look at alternatives. But thanks to another respected literary personality of that time, Syed Ahmed Shah Patras Bokhari (who was director general of All India Radio and a fan of Bedi's writing), Bedi got a job as a scriptwriter at the Lahore radio station in 1943. The job brought financial security as well as opportunities to showcase his creative talent. Bedi penned several radio dramas that proved to be good practice for film scriptwriting later in his life. His plays were published as *Saat Khel* and *Bejaan Chiizein*.

At the start of communal riots that preceded India's partition, Bedi moved to Ropar as a precaution, where Harbans was a lecturer in a college. It was scorching in Ropar, and the house where Harbans lived was also small. Bedi decided to go to Shimla. After arriving in the iconic British Raj town, he felt the need for money. There was also some talk of Harbans getting married for which money was needed. He decided to write a script and sell it to solve his financial problem. His plan of writing without being disturbed, was to go to the coffee house on the Mall, find a cosy table, order a cup of coffee and then begin writing. When more than an hour had passed, and he had not risen, the waiters would start casting frosty glances. He would order another cup of coffee. He played this game daily. When the script was complete, he took it to Delhi. Unfortunately, it did not sell. But on the brighter side, while living in Shimla, he saved a Muslim family when religious fanatics attacked them. He even protected Hafiz Jalandhari, who gained fame for his composition 'Abhi To Main Jawaan Huun' and later for his work *Shah Namah-e Islam* and also being the winner in a competition for composing Pakistan's national anthem. Hafiiz resided in Shimla at that time. He mentioned this incident later during a radio talk.

The time had come to leave Shimla and go to Delhi. Because of the enormous movement of people, the trains were jampacked. Satwant and the children were somehow pushed into a carriage. There was no room for Bedi. So, he rode on top of the carriage. After some time, the children shouted for him to come down as some men started teasing his wife. Bedi found a place. A man who looked educated asked him what his profession was. Bedi told him that he was a story writer. The man broke into derisive laughter. Inviting other passengers' attention, he told them, 'Look here, this man writes stories.' Everyone joined the laughter. Such was the appreciation for literature during those days!

In Delhi he tried to get the job as the lead editor of the magazine *Aaj Kal* but failed. The position was given to Josh Malihabadi at Jawaharlal Nehru's bidding. However, at the request of Sheikh Abdullah, who was chief minister of Jammu & Kashmir, Bedi accepted the offer of director at the Jammu radio station. Later on, he left this job due to personal differences with Bakhshi Ghulam Mohammad, Sheikh Abdullah's successor. Mumbai (then Bombay) was Bedi's next destination, where he lived the rest of his life.

Bedi invested thirty years of his life working in the Indian film industry, known these days as Bollywood, the mass producer of movies catering to popular taste. Starting with a low-budget movie called *Bari Behan* in 1949, Bedi achieved great success as a script and dialogue writer and later as a director of highly popular movies like *Daagh, Devdas, Madhumati, Mirza Ghalib, Dastak, Anupama, Satyakam, Baharon Ke Sapne, Mere Hamdam Mere Dost*. Bedi filmed his story 'Woollen Coat' as a movie, but it was not a commercial success. His son Narinder joined him, and he proved to be a successful director. But his untimely death at a relatively young age was a great shock for the family.

Aankhon Dekhi was the last film that Bedi produced. It had a Gandhian theme. He thought if the government waived the entertainment tax, the film would do better at the box office, but for him to approach every state government with the request to forgive the tax was a formidable task. However, if the Central government called upon the states, it was possible. Bedi thought of approaching President Giani Zail

Singh and seeking his help. Harbans at that time was serving as under-secretary in the Central government, and he was able to get an appointment with the president. A letter was drafted for the tax waiver. Bedi, his friend Surinder Sehgal and Harbans met with the president. As they entered his room, the president got up, embraced Bedi and asked him to sit by his side. After some casual conversation, Bedi told the president of his request and handed him the letter. The president said, 'I have no executive power, but I will see what can be done.' Bedi felt that he was causing him bother. The president said emphatically, 'Oh no, no. You are the treasure of our country!' He repeated the word 'treasure' more than once. Almost all the states issued the waiver. Unfortunately, the film was not released due to financial complications. Distinguished author and film director Khwaja Ahmed Abbas, best summed up Bedi's film career: 'Bedi spent thirty years in Bombay film industry, but the industry didn't spoil him as it spoiled many others. This is the reason why he is perceived as a failure. But I would say that this was the secret of his success.'

Although he was deeply involved in films, Bedi continued to publish his literary works—*Kokh Jali* (1948), *Apne Dukh Mujhe De Do* (1965), *Haath Hamaare Qalam Hue* (1974) and *Mukti Bodh* (1983). He was honoured with several awards: Sahitya Akademi Award for his novelette *Ek Chadar Maili Si* in 1965; Padma Shri in 1972; Ghalib Award for Urdu Drama in 1978; and *Filmfare* Awards for *Madhumati*, *Satyakam* and *Garam Kot*. Leading critics who commented on Bedi's literary contributions, either in magazine articles or in books, included Rashid Ahmed Siddiqui, Al-e Ahmed Suroor, Gopi Chand Narang, Baqar Mehdi, Upendranath Ashk, Joginder Paul, Khalilur Azmi and several others.

In Bedi's writings, noted critic Al-e Ahmed Suroor suggested, you get an image of new India—a country that is trying hard to modernize itself while it has not freed itself from the past. His characters carry the burden of the ancient ghosts, and they constantly struggle to free themselves from the grip of old phantoms. Bedi is not a silent spectator of this Mahabharata-like conflict. Instead, he tries to champion a spiritually and mentally enriched vision of life through his characters.

Ibadat Barelvi agreed with Suroor's assessment and added that Bedi's art is a matter of pride for Urdu lovers because it represents human life in all its dimensions, hues, and colors. He digs deeply, keeping his sight focused on the future and whatever he highlights is always a thing of great social importance.

Up to this stage, the senior critics cited above had made impressionistic remarks as part of their surveys of Urdu Afsana. It was Gopi Chand Narang who wrote the first detailed, well-argued structuralist analytic article, in 1965, on Bedi's art of story writing. Narang established that Bedi's creativity sought inspiration from the mythic roots or archetypal imprints of Indian culture. His concept of womanhood had footprints of Shakti or *mamta*—the one who suffered yet brimming with the life nurtured her creation. The article was published in *Nuquush,* Lahore, and *Aajkal,* Delhi and it created quite a tumult in Urdu literary criticism. Narang brought Bedi's writings to everybody's attention and a wider readership.

As it was mentioned above, Bedi earned great recognition for the female characters in his stories. His friend and literary critic Baqar Mehdi correctly summarized this aspect: 'In Bedi's stories, woman occupies a central place. She is not merely a fountainhead of dreams and fulfillment of desires, as she is often depicted in romance novels. She is harsh, and a grim reality with many facets, but the aspect that emerges most powerfully is that of a mother. Her melancholy looks and physical beauty that competes with the charms of blossoms enable her to hide despondency. She is the icon of latent pain and suffering, but she derives satisfaction in sharing her life's gloominess with others. She is the prisoner of rules and conventions that men have designed for her. But there is such magical power within her that she can easily shake up the most oppressive and abusive opponents. Some might deny this, but Bedi was very successful in highlighting this aspect of the men-women equation."

As time went by, several problems arose. Bedi's wife died in 1977. A greater calamity struck him when his son Narinder Bedi, a successful film director, suddenly passed away in 1982. Bedi himself was afflicted with a stroke in 1979, that affected the right side of his face.

Harbans recalls several incidents that happened during those years. 'I went to Mumbai to be with my brother. He had cancer. I knew that he was the disciple of Hazur Baba Sawan Singh of Beas. He often talked about God-realization and shedding the fear of death. One day, I asked him, "Brother, are you afraid of death?" After a moment, he replied, "Yes, I am afraid of death." I began to pontificate, "But, Brother, after dying you reach a higher, more beautiful, and a happier world . . ." He cut me short and said, "Harbans, it is I who have to die." Speechless, I realized how foolish I was.'

Bedi never lost his sense of humour, although there was little joy in his life due to several events that happened in

---

* Baqar Mehdi, 'Rajinder Singh Bedi: Bhola Se Babbal Tak' in *Jareeda* (special issue), 1984, p. 278.

quick succession. Once, he went to see Harbans in Dalhousie to escape the heat of summer. The brothers went for a walk to Charing Cross where people gathered for a stroll or socializing. Bedi spotted a person who had been his class fellow. They recognized each other, embraced and began to exchange some old memories. Bedi asked his friend what his profession was. He said he was the owner of a hotel. 'You must be making a lot of money,' Bedi said. 'Oh no. Due to the partition, very few tourists show up. I make no money; I am mostly sitting idle.' After some time, Bedi inquired, 'How many children do you have?' 'By God's grace, quite a few.' Bedi remarked, 'Oh yes. A man sitting idle looks very odd, indeed.'

Bedi's habit of chewing paan (betel leaf) was well known. When you chew paan laced with tobacco and other aromatic ingredients, you have to spit. Once when he was driving, he opened the door of his car and let out a jet of saliva. A vehicle following him speeded to come on a level with him. Looking in, the driver said, 'I knew it is Bedi Sahib.' The person was film star Pran. Sometimes, instead of moving towards his destination, he would suddenly take a U-turn and go a few miles to make for his favoured paan shop. He used to say that he knew his car's value only when he went searching for paan. Often the front of his shirt would get dotted with red paan juice. His daughter Surinder would tease him, saying, 'I know how Daddy gets these spots on his shirt front, but I wonder how he gets them on the back of the shirt also.'

As the end came near, Bedi was shifted to a nursing home. That very evening, his friend and famous writer Upendranath Ashk came from Allahabad to see him. Whenever Ashk came to Mumbai, he stayed with Bedi. Ashk was told that Bedi was in a very delicate state, and he should not be disturbed. When

Harbans and Ashk reached the nursing home, they saw one leg of Bedi was raised high, and other parts of his body were covered with tubes. Ashk sat down, and as was his nature started to talk loudly, boasting about several inconsequential things. Harbans told Ashk, 'Please don't talk loudly. Brother is in great pain; he can't follow what you are saying.'

The following day, Harbans went to see his brother. He was resting and looked calm. Harbans told him, 'Brother, Ashk Sahib had come to see you.' Bedi looked amused and said, 'Did he say anything sensible?' Even at the brink of death, he was in full possession of his senses. Not only had he listened to what Ashk had said but had analysed it as well.

After Bedi's death on 11 November 1984, a meeting of writers was held to pay tributes to him. The person who talked most profusely, Harbans recalls, was the one who had taken away Bedi's best books and cheated him of money on the pretext that he would write his biography, something that would make him famous. Fame was something that mattered a great deal to Bedi. Among the many messages of condolences received was one from President General Zia-ul Haq of Pakistan stating that Bedi's death was a loss not only to India but also to Pakistan. The Russian embassy sent a person to offer condolences. Later, a road crossing in Mumbai was named Rajinder Singh Bedi Chowk. Punjab state instituted a Rajinder Singh Bedi Award for Literature in his honour.

Bedi had many successes in his life; he faced some failures and suffered tragic losses, but he never lost the zest for life, sense of humour and love for his family and the people around him. Maybe during his final hours, he thought about death like Faiz Ahmed Faiz, with whom he shared a passion for the city of Lahore and love for the Urdu language.

kis tarah aaye gi jis roz qaza aaye gi
shaayad is tarah k jis taur kabhi avval-e shab
be-talab pehle-pahal marhamat-e bosa-e lab
jis se khulne lagein har samt talismaat ke dar
aur kahien duur se anjaan gulaabon ki bahaar
yak b yak siina-e mahtaab ko tarpaane lage
shaayad is tarah k jis taur kabhi aakihr-e shab
niim va kaliyon se sar-sabz sahar
yak b yak hujra-e mahbuub mein lahraane lage
aur khaamosh dariichon se b hangaam-e rahiil
jhanjhanaate hue taaron ki sada aane lage

How will it come the day death comes?
Perhaps during the early hours of the evening,
unwanted, pressing forward,
with a compassionate kiss on the lips,
magical doors start to open in all directions,
and from a faraway place
an unknown spring of roses,
without any good reason,
begins to torment the moon's heart.
Dawn rising from half-opened green buds
suddenly starts to flutter in the chamber of the beloved.
And from the silent windows
at the time of the departure
a tinkling sound comes from the stars.[*]

---

[*]   Surinder Deol, *Faiz: From Passionate Love to a Cosmic Vision* (New Delhi: Rupa Publications India Pvt. Ltd., 2021), p. 311.

3

A Creative Process

RAJINDER SINGH BEDI

I crave your indulgence for starting on a highly personal note. Maybe, I can seek it on the grounds that being an insignificant unit of the vast multitude that constitutes humanity, to understand it, I must first pass through the labyrinths of my mind to understand myself.

In the first instance, what constitutes expression in the short story? How and why did the writing bug bite me? Why only me and my friends, and not others? Why didn't I, like Fernandes, take to selling candles outside the church to feed myself?

Art does not gush forth spontaneously from the mind like a spring from the ground. Not that you go to sleep at night and find yourself a writer on waking up in the morning. No one can claim that a man can be a born writer. All that one can claim without any fear of contradiction is that a man may have the potential for writing, which may be an inborn gift and maybe cultivated the hard way. In the first place, a writer has a sensitive mind and feels more intensely than others; he can gloat over kudos that are showered on him and undergo mental pain as if he is being flayed or passing through a salt mine. In the second place, a writer should be like a bird that pecks on the ground, separating grain from sand and earth. The thought will not pester a writer that he has been extravagant in using electricity or has consumed ream after ream of paper. He must consider the fact that according to the law of nature, matter is ultimately indestructible. Besides, he should be thick-skinned enough not to let things easily go. He should not feel satisfied with his first draft but should go in for the revised one. He should also have some aptitude for other fine arts. For instance, he should have an ear for music. He must know why the maestro has strayed so far away on the musical scale, searching for the right note. He must also have an eye for line and colour and comprehend how the signature line has emerged from a medley of brush strokes. If he possesses all these faculties, he has in the end only to contend with one factor: if the writer's contribution comes back with a regret slip, the editor must indeed be a dunce.

Having said this, only one thing more remains to be said—anything can trigger a story. For instance, you may be going on your way when someone comes out of the blue and jerks your turban off your head, without any rhyme or reason. Or you may meet with an accident, throwing you off your feet, and you resolve there and then that you must become somebody, and to achieve your purpose, you struggle hard to find a place for yourself under the sun. It is a truism that until a man is confronted with danger, his potentialities do not fully come into play. He is not even aware that a vast treasure of talent is lying dormant in him.

All this happened with me when I was still a novice at this game, and I have reasons to believe that a similar thing must have been the lot of other writers, too, with slight variations. It is not unusual for people to meet with accidents, and they do land them in difficulties. It is also a matter of chance that people pursue some other vocation instead of taking to writing. Either they raise the banner of victory after achieving their objective or perish in the attempt and fall by the wayside. In other words, after facing constant humiliations and meeting setbacks in my endeavour to be a great writer, I also followed the example of innumerable youths of the country and took to writing ghazals. But to no avail. I was married at a very early age—I hope you have got my point. I had no sweetheart within sight to inspire me. If one came within my reach by sheer luck, she would take no notice of me, thinking that I was too young and callow for her to flirt with. Even if she tarried to give me the glad eye, my wife would run after her, slipper in hand and drive her way. I had read somewhere that love is first born in the beloved's heart, and I would keep waiting for that love to kindle in her heart. But I always stayed in vain.

During this period, I ran the full gamut of boredom, disappointment, jealousy and betrayal in love, which is the lot of all lovers depicted by poets in their verses. But all of them had a false ring. Then I realized *I* was my own censor; I was there to damn myself. My black-faced rival did not even venture near my house; he had, in fact, no need to do so. It was an essential condition of the unwritten matrimonial code of conduct that if a rival could not be done to death, he could at least be put in the police lock-up, there being no bar against it. There are indeed very few people of Faiz's ilk who could establish a healthy rapport with their rivals-in-love and become wise of their amorous traits. In short, I remained innocent of what poetry could teach me concerning life and its ways. On the other hand, Dame Life bestowed upon me a host of problems, such as domestic bickering and daily-living vicissitudes, which are no less arduous and intricate than the pain of falling in love. They created such a state of listlessness in my mind and sent a tremor down my spine that even the second-hand woollen coat which I had bought from Miranja & Miranja in the Lande Bazaar failed to shield me against these rigours of living.

I have had enough of it, and it is time I put a stop to this personal trivia. Some people know what I was in for after writing 'Garam Kot' (The Woollen Coat). They know more than me about what did not happen with me than what happened with me.

There is hardly any difference between poetry and a short story. If any verse written in regular metres is poetry, then a short story is also a poem, written in *longer* metres. Perhaps a long and sustained metre starts with the story and ends when the story ends. A novice is not quite aware of this and thinks it is easier to write a story than a poem. In Urdu poetry, especially in the ghazal, you address a woman directly or implicitly while there is no such stipulation in a story. You may be describing a man or a woman, and you are not very meticulous about language. The lines of a ghazal can never be rough and coarse, but the same can be rough-hewn in a story. Rather, prose, which comes later in literary evolution, linguistically speaking, can be less sophisticated. It could be distinguished from the language of poetry. If there is a place

for a beautiful woman in this world, there is equally a place
for a rugged or uncouth man in the scheme of things. Though
the decision is not entirely left to a woman, she is fascinated
by a wild male. She does not like a man who is effeminate or
apes her ways. If our critics have praised the short story, it is
via poetry and not via prose, as a result of which even the most
seasoned story writers went off the rail. The critics did not
have a hand in the derailment of the story. The practitioners
of the short-story form themselves loosened the nuts and
bolts of the storyline.

It is undeniable that story as an art form demands far
more labour and mental discipline to write. To deal with
such a long and sustained metre that runs through the entire
story requires excellent virtuosity and literary devices. The
other genres, including the novel, can be tackled piecemeal,
but the short story must be handled at one shot and as a
comprehensive whole. If all its ingredients do not march
abreast from the very beginning, the battle can never be won.
After completing the story, the writer may return to it only to
alter a line here or add a word there. I have not dwelt upon
this process of revision in a fit of absentmindedness. In a
short story, elimination is, in fact, more critical than addition.
You will perforce have to score out some of the passages you
consider to be most beautiful by themselves, but which take
away from the story's overall effect or cause your attention to
drift away from the central or focal point of the story.

Now I am going to say something startling. The Urdu
language has not developed adequately to cope with the
demands made by the short story; it has failed to carry this
sophisticated art form in its stride. To grasp the significance
of what I am saying, you will have to look back in time. This

backward glance will reveal that each past era had laid great stress on diction. If we try to delineate this fact in the form of a graph, we will find that the graph starts dipping down after Mir, Anis and Ghalib. We seem to have studied *Fasana-e-Azad* as nothing more than a novel or a long piece of fiction. We have gone to the extent of comparing it with *Vanity Fair* and stopping shortly after drawing that parallel in our audacity. We have called Agha Hashar the Shakespeare of India, which proves that we have studied neither. Or, if we have, we have not marked the difference between the two. It is a telling comment on the present state of affairs that I once asked a Poona Film & Television Institute candidate who was his favourite author, in an examiner's capacity. Prompt came his reply, 'Sir, I like only two—Shakespeare and Gulshan Nanda!'

There was a time when Ashiq Batalvi and Fayyaz Mahmood's stories found a place of pride in highbrow literary magazines such as *Humayun* and *Adabi Duniya*. Their stories almost leapt up from the pages of these magazines. But today, these poor fellows do not even find a passing reference in the history of the Urdu short story. By laying undue emphasis on the so-called powerful expression in the short story, we have done incalculable harm to the short story and their writers too, in the bargain.

Among the short story's creative problems, the main problem is deviation from conventional language so far as expression is concerned. Our ears, which are tuned to vociferation, regard deviation as a lack of command over the language. Even today, we go into raptures in aping the traditional style in trotting out philosophical lore in the story and mouthing heavy-going aphorisms through today's and yesterday's characters. To go into raptures has become second nature with us, and I am the last person to quibble over it. But it becomes a pain in the neck when we dub even sermonizers, historians and philosophers as storytellers.

The short story as a genre is not something indigenous to us. True, we wrote the Jatakas and *Katha Sarit Sagar,* and they travelled to the West, where they blossomed into a fine art form. There have been experiments galore, and we should not look askance at them, for we have also benefited from them. Why talk of the short story alone? To appreciate it, any art form should be visualized and judged on a universal scale. No art can be considered in isolation. It transcends geographical and national boundaries, provided, of course, you don't bracket Manto with Maupassant (1850–1893) and me with Chekhov (1860–1904). Of course, it is another cup of tea that I may like to identify myself with Kawabata (1899–1972). How would you like the idea if I say that Ram Lal (b. 1923) and Joginder Paul (b. 1925) are the Heinrich Bohl (b. 1917) of India and Qurratulain Hyder (b. 1927), the Han Suyin (b. 1916) of India? Indeed, I would have no objection if Han Suyin's countrymen also called her the Qurratulain Hyder of their country.

It is a funny state of affairs, isn't it? Urdu is getting highly *Urdu-ized.* A character in one of Bohl's novels says, 'There is no such thing as justice in a case as this. It is because the accused does not press for it. It is a state of affairs in which individualistic expression and ethical norms have become anachronistic.'

Only after dedicated labour and visualizing things in their universal perspective can the short story come into its own. And once this stage has been reached, writing becomes a part of writer's reflexes. You can collect the raw material for your stories without much effort. You find it scattered all over the place, at every nook, at every corner. Soon the writer starts suffering from a surfeit of it. In any case, after having mastered the art of story writing, the author gets the Midas' touch of Greek mythology. As we know, whatever Midas touched was transformed into gold. The only difference is that whenever we Indians feel gold, it turns into a story. The only snag is that even after having amassed so much gold, Midas died of starvation.

In writing a story, the process of remembering and forgetting goes hand in hand. Perhaps that is the reason why such erudite PhDs and DLitts fail to turn out a good story. They suffer from the disorder of not forgetting. Here I would like to allude to a letter Manto had written to me: 'Bedi, the trouble with you is that you are given to too much thinking. You think before you start writing, you think while writing, and you think after you have finished writing.' I caught his point. By telling me that I brooded too much, he was perhaps trying to point out more labour and less story in my stories. But there was little that I could do about it.

On the one hand, I had to contend with art and, on the other, with language. The custodians of speech have been such an insensitive lot that they did not even spare Iqbal. A man had gone to meet Dr Iqbal. On being asked what they talked about, he replied, 'I kept saying *Ji han, Ji han!*' and he kept replying, *'Han ji, Han ji!'* Now, things have become a bit easier, for we don't have to seek confirmation of this fact. The other day, Professor Narang told me that now a movement is afoot in Pakistan, which does not accept language that has migrated from the East and is being used by eminent writers such as Shaukat Siddiqui and is called genuine Urdu. In any case, I acted on Manto's advice and beat back the hand from my stories. But not for long.

For the hand kept appearing again and again. That facile and easy expression to which Manto had alluded, one learns only by annihilating oneself into the dust. But the same spontaneity and artlessness which exuded so much pleasure in Krishan Chander and Manto's stories could also be a bane of the short story writer. My plight was like Manto's female character, who wanted to be possessed and ravished and then wanted to wreak vengeance. When I discerned that playfulness in some of Manto's stories, I wrote to him, 'Manto, there is one great thing about your stories. You don't think before writing, while writing and after writing.' That put an end to our correspondence. He had not taken my remark amiss as I learned later, but he doubted how a man like me who had no experience of life outside marriage ever made a successful writer. And to cap it all, I not only drank buffalo's milk but also kept two buffaloes. How should I tell him that if Muslims can have an affinity with camel, Hindu with cow, why can't a Sikh have a relationship with buffalo?

The story is a feeling, a sensibility, a consciousness that can never be given birth to. It can be cultivated with diligence and hard labour, but even after having acquired it, one remains empty-handed. Some traits manifest themselves because they are so facile, and others because they result from mental quirks. The only consolation is that, till now, the story has not gone out of our hands and fallen into the editor's hands. We can still alter, add to and subtract from it. And if it comes to that, we are free to tear it up and throw it away. If Hemingway could write 500 pages and extract 96 pages from them, why can't we do the same?

Some excellent stories have been written in Urdu. They can no doubt be counted on one's fingers, and there is a reason for it. While meeting the demands of others, we overlook the fact that we are dishonest with ourselves. We do not realize that we have become the prisoners of our image.

4

In Front of the Mirror

RAJINDER SINGH BEDI

I'm nobody! Who are you?
Are you nobody, too?
Then there's a pair of us—don't tell!
They'd banish us, you know.

Emily Dickinson

I have not known until today who am I! This may create the impression that I am trying to be unnecessarily modest. It is far from reality because a man who does not bend before others or profess to a particular school of thought or ism, or if he is an adherent of a specific religion, he may be relatively modest. A man who kowtows to others or talks ingratiatingly may also be the worst example of rank egoism. For all one knows, a man who poses to be self-effacing may be hazardous. The Guru Granth Sahib says, 'A sinner bends head over heels like a hunter out to kill a deer.'

I know I am a modest, well-meaning and simple man, but there are moments in my life which, at first sight, one can erroneously attribute to my sense of egoism. Such moments generally come when bitten by the writing bug, when I sit down to dash off a literary piece. I am very much taken up with the subject. It is something refreshingly novel, and I feel the surge of inner strength to express myself engagingly. Then I feel as if I am someone out of the ordinary. Get out of my way, I'm sailing in! Beware, the lord of all he surveys, the king of kings, the emperor who rules over the whole world arrives in his resplendent regalia!

Since it is not easy to write without an upsurge of such feelings, it would appear as if this momentary egoism has supplanted my habitual modesty; both seem to be within a handshake of each other. At that time, nothing can intervene between me and the piece of paper lying in front of me. At that time, it hardly matters to me what others think of me. How is one concerned if sitting in my home's privacy, I regard myself as another Kalidasa or Shakespeare? Of course, after writing and before reaching the publisher, if I still labour under the illusion of being supreme, there couldn't be a greater fool than me.

For one thing, such a man is soon found out when he transfers his thoughts to paper. Failing that, his ever-obliging friends are there to tell him his real worth. And if they want to perpetuate an insult, they keep silent over it.

Well, who am I?

Generally, people ask who that man is or what he is, meaning what his vocation is in life. These two questions are entirely irrelevant in my case. People know me, and they also know what I do for a living, thanks to films that heaped disgrace on me. This is a world of publicity. People look wide-eyed at the publicized man. But few know the price the man had to pay to be pushed into the limelight. Maybe that's why people still aspire so arduously for fame. I am nobody. You had better ask our film heroes who cannot spend even a single moment of their lives naturally. They pose as great actors before their wives, who know them inside out and smile, and simply smile at their heroics even at home.

When I look at myself, I am reminded of that dog—mind you, I'm not deliberately modest—whom a director had cast in his film. The dog was caught in the sequences of the film. Having figured in scene number twelve, he was also required to appear in a war scene number fifty-one, which was shot months later. Being a well-meaning, run-of-the-mill type dog, he ran about in the bazaar sniffing for food in the garbage like any other dog. But after coming into the films, he had become a precious commercial commodity who could be bought and sold and whose price fluctuated, conforming to the business phenomenon of boom and bust. Hence the film's director kept him tethered all the time and threw food to the poor thing three or four times a day. He was given a comfy mattress to sleep on. If he caught a chill, a veterinarian was immediately sent for. The dog wagged his tail before all and sundry, treating every mortal for an angel, that is if a dog can distinguish between Satan and an angel. They proceeded with the shooting of the film, and the dog had a good time.

At last, the film was complete, and the dog was released from his bondage. But by that time, the dog had lost the habit of rummaging through the garbage in search of food. After wandering about, he would again return to the film studio, wag his tail, and on being kicked, run away howling—also, the same place, the same bleary-eyed wonderment, the same abuses. The film director was not a dog, but practically a man.

I am thinking of a man whose ego has been inflated by fame or who is hungry for fame, who wants to amass wealth, giving him the power to buy anything he takes a fancy to and be able to make law, religion, customs and politics his handmaiden. A person, who like the hero of *Lolita*, becomes the victim of some obsession, and enjoys life to its dredges. At the same time, people stand by acclaiming him and saying, 'These are the fads of big people.' Fame, status and wealth are all dangerous things that every wise and good man wishes to renounce after attaining them. In my case, as the saying goes, I want to get rid of the blanket, but it won't let go of me; it just keeps clinging to me. It can also be that a man may simulate that he wants to renounce things while he is enamoured of them.

Once, I ran into one of my admirers. He had read some of my stories and was one of those persons with an affectation of wisdom or knowledge but was regarded with scorn by others. After talking about some inconsequential things, he came to the point.

'Bedi Saheb, you are a great man.'

'Okay,' I said, a little flustered. Then my Punjabi self got the better of me.

'Oh no, I'm nothing.' And when he readily agreed with what I had said, it put me in a towering rage.

Who am I? His remark put an end to these questions at one stroke. Now that I think of it, these questions just don't apply to me. Instead, one should ask me, 'Why are you here? In other words, why should I exist?'

I am innocent of this too.

Millions of people are born in this world every day. I was also one of them who had suddenly come into existence. My mother must have felt happy over it. And so even my father. But the neighbour living on the right side of our house was unaware of my coming into the world, and it was all to the good, for it is not wise to take a neighbour into one's confidence. Later, the neighbour must have dropped in to congratulate my parents as a matter of formality. How could my birth have made him happy; one would want to know? Somewhat to his chagrin, he must have felt that one more rival was born to compete with his son Pannalal, and potential danger to his about-to-be-born daughter in this highly competitive world. So, it has become an empty custom to congratulate Rajinder Sigh Bedi when he is born, felicitate Chuhar Singh as soon as he sees the light of day, and beat the drum on the arrival of Dhallu Ram or Chumney Khan in this world.

Tagore says that children born galore in this world testify that God is not tired of creating human beings. How insensitive God is to develop human beings just because He is not tired of doing so.

You, idler, do something,
Stitch and re-stitch your pajamas, if nothing else.

Hence in deference to God's contention, the last stitch was put in His cloth at three forty-seven on the morning of 1 September 1915, at Lahore. Like man, Ram and Rahim also conveniently forgot that this world is an abode of sorrows. Otherwise, was it an act of kindness on His part to send me into this world? According to the shastras, I must have been sent into this world to atone for the sins of my past births, which, it seemed, even God lacked the power to condone.

Like all good parents, my parents also nursed the desire to see me ending up as a collector, a high government functionary. Why blame them? A collector was the limit of their reach. Little did they know that there are even higher government functionaries than a collector before whom even the latter bent his knee. That reminded me of a simple Punjabi Jat (peasant) who appeared before a tahsildar (revenue officer who commands great prestige in rural areas) connected with a dispute relating to land-revenue payment. The tahsildar gave his verdict in favour of the Jat. Much pleased, the Jat blessed him, 'May God make you a patwari (a petty revenue assistant).'

In this rat race, people are not tired of giving classic examples that are nothing but tailor-made conspiracies to dupe the gullible. For instance, they remind people that Lincoln was born in a log cabin and became the United States president. But the same people fail to give an example where a person had travelled from a squalid dwelling to the Rashtrapati Bhavan. The standard of Lincoln has ensnared millions of people who have ultimately died a dog's death. Why forget that the rising sun means the death of millions of stars? Despite that, if you persist in picking holes in the Redeemer and His ways, you do so at your own cost.

I was a sickly child, the son of a sick mother. While suffering from typhoid, I had to face severe jolts of which the patient is himself the progenitor. He feels as if he has been put in the sling of life and is being catapulted somewhere beyond the horizon of death. Burrowing my head into the pillow, I had seen thousands of colours blurring into each other and defying any definition. Some rainbows transcended all limits of description. I would lie on the bed, shedding tears that were neither sweet nor bitter and conformed to no sense of taste. Near and dear ones could not even wipe them off. Hundreds of times, I was left alone and in a sad state in arid wastes, and then suddenly I would realize with intense fear why nobody had stirred near me for eons. Scores of times, I had seen a marketplace in a city in England or a ghat at Banaras, where I was born in my previous lives. The Ganges would recede after flowing over its banks, leaving behind thousands of small channels, thinly flowing through red and yellow alluvium from which water gushed as my feet stamped over it. A small, nine-year-old swarthy child, a black thread tied around his naked waist, a tuft of hair over his head. It happened to be me.

Before I could grow up sufficiently to give my body a chance to go to rack and ruin through evil deeds and the hectic business of life, my body had already failed me. I would throw tantrums at the slightest provocation and start whimpering at the smallest complaint. My mother would throw me away in utter disgust because I would keep suckling at her breasts to the point of squeezing them dry. 'Ma, whether you live or die, I must have my milk.' Even today, I make the same demand, and mother is nowhere around. You know what I mean. No, she is nowhere. After throwing me away, she would again pick me up out of maternal affection. She could never decide whether to keep me or throw me away for good.

I died many a time and came alive many a time. Everything came to me as a surprise; every living moment drove me to distraction. There was no limit to my surprise, nor was there any boundary to my despair. My parents had many horoscopes made for me, as I learned later. According to my horoscope, Ketu marred my constellation, and Mars cast its shadow over Mercury from its own house. From this, the astrologer concluded that the child would become a famed artist though recognition would come to him late in life, maybe even posthumously. According to the astrologer, the Sun was located in the child's house of gain, and Venus was also found in the same house, as a result of which its light had been dimmed by the light of the Sun. Again, since Saturn overlooked Venus, a large number of women would come into his life. The confluence of the two planets may even take him to brothels. But since he enjoyed the protection of Mercury, he would not be defamed. Also, Mars and Saturn were together, and being at cross-purposes could lead to some harmful effects. But Mars was Mars, and thus no great harm would be done, except that Saturn would place some obstacles in his way to success, mainly because Mercury also happened to be weak. In the tenth house resided Rahu, which Mars overlooked. Such being the case, his wife would remain chronically ill. In other words, my father's wife and my wife would remain sick perpetually. The whole family was under a curse.

Hence, except for ruining my wife's life and marring the future of many children, if I have done anything worthwhile, it is scribbling over pages, writing books and then going out to buy them myself.

My mother was a Brahmin, and my father, a Khatri. In those days, such marriages could take place even in Gretna Green. (*Editors' Note:* You can no longer turn up to be married at Gretna Green, a parish in Scotland. The minimum period required for arranging a wedding is twenty-

nine clear days. This is how long it takes the Registrar to check
the documentation and draw up the marriage schedule.) But
it materialized in my parent's case. My father and mother
were highly accommodative, which was reflected in their
feelings and respect for each other's personal views. In one
niche was kept the Bhagavad Gita, and in the other, the
Guru Granth Sahib. The first stories that I learned in early
childhood did not relate to fairies and demons. They were
the condensed lessons obtained from each chapter of the
Gita, which we heard with great reverence each morning
from our mother's lips. I could easily comprehend such
things as Raja, Brahmin and the Devil, but many things
went over my head.

'Ma, what is this *gunka*?'

'Yes, it's something. Sit still.'

'Oh, no, you must tell me—this blessed thing gunka.'

'Be quiet!'

And then an expression would creep over her face, which
one could discern only on my mother's face when she found a
child's face was wilting.

'A bad woman is called gunka.'

'But you are a good woman, aren't you?'

'A mother is always a good woman. Every mother, any
child's mother.'

'Then who's a bad woman?'

'Oh, stop picking my brain, child. A bad woman is the
one who lives with several men.'

Mother's explanation duly registered on my mind. But
next day, I got a shoe-beating from her when I called our
neighbour Sumitra's mother gunka because many men,
such as her husband's younger and elder brothers and other

nondescript male relatives, lived under the same roof in their house.

The remaining part of my life reads like leaves from the same book. No sooner did I pose a question when life said, 'Be quiet!'

Even if I got a reply, it went over my head. And if I managed to get the head or tail of the question, I got the beating.

My physical rigidness, jangled nerves, half-hearted replies to my questions, or a lack of understanding in catching their ethical implications were enough to make me an introverted and supersensitive child. In life, apart from the darkness, there is also a great vacuum. Life is fraught with risks, dangers, disappointments and unknown fears, which send a tremor through the heart like that mild electric shock that can make the diaphragm tingle. The rest are typical happenings and experiences which writers encounter in their lives. The writer learns from them, experiments with them and then tries to reduce them to words.

In a sort of way, I had formed an acquaintance with the stories of the Ramayana and the Mahabharata and its characters at an early age of five. The Ramayana is a weighty tome swarming with all sorts of characters, many of them very noble and self-sacrificing. But of them all, Sugreev, whose brother Bali even carried away his wife while he stood there gaping helplessly, touched the most resonant chords of my heart. As a happy stroke of luck, if Lord Rama had not passed by just at that time, Sugreev would have been left high and dry. In the same manner, I have a favourite character in the Mahabharata—Shikhandi, the effeminate who acted as a smokescreen in the killing of Bhishma Pitamah, the great elder of the epic. But for this man, Bhishma Pitamah would have lived on until eternity.

My father often brought some books from the roadside lending library at one paisa per book per day for my ailing mother's diversion. He would sit by her side and read aloud from the book. I would unobtrusively worm my way into their presence and listen to my father. In this way, while still in school, I became familiar with Tod's Rajasthan and the exploits of Sherlock Holmes. Most of *The Mysteries of the Court of London* remained an enigma to me. I only remember that father used to read them with great zest, leaving me wondering why a particular character made some mischief to a woman. By then, I had learned that it was indecent to go after women. And that a woman was something terrible and vulgar. I would doze off thinking about this, feeling distraught.

Just about that time, my uncle bought a steam press, which brought a few thousand books with it as a part of its dowry or legacy. I had devoured all the titles between my primary and middle school. I was like that silverfish found in every old book or a bookmark that every publisher slips in between a new book's pages. In a theoretical way, I had become familiar with everything, but without a practical bias. It caused the same havoc as can be generated in anybody's life by the chasm between theory and practice. I was crucified at the cross of every new experiment. Perhaps it was a necessity in my case.

After having described the foundations of my life in such abundant detail, it is perhaps superfluous to write about the remaining episodes of my life. I passed my matriculation examination, joined college, wrote poetry in English and Urdu and stories in Urdu. After Mother's death, I took up a job in the post office, got married, had children, then my father died. I served in the postal department for nine years, joined the All India Radio, then came partition of the country, murders and destruction, bodies drenched in blood, a journey to Delhi on the rooftop of a railway carriage, appointed Station Director Jammu Radio Station and picked up a fight with the so-called democratic set-up of the state. Then I came to Bombay. I produced some good films and then some bad films and in between wrote a book of Urdu short stories with blood dripping from the pen held in my hand. There were harrowing ordeals that even the Buddha would not have tolerated in his life; the moments which I could not have lived through if I were a normal person. I developed apathy towards my wife, followed by a complete estrangement towards her. Why did this happen? I would say that particular things happen as one grows old. My elder son had a low opinion of my business acumen, and I considered him an irresponsible person who was blindly in love with dirty money and nothing else. Well, does it all add up to anything, makes any sense?

My convictions? None whatsoever. My aspirations, hopes and disappointments? None. I don't love a woman out of wisdom, and she doesn't love me out of foolishness, for the simple reason that I can differentiate between love and greed. In a detached way or without aspiring for it, I have only one compelling desire, and that is to write and go on writing. Not for money, not to enrich a publisher, either. I want to write for writing's sake. I do not want to take refuge behind religious scriptures. I don't need them. If it comes to that, I can write better than those that exist.

I am not in quest of a guru, a mentor and a bestower of learning. Every man can be his guru and his pupil. The rest is give-and-take of the marketplace. I have had a tête-à-tête with green leaves and jasmine flowers and have gone into raptures over them. I know the dog's vocabulary. My dog understands me, and I know him. I don't need salvation. If God can commit the folly of creating man, why should I, in my wisdom as a man, stoop to the nonsense of creating God? If reality needs me, I think it can rise above the past and the future and search me out in some moment of repose. I want to live my life as a simple man after comprehending the purpose of my life. I desire to reach some destination, but it should be in a state of desirelessness, which we call the relaxed state in a simple, unadorned language. This state comes only after knowing, and . . . the rest I don't know anything about.

PART II

Selected Short Stories

1

Give Me Your Sorrows

On the night of the wedding, things did not happen as Madan had anticipated. His plump sister-in-law cajolingly pushed Madan into the middle room, where he faced Indu—she was cloaked in a red shawl, indistinct from the darkness of the room. Outside, Chakli Bhabhi's laughter (chubby sister-in-law) and Daryabadi Phuphi (father's sister from Daryabad) and the other women broke the silence of the night like crystal candy slowly dissolving. These women understood that Madan was ignorant, although a grown-up man. When he was awakened, he exclaimed, 'Where? Where are you taking me?'

These older women had seen it all during their days. The echo of what their lusty husbands had said and meant on the first wedding night was a distant memory. They were well-established but were intent on setting up a new sister. To these daughters of the earth, the man was like a cloud to whom they must look for rain. If there was no rain, then they must entreat, promise gifts, perform magic. Madan had been waiting for this moment as he lay in a space, in front of his house, in a new neighborhood of Kalkaji. To his cot was tied his unlucky neighbour Sibte's buffalo, snorting and sniffling at Madan. At such a time, there was no possibility of sleep.

The moon, which guides the ocean waves as well as the blood of women, shone through a window as though it were watching Madan's next move. He stepped forward, conscious of the roar within himself, and pulled the cot into the moonlight so that he could see his bride's face. He hesitated, but then he thought, Indu is not a strange woman I cannot touch; she is my wife. Looking at the bride who was wrapped in red, he judged where Indu's face should be, and when he felt the bundle there, it was. Madan had thought that she would not easily let him look at her face, but she did, as though she had been waiting years for this moment, and some imagined buffalo's nudging had kept her, too, from her sleep. Though her eyes were closed, Madan could see that she had had her share of sleeplessness. He looked at her face again. It was round rather than oval, so round that the moonlight made dark caves between the cheeks and lips, seemingly between two blooming hillocks. The forehead was a bit narrow, with curly hair spontaneously rising from it.

Indu freed her face, as though she had granted the privilege of looking only temporarily. There were certain limits imposed by modesty. Madan raised his wife's face again, somewhat roughly to call out in an emotional voice, 'Indu!'

Indu felt slightly afraid. It was the first time in her life that a stranger had called her name in this way, and this stranger was destined to be her husband. She looked up for the first time but quickly closed her eyes and said only, 'Yes.' She felt that her voice had emanated from some region, under the ground.

Their conversation began very slowly, but it continued and never seemed to come to a stop once it started. Indu's father, Indu's mother, her brother, Madan's brothers and sister, his father, the father's Railway Mail Service job, the father's temperament, favourite clothes and food habits—all these people and subjects were surveyed. In the middle of this, Madan wanted to stop the conversation and do something else, but Indu disregarded any such inclination. Helplessly, Madan began describing his mother, who had died of tuberculosis when he was seven years old.

'So long as she lived, the poor woman, my father's hands were occupied by medicine bottles. We had to wait on the hospital steps, and little Pashi waited in the house. We were tired but sleepless with anxiety most of the time. Then finally, one day, on the evening of 28 March . . .' Madan was quiet. He was very close to crying. Frightened, Indu pressed his head to her breast. Thus, in a moment, Indu's unconscious sympathy achieved Madan's conscious wish! Madan wanted to know more of Indu—but she caught his hand and began to speak.

'I cannot read or write, but I have known my parents, my brothers, and sisters-in-law and scores of other people; I understand many things. Now that I am yours, I'd like to ask something of you.'

Madan was overcome with emotion. With impatience and quick generosity mixed in his voice, he asked, 'What do you want? I'll give you whatever you wish!'

'Do you promise?' Madan spoke without hesitation, 'Yes, yes, I promise.' But then doubts arose in his mind. His business, just begun, was still slow. If Indu had asked for something beyond his power, what would he do?

Taking his rough hands in her soft ones and laying her cheek against them, Indu asked, 'Give me your sorrows.'

Madan was relieved, but he was also surprised at the request. He couldn't decide from the expression of her face, whether this was a rehearsed sentence, tutored to her by her mother or by a girlfriend. Then he felt the warmth of a tear on the back of his hand, and he embraced Indu lovingly, saying, 'Given!'

But all this had taken his inordinate appetite from him.

The guests departed one by one. Chakli Bhabhi, her two children firmly in hand, descended the stairway carefully because of her third pregnancy and left for her home. Daryabadi Phuphi, who, upon losing her precious necklace, had wailed so loudly that she fainted and then in the washroom had found it, took away her dowry share of three garments. And the uncle left, after receiving a wire about his 'Justice of the Peace' appointment, and due to the excitement, he had nearly kissed Madan's bride!

The old father and the younger brothers and sister remained in the house. Little Dulari or Munni snuggled in her sister-in-law's arms. If a neighbourhood woman came to see the bride, Dulari was the one who determined the length of time the visitor could spend with the bride. Indu slowly settled into the house, but the people of Kalkaji still made excuses to stop in front of Madan's house while passing, hoping to see Indu. When she saw them, she quickly drew up the edge of her sari, covering her face. What they saw in this brief uncovered moment pleased them.

Madan was engaged in the crude turpentine business. Soon after the marriage, the pine and cedar trees, which were the primary source of supply, were caught in a forest fire and reduced to dust. Turpentine sent from Mysore and Assam was expensive, and people were not prepared to purchase the product at a high price. With his income decreased, Madan would close his store and the office, and come home earlier than usual. Reaching the house, he always tried to get into his bed. At mealtime, he placed dishes before his father and sister, and after they had eaten, he gathered up the utensils and put them by the washbasin. Because of Indu, Madan now found housework worthy of his attention. All understood this. Madan was the eldest, Kundan younger than him, and Pashi younger than both. When Kundan, to show his affection for his sister-in-law, insisted on waiting to eat with her, Dhuni Ram or Babu ji scolded him. 'You go on and eat. She'll get her food.' Then Dhuni Ram surveyed the kitchen. When Bahu had finished her food and turned her attention to the pots, Dhuni Ram stopped her, saying, 'Leave them Bahu, the dishes can be done in the morning.'

"No, Babu ji, I can do them very quickly now,' she said.

In a trembling voice, Babu ji would reply, 'If Madan's mother were alive, Daughter, then you would not be doing all this.' And Indu would stop the movement of her hands.

Little Pashi was embarrassed in his sister-in-law's presence because Chakli Bhabhi and the father's sister from Daryabad had performed a ceremony to 'make the bride's lap green.' They had placed Pashi in Indu's lap. After that Indu had felt that Pashi was not only her husband's younger brother, but her child. Whenever Indu lovingly tried to take Pashi in her arms, he protested and kept distance. By coincidence, Babu ji was always present at such times, and he scolded Pashi. 'What is this? Your sister-in-law loves you. Do you think you grew up for this?' But Dulari couldn't be chased away from Indu! Her obstinate insistence, 'I'll sleep with Bhabhi' seemed to awaken some demon in Babu ji. One night he slapped Dulari so hard that she fell on the uncemented drain. Leaping forward, Indu helped her, her dupatta falling from her head. Her hair, the red powder in her hair parting, the ornaments in her ears divulged.

'Babu ji!' Indu caught her breath, catching Dulari and pulling up her dupatta at once, acutely embarrassed. She brought the motherless child to her breast, making her feel as though she were lying on pillows and cushions, no hard bedframe, where nothing could hurt her. Indu caressed Dulari's sore spots and large, lovely dimples returned to Dulari's cheeks. Seeing these dimples, Indu said, 'Oh Munni! May your mother-in-law die! Look at your dimples!'

Munni looked up with diverted attention. 'You have dimples too, Bhabhi.'

'Yes, Munni,' Indu smiled.

Madan was angered by all this while he was standing nearby and listening. 'She may be a motherless child, but I tell you it's a good thing in some ways.'

'Why? Why is it a good thing?' Indu asked quickly.

'It is good. If no bamboo grows, no flutes will make noise. No mother-in-law, no quarrels.'

Indu was angered. 'You may go—please go to the bed. What business is this of yours? If a person is curious, then he quarrels sometimes, doesn't he? A quarrel is better than the silence of the burning ghat! Go away, what business do you have to enter the kitchen?'

Madan stayed, abashed. The other children had been put to bed by Babu ji. Madan stayed standing there. Necessity had made him stubborn and shameless. But when Indu reprimanded him again, he left.

Soon Madan was in bed, restless but thinking of Babu ji. He hadn't the courage to call Indu. His impatience reached its limit when Indu sang a lullaby to help Dulari sleep. 'Come, queen of sleep, you intoxicated one, come . . .'

This lullaby, which put Munni to sleep, made Madan sleepless. Disappointed, he pulled the quilt over his head. Holding his breath, he felt intuited he was dead. His bride, Indu, sat near him crying loudly, beating her forearm, and breaking her bangles, falling on the floor, and rushing, sobbing, while dashing into the kitchen to smear ashes on her hair; then going outside and raising such a lament that people in the lane could hear her. 'Neighbors! I've been ruined!' Now she did not care about her dupatta, her shirt, the red parting, and flower in her hair; the birds of her fanciful thoughts, it seemed, had flown away.

Tears were flowing rapidly from Madan's eyes, but he heard Indu laughing in the kitchen. Coming back to the real world, Madan wiped his tears, chuckling at himself. At a distance, Indu too was giggling softly. Out of respect for Babu ji she tried not to laugh loudly, as if there was something immoral about laughter. Silence, the dupatta, hushed laughter, the veiled face, this is what Indu had become. Madan imagined that Indu was sitting beside him, and he talked with her about many things. He loved her as he had never loved her before. He returned once again to his world of thoughts, and with the empty bed next to his bed, he called in a low voice 'Indu' and received no answer. Sleep, that intoxicating beauty, embraced him. He nodded, yet it seemed that Sibte's buffalo of the marriage night was with him, sniffing at his face. He rose in a restless mood, looked towards the kitchen, scratched his head, yawned two or three times, and once again lay down. He slept lightly; when Indu came, and her bangles jingled as she smoothed her bed, he woke up and sat straight. Rising so hurriedly intensified his desire and his whole body burned with an internal fire. He asked excitedly, 'So, you have come?'

'Yes.'

'Has that damned Munni died in her sleep?'

Indu started, 'What are you saying! Why should she die? She is the only daughter of her parents!'

'Yes, the only sister of your husband; Bhabhi's favourite!' Madan assumed a severe, authoritative tone. 'Don't encourage the little witch so much.'

'What is the harm?'

'Here's the harm.' Madan grew more annoyed. 'She won't leave you alone. Look how she clings like a leech. She never stops pestering!'

'Yes,' Indu said, sitting on the edge of Madan's bed. 'But you shouldn't revile your sister this way. She's only a guest. If not today, she will leave tomorrow; if not tomorrow then the next day; one day she must leave this house.' Indu wanted to continue, but she couldn't.

Before her eyes appeared her mother, father, brother, sister, uncle—all lost to her. Once, she had been their loved one. In the blink of an eye, she had become separate and something that didn't belong to them. Suddenly, they began discussing her marriage. They were doing it day and night as if a cobra's hole had been discovered in the house, and no one could relax and sleep until the snake had been caught and expelled. All sorts of snake charmers and magicians were called, even the legendary physician of the gods,

Dhanwantari. Finally, one day from the north-west came a colourful marriage procession, just like a storm. When it cleared, a vehicle stood there in which sat a bride, dressed in gold- and silver-embroidered clothes. Behind her, in the house, the monotonous playing of the *shehnai* sounded like the snake charmers *biin*. With one jolt, the vehicle left.

Madan's lousy temper had not abated. 'Women are so clever. You arrived in this house only yesterday, yet everyone cares more for you than for me!'

'Yes!' Indu affirmed. 'This is all deceit—they have been tricked!'

Oh? Tears came to Indu's eyes. 'Their love is a result of my deceit.' She went to her bed and, hiding her face in the pillow, began to sob. Madan was puzzled, but Indu got up and came to him, catching his hands tightly. She spoke directly, 'You are always making mean remarks. What's wrong with you?'

Madan decided on a display of husbandly dignity. 'Go on, why don't you go to sleep? There's nothing I want from you.'

'You don't need anything from me, but I must take my whole life from you!' She scrambled towards him, like a fish trying to climb the rushing waters of a waterfall instead of flowing with the current. Pinching, grabbing, crying and laughing, she said, 'Will you call me a deceitful woman again?'

'That's how all women are!'

'Just wait . . . you . . .' Her words were inaudible.

'What was that?' Madan demanded. Indu repeated it in an audible voice, and Madan guffawed in uncontrollable laughter. Then Indu was in his arms, saying, 'Men, what do you know? When a woman loves a man, she loves his relatives too, even his father, brother or sister.' Her thoughts jumped ahead. 'I'll even arrange Dulari Munni's wedding.'

'This is the limit! She's not one length high, and you begin to think of her marriage!'

'You see her one length high?' Indu put her hands over Madan's eyes.' 'Close your eyes a bit and then open them.'

He did close his eyes, and after some time, Indu said, 'Now, you must open your eyes! In this much time, I'll surely grow old!' When he opened his eyes, he felt for a moment that it was not Indu before him but Munni. Then he was lost in his thoughts.

'Up to now, I've put aside four suits of clothes and some cooking utensils for her,' Indu disclosed, and when Madan gave no answer, she shook him anxiously. 'Why are you worried? Don't you remember your promise? You must give me your sorrows.'

'Eh?' Madan was startled; then, his heart lightened as he felt that his burdens were shared. He hugged Indu, and this time it was not only her body but her soul as well.

To Madan, Indu was all soul. She had a body, but somehow it remained invisible to Madan. There was a veil made of dream filaments, coloured by breaths of smoke, dazzling with golden threads of laughter, which always veiled Indu. Madan's hands and eyes committed sacrilege, like Duhshasan outraging the modesty of Draupadi. Bolts upon bolts and yards upon yards of cloth to cover her nakedness came down from the sky, unceasingly. Duhshasan was tired and defeated; he fell to the ground, but Draupadi still stood dressed in a white sari. She looked like a real goddess. Madan's lusting hands were wet with the sweat of shame, and to dry them, he raised them, spreading the fingers wide, passed them over the burning pupils of his eyes. Through these twitching fingers, he could see the soft pleasantness of Indu's well-crafted body. For use, it was close, but for lusty misuse, it was far. Sometimes when Indu was caught on Madan's lustful mood, she would say, 'What are you thinking? There are young ones in the house. What will they say!'

Madan would reply, 'The young ones don't understand; the old ones are indifferent.'

During this period, Babu Dhuni Ram was transferred to Saharanpur. There he was made Head Clerk in the Railway Mail Service, in what was called a selection grade. A large house was assigned to him that was sufficient for eight families, but he stayed alone. Throughout his life, he had not been separated from his family. He enjoyed family life, and such loneliness at the end of his life distressed him. But it could not be otherwise; the children could not be taken out from their school in the middle of the year. They had to stay in Delhi with Madan and Indu. Under stress, Babu ji developed a heart condition.

After Babu ji wrote many letters close to the summer vacation, Madan sent Indu, Kundan, Pashi and Dulari to Saharanpur. Babu Dhuni Ram's world perked up. Before, he had been burdened with free time after his office. Now he had nothing but work! The children took off their clothes and left them here and there, and Babu ji picked them up. Separated from Madan, Indu grew careless like Rati. Indu paid little attention to her clothing. She behaved in the kitchen as though she were in a dog-pound, face turned outward-looking for her master. She would nap after completing her housework, sometimes lying on a trunk, sometimes near the oleander plant or the mango tree.

The months of *saavan* gave way to *bhaadon*. In the courtyard, young and newly married women swung happily and sang, 'Who has put up a swing in the mango grove?' In the spirit of the song, they pushed each other on the swing and played hide-and-seek. The middle-aged women stood close by and watched; Indu felt she was like these women. She turned her face away, sighed and went to sleep. Babu ji would not try to wake her. Instead, he took the opportunity to pick up her discarded shalwar, which she always flung over her mother-in-law's old sandalwood box and hung it on a peg. While doing this, he had to be careful that no one was watching him. Occasionally, while picking up one garment, he would see Indu's bra lying behind in the corner. At this sight, his courage failed him, and he would leave the room quickly as if a snake had appeared out of a hole. Then from the veranda, his voice repeating the Vedic hymn, '*Om Namo Bhagvate, Vasudeva . . .*' could be heard.

The tale of Babu ji's daughter-in-law's beauty was spread far and wide by the neighbouring women. When women spoke in front of Babu ji of his Bahu's loveliness and well-formed body, he responded happily, 'We were so lucky, mother of Ami Chand! Thanks, that a healthy person has come to our house.' Saying this, his thoughts went to his wife, who suffered from tuberculosis, her bottles of medicine, the hospital steps and the sleepless nights of his children. Then he would imagine many plump children tucked in Bahu's arms, on her thighs, hanging around her neck, and still more coming. Lying on her flanks with her face to the ground and her hips towards the sky, Bahu was releasing children one after another, of different ages or sizes, they looked alike, twins and more twins. '*Om Namo Bhagavate . . .*'

The neighbours knew that Indu was Babu ji's favourite, and jars of milk and buttermilk began to arrive at their house. Salam Din Gujjar made a special request to Indu, 'Bibi ji, please have my son made a coolie in the railway station. Allah will reward you!' It wasn't long after Indu's recommendation that Salam Din's son got the job, and that of a sorter, not a coolie. She helped people, and when she could not, she attributed it to fate or there were no more vacancies to be filled.

Babu ji took special care of Indu's food and health. Indu hated milk. At night, Babu ji prepared milk in a small pot, put it in a glass, and brought it to Bahu's cot. Indu pulled herself together, rising and saying, 'Oh no, Babu ji! I won't drink it.'

'Even your father-in-law will have to drink it,' he would joke. 'Please, go ahead and drink it.' She would laugh.

Babu ji retorted with faked anger, 'Do you want to suffer later as your mother-in-law did?'

'Yes, yes,' she said, but she pretended to be hurt by his words. Why not pretend? Only those who have no one to console them never pretend to be broken; here, everyone was ready to comfort her.

When Indu did not take the glass of milk from Babu ji's hand, he placed it near the head of her bed. 'Take it from here; drink if you wish.'

Back at his bed, Dhuni Ram played with Dulari Munni. Dulari rubbed a bare part of Babu ji's body with her body, and putting her face to his stomach, she made a *burr burr* sound. Looking in Bahu's direction, Dulari roared, 'The milk will spoil, Babu ji. Bhabhi isn't drinking it!'

'She'll drink it, she will, Daughter,' Babu ji hugged Pashi with his free arm. 'Woman can't bear to see anything go bad.'

Hardly was this sentence completed when, 'Shoo, you *khasmaan nuun khaani!*' exclaimed Bahu. As she discovered that a cat was coming for the milk, she quickly gulped it down!

Shortly afterward Kundan came to Babu ji, saying, 'Babu ji, Bhabhi is crying.'

'What?' Babu ji looked through the darkness towards Bahu's bed. He sat up, then lay down again and told Kundan to go on to sleep.

Lying on his bed, Babu Dhuni Ram could see God's garden through an opening in the sky, and he asked God in his mind, 'Of all those blooming flowers, which is the one for me?' The scene changed and became a river of pain, and he heard continuous wails. Hearing them, he said, 'Since the world was made, how much man has cried!' And crying, he went to sleep.

Within twenty days of Indu's departure, Madan began to lament her. He wrote, 'I'm sick of eating bazaar bread, and I've gotten constipated. My kidney is starting to hurt.' As if he were an office worker needing a leave, he sent a doctor's certificate with the letter and a letter of confirmation from a friend of Babu ji's. This brought no result. Finally, he sent an urgent reply-paid wire.

The money for the reply was wasted, but no matter. Indu and the children returned. Madan didn't speak nicely to Indu for about two days. His mood affected Indu as well. Finding Madan alone one day, she caught and held him. 'Why are you sulking like this? What have I done?'

Madan was annoyed with her and replied brusquely, 'Leave me, go out of my sight. You unworthy woman!'

'Did you call me back to say such things to me?'

'Yes!'

'Well, say them now or forget it.'

'Watch out, and this is all your fault. If you wanted to come, why did you let Babu ji stop you?'

Indu growled, 'You're behaving like a child. How could I say anything? Besides, I think that by calling me, you were cruel to your father.'

'What do you mean?'

'There's no mysterious meaning. He was enjoying life with his family.'

'And what about my life?'

'Your life? You can be wherever you want,' and she spoke mischievously, looking sideways towards Madan. His defense crumbled. He had been waiting for a good excuse, and he caught Indu and held her closely,

'Was Babu ji happy with you?'

'Oh yes, one day I awoke and saw him standing by my pillow smiling down at me.'

'That can't be true!'

'I swear by my life . . .'

'Not by your life, swear by mine.'

'I won't swear by your life, even for millions!' Madan was thinking. 'In books, they call it sex.'

'Sex? What's that?' Indu didn't know the English word. 'That's what is done between man and woman.'

'Oh, Ram!' Catching her breath sharply, she backed away. 'What a dirty thing to say! Aren't you ashamed, talking about Babu ji like that?'

'Shouldn't Babu ji be ashamed, looking at you like that?' Madan countered.

'Why?' Indu immediately took Babu ji's side. 'Why shouldn't he be happy to see his daughter-in-law?'

'Why not indeed, when the daughter-in-law is like you' Madan tried to change the topic.

'Your mind is dirty,' Indu went on angrily, 'that's why your business is crude turpentine. All your books are full of dirt; you and your books can see nothing but sex. When I grew up, my father began to love me more. Was that also that wretched thing, that word you used?' She paused and then continued, 'Why don't you call Babu ji here since he's not happy alone. He's sad. Doesn't that make you sad?'

Madan loved his father very much. As the eldest son, he had been profoundly affected by his mother's death. He remembered her very well. When thoughts of her came to his mind, Madan closed his eyes and began praying *'Om Namo Bhagavate, Vasudevay, Om Namo . . .'* Not only did he love his father, but he also didn't wish to be deprived of his protection, especially since his business was not yet established. But in a noncommittal tone, he said, 'Let Babu ji stay there. This is the first chance since our wedding to be free with each other.'

After three or four days, Babu ji's tear-filled letter arrived, 'My dear Madan . . .' The words *my dear* it appeared, were washed out by salty tears. He wrote, 'Bahu's being here brought back the old days for me. When your mother and I were newly married, she too was as playful and youthful. She threw her clothes here and there, undressing, in the same way. The same sandalwood box . . . the same household chores . . . I go to the bazaar, come home again, bring groceries, and sometimes curd or buttermilk, but no one is in the house. The place where the sandalwood box stood is empty . . .' And once again, half a line was blurred. Finally, he had written, 'Upon returning home from the office, entering these huge dark rooms, dread overcomes me . . .' And in the end, 'One thought about Bahu — don't put her in the care of an inexperienced nurse.'

Indu caught the letter in her hands. With a catch in her breath, her eyes opened wide and close to tears from embarrassment, she said, 'I could die! How did Babu ji know about that?'

Madan recaptured the letter. 'Is Babu ji a child? He's seen the world. He caused the birth of his children.'

'Yes, but . . . how many days has it been?' Indu cast a hasty glance at her stomach, which had not yet begun to swell. As if Babu ji or someone else was looking, she pulled the end of her sari over herself. Her thoughts wandered. Her face glowed, and she said softly, 'Your relatives will send sweets.'

'My relatives? Oh yes.' Madan followed her thoughts. 'But what a shameful thing—only five or six months, and this big fellow is coming!' He motioned towards her stomach.

'Is he coming on his own, or did you bring him?'

'You . . . it's all your fault. Just like a woman.'

'You don't like it?'

'Not at all.'

'Why not?'

'We should have enjoyed life for some more time.'

'Isn't this an enjoyment of life?' Indu was shocked. 'Why do men and women get married? God has given this without our asking, hasn't He? Ask those women who have no children—do you know what they do? They go to the saints and fakirs, tie their ribbons at tombs and shrines. All modesty leaves them and, naked, they cut reeds along the sides of rivers and raise evil spirits at the burning ghats.'

'All right,' Madan stopped her. 'You've begun a long story. Is there such a short life ahead in which to have children?'

'Then when he's born,' Indu's tone rebuked him and her finger jabbed at him, 'you can't even touch his hand! He'll be mine, not yours. You don't need him—but your father does, I know that!'

Abashed and shocked at herself, Indu hid her face in her hands. She had thought that the new life sprouting within her would evoke sympathy and love from its father, but Madan sat without uttering a word. Indu dropped her hands and looked in Madan's direction, and in the special voice of a woman in her first pregnancy, she said, 'Anyway, what we've been talking about will come afterwards. First, I won't survive, I've been afraid of this since my childhood.'

Madan was alarmed. This beautiful thing, who had grown more beautiful with her pregnancy. Could she die? He came up behind her and clasped her in his arms.

'Nothing will happen to you, Indu. I'll snatch you even from the jaws of death! It's not Savitri's turn now, but Satyavan's.' Clinging to Madan, Indu forgot that she had any regrets.

Babu ji didn't write for a long time. However, a sorter came from Saharanpur and told them that Babu ji had begun having heart trouble again and that he had nearly died during one of those attacks. Madan was fearful, and Indu began to cry. After the sorter left, Madan closed his eyes and began repeating with all his heart, *'Om Namo Bhagavate . . .'*

The next day Madan wrote a letter. 'Babu ji, why don't you come home? The children miss you, and so does Bahu.'

But Babu ji could not leave his job. He wrote that he was applying for leave. Madan's feelings of guilt grew.

'If I had let Indu stay with Babu ji, it wouldn't have hurt me . . .'

One night before Vijaya Dashami, Madan, in a state of anguish, was pacing the veranda outside the middle room. Suddenly, he heard an infant crying. He rushed towards the door just as Begum, the nurse, was coming out, saying, 'Congratulations! It's a son!'

'A son?' In a worried voice, he continued, 'How is my wife?'

'Perfectly all right! I've told her it was a girl, though, for if she were too filled with happiness, she'd have trouble recovering after giving birth.'

'Oh . . .' Madan blinked his eyes foolishly and moved forward to enter the room. The nurse stopped him. 'What business have you inside?' She went back in, closing the door firmly.

Madan's legs had not stopped trembling. Now, not from fear but from happiness, or perhaps because when someone comes into the world, all the people in his neighbourhood tremble. Madan knew that when a son is born, the doors and walls of a house begin to shake as if afraid that when the boy grows up, he might throw them out rather than taking care of them. Madan felt as though the walls were really shaking . . .

Chakli Bhabhi had not come for the delivery because her children were too small, but Daryabadi Phuphi had arrived. During the delivery, she had chanted '*Ram, Ram, Ram, Ram . . .*' later, the soft repetition died out.

Never in his life had Madan felt himself to be so superfluous and useless. Just then, the door opened again, and Phuphi came out. In the faint light of the veranda, her face seemed like that of a ghost, completely milky white. Madan blocked her path. 'Indu's all right, isn't she, Phuphi?'

'She's fine, she's fine,' Phuphi reassured him, placing her trembling hand on Madan, and hugging him. She moved on and went straight to the room where the other children were sleeping, lovingly placing a hand on each and murmuring something, with her eyes lifted to the roof. Worn out, she lay face down next to Munni. From her trembling shoulders, Madan could guess that she was crying. He was astonished, Phuphi had seen too many deliveries; why was she so shaken now?

The smell of burning *harmal*, a disinfectant, drifted from the inner room, like a cloud of smoke, enveloping Madan. He felt dizzy. The nurse came out with some clothes; lots of blood was on them, and a few drops fell on the floor. Madan was dazed. He didn't know where he was. His eyes were open, but he perceived nothing. From a distance came a faint cry from Indu and the crying of the baby.

The next three or four days were busy. Digging a hole away from the house, Madan buried himself deep within after the birth of his child. He stopped the dogs from digging too, and what happened after that, he remembered almost nothing. It seemed that from the moment the scent of harmal entered his nostrils, he had lost consciousness, and he regained it only after losing those four days. He was alone in his room with Indu . . . like Nand and Yashoda, parents of Krishna. Indu looked at the child and speculated, 'He resembles you exactly.'

'That may be true.' Casting a fleeting glance at the child, Madan continued, 'All I can say is thank God you were saved.'

'Yes,' she began, 'I always thought that . . .'

'Don't say anything inauspicious!' Madan intervened. 'After this experience I won't come near you again!' He pressed his tongue against his teeth in repentance.

'You'd better take that back,' Indu smiled as she said it. Madan covered his ears with his hands, and Indu began laughing gently.

After the child's birth, Indu's navel did not return to its proper place for several days. It rambled around looking for the child which had gone out into the world and had forgotten its real mother. But then a readjustment took place, and Indu gazed at the world peacefully. She emerged as a goddess, forgiving the sins not only of Madan but of all sinners in the world, and she made offerings of pity and compassion. She became slender after the delivery and seemed to Madan lovelier than before. As he gazed at her, she suddenly placed her hands on her breasts.

'What is it?' Madan asked.

'Nothing,' Indu said, trying to raise herself a little. 'He's hungry.' She motioned towards the child.

'He? Hungry?' Madan looked first at the child and then at Indu. 'How do you know?'

'Don't you see?' She looked downward. 'It's all wet.' Madan saw the milk oozing through her loose gown and smelled a familiar scent. Indu stretched her arms towards the baby. 'Give him to me.'

Madan reached into the cradle but hesitated momentarily; gathering his courage, he lifted the child as though it were a dead rodent and put him back in Indu's lap.

Indu asked shyly, 'Would you go outside?'

'Why? Why should I go out?'

'Please go,' Indu pouted and said modestly, 'I can't feed the baby in front of you.'

'What?' Madan was astonished. 'In front of me—why not?' And shaking his head as though he still did not understand, he went outside. Once at the door, he glanced back at Indu. She had never seemed so beautiful to him as at that moment.

Babu Dhuni Ram came home on leave, but he appeared only a shadow of his former self. When Indu put his grandson in his lap, he seemed happy. But he had developed an ulcer which troubled him night and day. If it hadn't been for the child, Babu ji's condition would have been far worse. Several treatments were attempted. One of the doctors gave him fifteen to twenty coin-sized pills to be consumed every day. The first day, he sweated profusely and had to change clothes three or four times. Each time Madan took the clothes and squeezed them out into a bucket, the sweat filled up a quarter of the bucket.

At night, Babu ji began to feel nauseous and called out, 'Bahu, bring my *datun*. The taste is terrible. Bahu came running, bringing his datun. Babu ji sat up, chewing his neem stick; he still felt nauseous. Blood started to flow. Madan helped him lie back on the pillow, but the pupils of his eyes had turned upward, and just in a moment, he had reached the garden of Heaven where he recognized his favourite flower.

This happened only three weeks after the boy's birth. But Indu scratched her face and beat her head and breasts until they were blue. Before Madan's eyes was the same scene which he had seen in the dream of his own death. The only difference was that Indu took her bangles off instead of breaking them; there were no ashes on her head, but dust from the earth and her tangled hair gave her face a desperate look. And instead of crying, 'Oh neighbours, I've been ruined' she cried, 'Oh neighbours, we've been ruined!'

Madan did not yet realize how great the household's burden had now fallen on him. He collapsed entirely until the next morning. Perhaps he would have been lost if he had not stayed outside and rested face down on the dampened

earth next to the drain, an act which somehow consoled him.
Mother Earth took her child to her breast and saved him. The
children—Kundan, Dulari and Pashi—were like tiny chicks
whose nest was attacked by a hawk; they raised their beaks
and chirped helplessly. If there were any feathers to shelter
them, they were Indu's.

Lying on the side of the drain, Madan thought, 'Now this
world is ended for me. Can I go on living? Will I be able to
laugh again?' He rose and went into the house.

The bathroom was under the stairs. Pushing in and
closing the door behind him, he asked, 'Will I be able to laugh
again?' And he was laughing loudly, though his father's body
was still lying in the living room.

Before lighting the funeral pyre, Madan lay prostrate
on the ground in front of his father's body. It was his last
salutation to the one who had given him life. But he was not
crying. Seeing this, the relatives and neighbours joining in the
mourning were astonished. According to the Hindu ritual, as
the eldest son, Madan had to light the pyre and later break
the burnt skull.

The women standing at the edge of the burning ghat
washed at the well and returned to their homes. When Madan
reached home, he was trembling. Whatever strength Mother
Earth had given to him changed to fear with the arrival of the
night. He needed support; support stronger than the power of
Death. The daughter of Mother Earth, Indu, like Sita coming
out of an earthen vessel, embraced this Ram in her arms. Had
Indu not given herself completely to Madan that night, his
terrible sadness might have killed him.

Within ten months, Indu gave birth to her second son.
Having pushed his wife again into the fires of hell, Madan

forgot his sorrow. Sometimes, he would think that if he had not called Indu back from Babu ji, his father would have lived longer, but soon he was busy making up the loss caused by his father's death. His business, nearly closed because of his negligence, now got off to a good start.

When Indu went to her parent's home, the younger baby clung to her breasts; the older boy was left with Madan. He proved to be very obstinate, sometimes getting his way, sometimes not. Indu wrote letters: 'I hear the crying of my son. Are you beating him?' This astounded Madan. She was an ignorant, illiterate woman. How could she write a thing like this? Once more, he found himself questioning her. Had she been tutored?

Years passed. There wasn't enough money for extra pleasures, but there was sufficient for the family's needs except when big expenses came up, like Kundan's admission fee or Dulari's engagement presents. On such occasions, Madan sat with a downcast face. Indu approached him and asked smilingly, 'Why are you worried?'

'Why shouldn't I be worried? You know Kundan's college admission fee . . . and Dulari's . . .'

Indu laughed. 'Come with me.'

Madan followed her to the sandalwood box which no one, not even Madan, had permission to touch. Sometimes this made him angry. He often said, 'When you die, you'll take this along, clasped to your breast.'

She always replied, 'Yes, I certainly will.'

Now Indu took from the sandalwood box money and put it before Madan.

'Where did this come from?'

'From nowhere special . . . You're concerned with eating the mangoes, not with counting the trees, aren't you?'

'Yes, but . . .'

'So, go to your work.'

When Madan pressed her, she laughed and said, 'I have a rich friend, don't you think that's it?'

Madan did not like this joke. He knew it was a lie. So, Indu changed her story, 'I'm a robber, a generous one who steals with one hand and gives to the poor with the other.'

In this way, Dulari's wedding was financed; Indu sold even her own ornaments. Debt was incurred and paid off. And Kundan's wedding was also celebrated.

In these weddings, Indu took the place of the mother and performed the hand-exchange ceremony. Babu ji and his wife looked on and threw down flowers that no one could see from the sky. But it so happened that they began to quarrel. Mother said to Babu ji, 'You have eaten the food cooked by Bahu, and you've had her serve you. I'm so unfortunate that I haven't even seen her!' This argument reached the ears of Vishnu and even Shiva. The gods supported the right of Mother and decided to send her to the world of mortals. She was put in the womb of Indu, and so a daughter was born to Madan and Indu.

Indu was scarcely a goddess, for she would even fight with Madan about matters of principle or the children. Angered at this streak of obstinacy, Madan called her 'Harishchandra's daughter'. Whatever the factual differences of opinion, Madan and the others in the family had to submit to Indu since her stand was always based on truth and dharma. Even if the quarrel was prolonged, and Madan was able to reject all her statements with husbandly sureness, in the end, he came to Indu and asked her forgiveness.

After Kundan's marriage, a new sister-in-law came to the house. Though she was a wife, Indu was first a woman, then a wife. In contrast, the younger Rani was just a wife. Because of Rani, the brothers quarrelled, and the household items were divided through J.P. Uncle's help. In this joint-family division, the property left by the parents and Indu's belongings was indiscriminately mixed. Indu suffered in silence and maintained her calm. After gaining a separate household, Kundan and Rani were still not happy. But soon in Indu's new house, neither happiness nor household goods were lacking.

Indu did not regain her health after the birth of her daughter. The child continually clung to Indu's breasts. While the others looked down on this small lump of flesh, Indu gave her loving attention, but sometimes, she, too, became distressed and thrust the child into the cradle. She scolded her, saying, 'Why don't you let me live?' The little girl would cry.

Madan started avoiding Indu. Despite his marriage's security and warmth, he still felt he had not found the woman he truly desired. The crude turpentine business was flourishing, and Madan spent money without informing Indu. After Babu ji's death there was no one to question him, he was completely free. It was as if his neighbour Sibte's buffalo sniffed at Madan's face once more. The buffalo of that wedding night was sold, but its owner was alive. Madan began to go with Sibte to those places where light and shadow made strange forms. Sometimes a dark triangle in the corner was quickly pierced by a four-cornered wave of light from the above. No view seemed complete. It appeared that a garment came from the side and flew towards the sky, or another garment completely covered the observer's face and the person struggled for breath. When the square wave of light formed a frame, a figure came and stood in it. The observer stretched out his hands—and the figure crossed to the other side as if nothing were there. From the rear a dog began to howl, but its voice was drowned in the beat of drums coming from above.

Madan knew the features of his ideal, but every time he thought he had found it, the artist had drawn one wrong line, or the sound of the laughter was higher than it should have been. Madan was lost in the search for pristine beauty and perfect art.

Sibte talked to his wife when she presented Madan to him as a perfect husband; not simple description in words but it seemed the words themselves had been thrown on Sibte's face. Sibte didn't take it kindly. He hit back in the same way, as if with a bloody watermelon whose nerves and fibres stuck in her nose, eyes and ears. Then shouting countless curses, the Begum took the kernel and marrow from the basket of her memory and threw them into Indu's clean courtyard.

One Indu divided herself into two. One was Indu, the real self, and the other was an angry, aggressive personality.

Whenever Madan returned home, he came to the house to wash, put on clean clothes, and chewed paan with spicy tobacco. One day when he returned, he found Indu looking different. She had dabbed powder on her face, rouge on her cheeks, and, not having lipstick, had rubbed pigment on her lips. Her hair had been done so beautifully that Madan couldn't stop staring at it.

'What's going on?' he asked with astonishment.

'Nothing,' she replied, meeting his stare. 'I had some leisure time today, that's all.'

After fifteen years of marriage, Indu had some leisure time for her make-up! During those years, wrinkles had come to her face, and two or three rolls of flesh showed below her sari-blouse. But today, her flaws were not visible under carefully applied makeup and lovely clothes.

'This can't be!' Madan thought with a jolt. He turned towards Indu for another look, as a horse trader turns towards a faultless mare. She was an older mare, but she wore a red bridle . . . Whatever fault lines existed, they weren't evident to his intoxicated eyes. Indu was magnificent even after fifteen years of marriage. Phulan, Rashida, Mrs Roberts and all the other women were but water carriers compared to Indu! Madan began to feel compassion and a particular fear.

Though the sky was not cloudy, it began to rain. The Ganges of domestic life appeared to be in flood, and its water overflowed the banks and took the whole valley and its inhabitants into its fold. The water flowed with such speed that it seemed even the Himalayas would be drowned. The baby began to cry, which was unusual, and upon hearing this, Madan closed his eyes not having the courage to bear what was happening around him. When he opened them, she was standing before him, now a young girl. No, no, it was Indu. Her mother's daughter, or her daughter's mother, who was smiling with the corners of her eyes and seeing from the corners of her lips.

In the room where one day the odor of burning harmal had made Madan dizzy, today a new fragrance confused him. A little rain could be more dangerous than a heavy downpour. Water seeped through the rafters and started dripping between

Madan and Indu. But Madan was still lost. In his excitement, his eyes shrank, and his breathing became abnormally rapid.

'Indu . . .' His voice was several notes higher than on the wedding night.

Indu, not looking at him, answered, 'Yes,' and her voice was several notes lower. It was Amavas, the darkest night without moon.

Before Madan's hands had reached out, she moved to him. He lifted her chin and examined her face, seeking all that was lost or found . . . Indu looked once at his darkening face and closed her eyes.

'What's this?' He was startled. 'Your eyes are swollen!'

'It's nothing.' She gestured towards the baby, 'That wretched *mother* kept me awake all night.'

The baby had been quiet, almost seeming to hold her breath and observe what was happening. The rain stopped— but did it really? Madan looked thoughtfully at Indu's eyes,

'Yes, but . . . these tears.'

'They're tears of happiness. Tonight—it belongs to me.' And she clung to Madan, laughing shakily.

With a surge of physical pleasure, he gripped her and said, 'Today, my deepest wish has been fulfilled, Indu, after so many years. I always wanted . . .'

'But you didn't tell me—you remember I asked something of you the night of our wedding?'

'Yes.'

'Give me your sorrows,' Madan replied.

'But you didn't ask anything of me.'

'I?' The idea was strange to him. 'What could I have asked? Whatever I wished, you had given me. You loved my family, looked after the education of my brothers and sister, and arranged their marriages, gave birth to my dear children—all these you have given me!'

'I too thought that that was enough,' Indu replied, 'but now I know that it isn't.'

'What do you mean?'

'Nothing . . .' she hesitated. Then, 'I kept back one thing.'

'What did you keep?'

She was silent for a time, looking away from him.

'My modesty, my happiness. You should have told me, give me your happiness, and then I . . .' She couldn't continue. Finally, she added, 'And now I have nothing.'

Madan's hands softened. He felt as though he'd been driven into the ground. This illiterate woman? Was it a tutored speech? But no, this had come from the furnace of life, and the fiery sparks were flying all around them.

After a while Madan spoke, 'I understand, Indu.'

Shedding tears, Indu and Madan embraced each other. Indu took Madan's hands and led him to a world, usually not reached by humans until after death.

2

Quarantine

The plague descended like fog, and made everything invisible, evoking fear, spreading its tentacles all the way down to the plains in the Himalayan foothills. Every child in the city shivered while hearing its name. The plague was dreadful, but the quarantine was no less frightening. People were not as harassed by the plague as by the need to quarantine themselves. That was why the Health Department had printed large-size posters asking citizens to protect themselves from rodents, and these posters were found on the doors, streets, and pathways. The message initially said, 'No Rodent, No Plague,' but later expanded to include, 'No Rodent, No Plague, No Quarantine'.

People's fear of quarantine was justified. As a doctor, I have a firm opinion about this matter. I can forcefully affirm that more deaths in the city were caused by the quarantine than the plague. I say this recognizing that quarantine is not a disease but a precautionary measure that requires demarcation of an area where healthy people during an epidemic are needed to separate themselves from those infected by the virus to contain disease. Although there were enough number of doctors and nurses during the quarantine, the excessive numbers of patients limited the care for all those who needed it. I saw many patients losing their will to fight the disease because they were separated from their loved ones. Many died because they saw others dying around them. Sometimes, some people whose condition otherwise was not serious died because they were breathing the same virus-infected air. And because so many people were dying, the dead bodies were being disposed of following a specially prescribed procedure. Hundreds of dead bodies were dragged like carcasses of dogs into mounds of fire. There were no customary religious services. The bodies were set on fire after the liberal splashing of petrol. At the time of the sunset, flames rising from the burning stacks of dead bodies merged with the sunset's redness, making the survivors think that the whole world was on fire.

Quarantine also became a cause of death due to the patient's family members' habit of suppressing information about the infection to save the patient from being forcibly removed and admitted into the quarantine facility. Every doctor was required to inform the health authorities about an infected patient as soon as they found out. This prevented families from seeking medical help. The neighbours came to know about an infected household only when they saw a dead body being taken out the front door amid cries and howls of family members.

During this time, I was working as a doctor in a quarantine facility. I, too, was much afraid of the plague. When I returned home, I spent quite a bit of my time washing my hands with antiseptic soap. I also gargled with a mouthwash that killed viruses, drank hot stomach-burning coffee, or consumed brandy. These routines had side effects: I suffered from sleeplessness and eye burns. Sometimes I took medicines that caused me to vomit to clean the inner recesses of my body. When scalding coffee created reactions in my stomach and made the vapours rise and enter my brain, I felt forewarned like any conscious man about the dangers ahead. Whenever I felt any minor irritation in my throat, I took it as an early sign of plague. O hell! I, too, will become a victim of this terrible disease. Plague—and then quarantine!

During those days, a recent convert to Christianity, William Bhagu, whose job was to clean the street, came to me and said, 'Babu ji, something horrible has happened. Today, the ambulance removed twenty plus one patient from our neighborhood.'

'Twenty-one? Ambulance?' I uttered these words showing my surprise. 'Yes, twenty plus one. They took them to qonteen. Alas! None of them will return alive.'

My inquiries revealed that Bhagu woke up at three o'clock each night. He gulped plentiful liquor, and then, as he was instructed by the Committee, he would start spreading lime powder in the streets and into the drains to stop the spread of the virus. Bhagu informed me that 3 a.m. had another significance. He was required to pick up any dead bodies that had been thrown into the street. He also ran errands for folks who feared the disease and were confined to their homes. Bhagu was not afraid of the disease. He thought if death came, he would not find an escape, even if he tried to hide.

During the days when everyone avoided close contact, Bhagu was there, covering his head and his mouth with a piece of cloth and tirelessly serving others. Although his knowledge was limited, he shared information with others like an expert. He talked about techniques for avoiding the disease based on his experiences and advocated cleanliness, the spread of lime and confinement at one's home. One day I saw him acting as a promotor for liberal consumption of liquor. When he came to see me that day, I asked him, 'Are you not afraid of the plague?'

'No, Babu ji. If she came uninvited, she wouldn't do any harm. You are such a big hakim, and you have cured thousands, but when I get the virus, your medicine and your instructions will do me no good. Yes, Babu ji. Please don't mind what I say. I'm telling you the right thing, and I'm very clear about what I speak.' And then, while changing the mode of conversation, he said, 'tell me about qonteen, Babu ji. I want to know about qonteen.'

'Yes, thousands are being admitted into the quarantine. We are offering the best care, which is possible. But there is a limit. Those who work with me are afraid of staying close to the patients for a long time. Fear is keeping their throats and lips dry. No one brings his mouth close to the patient's mouth as you do. No one troubles himself like you do. Bhagu, may God take care of you for your service to mankind!'

Bhagu lowered his neck and slightly uncovered his face by pushing the cloth covering aside, which revealed his face's reddish glow, fuelled by liquor consumption. He said, 'Babu ji, I'm worth nothing. If I can be of any help, if my useless body can serve someone's need, that would be my good luck. Babu ji, Rev. L. Abbey often comes to our neighbourhood to share the word of God. He tells us how much Jesus Christ emphasized the need to care of the sick by putting in all of one's effort. I understand this.'

I wanted to appreciate Bhagu's courage, but a surge of emotions stopped me. Looking at his self-confidence and action-filled life, I felt the presence of an envious drive in my heart. Following my inner desire, I decided that I would make a genuine effort to save quarantined patients' lives. I would provide comfort, even at the cost of my life. But there is always a giant chasm between one's thoughts and actions. When I saw patients' dreadful state on reaching the quarantine facility, and my nostrils felt the horrible virus-ridden smell coming from their mouths, my spirit retreated in self-defeat. I lost the courage to follow in Bhagu's footsteps.

Yet, that day I did a lot of work in the quarantine with Bhagu's help—this work required close contact with the patient and Bhagu did that for me, without raising any objections. I stayed away from the patients not only because I was afraid of death but also of quarantine. But was Bhagu bigger than death and quarantine? That day 400 patients were admitted into the quarantine and 250 of them died.

But because of Bhagu's fearless endeavour, I was able to increase the number of my patients. There was a map in the chief medical officer's room that showed progress in patients' treatment and it showed a consistent rise in the average well-being of patients under my care. Finding an excuse, I visited that room. I derived great satisfaction seeing a near 100 per cent increase in my patients' number.

One day I drank brandy, exceeding my usual limit. My heart rate jumped up, and my pulse started to race like a stallion. And like someone who had lost his mind, I began to move hither and thither. I suspected that the plague virus had finally caught up with me, and soon there would appear lumps in my throat or in my thighs. I was exasperated with this thought. And one day, I thought of running away from the quarantine. I shivered with fear as long as I stayed in the facility. That day I saw Bhagu only twice.

It was noontime when I saw Bhagu embracing a patient. He was massaging the patient's hands with great affection. Whatever strength that person had, he used to utter the words, 'Allah is the Saviour! He shouldn't bring even an enemy to this place. My two daughters . . .' Bhagu cut the person short and said, 'Be grateful to the Son of God, Jesus, my brother. You're looking good.'

'Yes, Brother, I'm thankful to God. I'm better than before. If I can leave the quarantine . . .' These words had hardly come out of the patient's mouth that his nerves tightened. Some liquid poured out of his mouth, and his eyes turned into stone. His body shook violently. The patient was showing improvement and was feeling better, but he lost his speech for a reason that could not be explained. Bhagu shed his invisible blood tears because no one else would mourn the patient's death. If any family member were present, he would have shaken the earth and sky with his wailing. Bhagu, it seemed, was the only relative present. He felt everyone's pain and was the only one who mourned. He prayed to Jesus to alleviate people's suffering, presenting himself as the one who was responsible for all the sins and moral lapses of men.

One day Bhagu came running to me, out of breath, unable to hide the anguish in his voice. 'Babu ji, this qonteen is hell; it is the same kind of hell that Reverend describes in his sermons.'

I told him, 'Yes, my brother. This hell is even worse than the other one. I'm myself thinking of finding an excuse for running away from here. I'm not feeling well today.'

'Babu ji, what more could we expect? Today, the patient who had lost consciousness due to the disease was thrown to the stack of dead bodies thinking that he had died. When petrol was sprinkled and the fire spread, I saw him moving his hands while his body was caught in the flames. I jumped and brought him out. Babu ji, he was badly burnt. My own right arm suffered burns in my attempt to save him.'

I looked at Bhagu's arm and found that his yellow flesh was visible under the burnt skin. The sight shocked and jolted me. I asked him, 'Was that person saved?'

'Babu ji, he was a good man. The world could not take advantage of his goodness and decency. Even in that traumatic state of shock, he raised his scorched face, and using his lifeless gaze, he thanked me.'

'And Babu ji . . .' Bhagu continued, 'After this, he was afflicted by so much pain, so much suffering, I have not seen any person go through it. And then he died. I should have allowed him to burn himself to death. I saved him for what? More hurt and more ache. He was not saved. I picked him up with my scorched arm and then dropped him at the mound of dead bodies.'

Bhagu fell silent after this. Trying to suppress his torment, he said, 'Do you know why that patient died? Which disease killed him? It wasn't a plague. It was qonteen. Yes, qonteen, qonteen!'

Although the thought of hell during this time of endless dread, agony and anguish was a source of comfort, the voices of grief-stricken humans frequently reached one's ears. In the urban atmosphere where even owls hesitated to utter their loud calling amid the night, there were lamentations of mothers, woes of sisters, bereavement of spouses and heartbreaking brooding of the kids which created a highly despondent environment. During these days, when even healthy people were depressed, one could imagine the despondence of those who were sick. And like someone suffering from jaundice, these people saw yellowed hopelessness from the walls of their homes. Those who were quarantined knew that it was their turn to die. They were not only watching the angel of death standing in person before them but also, they were staying alive like straws glued to a tree on the top of a hill amid a storm. At the same time, wild waves hit, determined to sink the mountain itself.

Maybe it was superstition—I missed going to the quarantine that day. I made an excuse for some important work, although it troubled me mentally. It was just possible that my presence would have helped some patients. But fear overpowered me. Before I went to my bed in the evening, I got the news that about 500 patients were admitted to quarantine.

I was just about to sleep after drinking liver-burning coffee when I heard Bhagu's voice at my door. When the servant opened the door, Bhagu came running to me, somewhat out of his breath, and said, 'Babu ji, my wife has fallen ill. Lumps have appeared in her neck. For God's sake, please try to save her. She is nursing a one-and-a-half-year-old child. If she dies, he will die too.'

Instead of showing sympathy, I replied in a sarcastic tone, 'You couldn't find the time to come earlier than this? Has the sickness started just now?'

'She had some fever in the morning when I left for qonteen.'

'She was sick at home, and even then, you decided to go to the quarantine?'

'Yes, Babu ji,' Bhagu said in a trembling voice. 'She was slightly unwell. I thought it must be a problem of the kind women generally have. She didn't have any other symptoms. Two of my brothers were present at home. And there were several hundred helpless patients in the qonteen.'

'With your excessive empathy and kindness, you have succeeded in bringing the virus to your home. Didn't I warn you that you shouldn't get too close to the patients? Look, for this reason, I didn't go there today. You are to be blamed. What can I do now? You think you're brave and heroic. You should pay the price now. There are hundreds of patients in the city that need my care.'

Bhagu replied with utmost humility, 'But for the Son of God, Jesus Christ . . .'

'Get away. You overthink about yourself. You intentionally inserted your hand in this fire. Why should I pay the price for that? It is late at night. What can I do for you?'

'But Rev. . . .'

'Go to Rev. . . . '

Bhagu lowered his head and left. After about half an hour, when I regained my cool, I felt ashamed of my behaviour. If I repented so soon, it meant that I didn't act thoughtfully. The best punishment for me was to offer my apologies to Bhagu while providing adequate care for his sick wife. I changed quickly into working clothes, and walking briskly, I reached Bhagu's home. I saw that the two of Bhagu's younger brothers were taking out the bed on which their sister-in-law was lying flat.

I faced Bhagu and asked him, 'Where are you taking her?'

He replied calmly, 'To the qonteen.' Then he added, 'When you refused to help me, Babu ji, I was left with no other option. She would get some care there. And when I go there to help other patients, I'll also take care of her.'

'Keep this *chaarpai* here. You haven't forgotten about other patients, stupid fellow!'

They took her inside. Whatever medicine I had, I gave it to Bhagu's wife and wondered how the deathless enemy within her would react. She opened her eyes.

Bhagu said in his quivering voice, 'I'll be forever indebted to you, Babu ji.'

I said, 'I'm sorry about my behaviour. God will reward you for the good work that you have done taking care of other patients!'

At that very moment, the enemy struck back, using its most deadly weapon. The lips of Bhagu's wife trembled, and her pulse was slowing down. My deathless enemy, who usually won every battle, threw me flat on the ground. I had lost. I lowered my head in shame and said, 'Bhagu! Unfortunate Bhagu! This is a strange reward for all your sacrifices. Alas!'

Bhagu cried like a broken man. How sad was that view when Bhagu moved forward and separated the sobbing child from the mother? I returned heartbroken.

I thought that given the dark abyss into which he had been thrown, Bhagu would stop caring for others. But the very next day, I found him helping patients. He saved lives, not caring about how fate had treated him. I, too, followed his example. After my work was done at the quarantine and in the hospitals, I used my spare time visiting poorer parts of the city. These were centres of disease due to the dirt and filth spread all around them.

At last, the city was free of the pandemic. It seemed that the city had had a shower bath. Rodents were a thing of the past. There could be one or two cases in the town that got immediate attention, and therefore, the spread of the disease was stopped.

The city life resumed its daily routine. Schools, colleges and offices were now open, and were delivering the expected services.

I felt that whenever I walked through the bazaar, I saw fingers pointing towards me. People looked at me with gratitude. When newspapers carried notes of appreciation for the work accomplished during the pandemic, they included my photograph. I was getting so much praise that I often felt self-gratified with a touch of vanity.

Finally, there was an important public meeting, and invitees included wealthy folks and medical practitioners. The minister in charge of urban welfare presided. I got the honour of sitting next to the chief guest because the purpose of the meeting was to honour my work and services. My shouldres felt heavy with one too many garlands. Although my presence in the forum was distinctive, I moved my gaze, filled with pride, this way and that way. 'In recognition of your work for the well-being of human beings, the Committee was offering a bag containing the "petty" amount of one thousand and one rupees.'

All those who were present were showering praises on my benefactor and on me. They were saying that my efforts and my care saved numerous lives. I worked day and night treating the citizens' lives like my own, my personal well-being as others' well-being. I had reached the patients in their homes and hearths and saved their lives.

The Minister for Urban Welfare stood up and standing on the left side of the table, he picked up a narrow stick and brought the audience's attention to the dark line that showed an uptrend in the display on the wall. The upward trend of the line showed the number of my patients who were cured of the disease. Fifty-four patients, who were my responsibility, were fully healed. That meant that my achievement was 100 per cent. The dark line had peaked.

After this, the minister appreciated my work and my dedication to my job. He also added, 'Given Bakhshi ji's services, he is being promoted as a Lt. Colonel.'

There was huge applause that came from all corners of the room. Amid this noise, I raised my head, filled somewhat with conceit. While thanking the chief guest and the audience, I delivered a big speech. I pointed out that the medical doctors' work wasn't limited to hospitals and quarantine places. They reached out to the poor in their homes. These were the people who couldn't help themselves, and they were worst-affected by the disease. We devoted our full attention to the complete eradication of the disease. When we were free after our work in the quarantine and the hospital, we spent our evenings in these dreadful places.

That day after the meeting, when I reached home, filled with great self-esteem after having earned the title of Lt. Colonel and feeling the weight of 1001 rupees, I heard a murky voice.

'Babu ji, many congratulations!'

Bhagu, while congratulating me, kept his broom on the cover of the water tank, and using both of his hands, he removed his face covering. I was taken aback.

'It is you . . . Bhagu, Brother!' I uttered these words with some difficulty. 'If the world doesn't know you, let it be. I know you. Your Jesus Christ knows you. Rev. L. Abbey follows you. May God bless you!'

I felt that my throat had dried up. Suddenly, the image of Bhagu's dying wife and her child came before my eyes. Because of the garlands' burden, my neck was hurting, and my overflowing wallet's weight was tearing apart my feeble pocket. After receiving so many awards and honours, I could not do anything other than feel sorry for the world that most generously showers accolades and praises!

3

Lajwanti

A simple touch makes you wither and droop,
O lajwanti plant!
A Punjabi folk song

After partition's bloodbath, the wounded, whose number was legion, wiped the blood from their bodies and, rising to their feet, turned their attention to those who, though looking unharmed, had their hearts full of anguish.

Rehabilitation committees were being set up in every lane and by-lane of cities with great enthusiasm. They tried to rehabilitate the uprooted people, who had lost their businesses by providing them access to land and shelter in their homes. But there was one aspect of rehabilitation to which they paid scant attention—the task of rehabilitating abducted women. This programme soon got underway with a slogan, 'Give them a place in your hearts'.

The committee set up for this purpose met with significant opposition, especially from the orthodox people living around the Narain Bawa temple.

To give this programme a definite shape, Mohalla Shakoor residents had taken the lead, with Babu Sunderlal being the secretary of the newly formed committee. He had been elected to this office with a majority of eleven votes. A prominent local lawyer was elected its president. In the opinion of the old petition writer of Chowki Kalan and other influential residents, they couldn't have selected a better person than Babu Sunderlal for the secretary's post. Being the husband of an abducted woman, he was expected to put his heart and soul into this work. His wife was still to be traced and restored to him. And by chance, her name was Lajo—Lajwanti.

Early in the morning, the rehabilitation committee members would lead a singing procession that went around singing, 'Lajwanti leaves droop at the mere touch of a hand.' Sunderlal's friends, Neki Ram and Rasalu would sing lustily, but Babu Sunderlal's voice would falter and trail into silence. He would walk in silence thinking of Lajwanti. Where was Lajwanti now? In what condition? Did she still think of him? Would she ever come back? Sunderlal's feet would shake as he walked along the hard and cobbled road.

A time came when he stopped thinking of Lajwanti. He had abandoned all hope of retrieving her, and his loss had become a part of the people's undefined loss in general. To drown his sorrows, he had taken to social service. Even so, when he raised his voice to sing in unison with others, he could not help reflecting on the frailty of the human heart. It could get hurt so quickly, like the lajwanti plant whose leaves curled up at the mere touch of a finger.

Sunderlal had been very harsh with his wife, Lajwanti. He was watchful all the time, and controlled where she went, where she sat, what she ate. He would beat her up at the slightest pretext.

And his poor Lajo! A simple country girl, she was delicate and slender like a branch of the mulberry tree. Her complexion had turned swarthy by remaining too much in the sun, and life in the open had filled her with animal spirits. She ran about with uninhibited grace in her village like dew drops on a leaf. Her slimness was not the result of ill-health but bespoke of her inherent strength.

When the heavily built Sunderlal first set his eyes upon her, his mind wavered. But later, when he saw that she could easily carry heavy loads without a scowl on her face and even put up with his beating without wincing, he felt incredibly reassured. It made him harsher still, and he increased the beatings, never caring for a moment to consider that anything carried beyond certain limits undermined one's patience and endurance.

Lajwanti herself played a part in blurring these limits. She would not give herself up to despair for long. After a beating, Sunderlal had only to throw a smile in her direction and she would smile back and towards him. 'Beat me again and see what happens!' she would say in mock anger. It was clear that she had already forgiven him for his beating. Like the other girls of her village, she knew that all husbands beat their wives as a matter of routine. If a woman rebelled, the other women would put their fingers on their noses and say, 'You call him a man. Do you? He can't even keep a woman on a leash!'

This beating was even canonized in songs. Sometimes even Lajo sang:

No city boy for me.
He wears heavy boots.
And I have such a slender waist!

And the irony of it was that she took a liking for a city boy the first time she saw him and ended up marrying him. The city boy was none other than Sunderlal.

He had come to Lajwanti's village as a member of a friend's wedding party. He had whispered in the bridegroom's ear, 'Your younger sister-in-law is a peach, very coy, very juicy. And so, must be your bride. Sour-sweet to make your mouth tingle!' These words had fallen on Lajo's ears, and she had immediately taken a fancy for Sunderlal, forgetting that he was wearing such heavy boots and her waist was so slim.

Such were the thoughts occupying Sunderlal's mind as he went round with the morning singing party. If only he could find Lajo again! Like a devoted husband, he would nestle her in his heart and impress upon the people that these unfortunate women were not to be blamed. They had fallen into the hands of those lechers and rioters to be exploited for their pleasure. They were the victims of circumstances, and a society that refused to take them back was rotten to its core and deserved to be wiped out of existence. Bearing in mind all those hypothetical cases, he would come up with a strong plea to rehabilitate these women and accord them a status, normally due to a venerable mother, a wife, a sister in every home. He would further urge upon the people not to blame these women even by a hint, about the sordid time they had passed through. He reminded them that they were sensitive like the lajwanti plant, which withered at the touch of a finger.

To propagate the idea of 'Give them a place in your hearts', the Mohalla Shakoor Committee took out singing processions, morning after morning. They would start at four in the morning, considered the ideal time for the purpose when it was so peaceful and quiet, and people were receptive to godly prayers. Even the street dogs who stayed awake all night acting as self-styled night guards had retired to seek the dying warmth of tandoors (ovens). Men whose bodies were lapping up the cosy warmth of winter beds would mutter on hearing the singing party passing in the street below, 'Oh, the same people again!' And then they would willingly lend their ears to Babu Sunderlal's harangue. Women who had managed to come across the border from Pakistan would lie sprawled in their beds like disintegrating cauliflowers while their stalk-like stiff husbands who lay by their sides would grunt, expressing their anger. Children who woke up momentarily would mimic the words of the songs and slide back into sleep again. The words heard at dawn leave their impression on the mind and keep buzzing in the ears throughout the day. Often a man keeps humming them without understanding their meaning.

It was the cumulative effect of these slogans and harangues that when Miss Mridula Sarabhai arranged for the exchange of abducted women between India and Pakistan, some Mohalla Shakoor men tacitly agreed to take their women back. The relatives of these rescued women assembled at the Chowki Kalan outpost to receive them. For some time, the abducted women and their menfolk eyed each other in awkward silence.

Then with a nod of their heads, the men signified their acceptance and walked off with bowed heads, their women following them. A new chapter had begun in their lives to rebuild their homes. Rasalu, Neki Ram and Sunderlal shouted, 'Long Live Mohinder Singh!' 'Long Live Sohan Lal!' thus lauding the men whose women had joined them.

Many of the abducted women whom their husbands, parents, brothers or sisters had even refused to recognize, why couldn't they have killed themselves? Some people asked. To save their honour, they could have taken poison or jumped into a well. They were indeed cowards to have clung to their lives when there were examples of thousands of women who had taken their own lives before giving the ravishers a chance to dishonour them. They forgot that even to live required great courage. What mental tortures they would have gone through, with what dazed eyes they would have struggled against death to live in this hostile world where one day their own husbands would refuse to take them back. These women would silently repeat their names to themselves—Sohagwanti, one who had the dignity of marital status. Once their names had great meaning for them, but now the same names had become a curse.

Locating her brother in the crowd, Sohagwanti said, 'Bihari, my brother, so you also refuse to recognize me? Don't you remember I had carried you in my arms when you were a little child?' But Bihari tried to slip away. While doing so, his gaze fell upon his parents, who had steeled their hearts and were helplessly looking at Narain Bawa, who was looking up at heaven. Heaven that had no reality; it was merely an illusion, a myth, a boundary line beyond which stretched a great void where there was nothing to see.

Miss Sarabhai had brought a truckload of Hindu women from Pakistan in exchange for Muslim women. Lajwanti was not among them. Sunderlal watched with great expectation until the last woman had got down from the truck. Sorely disappointed, he rededicated himself to the committee's work with greater zeal. Now he took out singing processions both in the morning and the evening. Periodically, he would also organize street-corner meetings. The venerable lawyer, Sufi Kalka Prasad, addressed these meetings in his halting wheezy voice, while Rasalu stood by holding a spittoon. Strange noises burst forth from the microphone as long as the lawyer's speech lasted. Then Neki Ram, the petition writer, would take over. He would go on and on quoting from the scriptures and the shastras to lend weight to his arguments. But with every sentence, he drifted away from what he wanted to say. Seeing that the meeting's real purpose was getting confused and that he was fast losing ground, Sunderlal would bravely rise to stem the rot but would sit down after spewing out a sentence or two, his voice choked, his eyes brimming with tears. A hush would fall over the audience. But his two sentences, which came from the depth of his anguished heart, had more impact than the meandering speech of the aged lawyer, Kalka Prasad. The audience's emotions drained out at the end of the lectures, and they returned home empty-headed.

One day, the committee people came out in the afternoon a little in advance of their usual time. They made an inroad into the temple zone considered the stronghold of fossilized orthodoxy.

Outside the temple precincts, some people were sitting on a cement platform under a peepul tree listening to a discourse on the Ramayana. Narain Bawa was narrating an episode from the great epic where a washerman had turned out his wife from his house saying that he wasn't Raja Ram Chander, who would accept Sita after she had lived for many days with Ravana. Ram sent Sita away from his palace, although at that time she was an expectant mother.

'Could one find a better example of Ram Rajya?' Narain Bawa asked his audience. 'This is Ram Rajya! Here even the voice of an insignificant washerman counted.'

The committee procession had stopped near the temple, and the participants stopped listening to the discourse. As he finished listening to the last statement, Sunderlal said, 'We don't need such a Ram Rajya, Baba.'

'Be quiet!'

'Who are you?' Someone yelled from the gathering. Sunderlal marched forward and replied, 'No one can stop me from speaking.'

There was a chorus of protests. 'Silence! No, we won't allow him to speak!' And then a voice came floating from a corner, 'We shall kill him!'

In a placatory tone, Narain Bawa said, 'Sunderlal, you don't understand the sanctity of the holy scriptures.'

'I understand only one thing,' Sunderlal retorted. 'In Ram Rajya, they listened to a washerman's voice, but in the present Ram Rajya, they refuse to listen to Sunderlal.'

The people who were going to rough up Sunderlal quickly cleared some place under the peepul tree by sweeping away the tree's berries. 'Give him a chance to speak,' they said, sitting down.

Rasalu and Neki Ram nudged Sunderlal to speak. He said, 'Shri Ram was a holy soul, an examplar for us. But how is it that he took a washerman's words for truth but refused to believe a mighty queen?'

Narain Bawa scratched his beard thoughtfully. 'Sunderlal, it's because Sita was his wife. You have missed the point.'

'Yes, Bawa, there are many things which are beyond my comprehension,' Sunderlal said. 'But I regard Ram Rajya as a state where a man does not suffer, nor does he allow others to suffer. To be inequitable to others is as great a sin as being inequitable to oneself. Even today, Lord Ram has turned out Sita because she was forced to live with Ravana. Was she responsible for what happened? Like so many of our sisters and mothers, wasn't she the victim of an evil design? Was it a question of right and wrong on Sita's part, or was it Ravana's palpable wickedness? Ravana, who had ten human heads and one big donkey's head. Today our own innocent Sitas have been thrown out of their homes. Sita . . . Lajwanti.'

Sunderlal broke down and started crying. Rasalu and Neki Ram held the banner on which school children had freshly pasted paper cut-outs bearing slogans. 'Glory to Sunderlal Babu!' they shouted. 'Glory to the great self-immolator Sita!' From a corner rose a lone voice '. . . and Shri Ram Chander!'

There were voices from all sides, 'Silence! Silence!'

Narain Bawa's discourse, which had been going on for the past many days, had suddenly come to naught. Many people rose from their seats and joined the procession headed by the lawyer Kalka Prasad and the petition writer, Hukam Singh. They marched on triumphantly towards Chowki Kalan, tapping their old walking sticks on the ground. There were still tears in Sunderlal's eyes as they were lost looking at the crowd. Today he had realized his plight as never before.

People sang with gusto as they marched: 'The lajwanti leaves wither and droop at the mere touch of a hand.'

The sound of the song was still echoing in the people's ears. The morning had not arrived, and Mohalla Shakoor was still lost in the morning haze. The widow living in House No. 414 indolently stretched her arms in a yawn and, finding that morning had not dawned yet, went back to sleep. Sunderlal's old village mate, Lal Chand, for whom Sunderlal and Kalka Prasad had obtained a ration shop through their influence, came tearing through the morning darkness.

'Congratulations!' he cried, sticking out his arms from under his thick cotton chaddar.

'Congratulations for what, Lal Chand?' Sunderlal asked, fixing a small piece of additive in his chillum.

'I've seen Lajo Bhabhi.'

The chillum fell from Sunderlal's hands, scattering the tobacco laced with additive on the floor.

'Where?' he asked, holding Lal Chand's shoulder, and shaking it when a quick reply did not come.

'On the border at Wagah.'

Sunderlal let go of Lal Chand's shoulder. 'It must have been someone else.' he said.

'No, Brother, it was Lajo. I'm sure of it. Lajo.'

'You recognize her?' Sunderlal asked. He picked up bits of tobacco from the floor and rubbed them on his palm. He picked the chillum from Rasalu's hookah. 'Tell me, how did you identify her?' he asked. 'Any distinguishing marks?'

'She has a tattoo mark on her chin, another on her cheek.'

'Yes, yes!' Sunderlal himself excitedly completed the description, 'and a third on her forehead.' He didn't want to be left in any doubt. He recalled all the marks Lajwanti had

got tattooed on her body in childhood. He was familiar with
her body—as familiar as with green spots on a lajwanti plant
that fades as the leaf droops. Lajwanti would feel embarrassed
on being reminded of those marks as if all her precious
secrets had been laid bare, rendering her naked. Sunderlal's
body shook with an unknown fear, and a wave of love surged
through his heart.

'How did Lajo manage to reach the border?' he asked,
gripping Lal Chand's arm.

'She came in an exchange of abducted women between
India and Pakistan.'

'What happened after that?' Sunderlal asked, sitting stiffly
on his haunches.

'Yes, what happened next?'

Rasalu sat up in his cot, coughing the rasping cough—
peculiar to a tobacco smoker. 'Has Lajo returned?' he asked.

Continuing, Lal Chand said, 'It was a fair exchange right
on the Wagah border. Pakistan counted out sixteen abducted
women and counted in the same number—sixteen on both
sides. But there was a rumpus. Our volunteers complained
that the women they were handing over to us were middle-
aged and old. People gathered on both sides of the border,
and it appeared they were heading for a fight. Then one
of their volunteers pushed Lajo forward. "Call her old, do
you?", he asked. "Have a good look at her. Is any of the
women you have passed on to us comparable to her?" And
Lajo Bhabhi stood there trying to hide her tattoo marks.
The discussion became heated so that both sides threatened
to take back their goods. I cried out, "*Lajo! Lajo Bhabhi!*"
But before I could approach her, our police fell upon us and
chased us away.'

Lal Chand bared his elbow to show where a stick had hit him. Rasalu and Neki Ram sat silent while Sunderlal kept looking into the distance. Perhaps he was thinking of Lajo, who was so near him and yet out of his reach. From his expression, it appeared as if he had drearily trekked across the desert of Bikaner and had sat down to rest under a tree with his tongue hanging out and with no strength left even to say, 'Please give me some water.'

He felt as if the violence that had marked the pre-and post-partition days had not abated. It had only changed its face. Now people had become outspoken. If someone asked, 'You know, one Lehna Singh was living in Sambharwala. There was also his Bhabhi Banto.' Pat would come the reply, 'Killed!' And the man would walk away without caring to note the implication of what he had said

People had now openly started buying and selling human flesh. They would publicly examine a woman, mark her complexion, the secret contours of her body, put fingers on her tattoo marks and watch the pale hollows their prodding fingers made in her flesh, the paleness merging into the redness of the coursing blood. The buyer would pass on while the rejected woman, holding her salwar string with one hand, tried to hide her face with the other and sobbed to express her humiliation.

Sunderlal was planning to leave for Amritsar on some business when he got the news of Lajo's return. The unexpected news almost swept him off his feet. He was in a quandary. Should he go to the border at Wagah to receive her there or wait at home for her arrival? He took one step towards the door and then retraced his step. He wanted to run out of the house, gather all the banners and placards he carried every day at the head of the procession and spreading them on the floor, sit in their midst and cry his heart out. But being chary of displaying his feelings so openly, he suppressed the tug of war in his mind and proceeded towards the Chowki Kalan police station where the abducted women were scheduled to be delivered.

Suddenly he found Lajo standing in front of him, shaking with some unknown fear. She knew Sunderlal, and he was the only one who could identify her. He used to treat her unkindly, and now as she stood there, she wondered what kind of fate awaited her when she was returning after living with another man.

Sunderlal looked up at Lajo. She was carrying a red dupatta commonly worn by Muslim women and flung over her left shoulder in Muslim style. Her mind was so preoccupied with Sunderlal's thoughts that she had forgotten to change her dress or not wear it in Muslim fashion. She was now standing there anxiously watching Sunderlal.

Her appearance gave Sunderlal a jolt. She looked fairer and healthier than before and had put on weight. All his conjectures about Lajo had proved wrong. He had thought she would miss him so much that she would be reduced to a bundle of bones. She would have become so weak and emaciated that she would not even be able to speak. It seemed to him that she had been quite happy in Pakistan. The thought made him sad, but he decided not to reveal his mind to her. But if she was so pleased there, why had she returned to India? Had she come against her wishes under the pressure of the government? But he could not understand why there was a touch of pallor on her face, and her body had become slightly flabby as if the flesh had refused to cling to her bones tightly.

The first glance at the abducted woman could lead to unpredictable results. There were some men at the police station who had outright spurned their women. 'We won't have the Muslims' left overs!' they said. But Sunderlal faced the situation boldly. Overcoming his disgust, he quietly accepted Lajwanti.

The discordant notes of those who had refused to accept their women were lost in the jubilant voices of Rasalu, the old petition writer of Chowki Kalan, Neki Ram, and others; Kalka Prasad's harsh voice sounding apart from others. Greeted by this medley of sounds, Sunderlal and Lajo proceeded to their home. The scene was reminiscent of what had happened thousands of years ago when Shri Ram Chander and Sita returned to Ayodhya after their self-imposed exile. People had lit lamps to celebrate their return, among whom many looked downcast and repentant at the privations and hardships the royal couple had suffered for no fault of theirs.

After Lajwanti's return, Sunderlal did not relax his efforts in propagating the objective of 'Finding a place in our hearts'. Instead, he intensified his actions in the same spirit in which he had started them. Until now, those who had considered him to be merely a bundle of emotions were impressed by his earnestness. Most of the people were pleased with this happy turn of events in Sunderlal and Lajwanti's lives. But others scoffed at the couple being united again. The widow living in House No. 414 turned her face against Lajwanti and refused to visit her.

Not that Sunderlal was worried at their inimical attitude. The queen of his heart had been restored to him; the void in his heart had been filled, for he had installed Lajo's image like a golden idol in the temple of his heart and sat outside zealously guarding it. Lajo, who was, in the beginning, afraid of Sunderlal's unpredictable behaviour, gradually opened out on noticing his change of heart.

Sunderlal now did not call Lajo by her name. He called her Devi—a goddess. She would feel so pleased, almost going into raptures over it. She felt like telling Sunderlal about her experience in Pakistan and by making a clean breast of it wash away her past sins with her tears. But Sunderlal was never in a mood to listen. Though communicative, Lajo still felt inhibited. At night when Sunderlal fell asleep, she would lie there staring at his face. When caught doing so, she would mumble out some incoherent explanation, which meant she was doing it just like that. Sunderlal, who was tired after the day's work, would fall asleep again.

Only once soon after her arrival, Sunderlal tried to draw out Lajo about her 'black days'.

'Who was he?' he had asked her.

Lajwanti had lowered her eyes and replied, 'Jumma.' Then she had raised her eyes and scrutinized Sunderlal's face, trying to decide what more to tell. But she had felt discouraged, for Sunderlal had given her a queer look. Caressing her hair, he asked her, 'Was he good to you?'

'Yes.' 'He didn't beat you, did he?'

Sliding forward, Lajwanti rested her head on Sunderlal's chest. 'No, he didn't beat me, but I was always scared of him. You used to beat me, but I was never afraid of you. You won't beat me again, will you?'

Sunderlal's eyes filled with tears. In a voice full of remorse, he said, 'No, Devi, I shall never beat you again.'

Devi! Had he said, Devi? Had he raised her to the level of a goddess? She began to sob.

She wanted to tell him everything, but he wouldn't let her.

'Let's forget the past,' he said. 'You did not commit any sin. It's our society to blame, which refuses to give women like you their honoured place. Thereby our society stultifies itself, not you.'

Lajwanti's secret remained locked in her heart. She had warily told Sunderlal how she had spent her days when she was separated from the family. She looked at her body, which after the partition had become the embodiment of a goddess. She was happy, thrilled. But the happiness was marred by doubt. She would suddenly sit up in bed as if, in her blissful moments, someone had distracted her mind, taking away her happiness.

Many days passed in this way. Doubt slowly edged out her happiness. Not because Sunderlai had again started maltreating her but because he was so kind and considerate to her, she suspected it went against his true nature. She wanted to be the same old Lajo to him who fell out with him at the offer of radish and patched up with him the next moment when bribed with a carrot. But Sunderlal gave her no chance to have a row with him; he always made her feel fragile like glass which would crack at the touch of a feather. She would look at her reflection in the mirror and ultimately came to believe that the Lajo she had known no longer existed. Sunderlal had given her shelter under his roof, but had he accepted her? She was living and yet rootless. Sunderlal had no eyes to see her tears nor ears to hear her sighs.

Every morning the singing party still wended its way through the streets. The reformer of Mohalla Shakoor even sang with Rasalu and Neki Ram: 'The lajwanti leaves wither and droop at the mere touch of a hand.'

4

Mangal Ashtika

Kartik, a Hindu calendar month that typically overlaps October and November, encompasses several festivals, including the twelfth day celebrated as Tulsi's wedding day. Tulsi is a highly beneficial and sacred aromatic plant, considered to be an embodiment of Goddess Lakshmi. This was the day chosen for Nanda and Vijay's wedding.

Nanda's beautiful and pink complexion could be compared to the work of an inexperienced disciple of a master colourist who had just coloured a cloth red. Her body was shivering from head to toe due to hidden emotions. In that moment of loss of consciousness, if she had shown any awareness of where she stood and what was expected of her, then without blinking her eye and with a constant gaze, she would not have looked at the lines drawn with white flour on *Purohit* Jiva Ram's face or the white feet of handsome Vijay. While she was circling around the holy fire, she should not have been standing upright. Because she was tall, her head was projecting upward of her husband's shoulders by standing upright. Before the marriage, her mother had strongly advised her to keep her body's posture lower while circling around the sacred fire. But Nanda had forgotten all this and several other things like how during the wedding, after the wedding, physically and in every other respect, she had to keep herself a step lower compared to her husband.

Vijay's habits were a pretty good reflection of the condition of his heart. His restive aspirations, visible through his eyes and changing from moment to moment like a nomad, were warmly embracing Nanda's white arms and her entire body that was visible to him through seven layers of her dresses. Sometimes, Vijay closed his eyes when he was deeply engrossed in his thoughts as if all joys of the future were collecting themselves in this very moment and Jiva Ram Purohit was second-guessing them.

This was the third couple that Pandit Jiva Ram was binding into a marriage today. Jiva Ram read the seventh mantra of the wedding. He didn't have to exert his mind while uttering these mantras because from childhood, when he learnt these mantras from Ravi Shankar Chattopadhaya, he had memorized them with such fervour that there was no scope for correcting the pronunciation, tonal quality of his speech, amplification of his voice, and its harmonic effect. He had inherited this skill from his ancestors. He was like a well-oiled machine that worked perfectly at any determined place. He would instruct people how to place money in the squares for Mars and Saturn drawn with dried white flour and throw vermillion powder and rice. In all these matters, he never made a mistake.

This job was simple like adding up two and two that allowed his mind to wander. That day he felt that he was standing on the top of a hill, and adjacent to the mountain, there was a beautiful lake. Ducks and swans were floating in the lake like small sailing boats, and at the edge of the lake, there were fertile fields, and at a little distance away, there were shacks of fishermen and farmers. These people were living such a joyful life that even kings would become envious of them. Further away, there were mansions of the rich. For them their wealth was no source of happiness, and they were feeling miserable. On the eastern end of the lake, there were blooming lotuses and the prickly yellow flowers known as *naag phani*. Under a delicate Indian redwood tree, a sannyasi was lost in creating heavenly musical notes with his conch-like long copper pipe and his attractive sound was reminiscent of something that humankind had forgotten since the day of its creation. Then Jiva Ram took a deep cold breath and told himself, 'With these hands, I have performed hundreds of weddings, and I have brought into being hundreds of new families. I have provided moments of bliss to even those who were sad and depressed. But I'm still a bachelor, I have no home and hearth, I am always an involuntary prisoner of loneliness, like the lotus and the prickly yellow flowers that need water to grow, yet they are not grimed by the water.'

Suddenly, he became aware that he was uttering *mangal ashtika*, the last mantra of the wedding, that ended with the word *saavdhaan!* (be alert!). The eighth mantra invokes the power and blessings of *Mangal* (Mars), whose colour is red and whose day is Tuesday. Mars is supposed to be the strongest in the Hindu zodiac system. Those born on the alignment of Mangal and other grahas are called *Manglik* and must be

married to other Mangliks only. He or she must be married to
a Manglik, though the restriction wanes at a late age. Because
Jiva Ram was a Manglik, it wasn't easy to find a bride for him.

With that word, the wedding concluded. There was
a cacophony of voices saying congratulations, and that
commotion attracted Jiva Ram's attention as well.

Jiva Ram repeated the word saavdhaan, and at the end of
this third wedding during the day, he experienced tiredness.
The greed for money that weddings satisfied was never a great
attraction for him. Jiva Ram raised his fatigued eyes upwards,
which manifested the heavy and dark bags under his eyes.
Jiva Ram stretched himself to minimize the spectre of those
bags. He looked at Nanda, who was snivelling. She was on
the verge of leaving her parent's home, while at the same time
Vijay was smiling. He knew he was going to be endowed with
all the joys of married life. During several body stretches,
Purohit briefly explained to Nanda and Vijay their specific
responsibilities—that they were being united with the fire,
air, earth and sky as witnesses. Nanda was told that she would
never be her husband's equal (although physically, she was
taller than her husband). Vijay was instructed to treat Nanda
as the queen of his home. Then Jiva Ram specially instructed
Vijay to protect and serve a Brahmin, a woman and a cow.
While reciting a part of the *Shivaratri* story, Jiva Ram said,
'Vijay, you too are a pandit, and you must be aware that every
hunter who wants to use an arrow has been instructed by the
animals.' Then he methodically elaborated his message.

When you kill ten sheep, it is equal to the killing of
one ox.

When you kill 100 humans, it is equal to killing one
Brahmin.

When you kill 100 Brahmins, it is equal to killing one woman.

When you kill 100 women, it is equal to killing one pregnant woman.

When you kill ten pregnant women, it is equal to killing one cow.

After having performed his duties, Jiva Ram wanted to leave. What for? To enter the prison of loneliness once again. To stay the same broken bachelor, and unnatural like lotus and the yellow prickly flowers that raise themselves, staying dry and arid, after the rain. He had performed so many weddings, like unstoppable rain, but he, without a wife, was much like the thorny yellow flower.

Currently, there was Nanda's unforgettable face, Vijay's wandering eyes in Jiva Ram's imagination, and there was the noise of the wedding attendees and the voices of songs and jovial conversations in his ears, but his emotional state was propelling him to leave quickly.

But what was that emotional state? It revealed no more forbearance for the sounds of drums, songs, hilarity and jocularity. The things that upset him included the changing facial expressions complexion of the bride due to the discomfort to which she was exposed, the furtive looks of the groom, the heartfelt cries of the bride at the time of departure from her parents' home, songs, soulful melodies, jokes and laughter. His heart pounded, listening to the wedding songs. Amid the commotion, he had a more distinct realization of his extreme bachelorhood and an utterly useless state of being. Whether or not it was reality-based, this belief had reached the limits of craziness. His body shifted sideways when he recited mangal ashtika and the word 'saavdhaan.' The more the bride's parents and the guests noticed his desire to leave, the more they asked him to stay. They would address him respectfully—the greater the pressure, the more robust and more vital his reaction.

There was another reason for Jiva Ram's self-humiliation. During an ordinary conversation, he had told me that this year during the full moonlight of the month of C*het,* which coincided with the Hanuman Jayanti celebration, he would enter his fortieth year. This reminded me that it was the day when Maruti Dev or Hanuman Ji was born. This meant that both Hanuman Ji and Jiva Ram shared the same stars. That also explained his body's healthy disposition and the mental state that was restive while being highly energetic. He couldn't sit still in one place for a long time. However, one thing separated them—Jiva Ram's shyness, modesty and secretive temperament. It is possible that there was some time difference in the births of Hanuman Ji and Jiva Ram. This might have changed Jiva Ram's *rashi* (the zodiac position of one's star), or a weak star altered the boldness into self-effacement. Jiva Ram had lived his life in loneliness, and that could also explain his reticence. By entering the confirmed and frightful bachelorhood status, he was hopelessly aware that if he fell ill, there was no one to take care of him.

As he didn't understand the feminine psyche, he was afraid of women. He knew only this much that women were the source of most worldly dissensions and conflicts. He also understood that women are emotional (as it was his nature too). They are shy and non-assertive. Hard to guess when something said in a routine manner might hurt their feelings. It was also confirmed that Jiva Ram had no knowledge of what was proper and improper in human communication. On many occasions, he had boldly said things that he knew were inappropriate. But since no woman had ever objected, it was an endorsement of his assertions.

During the transition from the twentieth to the fortieth year, he had considered the possibility of renouncing his bachelorhood in favour of a householder's life. But he was aware that bachelorhood conferred a higher social status on him, and he was proud of this. This desire to show off had stopped him from debunking this myth. By the time he reached his fortieth year, this idea of higher social status had lost its appeal. People were busy doing their daily tasks. Who had the time and patience to think about someone's bachelorhood? This was nothing but his own wishful thinking.

The domestic tales of misery, filled with conflicts, frictions, and disputations that he had heard from different individual sources had disheartened him. Even after an energetic and dynamic wedding, Jiva Ram fell into the abyss of his own thoughts. He took out a finger from his mouth and shook his head like an attorney who suddenly found a highly promising clue from the defendant's testimony that had the potential to change the case in his favour. While in doubt, he would inform himself, 'This is a good point, Brother. There is something positive here, notwithstanding all the cries and disappointments. People still live happily ever after. There must be some pleasure in this after all the dissensions and the deprivation of a peaceful state of one's mind!'

When Jiva Ram realized that he was forty years old and that he had not intimately seen a woman's face, for a moment, he didn't doubt this anomaly. Such a realization, however, also demolished the domain that his playful imagination had erected that he knew it all. To reconstruct that structure of self-satisfaction, he had to think of another magnificent wedding that exhibited the bride and the groom's disguised attraction for each other, the happiness of the parents at the wedding, songs and revelries, commotion and clamour. After Nanda and Vijay's wedding, the pieces that could potentially reconstruct his imagination's demolished dominion were vibrant enough to echo their presence to the sky.

After a few days, Vijay, the mischievous wanderer, who also lived in Rulna, and was a distant relative of Jiva Ram, came to see him. His eyes were more reddish than usual. It appeared there was a cauldron hidden behind them that was feeding the flames. Was that cauldron a symbol of one's youth? 'Youth is the act of burning in the fire of one's own blood,' Vijay uttered these words while he was reclining against the wheel of a Persian well.

'Say, Brother, why are you looking so sad?'

Jiva Ram tried in vain to hide his depressed state of mind.

'I'm not well since yesterday. I'm helpless. I've written to my brother requesting him to send my sister-in-law here for a few days. There is no one here who can give me even a glass of water.'

'Thinking of your sister-in-law during the days of harvesting! She must be busy in the fields. All your brother's earning happens during this time of the year. Prices are up, but if it rains, all will be lost.'

From a distance, Neel Rattan was seen coming. He was indeed the devil's incarnation. He laughed without any reason. If people cried, he laughed. This is what seers do, but he was no seer. That is why it was a dangerous trait.

When Neel Rattan came to know the subject under discussion, he said, 'That's right. Why would your sister-in-law think of coming here when she must take care of three kids of her own? Three adolescent girls. She must be spending her day taking care of them. If she comes, you will have to provide one-half of a cup of milk to the girls. It would be closer to a seer. Isn't it? I would say no less than two and one-half seer. Now you should calculate how much it would cost. And there will be other expenses. You will lie flat on the ground like a rat under the clutches of a cat.'

Then Neel Rattan changed the subject of conversation. He said, 'How was the wedding, Vijay? Are you happy with the bride?' Jiva Ram intervened, saying, 'Nanda is like a goddess, pure goddess. Wherever she goes, paradise follows.'

'You're right, Brother.' Vijay moved away from the wheel. 'Married life is like living in paradise. What more can I say? Nanda is real Nanda. I must have done some good in my last incarnation that I got a wife like Nanda in this life. I wish everyone a happy life like mine.' Vijay then added a note of information that Nanda eats only after he has eaten. If he had to go out somewhere, then she spends the whole day waiting for him. If he gets late, then he would find her in tears, and she would complain. Before sleeping, she massages his legs. More stuff like that. This was something that should have pleased the listeners, but Neel Rattan made a sad face and said, 'This happens, my son, for a few days. When it is more than two years, and there is a child, you will see a new reality. You won't see this merriment and celebration anymore.'

'Whatever happens,' Jiva Ram interceded, 'the home where Nanda goes, that home . . .' It was not clear what triggered a reaction, he added in a sad voice, 'It is not a life

like mine. If you feel sick, no one to take care of you. If I write
to my sister-in-law, she might not come due to the harvest or
her children. And if she comes, I'll need two and a one-half
seer, etc. Isn't this what you said, Rattan?'

Vijay and Rattan intensely felt Pandit Jiva Ram's
predicament. Neel Rattan winked and gave Vijay a specific
look. Vijay said, 'Brother, do you know why I have come
to you?'

'No, I have no idea.'

'I have come to learn mangal ashtika. I know all the seven
mantras. But when I recite mangal ashtika, I lose my flow.'

'Have you started doing the work of a purohit? Did you
leave the job you had?'

'Do you have any reservation in teaching me? I need it for
a special wedding.'

Vijay got closer to Jiva Ram and said, 'Brother, let
me tell you something. We have found a girl. She is very
beautiful, but at the same time as naughty as you. All women
are like that. We want that you should marry her. I'll do the
pandit's job—no need to show off. You will find comfort in
your married life. I realized the seriousness of your situation
the day you performed my wedding.' Both Vijay and Rattan
waited for Jiva Ram's 'yes' or 'no' response. There was silence
for some time.

Jiva Ram's answer was silence, which meant that he was
half willing.

Neel Rattan said in a whispering tone, 'Brother, that is a
good suggestion. Vijay is also a pandit. He can recite mangal
ashtika-*vashtika*. The wedding will take place without much
commotion. You will be happy. Now, it is up to you. I say
what is good for you. Let us not wait. The twenty-fifth day of

Kartik, Wednesday, auspicious timing, nothing but mangal ashtika and then saavdhaan!'

There appeared some moisture on the leaves of *naag phani* and the lotus. The pieces of Jiva Ram's mental construction flew toward the sky.

Jiva Ram Purohit's wedding took place with great fanfare. There were a band and the sound of the drum. Jokes were shared, and there was much laughter. Jiva Ram's heart ran faster than usual. If the walls of the chest were not there, his heart would have fallen out.

Vijay noticed that Jiva Ram's eyes were also wandering and fidgeting. He saw the bangles on his bride's white marble-like arms and her entire body, although she was dressed in seven clothing layers. His bride was also tall like Nanda, which meant taller than him. This was a matter of chance.

Vijay ritualistically placed Jiva Ram's hand over his bride's, and then he placed wet flour over it and recited the seventh mantra. There was a rainfall of rice from all sides. Like an experienced teacher, Vijay was asking guests to place money in different squares of the planets and deities like Mars, Saturn, Ganesh Ji, etc. With a quiver, Jiva Ram called Vijay's attention. While he was still muttering mantras, Vijay brought his ears closer to Jiva Ram's mouth. Jiva Ram said, 'Brother, my heart is really racing. I'm trembling. Don't you see that I'm feeling cold? Please tell Neel Rattan to give me support.' Vijay continued to recite mantras. A friend of Vijay said, 'Brother, Neel Rattan has gone to Giirhat, which is not far from Rulna. He must be on his way back.'

'Vijay, stop it.' Jiva Ram said in a hushed tone, 'Don't recite mangal ashtika yet. Let me think. I'm forty years old, and I'm a celibate pandit.' Vijay noticed Jiva Ram's reluctance.

His throat was getting dry, and he was madly moving his tongue to keep it moist. Vijay spoke slowly, but in a voice filled with loathing said, 'What a shame! There is no place in the world for weak human beings like you. Brother, the world makes fun of people like that.'

If this were within Jiva Ram's control, he would have saved his purity as a celibate Brahmin getting soiled by getting into a householder's life, but he noticed that his would-be-bride had kept his trembling hands down with tremendous pressure. Probably, she was wondering why his hands were trembling. Maybe this was her naughty self that was playing a game. She was youthful and a woman!

Then Jiva Ram waited for the quick recitation of mangal ashtika so that he was relieved of this mental torment as quickly as possible and got a chance to look at the face of his bride. The machinery of his imagination started its work. Once again, he imagined that he was standing on a fascinating hill. Next to the hill, there was a blue water lake with floating ducks and swans. Near the lake's shore, there were green fields and the shacks of fishermen and farmers. People were so happy that even kings might become envious of seeing this. Far away in the distance, there were mansions of the rich, but they were not as delighted as their poor neighbours. On the eastern edge of the lake, there were blooming naag phani and lotus flowers. Under the shade of an Indian redwood tree, a sannyasi who had given up the material world, was breathing into his conch-like copper instrument and producing such heavenly celestial notes which humankind had forgotten since the time the world came into being. Now he was not alone. Holding his hands, his wife was looking at the same view. Naag phani and lotus flowers were getting soiled by the water. Suddenly, the recitation of mangal ashtika caught his attention. Thanks to our ancestors that we got such a beautiful mantra. Someone said the word saavdhaan, and people started congratulating. Vijay gave his sermon, copying Jiva Ram. In the end, Vijay said:

> When you kill ten sheep, it is equal to the killing of one ox.
> When you kill 100 humans, it is equal to killing one Brahmin.

There was a mischievous boy sitting nearby who added:

> One mound is equal to forty seers.
> One seer is equal to sixteen *chhataanks*.

Vijay looked at him disapprovingly and asked him to shut up.

During the evening, that was the wedding night, Jiva Ram saw his bride sitting in the room's corner as a large bundle. His heart started to pound. He didn't dare to look at the bride's face. 'Maybe she wouldn't like that.' Jiva Ram repeated within himself. 'She is a woman, after all.' He tried many times but failed. He felt the presence of many people in the room. Jiva Ram extended his hand and then pulled back.

'A weak man like you gets exploited by the world.' There was an echo of Vijay's hurtful words. Gathering a lot of courage, Jiva Ram uncovered his bride. The bride stood up and started to clap like a crazy person. There was nothing but darkness in front of Jiva Ram's eyes. He found that he was still a bachelor though only recently married. Or was he a widower acting as a bachelor . . .

Some distance away, sitting on a charpoy and wearing expensive clothes, Neel Rattan was clapping. And from the outside, the words of mangal ashtika were pouring in, mixed with people's loud laughter, saavdhaan!

5

Kalyani

He was not afraid of roaming these dark and dusky pathways, numerous ditches filled with black water that always carried the Bombay industrial belt's dirt, and it had no place to settle down. The stones that had no discernable shape were a clutter and a jumble as if of their own volition to be useless, an obstacle in the walkway. And he—his legs used to tremble in the beginning, and he would stop if he found a dried piece of straw or a broken blade of grass in his track. He felt that everybody was watching him—the guy who made large bricks of indigenous soap at the end of the street and the barber next to him. They were laughing at him. At least, they were not crying. And the next-door guy who sold coal. He had probably never gone to the whorehouse himself, but still, his face was black.

Next to the whorehouse, there was a club on the first floor. They secretly sold rum, and the customers who gathered there played rummy. The windows opened inward like the eyes of a yogi, and whines and whimpers emanated from inside like cigarette smoke. People lost hundreds in gambling, but they saved money by smoking cheap cigarettes or simply smoked bidis, only bidis with the same relationship with cigarettes as penicillin had with tuberculosis.

Why did these windows open inwardly? No one knew. It didn't make a difference because anyone who entered the inner courtyard was nothing more than a shadow. A girl, expert in these matters, would come forward and take the customer inside. She would offer him a place to sit, and then she would walk out to fill a bucket of water from the pump that was in the centre of the courtyard, and it served both the shacks. Before she lifted the bucket, the girl would lift her skirt or tighten her saree grip and, while showing the pride of having gained a customer, communicated a few words with another girl in the same profession. 'O Girja, please take care of my rice that is boiling. I must attend to a customer.' And then she went inside and closed the door. Then Girja would talk to Sundari. What's so special about Kalyani? She had a second customer today. Instead of Sundari, Jari or Khurseed answered. It's her luck. They heard Kalyani closing the inner bolt of the door, and then there was silence. Sundari looked at the closed door with one eye and then tried to dry her wet hair with the towel while singing *raat jaagi re balam, raat jaagi* (I was awake the whole night, my lover.) Then she shouted at Girja. 'O Girja, Kalyani's rice is boiling. Don't you hear the gurgling sound coming from her pot?' Then all the three girls laughed loudly while hitting one another's shoulders. Girja would react forcefully. 'You struck me hard, you slut! You know I am hurting. I touch my ears. My kids nor I will make friends with a Punjabi.' Then Girja called a girl in the other shack.

'Gangi, what does your parrot say?'

She couldn't see Gangi, but her voice was heard. 'My parrot says, "*bhaj man Ram, bhaj man Ram.*"' (O my inner self, recite Ram's name!) Gangi had either lost her mind, or she had had no customer.

Mahipat Lal has come here after a gap of several months. To taste something different, he had been visiting a Nepali girl named Chuni-la, who lived nearby. After that, he had entangled himself with a Christian girl, who lived in shack number ninety-six. Her real name was different, but the girls and her agents called her Olga. Kalyani was unaware of all this. In her profession, the locational difference between a few shacks was like the distance of a few hundred miles. Girls came out of this place only to go to cinema theatres and then they returned.

Mahipat had gone to other girls for a change of taste, and it was the same drive that had brought him back here—the desire to taste something different. It was certain that after a gap of so many months, he had forgotten Kalyani, although he had given 200 rupees to Kalyani to visit her native place. Probably, he was drunk at that time, the same condition as now. After finishing a bottle of beer, Mahipat Lal was perhaps thinking of another woman, an incomplete image of a woman. He thought it was his job to complete that image like a painter, generally a man, and the image that is usually the woman.

Soon after entering the courtyard, he jumped over the parapet and walked down three-four steps. People think that hell or the netherworld is located somewhere under the ground, but they forget that its only two–three steps down. There is no fire burning over there, nor are there ponds of boiling water. Maybe after stepping down a few stairs, you enter a threshold, and then you see the infernal region, where such cruel punishments are meted out which a man can't imagine.

After stepping down, he went straight to the patio that faced the shacks. Although the courtyard was covered with bricks, there was a gutter that was always filled with water. It was the same condition as today, a year or year and a half ago. One had to be aware of this. Because the courtyard was open to the sky, the tenth day's moon was shining in the gutter water. The moon's reflection didn't care how polluted the water was. If someone poured some water from the pump, the moon's reflection wobbled. Briefly, the whole image of the moon swayed.

Some customers were looking at Girja, Sundari and Jari as if they were fully baked or half-baked water pitchers. Some of them were searching for their pockets. A mechanic was deciding to go with Jari because she was uglier than Girja, Sundari and Khurseed, but on the other hand, she was like the wall of eight bricks. The exciting thing was that the girls were not perplexed. They understood well, the madness of men. Mahipat looked at Sundari. She was dark-complexioned, but like all women from Konkon, she had sharp features. Her body below the waist fell into the *baap re* (O my God!) category. Precisely at that moment, someone pulled Mahipat's kurta. He looked back and found Kalyani, who was smiling while standing there, unabashedly showing her teeth. She looked slimmer. Why? No one knew. Her face was looking as if someone had left places for her two eyes and then covered the rest of her face in the same manner as leather is fastened on a drum. Fate and woman were the same things. That is why Mahipat followed Kalyani to the third shack.

Someone looked down from the club's window and not having luck with the pawn, turned the checkerboard over. Kalyani came out and filled a bucket of water at the pump, tightened her saree's grip, and then called. 'O Girja, take care of my things.' She took the pail and went inside.

From the nearby shack, Madam shouted. 'Is it one time or two times?'

Kalyani winked at Mahipat, and they looked at Madam's shack. She replied, 'One time.' She spread her palm in front of Mahipat for money. Mahipat took her hand and pulled her towards him, and then he imprinted a reddish stamp of his betel leaf on her lips. Kalyani cleaned it with the broad hem of the saree she was wearing. 'You're so impatient?'

Again, she opened and spread her palm. 'You give me thirty rupees. But I will tell Madam you were one time only. You shouldn't say anything to her. Understood?'

Mahipat moved his head. 'I understand.'

Kalyani's palm was still open. 'Take out the stuff.'

'Money,' Mahipat said.

Without giving a typical response, Kalyani smiled. She was feeling shy. She was a prostitute, but she was shy too. Who says that the woman who sells herself ceases to be a woman? Shame is both ornament as well as ammunition. This is how she gets massacred, and she kills too. Mahipat took out thirty rupees and put them on Kalyani's palm. Kalyani didn't count the money. She kissed the currency notes, brought them to her head and eyes. She bowed before the photograph of the goddess. She separated her share from Madam's, and then she went inside. Mahipat was in a hurry. He looked at Goddess Durga's photo. She was riding a tiger, and under her feet, lay the body of a dead demon. Durga had many manifestations.

In some, she carried a sword; in others, a lancet; in yet another, a shield. Sometimes she held a severed head of a hairy man. When Mahipat looked at it, the severed head looked like his own. In depicting Durga's profile, the painter had shown his mastery of how he illustrated the goddess's breasts, shoulders and thighs. The walls were broken. That would have been fine, but the wild growth over the walls and the hidden forms were revealed. This representation was mentally disturbing. The walls appeared like the Tibetan schools of instruction, showing maps and drawings of hell and heaven. Crocs were tormenting sinners and flame-filled tongues were licking them. The entire universe was caught in the colossal teeth of a ferocious creature with its mouth wide open.

He was going to hell. He was certain. 'Mahipat, let it be!'

Kalyani returned and started to remove her clothes.

This game of a man and a woman. If the woman was not hurt, it needed some evidence. And she was aware that the man would not accept it.

Mahipat started with a few bites here and there, and then he jumped from the bed. He wanted to have a look, not at Kalyani but the woman who represented the entire universe. Women like Kalyani come and go. Men like Mahipat come and go too. But the woman stays there. The man stays there. Why? We can't understand this, although there is nothing to understand.

One thing is sure. There was justice during Satya, Treta and Dvapara yugas, and yet women led secret lives. Why was Ganka a prostitute? There is injustice today, injustice everywhere. Then why are they stopped from sinning? Laws are applied to them. Why? The money that comes from the mint loses half of its value by the time it reaches you. Poverty needs money, more than any time in history. People hoard money so that this 'Lakshmi' doesn't go out. But money is a bitch goddess. When it gets into heat, it will go out.

Mahipat wanted to get confused, which is why he was entangled in the universal women's twists and turns. He asked for a beer. But by the time the dark shadow of Kalyani moved to call the boy, he had changed his mind. There is no need. He immersed himself in watching the view that was much more compelling than a drink. And then, for an unknown reason, Mahipat forcefully separated Kalyani's legs. She groaned in agony. Shocked by his brutal move, Mahipat loosened his grip. Now Kalyani was lying on the bed, and Mahipat was sitting on his knees on the floor. He was trying to say something. While lying straight on the bed, Kalyani was looking at the ceiling. She was looking at the fan that had gathered cobwebs, but it was still moving at a slow speed. Then suddenly, Kalyani felt something. The presence of Mahipat and his thoughts ran an electric current run through her body. She started to suffer like a winged insect that was being exposed to a burning match by a heartless kid.

Unable to manage his inner emotions that burst open, Mahipat came out of the room. There was great tension in his body. There was an electric current running inside that he wanted to get rid of. His hands' grip was so muscular that even a powerfully built person could not find an escape. He looked at Kalyani, who seemed out of breath. He couldn't believe that the weight of a sex worker's breasts could increase manifold within such a short time. The sheer expanse of the object and the distinctive spots found on top were diminishing the swelling centre. The marks of chickenpox were visible around her shoulders and thighs. In this troubled state, he forgot

about the universal woman and his ideas of masculinity. He
lost consciousness of the place where he stood. And where
was Kalyani? Where exactly did he stop, and Kalyani start?
He was like a killer who had just pushed someone from the
roof to die. The person who fell from the height was unable to
record a statement. Suicide was a good excuse. With a sudden
movement, he put his entire weight over Kalyani.

There was a heart-rending cry and incomprehensible
nonsense that followed. The moving wings of the fan were
casting their shadows on the damp and algae-ridden walls.
Who had increased the fan's speed? Mahipat was profusely
sweating and feeling ashamed because Kalyani was crying.
She didn't know how to deal with this kind of client. At the
same, she was also not ready to lose a valuable customer.

Pressing her head inside the pillow, Kalyani was lying,
face turned back, and her shoulders were visibly shaking.
Mahipat paused in amazement. He tried to capture Kalyani's
face into his hands by moving forward, but Kalyani pushed
him aside. She was crying. Mahipat's hands became wet with
tears. There was a constant flow. When a strong force meets
with helplessness, the result is a Holi played with the colour
of blood. Then eyes clean up the blood and bring it out to
wash the face. When this colour prevails, there is neither a
woman nor a man.

Kalyani freed her face.

Mahipat was doubly shamed. He apologized to Kalyani
repeatedly. Kalyani wiped her eyes with the bedsheet and
helplessly gazed at Mahipat. She got up and embraced him
with both of her hands. She put her head covered with
wrinkled Konkani hair on his broad chest. Then she started
to whimper. Mahipat in consoling her felt a strange sense of

belonging She rested in the embrace of her killer, and all was still. A man is, after all, a man. He is also a father and a brother. A woman is also a daughter and a sister.

And a mother.

A strong sense of repentance showed up in Mahipat's eyes, and it changed the dynamic. Now his head was on Kalyani's breasts, and she was showing her love. Mahipat wanted to leave the place before bringing this affair to its climax. But Kalyani was not willing to accept this insult.

Kalyani once again sought trouble for herself. She uttered a few words amid feeling great pain. 'O, my flower! For God's sake. I will have to get an injection.' Then very slowly, too slowly, while balancing the feelings of pain and pleasure, she exchanged the universal man with a child, and she lovingly embraced the child. She was kissing Mahipat very tenderly, with motherly affection, notwithstanding the foul smell of cigarette smoke and beer.

Mahipat reached for his clothes after washing himself, but Kalyani stopped him and asked for extra twenty rupees.

'Twenty rupees?'

She said that she would sing his praises. 'I have not forgotten the day when I went to my native town. You had given me 200 rupees for my travel. I stood on one leg and prayed for you at Kardar's big temple. I wanted God to protect my lover. Please give him a long life and lots of money.'

And Kalyani waited to see the outcome of her prayer with a hopeful gaze.

Mahipat's nostril was bloated with hatred. What a whore! You faked tears the last time you got 200 rupees from me. You had cried loudly as if I was an animal, a wild animal. Now twenty rupees more? What is the point of shedding tears? If you asked me in the usual manner, I would not have refused. You know it, I would not have said no. I don't know how to say no. For that reason, I'm grateful to God that I wasn't born as a woman. I give without anyone demanding from me. That way, you don't feel the guilt. Is this how you wait for a man to show up? And when he comes, you lie to him, try to rob him. You tell him . . .

I thought you would certainly come on a Tuesday. What's so special about Tuesday? On Tuesdays, I pray to God. This crying, maybe it is genuine. I allowed myself to be led like a blind man without thinking about it. The pain that I have inflicted, there is only one way to make up for that. Give me the money. But why? I've paid for two times, and I did it only one time.

Looking at the delicate situation in which Mahipat had placed himself, Kalyani questioned his thoughts. 'What are you thinking? Give me; my child will bless you!'

'Your child?'

'Yes, you didn't see?'

'No, where is it? Whose child?'

Kalyani smiled and felt diffident. Then she expressed her ignorance about the father. 'I don't remember faces. Who knows it might be yours?'

Mahipat took out twenty rupees and placed them on Kalyani's palm. She had not dressed yet. She was wearing a silver knick-knack around her waist that was shining.
Mahipat gave her a gentle push on her back and thought of something. Kalyani had just picked up her saree. 'Can I do it one more time? (I have paid the money.)'

'Yes.' Without any hesitation, Kalyani placed her saree on the bed. But the flesh was asking for help. It had no life. Its animalistic vigour had dwindled. Mahipat moved his head to say no. 'I'm left with no passion, no vitality!'

Kalyani agreed with him. 'I get many men, but I have not seen anyone strong and buoyant like you. After your visit, it takes time for my navel to find its balance.'

The moon had moved away from the ditch. One had to lie flat on the ground to see the moon. Kalyani caught Mahipat's hand and took him to the room where Girja, Sundari, Jari and other women were seated. Jari had serviced a mechanic and after that, a Bohra man. She had also quarreled with a Sikh. When she saw Mahipat walk in, she elbowed Khurseed. 'Kalyani's man is coming', she said, because whenever he arrived, he reached for Kalyani.

As soon as Mahipat entered the shack, he saw a bundle next to the bathroom. Girja was sitting next to it, and with the help of her hem, she was blowing air. Kalyani picked up the bundle and brought it close to Mahipat.

'Look, look, it's my child.'

Mahipat glanced at three, four- or five-month-old child. 'I have become like this by giving birth to this ruinous thing and feeding him. There is nothing to eat. On top of it, you come . . .'

Kalyani came close to Mahipat's ears and whispered. 'Look at Sundari. If you want, I will make sure that next time you get Sundari. No, no, I'll be alright the day after tomorrow. I'll put on flesh and fill these empty spots. She touched her breasts and shoulders. When you try to grab something, you should get something. If you want Sundari, please let me know. I'll make everything right. But you must come to me. Don't go to Girja. She's timid and playful.' And then, bouncing the child in her arms, she said she had named the baby Achmi.

'Achmi. Achmi, what?'

'I don't know that.' Kalyani answered and then slightly laughed. 'I had a customer who said that if he made me pregnant, I should name the child Achmi. I can't say that this is his child or someone else's. But I kept the name in my mind. He didn't come again, and you said nothing. Anyway, we shall see next time.'

Mahipat looked at Achmi and then around the room. 'This child will grow here. I know by coming here to these girls, I'm not sinning. If she expects ten, I give her twenty. But this child?'

'You can't breathe here, especially when you're about to leave.'

Mahipat took out a five rupee note and placed it on the child. 'The child has come to this world. It's my charitable welcome.'

'No, no, I'll not take this.'

'You must take it. You can't refuse to accept it.'

Kalyani gave in for the sake of the child. Mahipat placed his hand on Kalyani's shoulder and asked for her forgiveness. I treated you like an animal. But from his tone, there was no assurance that he would not do the same thing the next time. He would do the same thing. He was intoxicated with the idea. Beer was just an excuse.

Kalyani said that it didn't matter. 'You finished me today.' Her complaint was superficial. What else did she expect? That is how she earns her money to feed herself. No, when hunger hurts the stomach, then you realize it. All the world's men have died.

All the women have been killed too.

Mahipat inquired whether Achmi was a boy or a girl.

A strange streak of light appeared on Kalyani's face. It brightened her beaten-up countenance, and some buds blossomed. It's a lad.

In a quick action, Kalyani opened child's nappies, revealing his masculinity, and lifted him with her two hands as she presented him to Mahipat. With some hesitation, she asked him to look.

As Mahipat turned his face around, Kalyani asked him about his next visit.

Soon. He seemed to be bewildered as he answered her question. And then he quickly walked out to hide in places where there was light.

6

The Woollen Coat

I see many attractive suits hanging in Master Tailor Mirajuddin's showcase, and they make me painfully conscious of my worn-out woollen coat. Even if I am constrained for money, I must have a new coat for myself this winter. If I avoided passing the tailor's shop or did not go to the recreation club, I would remain blissfully oblivious of my well-worn coat. But when Sant Singh and Yazdani turn up at the club in smart worsted suits, I become intensely conscious about my coat's ripped condition and how badly it hurts my ego.

To keep the family going, a poor clerk like me must muddle through and do without many necessities in life. To protect his family from freezing in the biting cold, he must content himself by wearing woollens of a coarse variety. Last year, I bought this coat from a shop outside Delhi Gate dealing in second-hand clothes. The dealer had bought coats in bulk from a Miranja Miranja & Co. of Karachi. The label, Miranja Miranja & Co., stitched on the artificial silk lining below the inside pocket, gave away the game, but I consoled myself with the thought that I had bought the coat at a throwaway price.

But as the saying goes: Buy expensive, cry once; buy cheap, cry forever. My coat repeatedly threatened to fall apart.

One December evening during the same year, I decided to walk through Anarkali on my way back from the recreation club. I had a ten-rupee note in my pocket. I was left with ten rupees after paying for the monthly stock of flour, pulses, fuelwood, electricity bill and the insurance premium. If one had money in the pocket, passing through Anarkali was legitimate enterprise. One's anger subsides and one even starts to like oneself. As I passed through the bazaar, I saw the shop windows crammed with woollen suit lengths and saris. Or maybe I had an eye for these things only.

It was said that during the past few years, tons of gold had gone out of the country and, with the consequent glut of imported stuff, even the most inconsequential people had taken to wearing suits. They thought that this sort of sartorial embellishment did them proud. Little do we realize that clothing ourselves in beautiful garments and living lives of luxury are mere attempts to conceal our poverty. Rich people take themselves for granted, and they don't need to flaunt their riches.

The counters were piled high with rolls of fine worsted in the drapers' shops. I cast envious looks at them and found myself in a quandary: would it be right for me to spend ten rupees on a coat length of worsted and then starve my wife and children? After a brief struggle, I set my mind against the unholy desire to go in for a new coat. Grimly fingering the buttons of my worsening woollen garment, I set off at a fast pace, with every step increasing the distance between the shop and me. The brisk walk was a real warm-up, and the dreary cold failed to goad me into giving my desire a tangible shape. For that matter, now even my old coat seemed superfluous.

As I walked, I kept arguing with myself, trying to put my mind at ease. Didn't I know that the rich did not believe in ostentation? They wouldn't mind going without a shirt, not to talk of a tattered coat. Well, by that token, maybe I already belonged to the category of the rich!

This exercise in self-introspection, however, only added to my confusion. Hastily dismissing all further thoughts on the subject, I managed to reach home with the ten-rupee note still intact. My wife, Shami, was waiting for me. She was kneading the flour and, at the same time, blowing into the *chuulha* to get the fire going. The wretch Mangal Singh had supplied damp firewood and the wood would not come to the point of bursting into flames. The harder Shami blew into the chuulha, the thicker the smoke became.

I cursed Mangal Singh. The cheat! For my wife's beautiful eyes, I was prepared to take up arms against the whole world, let alone Mangal Singh.

After much fretting and fuming, the wood at last crackled into flames, and my wrath subsided. Resting her head against my shoulder, Shami playfully patted my coat and found her delicate finger coming out through a hole.

'The coat has outlived its life,' she said. 'Yes,' I readily agreed with her.

'I think I must put a few stitches,' she said, pointing towards the gaping hole.

'It requires some darning, too,' I said, trying to be helpful.

'But the lining is all gone,' she said, turning over my coat. 'Moths have been at it. Artificial silk, you know!'

'Forget about it.' I snatched it away from her. 'Instead of sitting in front of the sewing machine, sit by my side, Shami. I had a hard day at the office. Don't you see how exhausted I look? You'll have all the time for the machine when I'm asleep.'

Her engaging smile and my tattered coat!

Shami smiled. 'I've had enough of it. The blessed thing is past mending. It's worse torture than blowing into damp wood. Why don't you buy a new coat?'

Lo, she had me thinking again. To throw away money on a piece of cloth—it's a sheer indulgence, a sin. But Shami's eyes, those beautiful, smiling eyes. I could fight Mangal Singh to save those eyes from the pain. I could defy the whole world for her, purchase all the cloth.

I had just started thinking of a new coat when Pushpa Munni, my young daughter, came running into the house and started dancing on the veranda. Her antics were more fascinating than the movements of a Kathakali dancer. On seeing me, she stopped dancing.

'Papa, so you've come! Tomorrow our teacher is going to teach us how to make a tablecloth. She has asked us to bring a piece of casement cloth. And, also, an inch-tape to measure the cloth. Besides, I also require a piece of woollen cloth to learn cutting woollens.'

Shami slapped Pushpa because we were talking about purchasing a new woollen coat for me. 'The wretch is always ready with one demand or the other,' she fumed. 'She had fiddled around the whole thing just when I was trying to persuade you to get a new coat made.'

Poor Pushpa's tears and my new coat!

'Shami!' I raised my voice, against my grain. Shami trembled.

'Shami, go and mend my coat!' I barked, my eyes blazing with anger.

'Yes, right now! I don't care whether you do it willingly or with a whimper. You must take pains over it as you do with Mangal Singh's damp wood. Don't you see Pushpa is crying? Poppi darling, come here, my pet. What was it that you wanted? Tell me, my child. Casement cloth, wasn't it? And an inch-tape to measure cloth. Where is Bachchu? He must have fallen asleep, crying for a tricycle and a balloon. What good is a coat to me if it deprives him of a mere balloon? Shami, where's Bachchu?'

'He's sleeping,' Shami said, overawed.

'If you're ruthless with the children just because of my coat, then don't expect me to love you because of your beautiful eyes.'

Then I asked myself, why all this play-acting? Was I behaving in this manner for the sake of the coat? On whose side lay the truth anyway. Hers or mine? Or was it both? But one who's right has the edge over the other. I felt subdued.

'The other day, you said something about a pair of light-green enamelled earrings, didn't you?' I asked.

'Yes, I did, but . . .'

I imperiously brushed aside her unvoiced objection. The ten-rupee note in my coat pocket was to me like a vast treasure.

I found that Shami had mended my coat at the elbows the next day. But despite skillful darning, ugly wrinkles had appeared at the places where the cloth had utterly given way.

And that reminded me of Mirajuddin, the Master Tailor. I have a lively imagination, and that is my undoing. It often lands me in serious trouble. To buy or not to buy a coat, I was undecided. At Mirajuddin's there were suits, exclusive and elegant, which cost as much as five hundred rupees, including stitching charges. But I was an ordinary clerk, and it was futile on my part to pin hopes on such costly suits. They exceeded my means.

Finding me free from work, Shami came and sat by my side, and we began to make a list of things we could buy. When father and mother huddle, the children also flock around them. Pushpa and Bachchu burst upon us like a tornado.

Call it a quirk of imagination—or was it that I wanted to humour Shami? I began the list with a pair of light-green enamelled earrings. I looked towards the kitchen. The firewood was crackling and Shami's eyes were twinkling like stars. I learned that Mangal Singh had taken back the damp firewood.

'He has sent us mulberry sticks and slivers of packing cases,' Shami shared the information.

'And cow dung cakes?'

'Yes, those too!'

'Mangal Singh is God incarnate, a saint,' I said effusively. 'I must buy a piece of worsted for my coat to keep your eyes shining. Not from this month's salary, maybe next month.'

'Yes, when the winter is gone,' Shami laughed.

Pushpa had a long list of things she wanted—cotton cloth, inch-tape to measure fabric with, a yard length of green blazer cloth, DMC thread balls, gold piping. And, of course, some sweets: gulab jamun and *imarati*. I suffered from chronic constipation and wanted to buy a tin of Triphala Zamani from the Hakim's shop—a laxative to be taken with a cup of milk, the last thing at night. But Pushpa's formidable list edged out the laxative. Gulab jamun, I said to myself, must have top priority.

I decided to hide the gulab jamun under the staircase where the milkman often kept his milk can and tell Pushpa that I had forgotten to buy them. Oh, how she would miss them! It would be great fun to see her mouth watering at the thought of the desired sweet delicacy and then surprise her with the sweet.

And what about Bachchu? Since morning he had been bugging me for balloons and a tricycle. No, the tin of laxatives was out!

Shami was trying to appease Bachchu. 'I'll buy Bachchu a tricycle next month. My darling son will ride it the whole day. Poppi will get nothing. Bachchu will ride while Poppi will stare.'

I swore by Shami's beautiful eyes that until I had set aside some money for the tricycle, I would not venture near Nila Gumbad. To pass through Nila Gumbad and have no money to buy the machine! What abject helplessness. I may even start hating myself.

Shami stood in front of the Belgian mirror dressed in white when I rose and stood behind her.

'I know what you're thinking,' I said.

'I bet you don't.'

'You think that if you visited the District Officer's wife in this white sari and light-green enamelled earrings, her eyes would turn up in surprise.'

'No, you are miles off the mark,' Shami laughed. 'You admire my eyes, don't you? I was wondering what makes you admire them so much. You would have bought a woollen coat if you loved my eyes long ago.'

I put my hand on her mouth and my exuberance had suddenly changed into dejection. 'I assure you I'll buy a new coat next month,' I said in a faint voice.

'And by then, the winter will be over.'

I left for the bazaar; my mind filled with images of the small but joyful world created by ten rupees.

In Anarkali, every respectable man, except myself was wearing woollens. The neck of every lean young man was stiffened with a necktie and a hard collar like my younger brother's cat and his dog, Tiger. Looking at the suits, I said, 'I think people have become impoverished. No one knows how much of gold had been exported this month.' At a jeweller's shop, I examined several earrings. Endowed with a lively imagination, I could visualize how well the light-green earrings would go with Shami's outfit. But there was such a great variety that I could not decide which one to buy and ultimately came away without selecting any.

I ran into Yazdani, who was returning from the recreation club (which was in fact, a gambling joint). He had made a rich haul of fifteen rupees at the card table, and it was no surprise that his face glowed with joy. With one hand, I tried to cover up the bulge in my coat pocket, and with the other hand, I tried to hide a small patch, the size of a rupee coin, under the left-hand pocket. I wondered if Yazdani had noticed the unsightly wrinkles and the patch while placing his hand over my shoulder.

What did I care if Yazdani had noticed my coat, I argued with myself, trying to hide my unease. Would Yazdani care to give me a bag of cash? And how was he concerned if my coat was in tatters? Yazdani and Santa Singh have repeatedly told me they care more for their mental poise than worsted cloth.

Yazdani soon parted company, but I kept marvelling at his fine suit until I lost sight of him.

I thought that first I should buy sweets for Pushpa Munni lest I forget. Teasing her would be great fun. At the sweetmeat shop, kachoris were swelling up in a massive cauldron of sizzling ghee. My mouth watered. Though I suffered from constipation, I cast all discretion to the winds, and rested my elbows on the marble tabletop, and fell to eating kachoris with great relish.

After washing my hands, I searched for the money and there was nothing there! The ten-rupee note had fallen somewhere.

There was a big hole in the inside pocket of my coat where the moths had eaten into the artificial silk lining. As I put my hand into the pocket, it came out the other side—where the label, Miranja Miranja & Co. was sewn. The note must have slipped through this hole.

I looked utterly foolish—an innocent lamb freshly sheared of its precious wool. The sweetmeat seller guessed my predicament.

'Don't worry, Babu ji,' he said effusively. 'Pay me tomorrow.'

I did not say anything, for I had nothing to say. I had lost my tongue. All I could do was to throw a grateful glance at the sweetmeat seller.

In another cauldron, gulab jamuns lay soaked in syrupy glory. Through the smoky luxury of swollen kachoris I could also see a pyramid of golden imartis tantalizing me, and my mind darted back to Pushpa. The poor child!

I walked to Badami Bagh and trudging along the railway track for three-quarters of an hour. A goods train coming from the junction passed along the track and five minutes later, a shunting engine, belching blazing cinders. A gang of workers emerged from the nearby salt refinery after finishing overtime. I followed the track towards the bridge. Despite the cold, some college students were rowing in the moonlight.

'My fate, my unkind fate!'

I cursed myself under my breath. Was it a crime to dream of buying gold piping, cotton cloth, and gulab jamun for Pushpa and light-green enamelled earrings for Shami? Cruel fate! It had just demolished the small beautiful world of my imagination. I wanted to end my life which nature must have created in a thoughtless moment. Then I overheard the boy in the rowing boat telling his companion that the water in the river was never more than knee-deep in winter.

'Yes, they divert the water to the upper reaches of the Bari Doab Canal,' his companion said.

I retraced my steps and proceeded home. Feeling utterly distraught, I knocked on the door. It was a great relief to know that Pushpa and Bachchu had gone to sleep after waiting for me.

Sitting by the chuulha, Shami had been dozing fitfully while warming herself before the dying embers. As she saw me coming in empty-handed, she gave me a questioning look.

I put my hand in the inside pocket and wiggled the fingers through the hole below the label. Shami understood and I hung my coat on the peg. Shami sat down by my side, resting her head against the wall.

Yazdani and Santa Singh were playing cards at the recreation club. They had also downed a couple of drinks each. They asked me to drink, and I showed no interest because my pocket was empty. Santa Singh allowed me to take a sip from his glass. They could easily guess my financial dilemma. Or they were more concerned with their mental state than my concern for the worsted cloth.

While leaving for the club, I saw Shami in her white sari, which had tempted me to try my luck at the card table. If I had a rupee or two, I could have raked in much cash. What I carried in my pocket were four annas. Yazdani and Sant

Singh, who were wearing worsted suits, were arguing with the good-natured club secretary. The good man told them that he could not visualize the recreation club turned into a bar. At that moment, I put my hands into my pocket and uttered in a hopelessly constrained tone, 'To buy anything for the wife and kids is a crime against nature. With the same logic, one should be required to pay for the pleasure of gambling . . . *he, he, gee, gee . . .*'

I reached for my pocket and as I was about to remove my hand, I felt a piece of paper rustling against the lining near the back of the coat. Putting my fingers to work, I brought the piece of paper near the hole of my inside pocket.

And lo! There it was—the ten-rupee note. Slipping through the hole, it had got embedded somewhere inside the coat's lining.

That evening I tested my luck with a vengeance. I stubbornly refused to gamble at the card table. Instead, firmly clutching the note in my hand, I rushed home like a madman. If that day Shami had changed her white dress without waiting for me, I would not have gone crazy. My imagination had run berserk as if all that one needed to create a private world of one's own was a ten-rupee note.

I started to make a new list. Shami took the piece of paper from my hands and tore into bits. She said, 'Don't make too many castles in the air lest something happens to the currency note again.' Shami was right. If we don't make too many colourful plans, our suffering is less. I told Shami that I was afraid of losing the note once again. Your neighbour, Khemo, is going to the market. You should go with her to make all the purchases—the green enamelled earrings, DCM thread, inch-tape, etc. But don't forget to get gulab jamun for Poppi Munna.

Shami agreed to go with Khemo. That evening, Shami wore a lovely Kashmiri dress. I have little tolerance for the noise that kids make. But that evening, I spent a lot of time explaining to Bachhu the reason for his mother's absence. He was madly searching for her. I gave him hope. 'She has gone to buy your tricycle. No. A tricycle is a useless thing. She will bring home beautiful balloons.'

My daughter made fun of my distaste for tricycles. I took her in my lap and told her, 'Poppi Munna, you will have gulab jamun today to your heart's content.' I saw her mouth-watering. She jumped out of my lap, saying, 'I feel I'm gulping a very big gulab jamun down my throat.' Bachhu continued to sob, and Pushpa Munni practised her Kathakali mudras.

What could stop the flight of my imagination? I was afraid that the castles of my dream might crash and burn. That is why I had sent Shami to the market. I was thinking. She must be close to the veterinary hospital for horses. She must have crossed the corner of the college road. Now she must be nearing the dirty engine . . .

The door's chain moved slightly.

Shami had returned. She was standing at the door.

'I have spent more than I had bargained for,' she said as soon as she entered. 'I borrowed two rupees from Khemo.'

'Never mind the money!' I spoke.

Bachchu, Poppi and I eagerly followed her into the room. Shami had nothing else in her hand except a small packet. She placed the packet on the table and untied its string. It was a fine piece of worsted cloth for my coat.

Pushpa Munni wailed, 'Mother, what about my gulab jamun?'

Shami silenced her with a resounding slap.

7

The Scars of Smallpox

He was now standing at a place where no searching eye could find him . . . Behind an iron gate of large nails, a tall gate commonly found in urban locations, where animal waste was spread around, its foul smell, like the fog of the month of *Magh* (January-February), was floating parallel to the ground. Behind him, his sister was collecting cow's urine for a woman who had delivered a child. But Sakhia had seen his face. He had large and deep scars caused by smallpox, like big drops of rain found on thick sand in Matan Hel, her parents's village.

The way people lived in this new home was very traditional, and their dependence on the wisdom of a few who were willing to help was quite obvious. The walls were made of small bricks going back to Ranjit Singh's reign and like the protruding and sparse teeth of an older man in his nearly smothered gums, the bricks were stretched out. The mixture of cement, lime and mud that was supposed to bind them together had outlived its usefulness years ago. On one of the walls, a combination of mud and stubble was used as a base with a wash of lime on top to make place for some unattractive and large Nagari letters. Mehria (maid), who was sitting close to the pots and pans, was singing an out-of-place and out-of-tune song: *Apjas ki mat baandho ghathariya* (Don't try to fill a bag of sins.) Poor Mehria! She was showing repentance for sins that she had not perpetrated, and she was not even capable of carrying out. She was probably singing this because she had developed some grudge going back to younger son's wedding.

'O, my son! Why are you standing there in the cow-dung?'

The mother of the house called. At that time, the elder son took a puff of his mini hookah made of coconut shell while standing in the courtyard and laughed at the mother. She had finished her *Ram-naam path* routine. What was the use of this puja? You have finished *Ram-naam.* You're great, mother! Stay quiet. The big mama said with an unpleasant smile. Then to complete the last installment of her devotional recitation, the older woman picked up a worn-out chalice made of brass, filled it with water, and spread it around the roots of the peepul tree, that acted like a perplexed Brahmin of the courtyard. The tree quivered after receiving the cold shower on its roots. Or did this happen due to a whiff of cold breeze? Then she circled a red and yellow thread around the trunk and tied it firmly. The youngest grandson was very naughty. He was well known to all the neighbours; they called him a 'Sahib.' Despite solid objections by family members, he had adopted a puppy, thus soiling the good name of his ancestors. When Sahib got up in the morning, his pup also rose with him. The puppy would stretch, open his mouth, foam and seethe and then run towards the base of the peepal tree, lift one leg and showed his devotion for the tree in his unique way.

Sakhia's head was still heavy after having covered a distance of one-hundred miles. The lorry's ugly sound of *ghoon ghoon jhar jhar* was still echoing in her ears and her head was spinning. The eldest sister-in-law had placed lemon pickle on a china plate. '*Aa haa chhii!*' Sakhia said expressing her disappointment. These people use plates and bowls made of china and eat food in them like barbarian and uncultured Muslims, Sakhia told their niece who was standing nearby. Do you have a Moradabadi metal utensil? Bring some sauce in that. It will stop my urge to throw up. I'll never eat anything in a china bowl. And the bride showed her disinterest and nausea. The elder sister-in-law felt inner gratification. Now Amma is old. She can't tell the difference between the new and used utensils. But this . . . new stuff has now come into the house.

The sister-in-law took her plate and moved away.

Standing in the penumbra of the large urban gate, he was clearly visible to Sakhia. He had an English-cut hairstyle. The sister-in-law was saying in her rural accent . . . Jairam has done a BA from Lukhnow. He lived away from home, in a boarding house where single men lived. He didn't wear the sacred thread. He didn't have a *choti,* a long streak of hair on the back of his head to protect his highest chakra. Sakhia thought that this was the wisdom of the uncultured people. How do you reconcile the English style and the scars of smallpox? When this horrible face gets closer, it will be very troubling, and no lemon pickle would provide relief. Everyone will be asleep. I'll have to cope with this. What did my uncle see in these people? They pushed me into this hell. Sitting on her bed, Sakhia pushed her face towards her stomach and started to cry.

The women of the neighbourhood were still coming in to critically look at the bride. The bride was like gold and would pass every test. Because she looked sulky, the women gave petulant expressions. It's true that parents are like a precious treasure. One couldn't leave them in a day. One woman started to describe the time of her wedding, crying harder than Sakhia, surprising her. Until then, she had not missed her parents. The lower lip of this rustic woman fell like the hump of a camel's back. After some time, the naive woman realized that her crying was a bad omen for the house that had just seen a wedding. She wiped her tears with her headscarf. This is the way of the world. The young one, you should beg for the comfort of this home. Your husband is an incarnation of a cow. Jairam is a son, but he is more like a daughter. He doesn't speak much. He is so plain, calling day a day, and night a night. He will dance to your tunes.

'Today is very auspicious.' Amma of the house spoke. Amar, who lives in our street, got a child. Punjabis got a son thirteen days ago. The child will get a urine wash. This blessing is due to having a son. Sons are like the spring. They are born and are married. O Sunderi's mother. Where is your Sahib? When the eldest bride came, I put your Sahib in her lap. Three sons were born, one after the other. When I put him in the lap of the middle bride, Lala in the first year and Bitto in the second were born. Bitto is more loving than Lala. Where is he? I want to put him in the bride's lap.

Sakhia shrank like a pile of clothes. A son and the scars of smallpox!

A Gujjar came in to take away the animals. Another low-caste, scantily dressed sweeper was cleaning the courtyard. The fog was shyly dissipating, not able to compete with the sun's rays. And the bad odour was being taken care of by the low-caste person. Once the fog was lifted, the morning's moonlike face became visible. The eunuchs of the locality, dividing themselves in small groups, were coming to the home of the Punjabis, singing and dancing. At that time, the head cleaning-woman was decorating Amar's house. Sakhia was watching all this, but it was getting on her nerves.

After the courtyard was washed, he came to sit with the elder brother while playing with the puppy. But he gave the impression that he was trying to hide himself, trying to camouflage his face filled with smallpox scars. Sakhia felt compassion in her heart. O, Rama, never give an ugly face to anyone. Shame is hard to hide. I concede that this is not his fault. But was it my fault? My face made other women burn with jealousy. Even ghosts will refuse to dance when they look upon his face!

The elder sister-in-law brought pickle in a Moradabadi utensil. Sakhia took her fingers out of her Kashmiri shawl and moved towards the pickle. The sister-in-law looked at Sakhia's fingers and then her own, which resembled the stems of a cauliflower, and said that Jairam must have bestowed pearls in his past life. Fingers which resemble the tender stalks of mustard green. Tell me Sakhia Bhabhi, in what mould were these fingers formed?

So much love? Sakhia started to think. These relationships are of the kind that they generate love on their own. Because of these relationships everything starts to look pleasing. For this, you must bear whatever mother-in-law, father-in-law and sisters-in-law have to say. But when the man has a facial appearance of this kind, why should one care about what people say. One should consume opium and go to sleep.

'Will you play the utensil game?' Sister-in-law enquired.

Sakhia remained silent. She was shy about this ritual.

The sister-in-law put her hand under Sakhia's chin and lifted her face. Her eyes were closed as if she were musing. Her teeth were arranged like pearls and the upper lip's arch was pleasing.

The sister-in-law said, 'Tell me one thing.' Sakhia opened her eyes. The sister-in-law looked hither and thither. All women were busy doing their routines. 'Has Jairam seen you?' Sakhia wanted to ask her a counter question: who Jairam is, which would be truly amazing. But she turned her face away and shrank. The sister-in-law was a strong-muscled villager. She didn't allow the bride to shrink and repeated her question. Sakhia said 'yes' to avoid further questioning.

There was preparation under way for the performance of wedding-related rituals. Maybe the same old utensil game. In an open pan, they mixed water with milk and added coins. Kaka had brought the pouch that contained all the money. Sakhia would put her hand inside the pouch, and she would get nothing but currency notes. Sister-in-law pointed out that bride's hand was delicate. Kaka felt pleased. With one hand, the bride will take out as much as sixty rupees. The younger son-in-law of the house was standing next to Kaka. The elder one had not come. He was wearing a large turban of silken cloth, a long cotton coat, and a dhoti around his waist which made him look like an article of derision. Still, because of his position as a son-in-law he was being well taken care of. He commanded respect and if he didn't get, he would show his temper that made everyone uneasy, except Jairam, who was ashamed of his presence.

Everyone was busy doing their assigned task. The view from Sakhia's window resembled the bare breasts of a virgin, in undulating high and lows. The low-height green seedlings which were a little stretched, mirrored a bra. The ground had covered itself with fog to hide its nakedness, but the uncooperative sun slowly removed the cover, exposing the feeble land. Now he was closer, and Sakhia could see him easily. For two long minutes she looked at him. Jairam had another peculiar habit. He would frequently jerk his head as if he were saying, come here. That is why Jairam avoided getting too close to women. It seemed that the scars of smallpox melted after her two-minute gaze and Jairam's face looked clean and spotless. Sakhia thought that if after looking vacantly at the face for two minutes, the face could become spotless, living together for the entire life would make the face so familiar that smallpox scars would become invisible.

Now, it was noon and the day started to dwindle. Sakhia put her hand in Kaka's pouch and spread it widely and she captured around eighty-five rupees. Women started to laugh. O, Kaka, take care of your pouch! You daughter-in-law is easy with money. Another woman said, Kaka you have earned a lot selling milk, sufficient for seven generations. Kaka, will you take it with you to your samadhi? Amma came out in Kaka's defence. Do you think my Jairam is earning less? He gets three twenties and one. Just two of them. No liabilities. They can eat and enjoy.

It is good that Sakhia came to know how much he earned. It was not a bad pay. Is it easy to earn sixty-one rupees these days? Probably not. He had studied up to fourteen classes. It was not a big deal. Sakhia's cousin had done sixteen classes and on top of that he wandered around quite a bit in the province, came to know about law and then he joined a bogus company. The utensil game was next, but Jairam didn't show up. Maybe he sensed how much Sakhia hated him. Sitting all alone, he must be cursing himself. Mehria was singing her own gajal (ghazal). Sakhia said . . . don't sin. And Jairam was grappling with the same thought. This song mirrored his inner struggle. Everyone who listened to this song wanted to tell Mehria to stop singing. But before doing that, every man and woman was seeing a reflection of their lives, and before they told Mehria anything they were submerged in their feelings and emotions.

Sakhia saw Jairam approaching her in her thoughts. Her body below her waist was on fire. Her ears were flaming with fire so intense that the scars of smallpox were reduced to bone ash. Leave aside smallpox scars, even if he had the face of an African, even then Sakhia would not have felt anything. There was darkness around, or there were flames in which statues of a man and a woman were shining like gemstone jewels.

Amid these thoughts, Sakhia had forgotten what Jairam looked like. She was forgetful. Jairam didn't come to play the game. This thought obsessed her. It would have been fun despite the rising tide of hate, but what was the remedy for this hate? If we get close to someone, all deficiencies become assets.

He didn't come. How does he know that I hate him? As I wished his scars to disappear, they did disappear. Now the face of the man walking in the yard was not disfigured. This was first day of their married life, and she had already forgotten about the smallpox scars. So much . . .

Milk was boiling in the kitchen and then it spilt over and trailed snake-like on the floor. Oh, this bag of sins.

Amma called Mehria. Where are you lost? Can't you see that milk is boiling? Whore. When you want money, you climb over my head. I'll not give you money. I'll throw ash on your face. Amma said many things gurgling and babbling like a child.

At the end of the day, when it was close to the evening, animals entered the gate and no time was spared before they were milked. Cans filled with milk were placed on a wooden platform. Kaka, while seated on the wooden bench, was writing something in a red-coloured ledger with his son-in-law's assistance. His worn-out glasses were falling on his face. One of the temples of the glasses was broken and as such there was a thread that was providing the support and balancing the glasses. The broken lenses often gave the impression of two men when there was only one.

The women of the household were whispering. They were looking critically at Jairam. Sakhia sensed something. Why has he not come? Sakhia once again questioned herself. Her heart ran faster, and she remembered Matan Hel. And then Jairam . . . Women were telling him something. Like Amma, even she felt the need to defend him. But, but . . . If the beautiful face has a black mole, it looks even more beautiful. If the man is earning a good wage, if he is of good character, if he is healthy, if he is educated, then the smallpox scars can become a thing of beauty. Sakhia had finally found beauty in the smallpox scars.

Now, it was night. For another ritual, there was a search for Jairam. The eldest sister-in-law came, highly perplexed, and said, 'Sakhia sister, please don't mind my saying this. In youth, everyone is obstinate.'

Sakhia answered, 'What is the obstinacy here?'

'It is a childish outlook. As the time passes, wisdom will dawn.'

Sakhia gave a surprised look to her sister-in-law and said, 'Jiji, what are you talking about? I don't understand.'

'It could be anything,' Sister-in-law replied, 'Jairam has studied in college. He thinks that Sakhia has a long nose. That is why he didn't come for the play. And I don't think your nose is long. Let some time pass and things . . .'

The wedding night was coming—forcefully inching closer. Sakhia had gone beyond the smallpox scars and had discovered beauty. But Jairam had not forgiven her for her long nose, and the night that was cold, lonely and dreamless, lingered and frittered away.

8

A Father for Sale

I had not read it myself, but I was told that a funny advertisement had appeared in *The Times* issue for 24 February. It came to me as a surprise how a quaint ad of this nature could pass the scrutiny of the newspaper's advertisement department. I had never come across such an ad in the *Bought & Sold* column of any newspaper before. The advertiser had deliberately—or was it inadvertently—given it an aura of mystery. Except for the address, everything else in the announcement aroused the reader's curiosity, for it read: A father for sale, age seventy-one years, wheatish complexion, slim, asthmatic. Correspond with Box No. L 476 care of *The Times*.

'A father of seventy-one! He must have become a grandfather at that age.'

'People don't pay attention and then one day they are grandfathers.'

'If I buy a father, what would my mother who is a widow say? I will have a father and mother who are not married.'

'Someone has planned to walk the globe, walking backwards. In today's world everything is possible.'

'He will spread asthma.'

'Asthma is not contagious.'

'Yes, it is.'

'No.'

'Yes.'

The two men took out their knives and started a fight.

Some read the advertisement but laughed at the old man's idiosyncrasy. They would put the newspaper aside and pick it up to read it again, feeling a bit foolish, and then thrust the newspaper under the nose of the man sitting next to them.

'One thing is certain. The house will be immune from theft.'

'What makes you say that?'

'How can there be a theft if a man keeps awake while coughing the whole night?'

'I can see through the game. It's a conspiracy on the part of the manufacturers of sleeping pills . . . a father for sale.'

People laughed until till they were on the verge of tears.

Soon it became the talk of the town. People discussed it everywhere—at home, on the road, in the offices.

During January and February, the trees generally start shedding leaves. To see a crew of twenty sweepers sweeping dry and rotten leaves under a head cleaner's supervision is a common sight. They go crazy collecting and piling up these leaves. It irks them all. But they are not allowed to take these leaves home and make a bonfire of them to keep their children warm against cold. The ad seemed to have served the same purpose. A discussion had generated sufficient heat, and within no time it was likely to become a flaming bonfire.

'There must be a catch somewhere.'

'He must be filthy rich.'

'Nonsense. Then why would he put himself on sale?'

'It could be a clever device on the part of the children to get rid of their father. He could be a tyrant like Changez Khan or Halaku.'

'Did you read it, Mrs Goswami?'

'*Dhut!* Who has the time? My hands are filled with taking care of so many children. And then there's my husband, who alone is equal to so many! My Swami, *he, he, he!*'

'Fathers can be real bastards.'

A spate of letters poured into Box No. L 476. There was a letter from Miss Uni Krishnan, someone from Kerala who was working as a nurse in Abu Dhabi. She had a child and was keen to marry a man with a reasonable income and look after the mother and her child. Age, she added, was no consideration. It was evident that her husband had deserted her. Or some Sheikh of Abu Dhabi might have had an affair with her. Her letter was put aside, as being off the mark, as it did not even make a passing reference to a father on sale. After reading the bulk of the letters, it appeared all the readers of Agatha Christie and Hadley Chase had evoked interest in the ad as if they were hot on the trail of some mystery.

The man in charge of the classifieds suggested to the newspaper's general manager that the rates of the classifieds should be increased. But the young-looking old general manager or the young old-looking general manager shrugged his shoulders saying 'Shucks!' and threw his subordinate's suggestion in the wastepaper basket. From his attitude, it appeared he was trying to make amends for some past mistake.

Fearing that there was something fishy, the police arrived. The advertiser lived in Hindu Colony in Dadar. His name was Gandharvdas, and he confronted the police openly, declaring

that offering oneself for sale was not a contravention of the
law. He was chewing paan after paan and spraying the juice
carelessly on the walls.

The police investigation revealed that Gandharvdas
was a musician, and there was a time when his singing
was quite popular. His wife, with whom he was always at
loggerheads, had died. Both husband and wife had been
tied together in blind love. They could neither live together
nor live separately.

It was essential for Gandharvdas to reach home by eight
in the evening. Although they had nothing to do with each
other, this routine was well established. He sang lustily, simply
because Damyanti—that was his wife's name—abhorred his
singing. While he was singing, she would be in the kitchen
preparing *gaajar* halwa. She was pleased that her husband,
whom she gladly ignored, slept in the bed next to her, deep
in his sleep, snoring heavily. Snoring was the only music that
the wife understood.

After his wife's death, Gandharvdas forgot about all the
liberties his wife had taken with him, but he could not ignore
the cruelties he had inflicted upon her. He would suddenly
wake up at night and tearing his shirt he would run out like a
madman. In his last dream, his wife had raised a big hue and
cry because he had cast his eye on another woman. She had
run out of the house screaming. Gandharvdas had chased her,
but she had buried herself under the soft patch of the earth,
near the wooden staircase. But the ground kept moving and
fissures formed, which meant that his wife was still alive. In
a state of bewilderment, he had pulled her out of the earth,
but he was shocked to discover that her arms were missing
and her entire body below her navel. His wife, or what was

left of her, was clinging to him. Caressing that lifeless figure, Gandharvdas carried her upstairs.

From that time onward, Gandharvdas stopped singing.

Gandharvdas had three living children. The eldest was a well-known playback singer whose long-playing records were sold out the moment they were in the market. The demand on jukeboxes in Irani restaurants was mostly for his records, and no one cared for Gandharvdas's classical music. The second son was an offset printer, and he also made zinc plates. He earned about 1500 rupees a month from his printing press and enjoyed life with his Italian wife. He was just not concerned with others and kept himself in his family circle. When Gandharvdas stopped performing publicly, his son, who used to sing with him as an accompanist, also stopped singing. Gandharvdas suggested that he would like to buy the HMV gramophone records agency for his son.

'But why?' his son asked. 'What future do I have with you?'

His son's reply gave Gandharvdas a big jolt. How could he predict his son's future? Could anybody, for that matter? What Gandharvdas had meant was that they would swim and sink together. In any case, his son being young could not withstand the ups and downs of life. Sensing his son's attitude, Gandharvdas withdrew into his shell. He married off his daughter into an excellent Marwari family. Whenever the three brothers and their sister met, they called their father not a widower but a strong-willed and independent widower and patted their backs for having such inventive brains.

What happened?

Chatrak, a poet and an accountant, who had called on Gandharvdas in response to his ad, suspected that there must be something radically wrong with the older man. Otherwise, at least one of his three sons would have stood by him in his old age. Or was it that their proximity to one another had led to contempt and driven them apart?

Since Chatrak was an accountant who kept meddling with figures all the time, it created discord between his thinking and actions. Little did he realize that in India and worldwide, the family as an institution or as a concept was on its way out. To show respect to the elders of the family was now regarded as something feudal. The old folks would sit in some Hyde Park, cut off from the mainstream of life and shivering in the cold, hunting strangers with their eyes, hoping that they might stop to chat with them. They were like the Jews whom Hitler had shoved into the gas chambers. But before doing so, their persecutors would pull out their teeth with pliers for their gold. Once a lucky Jew escaped, and when a stray relative came to visit him in his attic, he found him lying dead and his dazed eyes still fixed on the door. The people downstairs, ignorant of the death upstairs, carried on their regular business of selling newspapers because the newspapers carried some fresh news each day. Ultimately, when the story of death goes around, a doctor will come up and confirm that the older man must have died a fortnight back, and the dead body had escaped from being decomposed due to the severe cold. After informing the authorities, the old man's relative quietly slunk away lest he should be asked to bear the dead man's funeral expenses.

Chatrak said that it was quite likely that Gandharvdas had frittered away all his savings on his children, and now he was left with nothing for his old age. Money saved for the old age was the language that was universally understood.

Acclaim in art and proficiency in music left the near and dear ones cold. Even if anyone reached extreme heights in his field, no one cared. The children were just not concerned with their father's achievements. They wanted him to spend his energy in pursuits, that brought *them* happiness. And they were good at coming up with excuses.

Gandharvdas was a cheerful type of person. He was always full of titbits and witticisms, which he generated at a moment's notice. He could laugh at himself as well as others. His jokes were generally smutty and obscene. Perhaps they were masks behind which he tried to hide his sexual frustration and inadequacy. A more plausible explanation could be that in old age, a man generally becomes more carnal and is not tired of narrating his imaginary sexual exploits.

Some people who responded to Gandharvdas's ad dropped out when they learned that he had a debt of 55,000 rupees, which had not been mentioned in the ad. This could perhaps be due to his crafty nature. Strangely enough, he was also having an affair with a girl who was younger than his daughter Rama. The girl named Devyani wanted to learn classical music, and Guruji taught it, devoting all his available time generously and made her achieve great success. Maybe due to the disparity in their ages, the emotional upheavals they experienced had reached a level Gandharvdas could not understand, what to say of others. Well, who would care to buy a father who had all the flaws and human weaknesses one could think?

And on top of that, he kept coughing all the time. He could stop breathing any moment.

When he went out, he drank on the sly. He even carried a quarter bottle hidden under his dhoti.

People say asthmatic patients live longer.

While teaching music, Gandharvdas would suddenly exclaim, 'I will sing again!' He overemphasized the point because his assertion lacked conviction even in his mind. When he was slowly building up the notes of a raga, the image of his dead wife would appear before his eyes.

'Still singing?' she seemed to be asking.

Due to an amalgam of positives and negatives, people had come to regard Gandharvdas as some scintillating object that left its halo behind, even when it had disappeared, or some other more shining object dimmed its lustre.

One Khurshid Alam said, 'I'm prepared to buy you provided you become a Muslim.'

'But I'm already a Muslim.'

'How come?'

'I've full faith in Allah. And what's more I've acquired music from Ustad Alaudin Khan's gharana (school or tradition of music).'

'You mean that you are a Muslim who recites the *kalma*?'

'A man's breath is the kalma which goes in and out of his body all the time. Music is my religion. Was it required of Ustad Abdul Karim Khan to become Baba Haridas?'

That was the last that they saw of Mian Khurshid Alam.

There were two or three women who showed interest in Gandharvdas. Like the one who had lived his life fully and had left no residue in his glass of wine, he told them, 'Perhaps you don't know that you want just opposite of what you are asking. You want to experience something new by which your body goes to sleep, and your soul wakes up. But I can see that you lack the courage to do so. You take shelter behind the facade of dharma, caste, religion and what not. But the body holds the soul in its iron grip and casts it aside. You fear the man lying under your bed, and at the same time, want to have him. You are like those virgins who keep harping on chastity and give themselves to lewd thoughts, placing no limits.'

Gandharvdas gave a mischievous smile and added, 'Even the spellings of your names are wrong.'

These women were convinced that being mothers, as far as they could remember, they were not searching for a father but the son of God. As for themselves, they already had three or four sons each, of course, lost to the business of this mundane world.

I'm talking about the day when the Lord's idol was stolen from a temple situated on the Bann Ganga bank. That day leaves were falling from the trees in great profusion, filling the temple precinct. The leaves were brittle and withered. Then some rain fell in the evening, and before the theft took place, moths in thousands immolated themselves hovering over temple lamps. Nature that had given birth to them was also the cause that turned them into manure. The same day, the temple priest, while gazing at Krishna's Radha, realized that she was much older than her lover and then in an instant looked smilingly at the cleaning woman, Chhabbu, who was even younger than the priest's daughter. She gathered all the leaves, flowers and seeds and carried them to her house.

The idol's theft caused no surprise as it was made of gold and silver and was studded with diamonds and sapphires. But nobody could assign any reason why Durve, the proprietor of Larsen & Larsen, should have purchased Gandharvdas. No words were exchanged between Durve and Gandharvdas. Only by a gesture of his eyes, Gandharvdas informed Durve, 'Son, buy me!' Of course, how could there be a son without a father? After that Durve could not venture to ask any further question. The terms and conditions of purchase were undetermined. But who can limit life by terms and conditions? Durve paid Gandharvdas's debt, helped him to rise to his feet, and then escorted him to his luxurious bungalow, Kirti Kunj, on Malabar Hill, where the old man was provided adequate medical care and comforts of the good life.

Durve's servant told him, 'Sir, you've brought home a headache for yourself. In what way, this decrepit, I mean this Babuji, is going to reward you for the troubles you are taking on his behalf?'

'No, nothing,' Durve replied. 'I expect nothing from him. What can anyone expect from a man who sits crossed-legged all day and does nothing but cough and cough? Or the man who chews paan laced with scented tobacco and spits all over the place? How can my wife and I, who are sticklers for cleanliness, stand such abominations? I'm afraid we might catch his bad habits. But have you seen his eyes?'

'No, Sir.'

'Then go and have a look at them—his weeping as well as smiling eyes. Just go and see what message they convey and how far they reach?'

'Sir, how far do they reach?' Jamunadas, Durve's servant, asked absent-mindedly, looking into the void. 'You are a scientist and understand such things.'

'Jamuna, I'm talking of science, of course. If plants, trees and fruits are necessary for man's survival, if animals of the jungle and children are necessary, older men are also indispensable by the same logic. If we ignore them, our ecological balance would be upset—spiritually if not physically. Humanity would become extinct.'

Durve's explanation went over Jamunadas's and another servant named Athavale's heads.

Durve plucked a leaf from an Ashoka tree.

'Ask your science to match the greenness and freshness of this leaf,' he said, holding the leaf before Jamunadas.

'Put Ashoka seed into the ground . . . ' Athavale suggested.

'Oh, no, I'm talking of the leaf, not the seed,' Durve said, shaking his head. 'If I start talking of the seed, God only knows where it will lead us.'

Getting closer to Jamunadas, Durve said, 'To tell you Jamuna, when I touch Babu ji's feet, you can't imagine how much peace of mind I get. I used to keep shaking with an unknown fear but not now. His presence is reassuring. I'm sure something similar must be happening to Babuji's soul.'

'Sir, I can't agree with you on this. These are nothing but hollow sentiments.'

'Just possible.' Durve flared up. He could have fired Jamunadas. But the mystery in the old man's eyes precluded him from taking such a drastic step. 'Say what you like, Jamunadas,' he added in a mellow voice, 'but you must know one thing—people bow to me wherever I go. They show me great respect . . .'

Durve suddenly trailed into silence. His voice became thick with emotion, and his eyes were clouded with tears.

'Sir, that's what I've been trying to tell you,' Jamunadas said. 'The whole world bows before you.'

'Exactly so,' Durve said while regaining his voice. 'I, too, wish to bow my head before someone.' Then he added an impatient note, 'Jamunadas, Athavale, please go. Don't disturb my puja. We have discovered God even in stones.'

The mango trees in Kirti Kunj had blossomed, and they heard the season's first notes of a koel (cuckoo) singing. And

Gandharvdas broke into a song for the first time in years: '*Koiliya bole amva ki daar* (Koel sings on the branch of a mango tree.)'

Someone remarked that his son sang better than him.

'*Aaisa* . . . Do you think so?' Gandharvdas asked in his typical Bombay accent.

'But don't forget that he is my son. If the father finished high school, shouldn't the son go one better and earn a graduate degree?'

The people who had lost their fathers would stare at Gandharvdas when he talked in this manner. Finding no frown on his face, they would provoke him.

'Your son often says that you are jealous of him,' a man told him.

'Is it true? My son says that?'

'Yes, he does. I'm not telling you a lie.'

Gandharvdas became thoughtful as if he withdrew into his inner cosmic world to complain to his wife about his son. After a pause, during which it seemed he had waited in vain for a reply, he said, 'It doesn't matter. My son . . . he too is a father.'

His mind went back to the time when his son had said, 'Father, I also want to learn classical music and learn to sing better than you. But only after I've amassed tons of money.'

Hearing this, Gandharvdas had patted his son on his back. 'Raju, things don't happen in this manner, not always according to one's wishes.'

Then he added, 'Either a man amasses wealth, or he excels in art.'

Big tears rolled down from Gandharvdas's eyes, and they got absorbed in his beard; they looked like prisms, their light breaking into seven colours. Durve saw it all from where he was seated.

Then as if the Devil had suddenly taken hold of Durve's mind, he got up and shouted, 'Get out, all of you!' The people in the room sprinted like rodents, falling upon one another.

Gandharvdas raised his hand and said, 'No, son, no!' Electric sparks were emitting from his hand.

On reaching his office, Durve found Philip, his works manager, feeding data into the computer. As the card emerged from the machine, his face turned pale. He winced and kept looking at the card. The card had predicted that Larsen & Larsen was going to suffer a loss of 41,00,000 rupees. Looking alarmed, he held the card before Durve's face. But there was not even a hint of a frown on his face. He only said, 'It seems the computer has been fed wrong data.'

'No, Sir, I've checked and cross-checked.'

'Well, it's a machine. Something could go wrong with it. Call the IBM people.'

'Modak, the chief engineer, has gone to the South.'

'Has he? But where in the South?'

'To Tirupati Temple. I have come to know that he has chopped off his hippy-like long hair and have offered it to the deity.'

Durve gave a faint smile.

'Did you feed the computer the information that we have a father living in our midst?' he asked.

Phillip thought Durve was joking or had gone mad. But Durve kept reminding him that they had the blessings of a mentor, adding that he should not forget that a machine was the handiwork of a man, someone who had a father, and that father, in turn, had a father. And ultimately, we reach a composite father, the Supreme Father of all, who could be perceived as a compounded whole or singular whole.

Phillip vented his anger in the form of a question. 'Does Devyani still visit Babuji?' he asked.

'Yes.'

'And Mrs Durve doesn't object?'

'In the beginning, she looked askance at these visits, but now she worships him. The fact is that Babuji is in love with the entire humanity. It appears Babuji has visions that made him delve into the mysteries of creation. As a result, he keeps smiling. Sometimes he winks.'

Phillip's anger was rising.

But ignoring his anger, Durve continued. 'Babuji is very fond of such words as *beti, bahu, bhabhi, chachi, lalli, mayyia*. Sometimes, he throws his arms around my bahu's waist and kisses her cheeks. In this manner, he seeks his liberation in imprisonment and imprisonment in liberation.'

'And Devyani?'

'Phillip, attach only as much importance to sex as is legitimately due to it,' Durve said contemptuously. 'Don't allow it to become an obsession with you. Music was perhaps a smokescreen for Devyani.'

'I have not understood you, Sir.'

'Babuji had told me that this girl had gone astray at an early age. She had seen her parents in a compromising position when she had just entered adolescence. She became someone like her mother. After her father's death, she went from one man to another in utter bewilderment. Her body fell apart, but her soul never found any satisfaction.'

'What do you mean?'

'Devyani was in a quest of finding a father.'

Phillip, who was a Catholic, felt galvanized. His eyebrows shot up, and his dilated eyes emitted hellfire.

'It's a fraud!' he cried. 'Mr Durve, it's an unadulterated fraud!'

Just then, Durve saw a blurred image of his acquired father, eyes moist with tears, standing behind the computer that was family heritage, and said, 'This morning Babuji told me, Phillip, don't try to understand the man. Only try to feel him . . .'

9

Jogia

Scantily clad in three-and-a-half garments after her bath, as was her daily routine, Jogia came out and stood before the almirah. I stepped back a little to have a good look at her. As my hand struck against the door it made a discordant sound as a faint murmur of protest. My elder brother was present in the room, shaving.

'What's it, Jugal?' he asked turning round.

'It's nothing, *mote bhaiyya* (Chubby Brother),' I said evasively. 'It's very hot. Isn't it?'

I was looking ahead of me. What colour of sari would Jogia select for the day, I was wondering? As a student at the J.J. School of Arts, I was obsessed with colours because I thought they speak, and in my thinking, they spoke more eloquently than men and women. This was my firm view. Sometimes men talk in their heads, making no sense. But colours always convey meaning.

Our house was situated in Kalbadevi neighbourhood of Shet Agiari Lane. The Parsi Agiari was way ahead at the mouth of the lane, but the rest of it consisted of houses facing one another. They huddled so close as if they were locked in an embrace and whispered to each other in soft sweet tones. It was like a mother talking to her child—sometimes ardently as lovers in a frenzy of passion, keeping lips close to lips, breasts touching each other, and minds brimming with thoughts, pure and dirty at the same time.

We could see from our place in the Gyan Bhawan what was going on in the private quarters in front of us. Bijor's mother was sitting in her room, chopping vegetables. Oops, she just cut her hand with the knife. Dinker Bhai had brought two tins of oil from Ahmedabad. The Punjabi woman had surreptitiously thrown away eggshells in the garbage can and was hastily retreating. Just as we could peer into their homes and invade their privacy, similarly what we were doing must be open to their gaze too.

Jogia's house was named Ranchhor Niwas, but I called it Banpu House for short because it was mostly inhabited by widows and abandoned women. Among them was Jogia's mother who worked in a tailoring shop and earned barely enough to make a living and pay for Jogia's tuition.

Jogia was a beautiful girl of seventeen or eighteen. She couldn't be called short, but being full-bodied, she gave the impression of being so. But nobody could believe that a simple and plain diet of dal and beans with a small helping of *shrikhand* thrown in once or twice a week could make someone sturdy and healthy. Perhaps, she was one among those girls whose bodies showed whatever food they gobbled up, not limited to deliberate choices, and it had the tendency to manifest itself in the wrong places. Jogia's face was broad like the frontal view of the Somnath Temple; her eyes like paper lanterns were guiding the wayfarers lost in the dark night to their right course. Her nose was like that of an idol and the lips were like a cased pair of emeralds and the rubies. Her hair measured up to her waist. Sometimes, she kept them loose, oily and wet, and sometimes they were dry, flying around, embracing her face. Her facial appearance was like the constellation of stars in which the moon waxed and waned according to the dictates of her feelings. Jogia was naive and simple, but she excelled in showing her physical charms to her advantage. She instinctively knew when to embellish herself and when to act straightforward. I think her education had a big hand in the way she came across and also how she had managed to look even prettier. Her complexion struck a discordant note because she was fairer than what was desired. It made some people uneasy. If the other elements of her personality had not revealed harmonious proportions, she would have knocked herself out.

I don't know the meaning of love. It might as well be an exotic bird. But the very sight of Jogia did something to my heart; I shook inside. Whenever we ran into each other I was taken aback by her silliness. She was friends with Hema, my niece. But it was a strange friendship because of the disparity in their ages. Hema was seven, while Jogia was eighteen. Perhaps only Jogia could fathom the reason for this kind of friendship, though I could make a guess. Chubby Brother and Bhabhi, my brother's wife, were labouring under the impression that Jogia had such affection for Hema that she visited her to help her with her studies. For that reason, she had become a teacher for every member of the family. I had just completed my training as an artist and therefore I was informal in my dealings with others, and I was also free with Jogia. But I had my limitations too. I was not an earner yet

and was a dependent on Chubby Brother. But the game of
hide-and-seek with Jogia had its own charm. Boys and girls
in Western countries hold hands and embrace each other
without any reservation. But do they get any pleasure out of
it? Does a tremor run through their bodies at an unexpected
touch of their bodies? Maybe they get some pleasure, which
is beyond my comprehension. But in my case a mere tactile
sensation and exchange of sweet nothings meant the whole
world to me. Its pleasure excelled love's consummation. My
hand might have inadvertently touched Jogia's body a couple
of times. It was only once I had kissed her, and I had done it
deliberately.

We would leave our houses at reasonable intervals,
keeping some distance between us. And then we would meet
near Parsi Agiari. Only the Parsi priest who sat in the garb of
an angel near the agiari, reciting his verses, knew our secret.
He was the only one who seemed to understand our angelic
intentions. Hence, when we passed by him, we always greeted
him with a '*Saheb ji*' greeting and then hurriedly proceeded
towards the hub of the world, where the Metro Cinema was
located. At that point, Jogia would follow the direction to
her college, and I would go to my arts college. Our talk was
trivial, but we derived great pleasure from it. Even if we talked
of love, it was about someone else's love affair in which Jogia
dubbed the male protagonist as *badmash* (a bad character). I
was irritated that although women didn't regard men with
respect, they couldn't do without them.

One day, we visited a solo art exhibition of a Western
painter at the Jehangir Art Gallery. No one in the city of
Bombay had cared to visit this exhibition, much less buy this
artist's work. Jogia and I had gone there, not to admire the

paintings, but to look at each other. There was no one there to sympathize with the artist. The colours from the walls leapt up to glare at our conspicuous presence. There was a painting captioned *A Morning at Juhu*. The upper part of the painting had been dabbed with red colour, bold and rough brush strokes, which were revolting to our senses. A stool was placed under the painting, and Jogia sat down to relax. Her breathing had become faster, and I realized that when one is in love even to plant one step forward could be a torture. It is like you must walk a long distance, but you were out of breath even before you had taken one step.

Disappointed, the painter went out of the hall to gauge the prospect of any stray visitor dropping in. In his irritable state of mind, he had frowned at our open demonstration of affection for each other.

Our solitariness seemed to have filled the whole hall.

That day I wanted to lay bare my heart before Jogia. This indirect profession of love through vague hints and gestures was becoming too much for me. I took one step forward and stood behind the stool where Jogia was seated. But all I could utter was, 'Jogia, may I tell you a joke?'

'Not while standing behind me,' Jogia said. 'Come in front of me.'

'But it's a different kind of a joke, Jogia,' I said hobbling. Without looking at me, she had guessed that my heart was in a state of flutter. Even her earlobes that quivered, mimicked her bemused smile. At last, I started to narrate the joke, 'There was a timid sort of a lover,' I began.

'Hm!' The way she perked up I could see she was interested.

'But he was not able to demonstrate his love,' I continued.

Jogia turned three-fourths to look at me. 'Are you telling a joke?' she asked me.

'Yes,' I was irate. Jogia sat up straight, expectantly.

It had become a long wait for her, making her tense, sparks flying in a vacuum. Just then some rays emerged from the red colour in the painting captioned *A Morning at Juhu* and a boat was spotted on the darkening sea.

I said, 'At last the girl lost her patience. The poor fellow had no guts. She thought she must give him a chance to make things easy for him. Accordingly, she invited her lover to her birthday party. The boy came with a bouquet of flowers.' "Lovely, aren't they?" the girl said accepting the flowers. "This splash of red in grey and green in red. I feel like giving you a kiss." She brought her face close to him. But the boy ran towards the door.'

'Oh, God!' Jogia hit her forehead with her hand.

'The girl asked him, "Where are you going, Lalli?" Turning at the door Lalli replied, "To get another bouquet."'

Before Jogia could smile and the time she took could stretch into eternity, I bent down and kissed her. In somewhat simulated anger, Jogia gave me a gentle slap, and wiped her lips clean together with another slap or two. She couldn't smile because she was faking anger, although I could see that she was quite pleased in her heart. In this aimless journey of life, a patch of earth had suddenly come into view and the showers of rain turned everything green. That day, if we had not been standing under that vibrant red painting, I doubt if I would have ventured to kiss Jogia.

Soon thereafter a patron entered the gallery and bought a painting which was hanging next to the painting in red. It was captioned *No One Belongs to Anyone*. It depicted a woman in tears, her head held between her knees. It had been painted in some mordant colours. Why had the man bought that particular gloomy painting when all the blooming colours belonged to us? Although we had no money in our pocket, we owned all the paintings. The entire exhibition was ours. Feeling satiated with this imaginary largesse, Jogia had already run to the exit. Standing at the door, she turned and looked at me, raised a fist, smiled and fled.

After trifling with the bright colours for some time, I too came out of the exhibition hall. That day everything looked rosy and bright. People have given names to colours—grey, white, black, blue and so on. But nobody has thought that there is also a colour which defies all classification, a colour in which all the seven colours of the rainbow remain dormant. This colour, which does not come in anyone's calculation, is called white. My throat was choked with gratitude. But gratitude for whom? With that one momentary touch, Jogia had become mine forever. I felt reassured. Even if she married some other person, she was mine. A woman filled with truth and vibrant passion; unlucky husbands don't get to possess such a woman.

So, on that day, I was speculating as to which colour sari she was going to take out from her almirah. If she had spotted me standing behind the door, she would have asked me through a gesture to indicate my preference. That would have spoiled all the fun. One certainly wants to know what consideration weighs with a girl in selecting a sari. When after her morning bath, Jogia stood before the almirah what made her decide to wear a purple sari that day? The process of a woman's thinking is nothing short of a mystery. It is so complex; it goes into depths that a man could never fathom.

It is said that moon not only affects a woman's blood, but also her thinking. And the moon has no colour of its own nor has it any light of its own. It borrows everything from the sun. That is why before wearing a sari, a woman asks her *sun* which sari she should wear.

Oh, no, it is not that she does not have a colour of her choice. Of course, she has. She makes her own decisions. She doesn't run up to the man for this determination. And the night? Even the night has a colour of its own. The day was intensely hot. Walking along the sand-coloured Agiari Lane people felt dehydrated like corns parched in a sand-oven. As a Marwari or a Punjabi wearing a turban passed by, the lane gave the illusion of an outsized cob of corn thrown out of the oven, cracked and puffed out.

From Gyan Bhawan, I could only see splashes of colour. But at a closer look they were saris from which Jogia was trying to select—for me, nay, for the whole world. She cast a cursory glance in my direction. Maybe her eyes were searching for me. But I had donned a magical cap by which I could see the whole world without being seen by anyone. That day it caused me great surprise when I saw that Jogia had selected a light blue sari. On a rather hot day the cool colour seemed to be the correct choice. If I was consulted, I would have suggested the same colour. It occurred to me that although I had done my best to hide myself from her, she had found me somewhere in her heart and had sought my advice. Again, the same separation in the beginning and union in the end. It appeared as a corpus of laws whose writ ran up to the end of the Agiari Lane. It was rigidly being applied to us. But from there on, we were free to observe laws of our own making.

Ambling up to Jogia I said, 'A beautiful sari! And what a gorgeous colour!'

'I knew you would like it.'

'How did you know it?' She didn't answer.

'Hm!' I was thinking. 'Today I don't feel like touching you.'

'What do you feel like doing?'

A victoria (a word commonly used for a horse carriage) came between us and it took ages to pass along. My eyes again started gliding over the lakes, throwing up water in jets. By then we had negotiated the Princess Street Crossing and had come to the Metro where our paths separated.

'Today I feel like resting my head at your feet and crying.'

'But why crying?'

'Our shastras say so. By crying, sins of our soul are washed away.'

'What sins your soul has committed?'

'Sins that my body could not commit.'

Such things are beyond a woman's comprehension. Or they comprehend better than what is required. Jogia was combating a thought of her own. 'Do you know what I feel like doing?'

'What, what . . .' I said impatiently.

'I feel like . . .' she pointed towards her blue sari. 'I feel like hiding you in its folds and flying towards the clouds from where I would not like to come back, nor would I let you return.' Jogia looked up at the light blue sky from where she had once descended.

Momentarily, I stopped in my tracks. My mind started to think of those fortunate ones whom Jogia-like fairies had carried to the blue skies, never to return. Even gods, if they passed by them, would have sighed, filled with desire.

As I turned to grab her attention, Jogia was gone.

Not to talk of the clouds, Jogia had left behind a helpless orphan, stranded on the hot and broken road. The realization dawned upon me. But it was too late to retrieve the situation. The heat had produced fissures in the road in which the big wheels of horse-driven carriages were getting stuck, making the sweat fall from drivers' brows. Just then I saw a pleasant whiff of a cold wave surging towards me. It was another young girl. Tall, slim, bouncing hair, and she too was wearing a light blue salwar.

As I proceeded further, I saw a few more women wearing light blue, out on a shopping spree. It was not my first experience. Once before I had seen women in large numbers wearing yellow dresses on their shopping rounds at Crawford Market. Their dresses, however, were not uniformly yellow. Some were wearing only yellow tops, others yellow saris, and still others yellow shirts. I started to think. What mysterious power had induced them to choose yellow, so that they all looked alike. If it was *maulsari* today, then it was orange the next day. What explains how a woman gets bored with one colour and then she changes to another; it could be mustard yellow, *champaaii, gul anari, kaasni, firozi.* But what is that wireless messaging system that conveys to one and all what colour to wear on a particular day, making groups of women displaying the same color in the bazaar, nay, the whole world. Maybe it is the season that dictates the choice of colour, or maybe it has something to do with the movement of the moon or cloudy skies. Or else, it is due to a hint dropped by an actress or a celebrity. No one knows. But women like to dress in dazzling colours to push a wave of different shades in front of men's eyes.

That day I was puzzled why all women were showing themselves in blue saris. As I reached the art school, I found that the class had ended, and students were coming out of their classes. Some of them came out in the open and stood under the Gulmohar tree. Sakshi was one among them. The colour of her skirt was blue.

If I had not met my friend Hemant, I would have gone insane. Hemant literally means autumn. But he was more like spring, always looking cheerful and bright. Seasons and colours changed, but Hemant always wore the same sardonic smile on his face. We used to tease him, *saaley,* try as you may, you will never become an artist. Have you felt the compulsion to tear apart your clothes and run wild? In your state of helplessness, have you thrown up your hands and plucked your hair? Why do you do that? Is it because myriads of worms are crawling over your body? Do bats attack you in the darkness of the night and put their mouths to your jugular vein to suck your blood? Did you cry like a child when your painting won the first prize in the art competition? Do you feel like an orphan despite your parents being alive? Do your friends pounce upon you one after another to hurl you down into a dark well? Do you know that Mansur who was crucified was none other than you? Your face is blotched and dark like ink and your features are hard, massive and repulsive like Mexican murals. For you, every oblong thing is a male organ and every knotty object its female counterpart . . .

I told him that the women of the city had emerged from their homes wearing light-blue clothes. Hemant bared his teeth as it was his habit, and he dismissed the whole thing with a sardonic smile. He made fun of me. He compared me to a man who had gone blind in the rainy season because everything was lush green. I pointed in the direction of Sakshi, whom we regarded as an artist's model. Until now she had not modelled for any artist, although her body was crafted for this purpose. 'Look,' I said, 'she is also wearing a light-blue skirt.'

Hemant didn't say anything. Dragging me by my hand, he took me to the lawn of the college compound that was surrounded by palm trees. He went and stood under a palm from where he had a good view of the road. In one direction, the road led to the Crawford Market and in the other to the Victoria Terminus and the Hornby Road. He wanted to prove that I suffered from illusions. There were no women to be seen around. If they had flown to the sky, hiding men under their saris, no men would be visible. But the place was swarming with men. They were going about looking blithely unconcerned as if they had nothing to do with women. There were tall and short, handsome and ugly, thin and rotund. They were going about as if they were in no way answerable to women. Just then a woman, apparently a native of the ghats, passed by. Firm and hard like steel, she was wearing a green ornament. Pointing towards her, Hemant asked me, 'Recognize your mother!'

'Leave these poor labourers alone,' I said. 'Let's not talk about them.'

'Then about whom do you want to talk about?'

'Those who have plenty of clothes to wear.'

Just then as ill-luck would have it, a sedan stopped in front of the Parsi wine shop. A middle-aged woman was sitting in the car, a fair representative of the class that had enough clothes to spare—clothes of such variety, quality and colours that you might wonder at their sight. Hence when women of her class stand before their wardrobe, they don't get wireless messages which ordinary women get. Rather their condition is like that of a customer before whom the cloth dealer unfolds bolt after bolt of various qualities of cloth, making it difficult for the buyer to make a choice.

Heavily made up, the woman in the sedan was wearing a flaming red sari. Although I was standing about fifty feet away from her across the road, I was feeling uncomfortably hot, and she was blissfully ignorant that she was the cause of my discomfort.

The woman's servant who had gone into the wine shop returned with a helper carrying bottles of whisky and beer in a basket. Opening the trunk of the car, he left the basket inside.

Hemant had already put me in a sullen mood. But to hide my temper, I said, 'Did you see those bottles of beer? The woman's husband must be finding the heat intolerable.'

To my discomfort, Hemant always got better of me, mocking and slightly contemptuous. It was rare that I scored a point against him.

One morning all the women turned out wearing grey. The colour of their dresses looked the same to me. But Hemant dragged me out of the room to prove me wrong. To my surprise I found that it was not uniformly grey, but each sari had a variation of that shade. All of them looked different. In the end, taking it to be a quirk of my character I stopped paying attention to such matters.

But easier said than done. I found that I just couldn't get rid of these fads. One day, Jogia came out wearing a black blouse with a grey sari. I couldn't help but marvel at her colour sense. Oh, what a blend of colours! Then I found that all the women were wearing that combination. The only difference was that it was either a grey sari and a black blouse or a black sari and a grey blouse, with threads of silver rippling through.

Seasons change. Autumn passed, and the spring came. I mean the kind of autumn or spring Bombay can boast of. Soon I discerned a queer emptiness in spring as if it were slowly on its way out like a last gasp of ennui, which turns love into pathos and spills emotions in the form of tears. Then the green turned into deeper green, bringing a wave of freshness with it. The river flowing with the first drops of rain, the fresh breeze wove a carpet of coolness over the sheet of water. The river flowing into the sea churned so much emerald that it turned into a rich blue body of water. As fish frolicked in the sea, their silvery scales scintillated in the light, and they looked like pieces of silver for the fishermen. Lightning and clouds clashed in the sky. The clouds roared, lightning flashed, and rain fell in torrents. During this time Jogia, changed into variegated garments—blue, yellow, lemon, grey, dark green and purple. She was in a hurry to mature from a girl to a woman, and then graduate into motherhood. I was convinced that a healthy and robust girl like her would deliver twins, nothing else. They could as well be triplets or quadruplets. But how would I take care of them? The thought made me laugh.

During those days, Jogia would touch her sick mother's feet like a dutiful daughter, cajoling her into giving her the permission to use lipstick. While our lives were slowly drifting towards a breakdown, they were at the same time blossoming into youth. True, Jogia had obtained her mother's permission to use lipstick, but how could she get such a large variety of shades to match her saris? One day, I gave her a Max Factor lipstick as a present. She beamed with joy as if I had placed in her hand a sesame to unravel a great secret. She forgot for an instant that she was standing by the Girgaum tram line. She just clung to me and hugged me. After that her eyes sank miles down into her sockets. They were damp with tears as they cast a brief look at me. I realized Jogia was a highly emotional girl. She had no need to show me, of all persons, her gratitude. Of course, it was a different matter that she didn't have a sari to go with the colour of the lipstick I had given her as a gift. I didn't have the money to buy her a new sari to go with the lipstick. In fact, I had stolen some money from Chubby Brother's wallet, and supplemented it with some money from Bhabhi's purse to make up the cost of the lipstick. A husband's younger brother *(devar)* is by convention allowed to extract money from his brother's wife *(bhabhi)*. There is some innocent romance at work in the relationship between devar and bhabhi.

The end of the rainy season brought a new development. Jogia secretly sold off a small carnelian precious stone dating back to her ancestors, lying forgotten in the house and she bought a new sari with the money, that matched my gifted lipstick. I would not have known about it but for Hema who deceitfully passed on the information to me.

Past the Parsi Agiari, we met in the untended Convent Compound which was in a bad shape. Jogia was wearing her new sari, its orange rippling into purple.

'Do you know what you look like today?' I teased her.

'What do I look like?'"

'A scarlet fly—the velvety insect that appears during the rains. They call it *beer bahuti.*'

Jogia's gleamed with mischief.

'And you? Do you know what they call you?'

'Yes.' 'You are *beer*, the gallant one. And I'm *bahuti*, the bride.'

Her face flushed, its red merging with the colour of her sari. She ran away, overcome with shyness.

That day all the women were wearing orange saris. Overwhelmed by the sight of this jovial procession, I wanted to share my experience with Hemant. This time Hemant humiliated me in the presence of three girls, and he did it without any compunction as we were standing by the roadside. I would have put up with it somehow, had not Sakshi appeared on the scene. She was wearing a see-through nylon sari in which she was showing contours of her body. Was she turning herself into a model?

How eager Jogia was to become a scarlet fly I knew from the very depths of my heart. But I could do nothing about it. I must take care of my training and seek a job. Or I must try to grow rich by selling my paintings to the connoisseurs of art, those who reside in the Malabar Hill and Warden Road neighbourhoods. But all these things required time, of which Jogia and I had plenty. But her mother had no time; she was afflicted with a serious disease.

I was waiting to reveal my intentions to Chubby Brother and Bhabhi, but I was saved this trouble.

'Kaka, why don't you marry Jogia?' Hema suggested this in the presence of my Chubby Brother and Bhabhi.

'*Dhut*!' I poured cold water on the proposal.

This *dhut* would have been inconsequential if others had not also picked up this refrain. A few days later, Chubby Brother and Bhabhi pulled aside Hema and slapped her so hard for her brashness that she went crashing and struck her head on the threshold. That day I had a foreboding that something ominous was in the offing. Maybe something untoward had already happened between the two families, of which I was not aware.

My conjecture proved to be correct. Jogia's and Birju's mothers along with that Punjabi woman broached the subject with Bhabhi. The women of the Banpu House were a nice lot and well-meaning. You were free to chat with them, on give-and-take terms, throw a broad hint without any fear, and sleep with them on the sly. But to have matrimonial talks with them—well, it was just not done. They looked askance at such matters. For that matter there were many other things, which were the bane of Gujarati families. They could have far-reaching consequences, like jumping into the well or ending life by taking poison.

Jogia's mother was in no position to offer her daughter much of a dowry. That is why when in our families a girl attains marriageable age, we give her despairing look and say, 'She has ripened enough to be our death.' To cut the matter short, I put my foot down when it came to the question of dowry. Bhabhi and the other women of Gyan Bhawan made incriminating remarks. Who was Jogia's father? They asked. Some volunteered the information that he was a Muslim. Another woman said he was a Portuguese who had lived in Baroda for a long time. These were, however, nothing but conjectures.

One thing which bore the stamp of authenticity was that Jogia's mother was the second wife of the Brahmin Diwan of Manadur, but not legally accepted as such. True, Jogia was the Diwan's daughter, but in the eyes of the people her mother was no better than a concubine. The Diwan's family saw to it that nothing should fall to this woman's lot from his assets. In the end, Jogia's mother came to live in Bombay. Jogia was of course innocent of all these things. She was born three months after the Diwan's death, whose affection she never received.

I was prepared to raise a flag of revolt against the inequities perpetrated against Jogia. If it came to that I was even prepared to live with her on the footpath. But most of the people were so callous towards Jogia's mother that they almost drove her to the verge of death. Now all she wanted was to offer her daughter's hand to some eligible young man and be done with it. Because of the inimical attitude of the people of my family, she lost confidence in me. In fact, my very sight aroused her ire. She had clearly told her daughter that if she ever broached the subject of her marriage with me, she would pour kerosene over her clothes and immolate herself. Jogia had stopped going to the art school and her windows in the Banpu House remained closed most of the time. She must be pining for a breath of fresh air.

One evening, I had a hard time. From early evening a bat started flapping its large wings over me. After a while, I felt a creature's mouth was resting over my jugular vein and was sucking away my breath. The harder I tried to drive it off, the more firmly its teeth dug into my flesh. Such evenings are neither bright nor dark. They have only one colour—the colour of calamity. Only those who fall a prey to such calamities know that they could find refuge only in their mother's or their beloved's bosom. But my mother was dead and thus Jogia could not be mine.

Oh, what suffocation, what despondency! Even despondency has a colour peculiarly its own—dirty grey and sparsely thin, like myriads of grains of sand stuffed into the mouth, and they stink, driving you to throw up. In the end, a man reaches a stage where he becomes insensitive to everything. He can't even distinguish one colour from another.

In the morning when I woke up, I felt like running away from my house, the city, nay, the world itself. If Jogia's mother had not been a liability on her shoulders, she would have agreed to come with me. And I would have surely taken her along. I thought of the hermits and Buddhist monks who renounced the world and lived by begging food. They sit down to meditate and intone, '*Om mane padme . . .*'

I really wanted to renounce the world. But just when I was going to put my resolve into practice, the door of Jogia's apartment in Banpu House opened and I saw Jogia standing there. It appeared that she had not slept for many nights. Her hair was dishevelled and fell over her face and shoulders in a disorderly manner. She picked up her comb and stuck it in her hair. Then she walked up to her almirah.

I was going to the art school. On the way, I found women wearing ochre-coloured clothes. Who had advised them to wear ochre colour? They looked so sad as if they had realized the emptiness of life and were overcome by a sense of renunciation. They were holding castanets in their hands and there were bhajans on their lips which no one could see or hear. Like the *bhikshus* (mendicants), they were going from door to door. Yes, they knocked on every door but in this big city of Bombay, nobody came out of their house to offer them alms.

As I reached my school, I found Hemant. He was smiling as usual. This time he forestalled me. 'What colour are the women wearing today?' he asked me.

I was in no mood to answer his question. He could be sarcastic. But I did say something. 'They have become mendicants,' I said. 'They have renounced the world and turned into nuns.'

I dragged Hemant and Sakshi from under the gulmohar tree and led them towards the bower of trees. There was a road in front, but the people appeared to be immobile. They had all reached the stage of renunciation. Wearing ochre-coloured robes they were staring into the vacuum with glazed eyes as if there was no man in this world nor any woman to whom they were answerable.

I pointed in the direction of a woman who was wearing ochre clothes and was holding a copper vessel. Hemant gave out a loud laugh at her sight. Sakshi joined him in his laughter. She was wearing jeans which clearly defined the outline of her hips and thighs. She had become every inch a model.

After he had finished laughing, Hemant said, 'Jugal, I hope you have not gone crazy. Just show me those ochre clothes. I don't see any. That woman is actually clad in a grey sari and what you call a copper vessel is her purse, a beautiful purse I must say.' Sakshi agreed with Hemant.

I stood there looking nonplussed. Just then a bus stopped, and a girl got down.

'How can it be?' I said to myself. 'She is a nun. And she's wearing ochre-coloured clothes. Surely, my eyes can't deceive me. I'm not blind.'

I stood there for some time to confirm that my eyes were not deceiving me. Convinced, that I was right, I looked back. 'Hemant!' I called.

But walking arm in arm, Hemant and Sakshi had gone inside, leaving their laughter echoing behind and I was derelict at the edge of this arid, sandy waste like a crazy person deserted by all. Their thousand mercies did not stone me, nor anyone called me a prophet.

Oh, yes, there was a girl walking in my direction. She had left me in doubt about the colour that was splashed over the world. Before I could call Hemant and Sakshi in a voice ringing with conviction, the girl had drifted closer to me.

"*Beer*!" I heard a voice calling.

I looked up startled. There was no question of any other colour. And she was none other than Jogia whom I had seen in the morning, selecting an ochre-coloured sari from her almirah.

I advanced a step or two in a dazed state and then stopped as if overcome by some strange helplessness.

'Tomorrow, I leave for Baroda,' Jogia said.

'Why, Jogia? What for?'

'My mother's place. I'm getting married—the day after.'

'Oh!'

'I had come to meet you.'

'Then meet me.' I was hardly aware of what I was saying.

At that time the corridor of the art school was crowded with students. I could also see Principal Sabri and some other people in the corridor. Just then, Jogia placed her lips on my cheek. It was so unexpected that I was almost thrown off my feet. In a brief moment she had grown from a teenager into a full-blown woman of forty. How passionate her kiss was! How pure and yet how full of lust.

Even if some people were watching, we did not see them.

'Even if they saw, did it really matter?' Jogia said as a parting shot, adding, 'If you cry after I am gone, I'll beat you right and left.' She raised her hand threateningly to drive home the point.

And she was gone.

In the morning, I saw a victoria in front of Gyan Bhawan and Banpu House being loaded with some suitcases and other household affects. The inmates of Banpu House had come down to the street level to see them off. But there was no one from Gyan Bhawan, except me. Not to talk of Chubby Brother and Bhabhi, who had locked Hema in the bathroom. The sound of her cries reached the street.

Jogia's mother came down supported by the Punjabi woman and Bijor's mother. She was walking with a staggering gait and was helped into the victoria. After recovering her breath, she folded her hands and looking wistfully at the people said, 'Time for me to go. May you live happily here!'

And then I saw Jogia. She was wearing a beautiful light-rose colour sari, a rose tucked in her well-groomed coiffure. She had just taken her seat in the victoria when the Parsi priest of the Agiari passed by.

Out of habit Jogia said, 'Saheb ji!' The priest responded with a 'Saheb ji' and smiled on seeing Jogia and myself standing side by side. Raising his hand in blessing and mumbling something from the scriptures, he quietly walked away. As Jogia resumed her seat, a smile was playing across her lips.

I, too, smiled.

10

Rahman's Shoes

After the day's hard grind, when Rahman reached home, he was feeling utterly famished. 'Jeena's mother, Jeena's mother!' he cried. 'Lay out my food. And be quick about it.'

The older woman was washing clothes, her hands drenched in soapy water. Without giving her time to wipe her hands, Rahman pulled off his shoes and pushed them under the cot. Then throwing a Multani *tehmet* of coarse *khaddar* around his thighs, he uttered *bismillah* and sat down cross-legged on the cot.

In old age, one's appetite becomes young. In this race between youth and old age, Rahman's 'bismillah' had already run past the plates of food while his old wife was still wiping her washing-soda and indigo-blue-drenched hands on her dupatta, which she had done for the past forty years, and which had irritated Rahman. But today he didn't mind her action because it was a time saver.

Rahman said, 'Jeena's mother. Be quick.'

And the older woman replied with her age-old conventional style, 'Oh, ho, Baba, you need to show some patience.'

Suddenly, Rahman's eyes fell on the shoes that he had hurriedly pulled off his feet and pushed them under the cot. He found that one shoe had mounted the other, which forbode travel. Rahman laughed.

'Today, my shoe has again mounted its counterpart', he said. 'Jeena's mother, only Allah knows for where I am bound.'

'You are going to visit Jeena, where else?' the wife said. 'I'm not washing your messy clothes for nothing. I've already wasted two *paise* worth of blue on them. You don't even earn that much in a day.'

'Oh, yes,' old Rahman swayed his head. 'Tomorrow, I have a plan to go to Ambala to meet my darling daughter, our only child, and therefore all the dearer to me for that reason. That's why these shoes refuse to separate from each other. A similar thing happened last year when I had to go to the district court to cast my vote.' He remembered that he had sensed a similar message and had watched one shoe lying on top of the other. He had to walk back from the district town because the prospective assembly member had refused to pay him the return fare. But the member had been properly served for his betrayal because when Rahman was about to place the blue mark on the ballot his hands were trembling, and in that confused state he had cast his vote for another candidate.

He had not met Jeena, who was married two years ago, and lived in Ambala. Rahman had spent the last few months in great trepidation. He could not stop feeling as if someone had placed something hot on his heart. However, if the very thought of meeting Jeena could bring so much solace to his heart, he could imagine how happy the meeting would make him. He felt excited about it. He would first meet his daughter and then her husband, Ali Mohammed, who was serving in the army. He would first cry, then laugh and then start crying again. He would lift his little grandson in his lap and take him to the bazaar. But why did he forget Jeena's mother in his scheme of things? While fumbling with a loose string in his cot, as was his habit, he said something about the loss of memory in old age.

Jeena's husband, Ali Mohammed, was a handsome young man. Joining the army as a sepoy, he had risen to the rank of a naik, and his fellow soldiers accepted him as their sardar. He played hockey with great verve, and because of his outstanding performance, his team had defeated the Railways, the University and the Police. He was scheduled to leave with his unit for Basra to quell Rashid Ali, who was getting out of hand in Iraq. Being a hockey player, he was singled out by his company commandant. This thought had a significant impact on him. Before being promoted to a naik's rank, he treated Jeena with kindness, but now he had become so swollen-headed that he overlooked her grovelling at his feet. There was another reason as well. While speaking at the prize distribution ceremony, Mrs Halt, who was the company commander's wife, had told Ali Mohammad something in English that was translated by the subedar as: 'I want to kiss your stick.' Ali Mohammad was confused about the word 'stick,' and thought she must have meant something else. The subedar was a jealous person, and his knowledge of English didn't go very far.

Rahman was full of misgivings about meeting his son-in-law. Leaning from his cot, he separated the shoes as if he feared making a trip to Ambala. Jeena's mother had placed food before him.

Today, contrary to the usual practice, she had cooked beef, which she had obtained with great difficulty from town.

She had cooked it with a liberal dose of ghee. Six months ago, Rahman had suffered from a severe liver complaint, and since then, had drastically cut down greasy foods from his diet. His breathing had improved after he drank liberal quantity of a local brew. His appetite had returned and the colour of his urine had improved. But his neck had stayed narrow, and his eyesight had shown no improvement. His skin colour had turned dark blue. He flared up at the sight of meat. Four or five days ago, she had cooked brinjals, and he didn't utter a word in protest, something that she misunderstood.

'The day before, you cooked masur dal, and I kept quiet over it. You want me to let you have your way in everything— that I should reduce myself to a clod of earth? I know your designs, Jeena's mother. You are bent upon killing me.'

The woman was expecting trouble the day she had cooked brinjals. She feared that he would get to her throat. But to her surprise, he had held his peace, and she mistook it for submission. The woman had sacrificed her taste for good food for the sake of her good-for-nothing husband. From the day she had aligned her fate with the fate of this craggy, skeleton-like man with a bloated stomach, she had known no comfort or happiness in life.

He was a constable in healthy condition in Ludhiana. But one day he slipped on the rind of watermelon and broke his knee. As a result, he had to take premature retirement. Now he stayed at home, doing nothing.

Washing the clothes, the woman said, 'Nobody is forcing the meat on you. Don't eat it if it does not agree with you. But why deprive me of a thing because you don't like it? I'm tired of eating bland, tasteless dal day after day.'

Enraged, Rahman thought of picking up his shoe from under the cot and smashing it over the hag's head, getting rid of whatever little thatch she was left with. It would also relieve her of the perennial bad cold she had suffered from. But after eating a few morsels, he relented. The liver be damned! The meat was so delicious. This woman at least knew how to cook. He shouldn't be ungrateful to her. Rahman savoured the dish, munching every morsel. A piece torn from the chapati and dipped in the rich gravy did its magic in his mouth. He guiltily thought that all his life, he had done nothing to make his wife comfortable. He wished that he could get a peon's job in the tehsil office so that he could bring back good old days.

After finishing his meal, Rahman wiped his fingers on the end of his turban and got up. Propelled by some subconscious thought, he picked up his shoes from under the cot and placed them in the courtyard, taking care to put each shoe apart from the other. He felt it had become imperative for him to undertake this journey, although he had to irrigate his eight-day-old maize crop.

While sweeping the courtyard in the morning, the woman carelessly pushed aside her husband's shoes, and coincidentally, the heel of one shoe was later found on the other. In the evening, one's resolution generally weakens. Until Rahman went to sleep, he kept vacillating about his trip to Ambala. He must first weed and irrigate his crop before making the trip. Besides, yesterday's rich, ghee-soaked food had upset his stomach. But when he woke up the next morning, he saw the way his shoes were positioned, and decided that the trip to Ambala was now inevitable. He may say 'no' a hundred times, and yet destiny would drag him on to Ambala. His shoes determined that.

It was seven in the morning. At that time of the day, one's resolutions take on a more determined character. Rahman placed his shoes the correct way and got down to sorting out his clothes and preparing himself for the trip

The washed clothes treated with blue had dried up during the night and were looking white and clean. The blue, it seemed, had sucked away all the dirt and had manifested itself on the surface in the form of pristine whiteness. It was not so when the blue was not used; the clothes looked as if they were washed in the pond's dirty water.

For the last three days, Jeena's mother had been pounding barley in the mortar to make sweet balls with it. She had a considerable stock of jaggery to make balls and had placed the material under the sun to divest it of insects. Besides, she had collected a supply of dry corn cobs. It appeared that she was silently preparing for the journey. The natural mounting of shoes one over the other had confirmed that a trip was in the offing. Her preparation would include food for Rahman during his travel and a gift for the daughter too.

'Jeena's mother, what name have they given the little one?' Rahman suddenly asked.

'Sahiq (Is-haq), what else?' the old woman laughed happily. 'Your memory has become feeble. Sahiq—that's the child's name.'

How could Rahman remember a name like Is-haq? When he was young, his grandfather had forgotten Rahman's name. The grandfather was still in his senses. But he got the name Rahman engraved on a silver plate in Arabic letters and it was placed around Rahman's neck. He didn't know how to read. He simply laughed looking at the plate. The village names during those days were nothing better than Shera,

Fattu, Fajja, etc. Names like Is-haq, Sho'yeb were creations of urban folks.

Rahman thought that Is-haq must be one-and-a-half years by now, and he was sure that he could hold his head so that it did not roll over his neck. When the child would meet him, he would look steadily at him, wondering from where this older man had descended upon his house. Little would he know that Rahman was his grandfather, and it was the old man's flesh and blood that had gone into his physical make-up. He would shyly hide his head in Jeena's lap, at which point the older man would feel tempted to hold both mother and son in his lap. Rahman laughed at his thought as no father did such a wild thing—to hold a grown-up daughter in his lap. It was not done. Oh, how big his daughter had grown. In her childhood, when she came in prancing after playing outside, he would lift her in his lap and laugh happily as she snuggled against his breast. But now, he must content himself by looking at her from a distance. Or he can bend down and airily brush his lips against her forehead.

Rahman felt that he would get so overwhelmed at their sight that it would bring tears to his eyes. He would try to push back the tears, but they would well up all the same—not only because Ali Mohammed was in the habit of beating his daughter. Tears were more eloquent in expressing his feelings than those long-winded words coming out of his lips. He had suffered much on her account and undergone untold hardships in bringing her up. Once, he had fallen out with Chaudhry Khushal, and the latter had given him a severe beating which had damaged his back, taking him almost to the verge of death. That would have been the end of him, and she would have missed her Abba forever. But a man does not

die until his time is up. Perhaps it was due to Is-haq's pious
deeds or of his daughter that he was still living.

Blood, as they say, is thicker than water. No sooner the
little one saw him then he would jump into his lap. 'Sahiq, my
child, see what I've brought for you? Sweet balls made with
jaggery, and toys. A lot of things. What else can the poor
village people offer as a token of their affection?' The little
one would have to make a real effort to dig his tiny teeth into
the corn cob. If it came to a showdown with my soldier son-
in-law, I would give him a big tongue lashing. What does he
think of himself?

Just a squirrel and posing so big! Of course, he would get
into a rage and threaten to throw my daughter out. But I'll set
him right. I'll go about the bazaar, the little one perched on
my shoulder, and his father will miss the child. He'll have to
climb down from his high perch and come to terms with me.

Entrusting the care of his field to another farmer, and
taking a loan against the standing crop, Rahman collected his
things for the journey and got into a horse-driven cart. His
wife gave him some food tied in a bundle. Entrusting him to
the care of Allah, she said, ' Ali will be departing for Basra
in a few days' time. Bring back my Jeena with you and my
Sahiqa. I may breathe my last any day.'

Getting into the train at Malka Rani until he reached
Manikpur, Rahman had purchased many things for Is-haq
en route. A small looking-glass, a Japanese celluloid rattle of
which half a dozen tinglers rattled all at once. At Manikpur,
he also bought a wooden baby walker for Is-haq. Sometimes
he wished that the child had already cut his teeth, firm enough
to eat corn cob with. At other times, he hoped that the child
was still too small to walk and that neighbours should say that

child had learned to walk with the help of the walker brought by his grandfather. He wondered what kind of likeness he would prefer for his grandson—a kid in the image of a grown-up or a grown-up in the image of a kid? Sometimes he wondered whether Jeena, who was now a town dweller, would like the rustic presents he was carrying for the child. She may not like them and yet go into raptures over them to please him. But there was no reason that she should not relish the sweet balls. Didn't he know his daughter? Of course, he could not be so sure of Ali; he was not the flesh of his flesh.

It was a tiring journey. Rahman had started feeling physically exhausted and mentally tired, which induced drowsiness. The meat that he had eaten seemed to have played havoc with his stomach. His eyes burned. He pressed his stomach. The place where his spleen was supposed to be located seemed to have gone stiff. In the train, the westerly wind was coming through the windows in great spurts. The trees flew past. As Rahman opened and closed his eyes, watching the trees as they flew past, he had the queer sensation as if the train was rocking like a swing. He dosed off while the train sped past three stations. It was reaching Karnal when he was fully awake. To his horror, Rahman discovered that his bundle was not under his seat. But for a small number of sweet balls and a few corn cobs which he had tied to the end of his chaddar to be eaten on the way, and the wooden walker resting between his feet, everything else had disappeared. Rahman looked around frantically and then raised a hue and cry. Two impressive-looking men occupying the opposite seats who were engrossed in reading their newspapers gave him angry looks. 'Old man, won't you stop making noise?' One of them scolded in a sharp voice.

But there was no stopping Rahman. He kept wailing loudly over the loss of his valuables. A police constable with a thick curled-up mustache was sitting in front of Rahman. He caught hold of the constable. 'You have a hand in it.' Rahman cried, hysterical with anger. 'You have had my things removed.' The constable gave him a violent push sending him sprawling. Rahman got up, panting.

'You are to blame,' the man who was reading the newspaper said. 'Why did you fall asleep, Baba?'

'You should have kept an eye on your things,' the other man said.

Rahman was in a nasty mood, ready to fight with the whole world. He went for the constable and tore off his uniform. In retaliation, the constable pulled out a rod from the walker and started beating Rahman with it. Just then, a ticket checker entered the compartment. Siding with the two impressive-looking men, he pulled up Rahman for disorderly conduct and ordered him to be removed from the train as soon as it reached Karnal. He would be handed over to the police. In a scuffle with the ticket checker, Rahman received a kick in his stomach, which left him prostrate on the compartment floor.

As the train arrived at Karnal, Rahman was shoved out of the compartment, and he landed on the platform along with his walker and his chaddar. A rod of the walker lay at some distance from its main body. It was smeared with blood. The corn cobs had spilled out of the chaddar and lay scattered on the platform.

The ticket checker's kick in the stomach had hurt Rahman badly. He was placed on a stretcher and carried to the railway hospital.

Images of Jeena, Sahiq, Ali Mohammed, Jeena's mother, one by one, passed before Rahman's eyes. How life's movie is abridged. It can hold only three or four images at a time. There may be other men and women hovering at the periphery of the film, but one hardly ever remembers anything about them. Only Jeena, Sahiq, Ali Mohammed, Jeena's mother mattered. Or sometimes, the moments of struggle and strife show up big in one's life story. For instance, a child's walker lying on the station platform and the corn cobs scattered alongside, which the porters, watchmen, signal men, urchins scurried off with, as they revealed their white teeth gleaming in darkness and the sinister laughter on their faces in the diminishing daylight. Far away, a policeman was recording something in his diary.

'And then, he kicked me again.'

'Eh! did he? I can't believe it. So, he kicked you again? And then . . .'

And then the hospital cot, its white sheet gaping wide like a coffin. The cot was reminding him of the grave, the angelic nurses and doctors.

Rahman saw that his chaddar in which he had tied the sweet balls was lying on the cot near the pillow. Of what use was this to him? Rahman thought. They could have as well left it on the platform. Now he had nothing but his chaddar.

The doctor and the nurse standing by his cot, moment by moment, kept pulling the white hospital bedsheet over his body.

Rahman felt like vomiting. The nurse immediately placed a basin near his cot. As Rahman bent down to throw up, he remembered having removed his shoes and had placed them under the cot. He bent further down to look under the cot and saw that his one shoe had mounted the other. Rahman gave a thin smile.

'Dakdarji,' he said. 'I've to go on a journey. Haven't you noticed it? My one shoe has mounted the other!'

The doctor smiled in reply. 'Yes, Baba, I know,' he said. 'You have a long journey ahead of you.' And then the doctor looked carefully at his chaddar. 'But your food is so meagre. Only a handful of sweet balls, and you have a long way to go.'

Jeena, Jeena's mother, Sahiq, Ali Mohammed, and then everything blotted out as if by a sad accident.

Rahman's hand clutched at the provisions as he started his long journey.

11

Babbal

Darbarilal had been sitting at home indulging himself with Sita since early in the evening. Indulgence in his language was a state of mind in which his eyes idly rolled over the pages of the *Evening News*, or he read Ghalib's ghazals, while his mind derived pleasure from the image of Sita, his sweetheart.

Sita had told him that he would find her standing at the corner of the road coming from the Aurora Cinema precisely at six o'clock. She would be wearing a maroon sari. But . . .

Darbari lived at King's Circle, recently rechristened as Maheshwari Udyan. He worked in a firm that sold loudspeakers, and although his salary was not handsome by any measure, he had never felt a scarcity of cash. By a stroke of luck, his father, Girdharilal Mehta, had raked in a couple of lakhs in a single day's forward trading, and after that, had withdrawn into a shell. Even his friends at the Cotton Exchange cursed him for slipping away like a strand of hair from a bowl of butter. But Mehta laughed away these comments. He would give a complacent smile, which comes to a man when he happens to have a couple of lakhs in his coffers.

Darbari's elder brother, Bihari Lal, had married into a family of Marwaris, and consequently, his sister-in-law had brought in the jewellery of colossal value. After one year, Darbari's sister, Satwanti, eloped with a rich Ismaili Saleh Mohammad and married him, choosing Nikah, the Muslim ceremony that binds couples. This became the talk of the town. Mehta Sahib banned his daughter and son-in-law into Prem Kuteer, their family residence, but matters were sorted out later. The boy's parents insisted that Satwanti had embraced Islam and that her new name was Kaneez Fatima. Mehta Sahib didn't take this insult lightly and changed his son-in-law's name to Sardari Mohan. It didn't make any difference because it yielded the same initials, S.M. Nawab—that is how he wrote his name. In a helpless state, family members started calling him '*Kyon Bay Saaleh* . . .' used in the sense of an abuse or a put-down.

Today, Saleh (or Sardari) and Satwanti were present at home along with their children. Bihari and Gunwati, the sister-in-law, joined them in discussing prospects for Darbari's marriage. While his sister, Satwanti, and his sister-in-law, Gunwati, held forth on what constituted an ideal husband, his brother-in-law, Sardari, tried to pinpoint the qualities of a perfect wife. This led to a war of words. Darbari, who was sitting in the veranda listening to this conversation, got up, and putting his head through the window loudly proclaimed that Darbarilal by name, son of Girdharilal Mehta by caste and resident of Bombay, forcefully rejects the idea of marriage. His pronouncement silenced everyone, including the women and children.

Resuming his seat in the veranda, he started scanning the pages of the *Evening News,* his gaze frequently traveling to the corner of the road, searching for a maroon sari near Aurora Cinema.

People inside the house resumed their laughter, and now among them was the sound of his mother's chuckling, higher than the others in decibel. So, she has also joined them! Darbari was the blue-eyed boy or darling of the family. The way he rubbed hair tonic in his hair, the meticulous care he took in grooming and the time he took in trimming his mustache's points proved the adage that before marriage, boys behave like girls and girls like boys. Watching him, the ladies of the house affirmed that this was a clear sign of his desire to get married, while the men were not sure; they saw signs of forboding disaster.

A Sikh carpenter had started work in the veranda to put up a wire-mesh covering around it. He was selecting coarse pieces of wood, and with his tools, smoothened their surface. The fluffy flakes of wood were seen flying everywhere, making it hard to walk bare feet.

A bell started ringing at the Don Bosco School, located opposite Darbari's house. Hordes of boys, wearing blue shorts and white shirts, spilled out of the hostel rooms, and fell upon one another. They were probably rushing to the chapel for the evening prayer. A priest, wearing a long robe that kept flapping over his knees as he ran about supervising a football game in the school playground, blew his whistle and brought the game to a close. Still, there was no sign of Sita.

A few cows had entrenched themselves on the road leading from the cinema, and they were leisurely chewing the cud. A car took a sharp turn and stopped at the back of the building. Then a fat woman came into view, who was following Ramaswami, the proprietor of Udupi Hotel, at a safe distance. But to Darbari sitting in the verandah, they created an illusion of proximity as if they were engaged in jostling each other off the road.

Then instead of Sita, he saw Misri coming from the opposite direction. As always, she was carrying a child in her lap. Babbal was a healthy child, round like a globe, soft as if made of sponge. He had cut a few teeth, two in front, which were holding to their pride of place. He looked like Disney's rabbit when he laughed. It was hard to find anyone who would not laugh at the child's laughter. Misri, his mother, was finding it difficult to keep him under control.

'Babbal!' Darbari called him and stretched out his arms. The child perked up in his mother's lap. At that moment, he forgot that he could have missed Sita if she had appeared while his attention was diverted. The child's emotional state changed as Darbari approached him. He had become serious as if he was saying that this was all deception. But as Darbari came closer, the child's grinning resumed.

'Wait!' Darbari went inside to fetch some puffed rice.

Misri, Babbal's mother, was a street beggar who had taught him the art of begging. She would stop by the side of someone who looked like a low-class office worker. Like a thoroughly rehearsed actor, Babbal would tug at the stranger's shirt or dhoti and make a gurgling sound, pointing to an object in a nearby shop. Amused, the man bought him what he desired. After the man left, Misri would exchange the item with the shopkeeper for a coin or two, not caring for the child's relentless crying. Misri could not sell puffed rice back to Darbari. Babbal had no interest in the cash that the mother valued.

Darbari took Babbal in his lap and held out his palm, from which Babbal collected a fistful of puffed rice and turned towards his mother.

'*Kameene Saleh . . .!*' Darbari laughed. Saleh (or Sardari) inside heard his first name and responded, 'What's the order, Sir?'

'I wasn't talking to you . . . the scholar of Persian poetry,' Darbari said, facing his house. He touched Babbal's cheeks and returned him to his mother.

'Selfish. No greetings, no thank you . . . Only interested in serving your self interest.'

Decorum had no meaning for Misri, who was hardened by the life of living on the footpath. 'All males are like that, Babuji,' she smiled and then stood there, waiting for the usual four-anna coin from him. As usual, Babbal was partially naked; he was wearing a black thread around his waist from which hung a talisman. Happy in his nakedness, he snuggled against his mother's bosom, occasionally looking around, as if to say that he was feeling secure as in a fortress.

Misri was a swarthy woman while Babbal was fair-complexioned. What was the secret of it? Darbari never asked. Maybe while she slept by the roadside at night, some unknown person had planted his seed in her, giving her eight annas or a rupee as a thank you gift.

'Babuji, it is strange that he doesn't mind going to you,' Misri said. 'But he dislikes men in general.'

'Why?' Darbari asked, surprised.

'I wish I knew.' Misri cast a loving look at her son. 'Of course, he doesn't mind being picked up by women.'

Darbari laughed. 'A wicked fellow! If he has a liking for women now, what havoc would he cause when he grows up?'

Misri's face reddened on hearing this. She felt that she was carrying a Kanahiya in her lap, who would grow up to be the favourite of *gopis,* who would encircle and dance around him.

'His father?'

Misri took time to answer. 'He is not . . .'

It was an incomplete answer. Was he dead? Or was he even worse than dead? She moved her gaze away from Darbari and said, 'He came once. I felt that he was the man. But I could not be certain. Up to that time, the child had no name. I used to call him Gopo or Naria. Then, he put a five-rupee note in his palm and called him by this name, Babbal. From that day onward, I started calling him, Babbal.'

Misri continued talking as if she were talking to herself, 'If he was not the father, why would he give him five rupees? It is also possible that Babbal is the child of a currency note.'

Darbari put an eight-anna coin on Babbal's palm. The child clutched hard at the coin, shrugged his shoulders, and threw it away. Misri picked it up, rushing before it fell into a utility hole.

'Naughty!' she said, kissing Babbal. 'Babuji, I say he's my man.'

'Your man?'

'Yes. He earns, and I eat,' said Misri as Babbal was pulling her head-covering. Misri was talkative; once she started speaking, she could go on for a long time.

Darbari saw the maroon colour fluttering across his eyes. He brushed aside Misri's ebony-black richness and Babbal's white-looking innocence. 'I'm going, *Saleh Bhai, achha Bhai* . . .' He walked away, cleaning chips of woods that were clinging to his trouser. Soon he was with Sita.

Facing the sea in a place near Shivaji Park, a little away from the bhelpuri sellers, Darbari and Sita sat down on the sand, leaning against the wall. Sita was eighteen and fatherless. She was living with her mother, who owned a house, a portion of which they had let out on rent to generate extra income, but the rental income was no certainty. Sita's mother wanted her daughter to marry, but she desired a son-in-law who was imposing enough to keep the tenant from defaulting on rent and thus keep the wolf away from the door.

Sita had told her mother about Darbari. In the beginning, Mother was lukewarm, but when she learned that the boy was a Mehta, she relented, knowing that in Bombay, those who collected rents were known as Mehtas.

Though of average height, Sita was attractive enough to make uncouth men whistle at her. She had good features. But her eyes remained wet as they had receded a bit into their sockets, and the eyelids kept drooping over them for protection. Because of her sunken eyes, Sita thought that she could delve deep into a man's heart. She seemed to know everything without being told. Her hair was very long, and Darbari wondered whether any of her ancestors had married a Bengali damsel. And Sita surprised Darbari by telling him that she was a Bengali and her full name was Sita Mazumdar. Darbari scolded her, 'O, you're *Sita mazedaar . . .*' Sita laughed. She was happy that she came up to Darbari's shoulders so that she could rest her head with its dark glistening hair against his shoulders; to find relief from the miseries of day-to-day existence by entrusting her inner being to him. She was keen to bridge the gap between *pita* (father) and *pati* (husband).

Sitting besides the shadow of the wall, Darbari was flirting with Sita, who was carefully trying to limit his excesses. When he circled his arms around her, she was alerted. She tried to engage Darbari in a conversation. She took out a small container from inside her blouse and pushed it closer to Darbari's face. 'See, what I've brought for you.'

'What's it?' Darbari said, removing his hand from her waist. 'No. Not like that,' she said, holding the box away from him. 'I'll show you what it is.' She once again held the box under Darbari's nose. 'Smell it!'

Darbari inhaled and started sneezing. The love game suddenly stopped. Taking out his handkerchief, he blew his nose hard. Sita looked at him bemused.

'What kind of joke is this?' Darbari again sneezed. 'Snuff?'

'It's no joke. It's snuff. It costs twenty rupees a *tola.* You look wonderful when you sneeze.'

Darbari looked at her as if she had gone mad.

'Remember, where you met me for the first time?' Sita gave him a loving look.

'No, I don't remember that.' Darbari shook his head and added. 'I do remember that I did meet you somewhere.'

'It was over there,' Sita pointed her finger towards the Mahatma Gandhi Swimming Pool. 'You were bathing and sneezing. There were three other girls with me. We had a half-day off at work. We were out on a stroll and had strayed in this direction.'

'Why in this direction?'

'Just like that,' Sita said. 'When we are off from our work, something queer happens to us girls. We can't stay confined within the four walls. We must go out, tense in the hope that something extraordinary might happen. But nothing ever happens. All we do is drink Coca-Cola.'

Sita laughed, and Darbari joined her. 'We were watching you,' Sita continued. 'You made us laugh, the way you kept going from the fountain to the diving board and back again, sneezing and kicking your legs all the time as if you were performing some stunts. I felt like wiping your nose with a corner of my sari, giving you a playful slap, as one does to a child, and then say, go and swim. Have a nice time.'

'Who were the other girls?' Darbari asked.

'There was Kumud, and there was Julie. She lives in Mount Marie, across the Bay. And the third one . . .' she suddenly stopped. 'But why do you ask?' she said.

'Oh, I was just asking. Well, forget about it. These girls are not equal to your shoes.'

'Have you seen them?'

'No, I haven't.'

Sita's face had momentarily become animated, but it suddenly lost its verve. Darbari succeeded in suppressing another sneeze and investigated the distance. 'Won't the sun ever set today?' he said.

The high tide had started. The waves came crashing towards the shore, bringing in their wake innumerable servings of bhelpuri, sugarcane bits, monkey nut husks, coconut shells, interspersed with pieces of charcoal, which the distant boats had unloaded on the sea. Like discarded sin, patches of oil from diesel boats rippled across the beach, darkening the sand. Sita turned to look and found Darbari strangely watching her, with a shadow of a frown on his face.

The sun was setting, stretching its long arms around the whole earth, trying to grab everything, a pile of golden light dipping into the sea's western direction. Soon its pride was lost in the horizon. The houses and people standing on the shore were bathed in the light that was reflecting from the wayward clouds. It was making a place for darkness and murmuring, 'Go, you are in charge now. Go and enjoy.'

The sneezing which had created a distance between Darbari and Sita now brought them closer. Sita trembled. Darbari breathed heavily. As darkness deepened, the light from the streetlamps shivered on the road. 'Darbari, what are you up to?' a voice kept echoing against the wall.

'You don't love me?' Darbari said, brusquely pulling away his hand that was groping Sita.

'Love doesn't mean all this.'

'I know, I know.' Darbari rose to his feet, smoothing and straightening his clothes and tried to leave.

'Where are you going, my moon?' Sita said in a voice full of entreaty as she looked up at him from where she sat and then clung to his legs.

Darbari jerked his feet free from her hold. 'You bitch! Trying to show off as if you were a pure virgin?'

'I think of nothing except you.' Crawling forward on her knees, Sita tried to retain her control over his legs. 'I'm yours, the moon of my life,' she whined. 'Every fibre of my body is yours. But I'm the daughter of a widowed mother. I'll give you my love, my whole being, but you have to marry me first.'

'Forget about it,' Darbari said in a harsh voice, 'Is my word not good enough? What good are these mantras, this mumbo jumbo? And these stale customs and rites? Are they necessary?' Darbari stopped and looked hopefully at Sita that she would allow him to continue with his advances.

'Yes, they are necessary,' Sita said in between her sobs. 'You and I haven't made this world.'

Darbari was getting desperate. 'If something stands between the two of us, we can't call it love. If there is any veil between us, any precondition, I don't recognize it. If our souls meet, then our bodies should meet too. God is present wherever there is love. It is written in our shastras . . .'

'It might be so,' Sita said. 'Wish all people thought like you.'

'I don't care what others think,' Darbari stamped his foot on the sand. Pulling it out from the sand, he walked off. Sita ran after him and called, 'Listen!' Darbari had not crossed the wall yet. They could still sit under its shadow and embrace the darkness. A few boys looked at the commotion. And a *chana* seller, who carried a roaster for his trade, came in between. The breeze coming in from the sea was making the roaster's flames shoot up.

Sita fell at Darbari's feet and placed her loose hair, eyes and lips against his leg. Raising her head, she looked up at him. Darbari was on fire. He was trembling with the heat coming from within. Licking his feet, Sita pleaded, 'Do you think I'm made of ice or stone?' she said. 'Don't I have feelings? Don't you think that I, too, wish to unite with you? But what do you know of a girl's anguish?' She trembled with an unknown fear. 'I don't say that you have caused this suffering. This is a gift from God. He is the one who cheated on women.'

'I know everything,' Darbari said, struggling to release his leg from her hold. 'Man can stand anything but not insult.'

'What insult?'

Instead of replying, Darbari kicked Sita, and she fell on the sand. Taking long strides, he walked towards the road.

Sita was trembling with an unknown fear. She had not felt it at even the death of her father. Putting her head on her mother's bosom, she had overcome the shock as if burning wounds get relief with the touch of someone's fingers. When her mother put her hands on her head, she thought it was the end of her misery. As she lay sobbing on the sand, she occasionally raised her head to take stock of her surroundings. Was anyone watching her? Was there a gentleman coming to her rescue? She saw a shiny object and picked it up. It was the silver snuff box filled with sand.

It was true that Darbari loved Sita but not as much as she did. Sita had come to the world to prove herself. Lying in the Ashok Vatika where the demon king Ravana had imprisoned her, she was waiting for someone to drop an engagement ring from the sky. But that story belonged to ancient times. Now we were living in modern Western times, and Darbari was taking full advantage of that change.

The wire-mesh work was going on in the veranda. The Sikh carpenter had abandoned the job after three days of causing frustration to himself and others. Sitting on the porch, Darbari was looking up the road where he used to see maroon, paddy-green, or reddish colours rippling across his eyes. Near him, his nephew Mahmud (also known as Banwari) played with an ugly toy made of cheap metal. It was dangerous with sharp corners that could cause an injury to the child. That is why Satwanti (or Kaneez) came running from the inside and took away the toy. The child started to cry, making a fuss.

Darbari protested. 'Hey, what are you doing, Sister?'

'You stay out of this.'

'Ok, don't you see how the child is crying? He is shaming Lord Kitchener. Give the toy back to him.'

'How can I give this to him. What if he hurts his eye?'

'Children have been playing with dangerous toys. Not many have lost their eyes.'

'He's a real devil.'

'All mothers say this.'

Mahmud (Banwari) had continued his loud crying, turning the whole place into hell. Darbari got up and gave the child a Japanese cat that when wound up, started to run and jump around, which was entertainment not only for kids but also for adults. But children want the same toy that is taken away from them. Darbari made faces, made weird sounds, acted like Hanuman, Johnny Walker, Agha . . . but the child didn't stop crying. He wanted the same toy. Darbari tried to hit him, but he was afraid of intensifying the howling and whining. Losing his patience, he said, 'Stop it, *Saleh!*'

Someone answered from the inside. 'Let him cry, *yaar.*' The sister returned.

'Hey Ram!'

'Why don't you say Hey Allah?'

'For Bhagwan's sake, be quiet.'

'Say for Khuda's sake.'

Satwanti (Kaneez) returned the toy. 'Take it, my father,' she said, pushing the toy towards the child. Then she picked him up and soothed him. She cleaned his face with her shirt; kissed him, licked him. Then she cursed herself. 'Such a mother should die! She should not be in this world. How cruelly she has treated the jewel.' She looked at her husband, 'Look how relaxed he is sitting.' Saleh got up and looked not very relaxed.

Darbari teased her. 'Now he can cut your hands or even the neck.'

'Let him,' his sister said. 'When I die, you will not feel any pain.'

'We don't know that.' Darbari added, 'It is said that the ignorant does the same thing as the wizard, but after making many mistakes . . . Imagine you had not done the stupidity of snatching the toy from the child!'

'Yes, I'm stupid!' Sister grabbed the child and went inside but after saying, 'To be a mother and to be a wise person are two very different things.'

Just then, Darbari saw a hint of orange near the Aurora Cinema. He quickly adjusted his clothes, straightened his cap and hurried out. Sita was standing at the corner of the road. Seeing Darbari coming, she looked away. Her eyes had sunk a little deeper into their sockets, and her eyelids were moister than usual.

'Huzoor, I await your orders!' Darbari said in a mocking tone.

Sita didn't reply. Darbari fixed her with a steady gaze.

'So, if you're in no mood to talk . . .' He turned to go.

'Listen . . .' Sita looked at him. 'You must forgive me. That day I committed a big mistake.'

Darbari stopped and looked hard at her. 'It won't happen again.'

Sita shook her head in agreement.

'You'll go with me wherever I take you? You won't hesitate?'

Sita nodded. She turned away her face and quickly wiped away a tear from her eye.

Darbari held Sita's hand in his rough palm.

'Don't be afraid of me, Sita,' he said in a placatory tone. 'You always make me feel so mean.' Sita wanted to hear this.

'No, it's not that,' she said promptly.

Once again, Darbari and Sita were sitting against the wall near Shivaji Park. The day had ended, and there were no clouds in the sky to deflect its light towards the earth. In the descending darkness, the Mahatma Gandhi Swimming Pool's railing got etched against the sky and was then swiftly blotted out. Sita was sitting tongue-tied, feeling uneasy at Darbari's emotional tone.

'You should smile and say something.' Sita smiled. Darbari mocked her for her fake smile. Sita burst out in laughter, and Darbari said, 'Don't you trust me?'

'No, it's not that,' Sita replied. 'Even if you marry me, you'll look at me with contempt. You will take me for a cheap girl.'

'No, Sitey. I'll never do that. Never.'

They saw some men approaching, holding long iron rods. Darbari looked at them, alarmed. His fear subsided when they started plodding the sand with the rods, looking for smuggled goods, which they had buried there a few days ago. They wanted to retrieve them before the tide set in.

Darbari and Sita got up and shifted to the other end of the wall. As they looked around, they were confronted by a group of upcountry men who made a living by cleaning utensils. They were in a hilarious mood and were jesting with one another. Darbari ignored them as harmless creatures, but Sita became nervous, and she was dependent on Darbari. She had no desire of her own. She wanted to smoothen her relationship, and for that, she was willing to pay any price.

Some good-for-nothing types passed by them, singing lines of a popular film sing: . . . . *ae mere dil kahien* . . . Then a cop was seen.

Darbari got up, peeved. 'All right let's make a move,' he said.

'We'll go to Juhu.'

'Juhu?'

'Yes, get up. We'll take a taxi from Kendall Road.' Sita followed him.

Sita and Darbari felt uneasy roaming around Juhu beach. Every few days, there was news of something terrible happening. A murder took place a few days ago, and then a couple was traumatized by bad characters. That day, all Juhu hotels and cottages were filled with customers. After wasting a couple of hours, they walked to the fort. Sita said something, Darbari's response was incoherent and indifferent as if he were chewing an intoxicating pill in his mouth, making his tongue swell.

Passing through Haji Ali, their taxi entered Tardeo, then took a turn towards the Opera House and finally reached Hornby Road, which had now become Mahatma Gandhi Road.

'Do you have a room?' Darbari asked the hotel manager. The manager gave Darbari a scrutinizing look as if he were looking at a person who had just committed a crime or was going to commit a crime. Sita, who was standing behind him, was trembling while looking at the ground. Both were facing a new situation, which made them lose the balance of their minds.

'Where are you coming from?' the manager enquired.

'From Aurangabad,' Darbari said with tutored alacrity.

'Well!' The manager first looked at Sita and then at the darkness of Darbari's face. 'Where's your luggage?'

'We don't have any luggage.'

'Sorry, we have no room for you.' The manager said as if he was trying to avoid contact with something toxic.

'What do you mean. Just now, you were saying on telephone . . .'

Waiter Number 27, who was carrying wafers, a salty snack, soda bottles and a key to a room, intervened, 'Sahib, this hotel is for use by respectable people.'

Darbari could not say anything, although he knew that the worth of this waiter was no more than one rupee, and the manager who was acting like a respectable man could be valued no more than five rupees. They were showing themselves off as icons of virtue. Whatever claims they might make, one needs to be alert. One must show off professional courage, openness and audacity to challenge the ethics of others. Darbari knew he was weak inside. He was an uncut jewel. He uttered abuses in English as he walked away, unsure whether he wanted the hotel management to hear them.

'Let us go, Sita,' Darbari said. 'We shall try another time.' They took a taxi and went home. Life seemed to have suddenly lost its savour for Darbari. Defeat rankled in his heart. He thought of people who were heroes in his eyes, but slowly they fell to his feet.

Today, he was not thinking of going anywhere. Nothing had been planned. He had been feeling distraught and left his office early. He had regained strength after the insult he had suffered on the evening he was refused a room at the hotel. This fire should not have arisen. That is why sane people give a lot of importance to controlling one's mode of thinking. These sensitive folks who have no influence on their thinking should not be born. But if they are born, they can't be ignored. You can't butcher them or strangulate them. The punishment in both cases is death. These people always hide in the corners of their brains. They will come at you when you are defenseless, not ready to use your hands or feet, like a dead body that is being prepared for the the burial.

Darbari was sitting on the veranda, and he was looking at the trees in the Don Bosco grounds. Under their shades, motor cars belonging to the rich folks were taking a nap. Some belonged to the rich office workers who shuttled between the office and home and often picked fights with their wives for their satisfaction. Some belonged to folks who had turned them into whorehouses on wheels. Their drivers were paid a handsome salary for keeping them polished and shining. They were like Waiter Number 28.

Darbari overcame the feeling related to his insult at the hotel by hoping that the privacy offered by a car could be a solution to his problem. But what was the use of this thinking? Hope doesn't get you a car. Father Girdharilal Mehta was a miser who didn't flaunt his wealth. He would sit on his treasure like a snake even in his next birth.

Saleh Bhai (or Sardari) had gone back to his place with his wife and children. The strong-armed and childless sister-in-law remained behind. She often complained to his brother about not having a child. She blamed him and implored him to consult a doctor. She said he had a problem, but the brother blamed her. The unborn children looked at the blame game and felt frustrated.

Darbai was feeling bored. If he stayed in the house, Mother would come out with a recital of the latest proposals that had been received for his marriage. He had no intention of getting married. He wanted to enjoy life.

Marriage would happen one day.

But marry whom? Sita leapt to his mind. A good girl, no doubt, and not bad to look at. Though showing great attention to detail, she seemed to have no will of her own. To take her as a wife—well, that was a different matter altogether. Sita was good, and he didn't mind associating with her. A wife ought to be the epitome of cheerfulness. She should look here and there so that the husband is compelled to tell her, 'Look at me.' And a widow's daughter. She would cling to him as if he were her father and not her husband. I'll be wasting my money on useless travel. But for short-term enjoyment, Sita was better than others. What a beautiful body she possesses!

Then he saw Misri coming with Babbal. On seeing Darbari, Misri was forcing Babbal's attention on 'Babuji' meaning Darbari. Babbal made a gurgling sound and bounced like a ball as if a new life was surging through him. It became difficult for Misri to hold him. He wasn't wearing God's apparel, but a man's—a torn undershirt and nothing underneath. As he approached Darbari, Babbal opened both his hands.

'This niggardly kid thinks that while standing here, I was dying to see him.' Going inside and then coming out bringing something for the child was like fulfilling a religious ritual. When Darbari returned with puffed rice, a thought flashed in his head for the first time. Misri is the mother, and Babbal is her child. The relationship between mother and child was indeed divine. Among the poor, a father, Darbari thought, plays an important role. The present situation was a source of pain. He was thinking fast, and his thought process was moving circles. A revelation hit him. He opened his eyes wide and then closed them. Darbari gave the puffed rice to Babbal. But the child was not accepting it. He was thinking why Babuji was not holding him today. He was shy. Like a rubber ball, he was hitting the wall and bouncing back. I don't want puffed rice, not even heaven's kingdom. Hold me, Babuji. Why are you hesitating?

'Misri, how much have you earned today?' he asked timidly given the nature of the question.

'About fourteen annas!"

'Why only fourteen annas?'

'Today, my man had gone to Nagpara,' Misri replied, gathering courage.

'Your man?' Darbari was surprised. 'Have you taken a man?'

Misri smiled, and while lifting the child, she offered him to Darbari. She said, 'He is my man. He is my man who earns for me. His aunt had borrowed him and taken him to Parle's Chuna Bhatti. She gave him this undershirt, which he doesn't like to wear. He moves his shoulders as if he was carrying the weight of the whole world.' Darbari understood the situation and laughed. He had not held the child yet. Forgetting the treat, he was trying to get his attention.

Misri said, 'He is getting used to going around naked. What will he do when he is an adult?'

'He looks fine this way, Misri.'

Babbal seemed to be saying, *false* . . . If you like me like this, then why don't you hold me? He was making noise, *hu, hu, hu* . . .

'When you carry Babbal, how much do you earn?' Darbari asked.

'This one?' Misri lowered Babbal. Her arms were hurting. 'When I carry him, then I can earn three or four rupees.'

Darbari took out a ten-rupee note from his pocket and offered it to Misri.

'Why this, Babuji?' she asked as her face reddened.

'You take it,' Darbari told her as he looked around. 'Take it quickly lest someone sees us.' Misri looked hither and thither. Her face now had a crimson look. She took the ten-rupee note, placed it in the narrow gap of her lower garment, and waited to hear something that people told her three or four times a year. Her face blackened as she heard Darbari's reasoning. 'I love him a lot. I love Babbal. I want to have him for a day or two.' Misri was puzzled. Darbari added, 'I'll treat him with great love, Misri, with great love like that of a mother. Like you, I like him a lot.' Misri handed over Babbal to Darbari.

Babbal jumped in delight. Holding puffed rice, he moved his head like a peacock. Then his well-built arms started to move like a bicycle. Darbari placed some puffed rice in his mouth. Babbal accepted it the same way as he did when his mother fed him in a somewhat mischievous manner. He wanted to be let go. He tried to touch the ground or demanded that he be picked and embraced next to his mother's bosom. He looked at his mother, and then he turned his face towards Darbari, and he playfully started to tease his mother as he used to tease Darbari before. Misri was standing confused while watching somewhat hard to believe interactions of a father and a son—who were not a father and a son.

'What would happen if he soiled your clothes?'

'Then nothing.' Darbari added, 'Everything relating to children is like nectar.' Misri's eyes turned moist. She got her man, the most precious thing. No, a child has found his father. She looked askance at both. The second thing was much bigger than the first one.

'I'll feed him, Misri.' Darbari held out a promise. 'You can come at ten o'clock to take him back.'

'Fine!' Misri moved her head to show her consent.

Misri left, but then she stopped to look at the child who was busy playing in Darbari's arms. He was trying to open Darbari's palms and showing frustration for failing. Misri called his name. Babbal looked at her. But today, nothing else mattered; neither mother nor father. Misri disappeared, leaving her heart behind. Satisfied that Babbal was in safe hands, she walked briskly. After some distance, she took out the ten-rupee note and looked at it as if she was looking at her man, not a piece of paper.

Darbari took Babbal inside, who looked at the room filled with many attractions. Everything that he saw was new to him. He wanted to put every little thing into his mouth to taste it, seeking limitless pleasure. Then the mother walked in and was taken aback, seeing Darbari holding a child. She put one of her fingers on her nose and said, 'Hey Ram, what is this?'

'Babbal is Misri's child. I like him a lot.'

'Where is the mother?'

'She has gone away. I borrowed the child to play with him. It's a loan. The mother gave birth, and her job was done.' Darbari looked at his mother.

'Keep your thoughts to yourself,' Mother replied. 'Mother is needed only for six or eight months, then stupid ones like you take over.'

'Alright, Mother,' Darbari pleaded. 'I'll take him to the ground facing Podar College. I must return Jagmohan's books as well. Please hold him for me.' Mother showed her strong disapproval. 'He's dirty.' She moved her hands and said, 'I won't touch him.' The sister-in-law who had arrived and was watching this added, 'If you're so fond of kids, then why don't you get married.'

'No, I like kids of others,' Darbari gave a strong response.

The sister-in-law sighed and said, 'If God does not provide, then what's the option.'

Darbari placed Babbal on the floor, where his attention diverted to a German silver spoon. Darbari went to another room, leaving Babbal to suck on the spoon. Maybe he was in the process of cutting his milk teeth. Suddenly, Babbal felt alone. He moved his hands first toward the mother and then toward the sister-in-law. Mother went away saying *chhe chhe* . . . The sister-in-law hesitated, but then she picked up the child spurred by an inner urge. She put him next to her bosom and started to move rhythmically as if she had fallen into a swing that was giving her divine pleasure. Babbal's dirt didn't bother her. Lost in her thoughts, she bathed the child and dressed him in silken and superior cotton clothes. This boy is so handsome; he could be dressed as a girl.

Darbari took out a suitcase and filled it with some clothes and books. He quickly closed the suitcase and rushed to the living room. Babbal's head was lost in Bhabhi's bosom. He looked up, sensing Darbari, and gave him the look of a warrior and moved his hands toward him. Darbari held Babbal in one hand and the suitcase in the other while saying, 'Alright, Bhabhi,' he walked out.

On reaching Dadar, he bought a shirt and short underpants for Babbal. He liked the shirt and made no fuss wearing it, but the underpants were another matter. He shouted and cried. He was running the bicycle with his legs. Sometimes standing up and sometimes falling. He tested Darbari's patience. And Darbari was thinking, 'What a strange man am I? I can't handle a child.' A light bulb caught the child's attention. He moved his hand to catch it, but nearly poked his finger into the netting of a table fan. He might have lost the finger if the shopkeeper had not shown presence of mind. Babbal didn't like the way his finger was struck. This meant more crying. As Darbari picked him up, the child pointed his finger to the shopkeeper to complain.

As they sat in the taxi, Babbal felt uneasy. His underpants were hurting him. Darbari was at the end of his nerves. Nothing in life had prepared him to handle this challenge. Darbari tried to put him on the seat next to him, but the child insisted on sitting in his lap. He eventually succeeded in removing his underpants which by now were severely wrinkled. The child looked relieved and stared out of the window to get a clear view of the world.

When Darbari reached Sita's place, he was disheartened to not find her there. Her mother told him that she had gone to Prabha Devi to meet Kumud. Prabha Devi was not far, but he didn't know Kumud's home address. When he questioned the mother, she wanted to know why he was looking for Sita. It was better to stay silent. Then the mother complicated matters by mentioning that one of her first-floor Sindhi tenants had served her 'nost' meaning a notice to terminate the tenancy agreement. How should she handle the matter? Darbari listened to the older woman's travails and during conversation informed her that Babble was his nephew. But mother showed no interest. She tried to converse with the child once, and he responded, but then she didn't say more. She went back to his personal story.

'The Committee says that you should spend so much on the repair of the property. Now one faces a difficult choice between repair costs and one's living costs. What kind of laws have been enacted? The Congress Party is there to drown you deep in the water. What will happen when Asht Grahi, the confluence of eight stars, occurs? I should have gone back to Jagadhri, my parent's home. When do you plan to marry?'

In few moments, even Mother was overcome with boredom. She said, 'I don't know when Sita will return. You have come in a taxi. Why don't you drop me in Mahim?'

'Mother, I'm not going in Mahim's direction.'

'Then, where are you going?'

'Towards the city.'

'That is good. I have some work in Parel too. *Hindolas* are coming. I need to buy some *mauli*. Do you know what is mauli?'

Darbari had it by then. Babbal was causing trouble too. And the taxi's meter was running. He hit his head and said, 'Mother, I'll drop you in Parel. Is Kumud's place on the way?'

''Yes, it is. But one should put these Bombay streets into the flames. I have gone there twenty times, and all those twenty times I didn't find it.'

'Now, let's try it for the twenty-first time.'

'But where do you plan to take Sita?'

'To my sister's.'

'But she is a Muslim. Isn't she?'

'What are you talking, Mother?' Darbari stopped the mountain from falling. 'Have you heard Satwanti as a Muslim woman's name?'

Sita returned like a spring breeze, surrounded by green leaves and flowers to save the situation from getting out of hand. She was wearing a tight blouse of deep grey colour and a handloom sari with the colour of cooked Begumi rice. Her entire body was in a flow. She was the spring but a messenger of autumn for Darbari. His inner garden was drying up, and the wild winds took away dried leaves. What remained, it conflicted with itself. Sita noticed Babbal and gave a pondering look, 'Whose child is this?' Then she approached the child. 'How sweet. He's like a Bablu.'

'Yes, his name is Babbal. How did you know?'

'How could I know this?' Sita clapped and invited the child to her lap. 'I can recognize a child by the looks. You can't guess?' Sita rubbed her hands against the child's cheeks and muttered something. Looking at the taxi parked outside, she asked, 'This is for us to go?' Darbari moved his head in agreement. The taxi driver, who was getting impatient, felt relieved. He got out and opened the back door. When Darbari, Sita and Babbal were seated, Sita noticed the suitcase. The shadow of suspicion appeared on her face. 'What is this suitcase for?'

Darbari answered the question with a simple, 'Yes.'

'Are we going to your sister's place?'

'Wherever we are going, don't be concerned with that. Didn't you say wherever I take you, you will come with me?'

Sita was trying to make sense. Darbari's facial appearance, suitcase, and the child—fearing Darbari's wrath, she put Babbal beside her and, expanding her nostrils, replied, 'Yes. I said that.'

Sita quickly looked at Darbari to watch his reaction and then lowered her eyes. She had an unpleasant feeling. She wiped her quickly reddening face with a corner of her sari. Darbari looked at Sita with a drunken gaze and said, 'Sita, you are starting to behave like that day.' Sita was filled with fear. She said, 'No, not like that.'

The taxi was passing by Haji Ali. The ocean's colour was the same today that one observes before the rainy season—

dirty, dark, and moist. Maybe it was raining at some places, and all the dirty water was draining into the ocean. Once again, it was the same trip—Tardeo, Opera House, Mahatma Gandhi Road, Flora Fountain and the hotel.

It was a different kind of hotel. A waiter was standing outside; he saw the passengers and came forward to open the door. Darbari stepped out and paid the taxi driver, and then he directed the waiter to take care of the suitcase. Sita, too, got out. Her gaze was lowered, and she was showing hesitation in taking care of the child.

'Hold him,' Darbari said, pointing to the child. 'This is a woman's job.' Sita wasn't ready, but she was helpless. She was afraid of Darbari getting angry and losing his temper. She picked up Babbal, but there was no love in her action. She was emitting sour and dirty air.

The hotel was one floor up. Darbari felt no need to ask whether a room was available. He was confident and unafraid. Sita saw drums containing oil or ghee stacked on the stairs. The rope on the side had become filthy with the touch of a multitude of people. There was a stale smell in the place. Without touching the string, Sita climbed the stairs following Darbari.

When the manager saw three customers, he showed some sanctified brightness on his face. He came from behind the counter and said, 'Welcome, Sir.' Today the doors of all the rooms were open for Darbari and Sita.

Darbari informed the manager, 'We're coming from Bil Mor and are in transit here. Tonight, we shall be travelling via Punjab Mail to Agra to see Taj Mahal, which Shah Jehan had built for the love of his life, Mumtaz. I think the emperor didn't love her that much; he did it to overcome his guilty feelings.

He made the love of his life produce sixteen or eighteen kids. He wanted to compensate her for his excesses . . .'

But these facts were unnecessary. The manager was repeating, 'Sir, Sir . . .' He was all smiles, more than what was proper. He was moving his head and lowering it too. After signing the register, Darbari reached the room and saw Babbal munching a biscuit.

'Who gave this to him?'

'The waiter.'

'And this ice-cream cone?'

'Someone in the other room.'

The waiter was bringing milk for the child as if he was without any work for centuries, and now, and now he had found some work to do—never-ending work that would never free him. Tip income had no meaning. He was standing there holding a bowl containing milk, waiting for recognition before he left.

'Alright, waiter,' Darbari said, dismissing the person. 'We are tired; we have been travelling for a long time. We need to take some rest.'

'Yes,' the waiter answered. 'Sahib, if you need me . . . '

Darbari closed the door before the waiter completed his sentence. He felt tired, breathed deeply and fell on the bed. He didn't like the way Sita was feeding Babbal. But he couldn't say anything. At that very moment, Babbal through a playful action hit the bowl with his hand and all the milk fell on the ground.

'Pitiable! What a dirty act!' Sita wiped the child's face with a handkerchief and took a broom to wipe the floor. Babbal stood up, holding on to Sita, who was worried. There was an uneasy feeling inside. Darbari appeared embarrassed.

'This hotel is no good,' he said to start a conversation.

'You're right,' Sita spoke with some indifference. Darbari smelled something. 'There is a bad odour.' He wiped his sweat from his forehead and said, 'Now, you should leave him alone.' Sita was making Babbal sit, but he was resisting. Darbari gave him the ashtray, and Babbal thought it was a toy and started to play with it. Then Darbari moved forward and grabbed Sita's hand in an amateurish manner that lacked decency.

'For God's sake!' Sita pleaded, gesturing toward Babbal, but Darbari did not understand the subtle hint. He did not see anything. He was filled with desire for a fresh-looking and enticing girl, and his breathing was getting faster. He put his hands around Sita; they were hands composed of flesh and blood. They had a wooden feel, and they were hurting Sita. She was not stopping his advances. While in the fold of his arms, she was shaking and quivering and getting lifeless. She wanted to let herself loose.

Babbal fearfully looked at both. Darbari noticed Sita's tears. 'It is clear. You don't love me.'

'I don't love you. I don't . . .'

Babbal had defaced himself with ash from the ashtray, and he had started to cry.

'Stop it, rascal!' Darbari expressed his anger and frustration. Sita felt like running away as her arms had lost their vitality. Babbal started to cry louder. Darbari in his blind rage wanted to catch the child by his throat and silence the voice that was coming between a man and a woman. He hit Babbal hard, and the child fell some distance away.

'Aren't you ashamed?' He heard Misri's voice coming through a void. Darbari turned around. It was Sita, not Misri, who was partially naked. She picked up Babbal and brought him closer to her bosom. Babbal put his head there and continued to cry and sob. He lifted his hand and with a finger pointed to Darbari, identifying him as the culprit. 'He hit me.' Although he was dressed in clean clothes, Darbari saw him as a filthy child. He wasn't so upset with Sita as with Babbal. He had his reasons.

Feeling ashamed and regretful, Darbari came forward to hold Babbal. Had Sita been free to make her decision, she would not have passed on the child to him. Once Babbal was with Darbari, he was pointing his complaining finger towards Sita. Both Sita and Darbari were at their wits' end.

'Sita,' Darbari called her.

She didn't answer, but she tried to cover her nakedness with her sari.

'Sita,' Darbari said again. 'Will you ever forgive me?' And then, to remove any doubt, he added, 'We shall get married first.'

And then, gathering courage, he put his arms around Sita. She looked carefully into Darbari's eyes, and then she embraced him and cried like a baby. Darbari cried too. They combined their pains and miseries, their joys and delights into something singular. When Babbal saw their sobbing, he stopped his cries. Then he laughed aloud as if nothing had happened. In search of his favourite rice puffs, he tried in vain to open Darbari's fist.

12

For a Cigarette

It was nearing four in the morning when Sant Ram woke up. In the adjacent bed, Dhobin was spread on her side, fast asleep. Sant Ram called his wife, Dhobin—a washerwoman. She had a nice sounding name, Debi. But Sant Ram had nicknamed her Dhobin because she refused to give clothes to the laundry for washing and instead insisted on washing them herself. They were affluent and had many servants. But right from a flimsy handkerchief to a heavy bedsheet, she washed everything at home. When tired, she would squabble with everyone in the house; these squabbles proved more expensive in the long run than the laundry charges. Before going to sleep, she would ask Sant Ram to gently massage her body. But she said it in a way that it was difficult to comprehend whether it was a request or a command. Not to talk of Sant Ram, even her children were irritated at her requests, that were more perennial than occasional in nature. They didn't mind doing this favour for five or ten minutes, but to stretch it to an hour—well, it tested their patience. In the end, exhausted they would lie by her side to regain their stregth. One day, her daughter, Lado, went to the extent of saying, 'Mummy, it's so tiring. Now you massage my body.'

There was one great problem. Dhobin could not decide with certainty where her body ached. Wherever one dabbed one's finger to locate the pain, the pain was always somewhere near it or somewhere else. It could be a little up or down on her body. In the process of trying to locate the exact spot, she would get a whole-body massage. Not that it was a subterfuge on her part. She really couldn't tell where her body was aching and ended up saying that it was aching all over. Dhobin did not mind extending this favour to others, but nobody showed any interest in availing her service. She had an iron-like control over her body, but it was her arms, muscular and powerful, that had the pull of a wrestler's and family members were afraid of the strength with which she touched others. Sant Ram was scared of what he called her 'dhobi-wrench.' A washerwoman, indeed!

He had given his wife this name because in his childhood he had seen a 'dhobin' weighing nearly twelve maunds in a bioscope. Lying half naked on her side, holding a peacock feather fan in her hand, she looked buxom. The guy with a bioscope would appear in Sant Ram's Lane with fanfare, beating a drum and announcing, 'See a night in Paris as gay as the marriage party!' Then changing his tune, he would say in a sing-song manner, 'Look at a washerwoman, a dhobin, weighing twelve maunds. She is fair complexioned! Fair . . . Oh, how fair!'

Taking a paisa each from their mothers, children would run out into the lane and dump the coin in bioscope operator's hand and then close their eyes on the aperture in the magic box. They would watch the cavalcade with great fascination—the city of Paris, a wedding party, a white bear. And finally, they would see a 'dhobin' and a circus clown. More than anything else, they were intrigued by the image of the flabby dhobin. How could such a sprawling woman manage to imprison herself to a box? Even a month ago, she was reclining in the same posture. Didn't she get tired? Children were enamoured by her for an unknown reason. She would stay lodged in their minds only to come out after fifteen or twenty years.

Lado, Sant Ram's married daughter, who had returned from her in-laws only the day before, was sleeping in the adjoining room. She was lost in deep sleep as if she had no husband to take care of. Her mouth was open because her mean little son, Bobby, did not let her have a wink of sleep earlier in the night. Sleeping soundly now, she wanted air to breathe. She had not changed from the person she was six years ago when she got married. She had the bad habit of spraying her saliva over the other person's face as she spoke. Her habits had not changed too; it took her a moment to get angry and soon after, be conciliatory. Sant Ram and Dhobin were worried: how would they find a husband for their naive and simple daughter? What if she got a difficult husband? Luckily, the husband she got made no demands nor did he reveal any intention of doing so in the future. While her parents continued to hold strong negative feelings for each other, her in-laws suffered from a surfeit of love. Hovering between two contrasting families, she and her husband were tied in a strong bond of love, more so, because of the compatibility of their temperaments. The appearance of a rodent in the house would send both squealing into each other's arms. Sant Ram was glad that his daughter and his son-in-law had the valour of a sparrow.

Sant Ram knew that negative qualities could be of immense value in life. For instance, qualities like shame, fear, niggardliness were not bad. But to his regret he saw that these qualities were also percolating down to his grandchildren. Lado's little son, Bobby, was sleeping with her, his arms curled round her neck. Whenever he came out of his sleep momentarily, he would start rubbing her earlobe—a most irritating habit which only a mother could tolerate. Whenever Sant Ram, out of grandfatherly affection, took his sleeping grandson to sleep with him, he returned him to his mother, losing no time. When the child rubbed his earlobe with his moist flabby hand, he felt nauseated as if a centipede was crawling over his ear.

Sant Ram's two younger children, a boy and a girl, had gone to Gurgaon to spend time with their maternal uncle. Their beds were lying empty. Only his eldest son, Pal was here, as testified by his loud snoring. Sant Ram wondered how tall Pal looked! It seemed he had grown taller when no one was watching and consequently he had gone out of Sant Ram's control. In the beginning when Sant Ram checked him for his mistakes, he would express his resentment in many ways. He would squabble with his mother, and sometimes threw the cup of tea out of the window. But nowadays, he submitted to his father's exhortations without any reaction, which annoyed Sant Ram more. He wanted his son to retaliate and hit back. Perhaps Sant Ram was not clear in his mind what he expected He wished his son could defy him, but he did not. Perhaps it was six years ago that he had slapped him, and that imprint had been obliterated long ago. In fact, he was afraid of physical violence inviting the same kind of reaction. As on other nights, Pal had come home at two o'clock after gulping three or four pegs of Diplomat whiskey. Its smell might have disappeared from the others who drank with him, but it was still lingering in Pal's breath.

Pal was a lean young man of around twenty-six. But he was still given to behaving like a baby crying for attention. He was also skinny. But he made the grade as a grown-up man because of his facial cut and the style of his moustache. Women liked him because he showered affection on their children. He had a great zest for life and was highly ambitious. Egotistical to a fault, his nostrils would flare up with an exaggerated sense of his own importance. He introduced himself with a flourish as 'Pal Anand' as if he was the precursor of a tradition whereas the fact was that he was only following in the footsteps of his father, Sant Ram Anand, who had brought him up like a princeling. Sant Ram had pampered him by giving him extra pocket money to spend as he pleased. This was against Dhobin's wishes and the cause of strained relations between husband and wife. Excessive indulgence and an assured place under the family's roof had inculcated in the son a false sense of security, making it increasingly difficult for him to withstand the ups and downs of life.

Sant Ram lived in a big house, with three bedrooms and a large drawing room. Its walls were decorated with paintings of renowned artists. Pal changed his dress twice a day, conveniently forgetting that his lavish wardrobe had been assembled with his father's money. Not only was he ungrateful, but Pal hated his father. He would pass by Sant Ram without taking any notice of him, as if he was not his father but an odd piece of furniture. Sant Ram owned an advertising agency. If the government passed a legislation inimical to the interests of the company, and as a result the business suffered, who would Sant Ram blame? Business never runs an even course; it oscillates between boom and bust. It is the way of the world to stick to a man when the going is good and share the fruits of his labour, and desert him when he gets into financial trouble. People might heap derision on him for being a loser.

Pal being a modern man attuned to new thinking which was much in vogue, could show respect to a man who was rolling in wealth, one who had a flair for minting money, erecting huge buildings and buying cars like an Impala. Once Pal had expressed such views to his father. It had greatly hurt the old man's feelings. Something seemed to have snapped within him without his being aware of the extent of the damage his son had wreaked upon him. How much he had wished to rob a bank and rake in bags full of money to throw at his son or wife and thereby retrieve his prestige! One could never create excessive wealth by fair means; it could only be gained through unfair means, of which he was not capable. The irony was that when he ran into a loss, neither his wife nor his son even offered him a word of consolation—oh, dear Husband or dear Papa, please don't take it to your heart. It's all a game. Money comes and goes. Not all who lose money are fools or those who make money necessarily wise.

The family had started ignoring him as if he were a doddering old fool, who had already played his innings. He felt lonely and forlorn in his own house. By the logic of it, it meant that if his financial condition improved, he could take it out on them, by beating them black and blue, starting with his wife. But, no, to harbour such vengeful feelings was not appropriate for a husband or a father. But why should one presume that a father's job was only to bestow affection but get nothing in return? As if he was not in need of love. But who could do without love? A one-year-old child needed it as much as a hundred-year-old man. Even his cocker spaniel, Jimmy, who would presently be sleeping in his kennel, loved to be patted. When someone gave him a loving glance, a message ran from his brain down to the end of his tail. His tail started wagging and along with it his entire body. If he was denied his share of love, he would even refuse to eat and pose as if saying, 'Look, I can bear the pangs of hunger, but I can't forego love.' And here was his family—Dhobin, Lado and Pal who considered him a notch lower than Jimmy.

Maybe it was because all his life Sant Ram had only learnt to give to others, a habit which had in time become second nature; he lived only to give to others. He did not feel so sore about his financial losses as the fact that he had lost his capacity to give. When a member of his family passed by him, without as much as giving him a nod, he analysed the meaning of their silence, not realizing that even receiving could become his second nature as much as giving.

In fact, Sant Ram did not mind Dhobin's round-the-clock nagging and pontificating. She more than made up for her lack of education by her hard work and flair for keeping her house in good condition. One night in response to his feeble lovemaking, she withdrew her lips from him because Sant Ram's mouth smelled of tobacco. But smoking was nothing new; he was smoking from his younger days. Why should she express her aversion to his smoking so late in life, a time that had a feel of having lived together for few centuries? Was it a hint for his sense of inferiority? Or maybe Dhobin had herself grown old, dry and cold. It is only the heat of youthful passion which drives away all smells. But if Dhobin had become old and cold and had run dry, he himself was no longer young. His lips were devoid of the sap of youth and were only good for uttering taunts and vituperations. Even a simple woman like Dhobin knew how a man squirmed when a woman withdrew her lips from him.

Perhaps Dhobin, the 'dhobin' of the magic bioscope, had entered her menopause. Her attitude to life seemed to have changed. Getting out of her 'conjugal bed', she had flung away her peacock fan and had turned her face against her silent admirers! Now there was no magic box operator, nor the watchers of that peep show. As in the case of old men, a second phase of youth had descended on Sant Ram when only a thin line kept him from ignominy. A simulated sense of potency coupled with experience and finesse had taught him to remain self-contained and self-assertive which generated a kind of miasma within him in which he wallowed like a buffalo enjoying herself in a muddy pond. His setback in business could as well be the reason for it. It often happens that the fear of financial insecurity generates diffidence in love.

There was no point bringing Lado into the picture. She was married and was settled in life. The memory of her youthful days which she had spent in her father's home was akin to that of a songbird which pecked at the grains in her father's courtyard and flew away. But Pal was still entrenched here as if glued to the house where he had to bring his bride and help her to set up a home. By shifting to some other place, father's roof did not change. Why didn't he understand such simple things? Perhaps he did not wish to understand them. Why couldn't he spare a few moments for his father, mother, brothers and sisters? Had he become a demi-god on securing a job in an American business firm? Why didn't he consider it a wrong thing to make money on the sly through private contracts while still doing his regular job? It was incumbent upon him to sit and chat with his father once in a while. Surely, his father did not covet his money. He was only hungry for his son's company. That the souls which had affinity with one another should merge together. That they should sit together and divert their minds by talking of things in general. For instance, about the new system of education which had left even the highly educated people of the old generation far behind in the race of life. Let the young have a glimpse of the old world and the old ones be allowed a glimpse of the new world. Let the young ones know that education is not everything, experience counts for more.

Sant Ram didn't mind if Pal conducted himself in this manner out of carelessness or ignorance. But he was an intelligent young man and should have known better. He could reach the heart of the matter in no time. For instance, last year when negotiations were going on for his marriage with a rich man's daughter, an only child, he had immediately put his foot down. He said, 'It has taken me ten years to free myself from your stranglehold. Do you mean to say I should waste another ten years in liberating myself from the clutches of a rich man's daughter?' What Pal said had indeed some validity and that he had said it so clearly had left Sant Ram amazed. He had felt proud of his son. How intelligent and how self-respecting! But at the same time, he did not miss the sharp edge of his son's remark. What did he mean by freeing himself from his father's stranglehold? Can a son free himself from his father's hold or a father from his son's hold? They are not made to wean themselves away from each other. Even if they lived continents apart, they were not separate from each other. After the father was gone, a son might say that his father was a good-for-nothing fellow and the legacy that he left behind was that of heavy debt. Even then the invisible bond between the father and the son is not snapped—the relationship of a good-for-nothing father and a worthy son survives.

Sant Ram thought he could not die unless he left some wealth for his children. If he died a pauper, Dhobin would chase him, even in the next world and wring his soul dry. But if one came to think of it, what did his father leave for him? But his respect for his father had not diminished. Does a man deserve to be called a father only if he leaves property and money behind for his children? Even arithmetic can be used to pick holes in this argument. As they say, one man's loss can be another man's gain. It is only by driving a man into debts that a creditor can amass wealth at the debtor's cost. Well, he still owned a nice bungalow on Tughlaq Road. True, he had to raise money by offering it as security to cover up his business losses. He was passing through lean times, but he was confident that he would be able to liquidate all his debts before dying. He owned two hundred bighas of very fertile land in Jagdal village, part of it ancestral and the rest purchased with his own money. Didn't it speak for his prudence and guts that in spite of his bad circumstances he hadn't sold even an inch of this land? He had not sold the land lest it should cause pain to his forefathers' souls. And he had also to think of his family. They would have cursed him for being thoughtless and selfish. Besides, he had a sizeable life insurance policy. If he took that into his head, he could commit suicide for the sake of passing its benefit to his family.

Sant Ram recalled his own father's death. His death had indeed made him sad but at the same time he had felt a vicarious sense of joy at his passing. Henceforth, he would be on his own, answerable only to himself for all his actions and let nobody question him for his actions. This thought almost absolved him of all responsibility towards Pal. Which son does not secretly wish for his father's death?

The thought gave him great mental relief. Going into the adjoining room he switched on the zero-power lamp and looked at Lado, her son Bobby and then his eyes came to rest on Pal's face. He was alive in his son, and he would soon be living in his grandchildren.

Just then Sant Ram felt a strong urge for a cigarette. *Arre, yaar*, what a wonderful thing a cigarette is! Whoever invented it, had performed a miracle. A tiny companion of solitary moments which constantly keeps reminding one of someone else's presence. One never feels alone when a cigarette is lit. A cigarette is life itself whose one end keeps burning slowly like one's own life, the other end remaining stuck in the jaws of death. Dying and living with each single breath. It brings one's scattered thoughts to a focal point. And by then one has divined some important secrets of life beyond which one need not know anything more. People say smoking causes cancer. It might be true. But those who do not smoke, do they live as long as Methuselah? Every person has to attribute his death to one cause or the other. Why not attribute it to cigarette smoking?

Last night while coming home, Sant Ram had forgotten to buy a pack of cigarettes. Now he badly needed a smoke, and no shop was open at four-thirty in the morning. And Sant Ram's urge for a smoke was getting more pronounced with each passing moment. He saw a packet of cigarettes lying on Pal's side table, a box of matches resting upon it. Being the lordly type, Pal did not smoke anything less than State Express. Unlike him, his father smoked anything he could

lay his hands on—Charminar, Scissors, Gold Flake. Should
he go for the State Express? But why couldn't he wait until
six-thirty when paan–cigarette shops generally opened? But if
he waited, it would be like waiting for a glass of milk and not
for a cigarette, the urge for which was most insistent. Sant
Ram stretched out his hand towards the packet. In the dim
light of the zero-power lamp, he found that there were only
two cigarettes left in the packet. Pal would certainly require
one for his morning ablution in the toilet. And the other?
Maybe he needed more than one for this purpose. Possibly he
smoked right after his morning shave or soon after breakfast.
State Express cigarettes were not available in that area and
could not be replaced easily, not before nine or ten in any case.
One would have to go as far as Connaught Place to buy them,
which meant wastage of half a gallon of petrol for nothing.
And for a packet of cigarettes at that! No, he must wait for
the shops to open.

But mister, when a cigarette calls, it calls at the top of
its voice, splitting your ear drums. Those who do not smoke
cannot hear this sound. Their ears are not attuned to this
sound. Why not ask the servant, Bhiku, for a cigarette? But
the fellow only smoked bidis. Well, a bidi should do as well
under the circumstances. But there was a snag. Who could
wake up Bhiku from his sleep that was mythic, lasting ages?
It was like digging up the whole mountain for the sake of a
pebble. Bhiku always woke up in a huff, muttering, 'What
happened? What happened?' which brought the roof down,
disturbing everybody's sleep.

Oh, yes, the night watchman was there. Sant Ram opened
the door and surveyed both sides of the road in the light of
the streetlamps but there was no sign of a night watchman

anywhere. It was going to be 4.45. Thinking that his duty was over, he must have gone away to steal some sleep and must be lying down by the side of a frustrated thief. The residents of the locality wasted money on him for nothing. There was not even a remote possibility of brigands descending over the place, especially when the police station was nearby. At last Sant Ram decided to take a cigarette from his son's packet and be done with it.

He lit the cigarette and took a long puff. It reduced his misery by half. The second puff reduced it by another quarter and the third puff still further. At this rate, the fourth puff should have given him complete satisfaction. But the law of diminishing returns also operated in smoking. One has to smoke more and more with less and less satisfaction. But he really enjoyed his smoke. Not as harsh as the brands he was accustomed to, but it was quite nice and mellow and smooth.

After finishing the cigarette, Sant Ram was overcome by a sense of guilt. Couldn't he do without a cigarette for some more time? In one's youth, one could keep one's desire under check, but not in old age They get the better of one's weak will. But why this sense of guilt? It should have made him happy that he had smoked his son's cigarette and Pal, being his son, should have also felt pleased. A petty, innocent theft is such fun. Just then Sant Ram heard Bobby muttering, 'I'll kill you! I'm going to kill you!' He was quarrelling with someone in his sleep. Lado started patting him in her semi-awake condition, sending the child back to sleep. Pal was not aware of what was going on in the bed next to his own. His snoring had stopped, but he had started whistling through his nose as if something was stuck in it.

Dhobin's voice came from his bedroom, 'Are you smoking?'

'Yes,' Sant Ram replied from where he was standing.

'You start smoking even before the day has begun. If you keep burning your liver like this, won't you fall ill?'

Sant Ram muttered to himself as if she cared for his health. These people were a curious lot. They ignored him when he needed them most and started pestering him when he wanted to be left alone.

Turning his face towards the door he said, 'Go to sleep. It's only quarter past five.'

Dhobin's voice came as if filtering through her yawn.

'No sleep for me. I've to put on the heater to boil water for bath. And there's such a huge pile of clothes to be washed.'

He heard Dhobin getting down from her bed. Yes, when women decide to leave their beds, they don't care whether someone is being disturbed. He heard her noisily flapping her bedsheet as if layers of sand were sticking to it. Then he heard the creaking of the almirah. She must be taking out money for the morning's milk. Then there was the click-clack of her sandals which pleased him no end in his younger days and did something to his heart, but now it felt like hammer strokes.

While flapping the bedsheet she had kept muttering, 'Oh God, my head is bursting with the smell of cigarette!'

'Well, well,' Sant Ram retorted, 'you're always smelling things.'

Truly enough, these days Dhobin was always complaining of smells. Maybe it had something to do with old age. Someone may be smoking three rooms away and yet the smell of the cigarette would reach her. Similarly, the smell of whisky reached her with its very first sip. Her cantankerous nature coupled with her insistence on bland food showed everybody in a bad light. Thus, already damned in her eyes, Sant Ram and the children would indulge in indiscretions to their heart's content and then gloss over it as if nothing had happened. But nothing remained hidden from Dhobin. Sometimes Pal came out in the balcony to have a puff or two, pretending that he was taking the morning air and when he turned back to look, he would find Dhobin standing behind him which killed all the pleasure of smoking. Now he had started smoking openly. He had even gone one better. He would keep a bottle of Scotch handy. On reaching home from the bar if he thought he could do with one more peg, out came the bottle. His mother often had a row with him over it, but she had ultimately given up in despair. She said, 'Not that it matters to me in any way. But the girl who falls to your lot will bemoan her fate.'

Cigarette! In fact, according to Sant Ram, the way a man or a woman's mouth smells should be similar. Otherwise, the relationship is ruined. It was on the basis of this notion that Dolly, Sant Ram's typist, was the first person whom he had chosen to offer a cigarette.

What would Pal say on getting up? Sant Ram kept mulling over this thought. Not that it really mattered. What really mattered was the want of satisfaction and lack of satiation. It was like a third person butting in between two lovers. For one thing, Sant Ram had to reckon with the fact that Pal was mean in many ways. Once he had mistakenly used Pal's shoes. A small matter, but Pal had a problem with it. He had almost discarded the shoes saying that they had become loose and were now of no use to him.

Sant Ram had felt greatly hurt. What if he had used his son's shoes just once? Hadn't Pal used his chappals scores of times and he had never grumbled over it? Rather he had felt pleased. There was an old saying that if a son started wearing his father's shoes it meant he had come of age and now could lend his father a helping hand.

The other day Pal had bought a smuggled German jersey to which Sant Ram had taken a fancy and he had tried it on himself just for the fun of it. But Dhobin spoiled the fun. She smirked as she saw him in the new outfit.

'What's the matter?" he had asked.

Suppressing her laughter Dhobin had said, 'It's nothing,' and then remarked, 'Oh, look how you strut about! Like a cock around a hen.'

This was her master stroke which pulverised him flat into the ground.

Pal, however, drove the last nail into the coffin. After wearing it for a short while Sant Ram had put the jersey back in Pal's wardrobe with great care. But next morning Pal came to him holding the jersey.

'Papa, did you wear it,' he asked.

'Why?' Sant Ram asked in a guilty tone. 'Why don't you wear it?'

'It is of no use to me now,' Pal replied. 'Just look at your stomach. Due to overstretching, the jersey's lining has lost its elasticity.'

Sant Ram felt angry and went after his son.

'Don't forget I'm your father,' he said. 'You mean I've put you to loss by wearing your jerkin just once? And what about you who have put me to loss hundred and one times? But I always glossed over it, thinking that it was all in the game. You have used my shirts, my shoes many times. I always said to myself, it's okay, my son is wearing them. That day, you flung that three-horse bosky shirt in my face . . . You are a mean, shameless brute!'

Instead of feeling contrite, Pal started to argue.

'You eat paan,' he reminded him, 'and however careful you might be, a drop of paan juice is bound to fall on the shirt. After that, the shirt is of no use to me.'

During those days his daughter, Lado, had come with her children to spend some time with her parents. She was standing there watching both father and son squabbling.

'Papa is very much like me,' she chipped in.

His younger daughter was making his bed with Bhiku's help.

'Yes, when Papa talks, he sprays paan juice over the person he is talking to,' she said. 'The real fun starts when Lado Didi and Papa are standing face to face and talking.'

'Don't forget I'm Lado's father,' Sant Ram said trying to make light of the situation. 'Can't a father take after his daughter?'

Lado laughed. Even the little Duman laughed a miserly laugh. His lungs being congenitally weak he could never laugh heartily.

'Hey, hey, Papa chews paans,' he laughed. 'It is not surprising that his shirt's front gets stained, but why the back of his shirt?' They were implying that their father ate paan not with his mouth but with his shirt.

Just then Dhobin appeared on the scene. Instead of siding with her husband against her children, she also had a dig at Sant Ram.

'Don't ask me,' she said. 'He's another Bobby. When he sits down to eat, he spills food over his shirt and when he sits down to write, he stains his clothes with ink. He gets away so easily, but it is me who has to bear the brunt of it. My hands become stiff like wood with all the washing that I've to do the whole day. My bad luck, I've wasted away my life in removing these stains.'

It was only Bobby who hadn't had his say until then. Brandishing a small bamboo stick in the air he was chasing away an imaginary foe. 'I'll kill you! I'll kill you!' he shouted. One would think it was the grandfather who was being addressed as the enemy.

Then they heard Jimmy barking. Call it a coincidence, Bhiku had just gone away to pay the electricity bill. Otherwise, he would have also commented in his Maghi accent, 'I don't believe in intruding into a husband–wife quarrel.' Obviously, his verdict would have gone against Sant Ram.

The entire family seemed to be unhappy with him. It was not so a few years ago. But his world had changed since he had started incurring losses in business. Nobody seemed to appreciate what he said. Perhaps they thought he was getting senile, that he should not inflict his presence on them but keep out of their sight. Better still, he should oblige them by departing from this world. But where was he to go? He had sacrificed his life, his everything for the family. Work, work, work and no recreation. A work maniac, perhaps he was going insane. If not, he had become highly idiosyncratic for sure. Does a man know that he is going mad? It is only his expression that betrays him to others.

May God protect a man from incurring a financial loss. If he has to face this misfortune it should be while he is in full vigour of his youth and not in his declining years. He was sorry that his fatherly image was gradually getting tarnished in the eyes of his children and his wife.

Pal woke up at eight. Seeing him, Sant Ram felt a bit unnerved. A man who says he is not afraid is really afraid at heart. Sant Ram knew in his mind that he was afraid of his son. He didn't wish matters to come to a head. His son should not declare openly that he wanted to live separately from the family. Pal was of course always looking for an opportunity to find fault with his father. Sant Ram had smoked his son's cigarette and how upset he was over this trifle. People would laugh at it. But what a mental tug-of-war?

Before lifting his morning cup of tea, Pal shot a quick glance at his father and wished him to which Sant Ram responded with a gentle nod of his head and lowered his eyes. He wanted Pal to turn his face in the other direction so that he could have a good look at him. But Pal did not turn his face; it remained lazily fixed in his direction. Unnerved, Sant Ram hid his face behind a copy of the *Hindustan Times*. Shifting the newspaper away from his face Sant Ram stole a glance at his son—he found him slurping his tea and then putting the cup back in the saucer. Picking up the packet of cigarettes he proceeded towards the toilet.

So far so good. Pal had not opened his packet in his presence. He would only find out when he was in the toilet. Anxious to watch his son's expression when he returned from the toilet, Sant Ram lingered there.

'Aren't you going to have your bath?' Dhobin asked him.

'Yes, I'll go,' Sant Ram replied testily. 'Perhaps my last bath.'

Dhobin looked at Sant Ram in surprise. And then realizing that his bark was worse than his bite, she got busy in preparing breakfast.

After a while when Pal returned from the toilet, Sant Ram found that his teeth were clenched, and his forehead seemed to have receded a little. He was hurriedly soaping his hands at the washbasin. Was he in a hurry to go somewhere?

Sant Ram watched his son's face in the mirror. He seemed to be frothing at the mouth. No, it was the soap foam that had settled on his face while he was washing his hands.

As Pal was returning from the washbasin, Dhobin called out to him, 'So you again drank last night before coming home?'

Pal made no reply. Then he said, 'And I'll drink again tonight.'

Dhobin became tense. She was not the one to get cowed down so easily. 'If you come drunk today, I'll not allow you to step into the house,' she said.

'Who wants to step into your house?' Pal retorted. 'In this prison house? I'm going to fix up a room in Golf Links.'

Dhobin's powerful voice hit him, 'Get out! Get out just now!' Sant Ram felt as if life had departed from his body.

'Keep quiet!' he barked at Dhobin, gathering his wits. 'What rot are you talking? Is it your house?'

'Yes, it's mine!' Dhobin replied, her voice fixed on the same octave of the musical scale at which Sant Ram had addressed her.

'If he wants to go, he is free to leave. You can also go if you like. I'm grateful to you, father and son, who have taught me to live,' she started nagging.

What Sant Ram feared most had come to pass. He would keep smouldering at his son's ways, but he never gave vent to his feelings openly. It is quite easy to say, 'Go away' but more difficult to say, 'Come back'.

Pal attended to his morning chores with quick despatch. He was shaving so rapidly that it left many nicks on his cheeks, drawing blood which he quickly wiped away with his towel. Why was he so gruff with his mother? When he spoke harshly to his mother it pained Sant Ram and when his mother paid him back in the same coin his distress was no less acute. But the relations between mother and son were of a different kind and came naturally to them. They fell out and patched up without leaving any rancour behind. But today, Pal's tone was different. If he went away, he would be gone for good.

'Who wants to return to his prison house?'

What did he mean by that? Pal had not said it in so many words, but Sant Ram could see he was greatly annoyed when he could not find his things. He was very touchy in such matters—shoes, clothes, cigarettes.

He rushed through his bath, dressed quickly and passed by his father on his way out. Sant Ram called after him, but he feigned as if he had not heard him. He had not even glanced at the morning's newspaper. Contemptuously throwing his State Express packet out of the window, he moved towards the door. Since Dhobin had had a row with him she did not remind him about his breakfast. But Sant Ram tried to stop him.

'Son, have your breakfast,' he said.

'No!' Pal replied gruffly and barged out. The way he banged the door behind him shook Sant Ram's very soul.

Pal was gone when Sant Ram and Dhobin started squabbling. He reproached her for her indecorous behaviour while she kept cursing him and shedding tears. She raked up old memories. From what she was saying, it appeared that she hadn't spent a single happy day since coming to this house as a bride. She regarded herself as a most unfortunate woman while on the contrary Sant Ram believed that he had given her all the comforts of life. If she had at all seen some bad times, he had softened the blow by sharing her tribulations and woes. But as her recital revealed, she was making him responsible for all the family ills.

She said, 'First you made me a drudge for your orphaned brothers and sisters. Then you foisted your friends on me for there was always one guest or the other arriving to stay with you. I cooked with one hand and held the baby with the other. I did all this for those ungrateful wretches. Now you have thrown me before these butchers. You were so liberal with your money that these favourite children of yours are given to extravagance and they have turned into nincompoops. Yes, all of them. And look at your son's audacity! How he glared at me and that too in your presence!'

Instead of going full force at Dhobin, Sant Ram adopted a defensive attitude. Was he really worth his salt, he wondered! If he wore the pants in the family, why couldn't he shield his wife against his children, and his children against his wife's onslaughts?

Lado, who had just emerged from her bedroom was watching the goings-on with interest. If only she had woken up a little earlier and stopped her brother from going. While asking her mother to calm down, she gave her father a meaningful glance which unnerved him more. Bobby had started crying. She phoned her husband to come and take them away. A hush fell over the room which was punctuated only by Dhobin's sobbing. Lado and the other children had realized that being an everyday affair it did not merit much attention. Sant Ram thought he was not the only person involved in it and hence why should he of all persons rake his head over it? Pal had been seething with anger which had in fact exploded in a verbal duel with his mother. Dhobin had only sparked off action; Pal had been waiting for any handy excuse, and his mother had obliged him in this regard. Since the morning, he was angry, maybe because he had found only one cigarette in his packet.

Sant Ram entered his office without acknowledging his staff's greetings. But they didn't mind. The saheb must be in one of those sullen moods. 'Again?' someone quipped. 'As if he's ever in a good mood!' his colleague remarked.

On entering his office, the first thing that Sant Ram did was to ask his peon Chandu to get him a packet of cigarettes. Normally, Chandu always kept a packet handy in anticipation of his master's demand.

Hanging his coat on the peg and tearing off the celophane wrapper, Sant Ram took out a cigarette from the pack. After lighting the cigarette, he got down to work but his mind was not in his work. An unknown fear seemed to have dulled his mind. Reclining back in his revolving chair, he placed his legs on the table and took a few long puffs at the cigarette. Was he really responsible for ruining his family's life? he asked himself. In spite of his age, he had kept abreast of times. Instead of being a father and a husband he had been a friend to them. Maybe this was where he had gone wrong. He had often behaved in a manner which was alien to the old-fashioned thinking of men of his age. When Lado had started going to college, he had warned her by saying, 'Lado, there's co-education in that college. There will be boys rubbing shoulders with girls and they will try to come closer. These days a new trend has set in our lives. They call it "having a good time". A good time is a basic difference between boys and girls. No responsibility devolves upon the male if he refuses to accept it in the light of his own norms. But a woman is weighed down by such responsibilities for the simple reason that it is she is the one who has to bear the burden of the child. For this reason, women are inherently conservative in their outlook; it is in their very nature. It is correct in a way that women should not cast their lot with men who cannot take care of them and their children.'

Through the haze of cigarette smoke, he visualized the face of his daughter as she had sat there listening to him, half understanding his message. Perhaps she was wondering what rot Papa was talking about. What he was trying to put across to her was known to every woman. How outmoded his thinking was, she seemed to be saying. But Sant Ram argued with himself that if he was dubbed as outmoded in his thinking why he kept hearing things which were true in the times of the Buddha as much as his own. There were some things which were eternally true. Did man learn only through experience and by making mistakes?

Pal was going on to be twenty-five. When Sant Ram directly asked him if he had any experience of women, he had made a clean breast of it. Apart from being his son, he was also like a good friend to him. That had set Sant Ram worrying about the escapades of his son. Sex, as he knew, could lead to serious consequences. One false step and it could cast its shadow over his son's entire life. That is why they have erected a wall between men and women in the matter of friendship and matrimony.

After answering Sant Ram's question, Pal watched him with a deadpan expression. Maybe he was even laughing up his sleeves. Talking of experiences—was Papa living in the nineteenth century? All the same, it was clear to Sant Ram that though the world lay open before his son, he was still ignorant of many things, and it was his father who had removed the cobwebs from his mind and made him capable of facing the complexities of life. And today just because he had stolen a cigarette from his packet, he had turned his face against him.

Perhaps he was mistaken, Sant Ram thought. Maybe his son was so preoccupied with other things in the morning that he had left home in a hurry. Normally he left the house at ten but that morning he went away at half past nine.

Sant Ram was negotiating a high-stakes deal. If the deal came through, it would put everything straight. Pal would become his cheerful self again and lose his ire against his father. They would all make a holiday trip to Kullu.

A cigarette! Just one cigarette!

Sant Ram's blood boiled again and again. No, he hadn't forgiven his son nor condoned himself. A father who hated his son, sure enough, hated himself also. The reverse of it could be equally true. A son who hated his father hated himself also as much. Pal in fact did not hate his father. He only hated himself because in this rat race he had not been able to forage ahead of his father. He would not relent until he had achieved his purpose and proved to his father that as compared to him, the old man was unworthy of his business. Sant Ram rang the bell for Miss Dolly, his secretary.

Today she had permed her hair and had draped a white sari around a tight blouse. She knew Sant Ram had a liking for white colour. Sant Ram did not look up at her. She knew these days the boss was a bit indifferent towards her and she had in turn adopted a business-like attitude towards him. It was out of sheer goodness that she deigned to talk to an old man like him. She worked for him and was paid for it. Why should extraneous considerations intrude upon her work?

'Yes, Sir?' Dolly tried to catch his attention.

Sant Ram looked up from his papers. 'Dolly, you look charming!' he wanted to say but desisted. But next moment his heart which was fluttering to escape from the morning's travails got entangled in Dolly's attractive hair. Women are a strange lot. If a man's heart does not flow with the current, the women would drown it in the stream's crosscurrents. But Sant Ram quickly took his eyes off the dark mass surging down Dolly's head and turned his attention to the Drakshava calendar hanging on his right as if he was looking for a date. Women understand men's ways and they keep their eyes fixed on their prey. And a man knows to his cost that the moment he looks straight into a woman's eyes he is doomed. Therefore, he looks into the void to find an escape. But for how long? For the hundredth part of a minute, he inadvertently glanced at her and that was the fateful moment when his heart stopped fluttering for good.

'Where's Perkins these days?' he asked. Perkins was Dolly's brother—John Perkins.

'He is here,' Dolly replied, forcing a faint smile on her face. She regarded the question as an overture a man makes before coming to the real issue. But she still wanted to be strictly businesslike. What kind of fun was it? Call, when you feel like it, spurn when your mood is off! He had completely ignored her for the past so many days and today he was trying to humour her by asking about her brother.

But how long could she hold on to her businesslike pretence?

In a moment of absent-mindedness, Sant Ram offered Dolly a cigarette. A tremor ran through Dolly's body, more agitating than her wavy perms. Holding back her advancing hand she said, 'No, thanks!' her bosom heaving in anger.

'Dolly!' Sant Ram fixed his eyes into hers.

Perhaps he wanted to tell her that his family and for that matter the whole world had given him a raw deal and she was the only one who professed love for him even though it was nothing but a pretence in expectation of a raise in her salary. 'Of course, you understood me all right,' he said to himself, 'but for a moment I thought it was genuine love, something divine. There was the same difference in it which one finds between an ordinary kiss and a stolen one. In which the past loss and the prospects of future gain blur into each other.'

Dolly looked at Sant Ram but for which he would have grown still older and sustained many more losses. It would have equally recoiled on Dolly, putting her job in jeopardy. She reflected over the matter from the deep layers of compassion which had a motherly touch. As a woman she was mother to Sant Ram, in fact to all the males of the world, irrespective of whether they were young or old.

'All right,' she said, taking the cigarette from Sant Ram. He lighted the cigarette for her. She took a long puff at her cigarette and taking a step forward looked at Sant Ram through the smoke screen.

'If Perkins is in town ask him to . . .'

Dolly stopped in her track, waiting for Sant Ram to complete his sentence.

'. . . ask Perkins to get me a carton of State Express. I'll pay him later.'

'All right,' Dolly said and stepping back, walked out of the room.

As Sant Ram reached home, in spite of being armed with a carton of State Express, he found himself rushing in with great trepidation. Dhobin or Lado would not have understood the state of his mind.

Pal arrived soon after. The uncertainty which had gripped Sant Ram's mind suddenly ceased. On the other hand, he felt so calm and composed like a man who on entering a heated room in winter suddenly stops shivering. Then a fear again gripped him. Had Pal come to collect his things to move into his room in Golf Links? But he saw no signs of it. Then why had he returned so early? He never came before one or two at night. Was it the prodigal son returning? Had he suddenly turned a new leaf? But why was he so withdrawn and reserved. He could chat with Lado, play with Bobby. The mean fellow, he must be full of animus against him. Pal went to his room and returned immediately. He took out a packet from his pocket and held it before his father.

'What's it?' Sant Ram asked. 'Russian Sobroyan.'

'You mean Russian cigarettes? And a full packet?' Sant Ram's face was flushed. His son was taking it out on him! In lieu of a cigarette, he was offering him a full packet. In other words, he was slapping him in his face. Sant Ram flung the packet in his son's face.

'Wretch! Ruffian! *Harami!*' he cried. 'You think I can't buy my own cigarettes? I can even buy them for you. I've not sunk so low as you think. Even now I can buy a hundred skunks like you and walk off carrying them in my pocket. Bastard!'

Pal looked on, utterly bewildered. His hand went to his face where the packet had hit him. A blood mark had appeared on his cheek.

'Papa!' he said.

Lado came running from her room. 'Papa!' she cried trying to figure out what had happened.

'What's going on here?' Dhobin said emerging from her room.

'Nothing, nothing!' Sant Ram said pushing them back. 'Let me first settle account with this wretch. His back is itching for a beating.' Then he got scared at the sight of blood on Pal's cheek. He almost lost his wits for it was not easy for him to bear the sight of his son's blood. To the onlookers it was his son's blood whereas in actuality it was his own blood—the blood of his own blood.

Frothing at his mouth he advanced towards Pal. 'I'm going to kill you!' he cried. 'Leave me, leave me alone! Today I'll set an example.'

'Sons have been murdering their fathers. Today it'll be a mother murdering a son. Wretch, what haven't I given you in life? When you went away to pursue your studies, I sent you 400 rupees every month. Then you dropped out midway and my friend maintained you for two years and induced you to complete your studies. He did it out of consideration for me. Otherwise, who cares for a rag that you are! Even then I kept sending you money so that my dear son may not run into difficulties. And what did you do with that money? You wasted it by leading a fast life—hotels, restaurants and all that. As you yourself boast, your friends called you Prince—a prince enjoying life on his father's money! You got a compartment in BA and failed to get your degree for having failed in Hindi, yes, in Hindi of all subjects! I pleaded with you again and again that it was a question of just one subject, and you should make one more attempt. But you were dead set against it. It seemed you had become allergic to my suggestion. Despite that I maintained you, an idler that you were. Had it been some Western country, your father would have kicked you in your buttocks and showed you the door the moment you crossed eighteen. It is only in our country that one can get away with such foolhardiness. When you happened to be out of pocket, I would slip ten or twenty rupees in your pocket when your mother was not watching. Now she turns round and says I am responsible for spoiling you people. Well, to quote your own words, you had yourself once said that a concubine would be anytime better than the kind of woman father had for a wife. Tell me, didn't you say so? A son who can talk such sacrilege about his mother what regard can he have for his father? Do you know when you abuse your mother it boomerangs on you? You must know I'm again going to make good one day. You will feel proud of me and draw your chair near mine. But I know you too well by now. I'll not indulge you anymore.'

Pal's lips quivered. 'Papa, what have I done?' he asked in a subdued voice.

'You?' Sant Ram said raising his voice. 'You have called me names, something which nobody has dared to do. They all know I can tear them apart to pieces with my bare hands. And look at your bravado. You fling a packet just because I've smoked one of your cigarettes.'

'A cigarette?' Pal asked.

'Yes, a cigarette,' Sant Ram said. 'Surely, you know it. I had smoked one of your State Express in the morning.'

'No, I know nothing about it.'

Sant Ram's body shook. But before he could fall, Pal held him in his arms and burst into tears.

'Papa, forgive me,' he said between tears. 'Papa, forgive me.'

The next morning, on waking up as usual, Sant Ram again felt the urge for a cigarette. Without disturbing Dhobin in her sleep, he walked into the adjoining room where Pal, Lado and her son were sleeping. He switched on the zero lamp and looked at their faces. In the dim light of the lamp, they looked angelic—one face more beautiful than the other. Today Bobby's arms were not around his mother's neck. He was sleeping peacefully without a care in the world.

Sant Ram thought to himself that before sending Lado to college he had given her a massive dose of advice. But if she had done something indiscreet, would he have thrown her on the road? Had Pal's escapade miscarried wouldn't he have put him through his paces? This talk of morals and culture were idle words. And his progeny and those living outside were like children at play who fell and got up to play again.

Dhobin was a fool. She knew nothing except washing clothes.

Sant Ram took out the carton of State Express and placed it by the side of his son's pillow. Because of the fight with him, he had not been able to give it to him last night. On waking up when he would see the carton lying by his side how happy he would feel?

Then Sant Ram took out a Russian cigarette from his pocket and lighting it took long pulls at it, blowing smoke from his mouth. A zero-power light is quite dim, and the haze of cigarette smoke made it dimmer still. In that light his children looked even more angelic. Sant Ram felt like bending down and kissing Pal's face. But then he remembered the saying that one should not kiss the face of a sleeping child.

The Russian cigarette's fourth puff proved quite heady. Sant Ram's eyes became dazed as he looked at his son as if he was getting intoxicated. Waving away the smoke he again looked at his children's faces and proceeded towards the puja room to pray.

13

Maithuna

The bazaar had become more extended, or the business seemed to have shrunk. The road rose a little bit towards the west, embracing the sky, and then it fell, indicating the shore where the world ended. That point could be reached with a single giant leap. We can die with the same hands that provide us the support for living.

After tirelessly spending the whole day searching for things, Magan Takley, a dealer for original or recycled art objects, had found only two things—a Florentine statuette and a Jamini Roy painting. There was a slim chance that a film producer might rent the figurine. But he was not very optimistic about the Jamini Roy painting. Perhaps even that would not be a dead asset. He would tuck it away somewhere in his shop, and one day, his sons or grandsons would rake in a fortune from its sale. He had heard that an undiscovered Leonardo da Vinci could fetch millions of dollars. His eyes shone with excitement at the thought of making millions. But he forgot that he was a balding man on the wrong side of forty. And a bachelor at that. There was little chance of his having a son now, not to talk of grandsons. But, like any other Hindu, despite wallowing in the spiritual tradition, he was a money-grabber at heart. Outwardly, he professed that money was contemptible—akin to the dirt of his palm—and yet he secretly lusted for it. There was nothing strange about it. No one surpasses a Hindu in the worship of money. On a Diwali night, one could find a one-rupee coin tucked under the platter, along with the lit lamp and bathed in milk. On Dussehra day, the car of a Hindu is decorated with one hundred kinds of flowers. Men and women gather to go to the Lakshmi temple for prayers. For the money, a loving brother like Joseph and a beautiful wife like Padmini are available for sale.

In front of Magan's shop was Saraja's store who sold Eve's batteries. The shop was partially hidden behind a peepul tree at whose roots flabby, jelly-soft Hindus poured jugfuls of water-diluted milk every morning, making the front of the store slushy. Saraj did not protest. After the partition when his family decided to stay in India, Saraju was under pressure to show regard for Hindu customs. All the same, he looked indulgently at the street dogs who pissed at the roots of the tree in passing, idly raising a hind leg. They must have been Muslims in their past lives and were now paying back the Hindus for butchering them during the communal riots of forty-seven.

Saraja looked as if he was eating droppings of the peepul tree. The reason for that was not the sluggishness of the business or hunger. Saraja ate everything that was taboo for Muslims, the circumscribed ones, fond of eating and drinking and sex. Whatever their mental level, they think and behave like wanderers. When they live in India, they talk about

Pakistan. When they live in Pakistan, they continuously harp on the tune . . . my Maula please call me to Medina. They are not interested in anything else. Magan Takley always thought about it. Their Allah must be having a good time. And our Bhagwan lives in the skies, away from the world. Saraj unconsciously could be a tantric—those who seek a drop of immortality by waking up their kundalini. They try to transcend both the sexual and spiritual planes by engaging in deeply meditative practices, including indulgence in intimate sex. What happens to a woman is not their concern. How can you achieve moksha when your partner is thirsty and hungry and tortured? How can you attain godhood in this manner? Man can find that drop, but what about the woman? A water drop is not the pearl as the seashell is not the pearl. A pearl is formed when the water drops fall into the seashell.

The night was fast approaching. Along with the darkness, the outer world had crept closer. Waliati Ram, the silk merchant, Budhashab, who hailed from Kashmir, and even Chakrapani from Udipi, who ran a refreshment shop, had closed for the day. Maybe Chakrapani ran out of idli dosa, sambhar, rava masala, etc. Only Saraj's battery shop was still open. Who knows what he was expecting? People need batteries at night. He opens his store in the early hours, which are part of the night—the last part of the night. There was no morning anymore. Communists have taken it away by talking about the dawn of revolution. Maybe, Saraj was waiting for the tourist agent, Michael, to plan a trip to Khajuraho to make some money on the side. Money was not Michael's primary concern in making the trip. Saraj was also not after money. He had an eye for Western women looking for a lover who could elevate them to the level of a Mumtaz Mahal, with the help of a local man who possessed a Shah Jahan's temperament. The purpose was to awaken the *maithuna* (the image of sexual union of a male and a female, mostly of Shiva and Shakti, or the symbolic act of energy transfer through the union of opposing forces) of Khajuraho.

'Hello, sweetie pie!' Saraj startled Magan, who turned and looked at the speaker. Saraj was illiterate, but he had picked up some English expressions from foreign tourists.

It must be a signal that Kirti had arrived, Magan thought. Kirti was dark and slight but firmly built; she perpetually wore a sad expression on her face. Wearing a striking magenta sari, she approached Magan. It was as if a fragment of darkness had taken a definite shape. She always came after nightfall, as if she were trying to hide from her shadow. She still found Saraj standing outside his shop, his whistle chasing her. And she always walked past him without a side glance. Kirti was not given to too much talking. One had to ask questions, and then she would reply in monosyllables, 'yes' or 'no'. Magan disliked Saraj for trying to take liberties with her. Many a time, Saraj had thrown hints at Magan. 'I don't know whether you have fallen for her or not? What are you waiting for? She's game and so young. Have a go at her. If you keep hovering around her like a pigeon, she'll fly away.' Angered, Magan had bluntly asked Saraj to shut up.

Magan was in a tricky business, having many layers where truth and falsehoods overlapped. When Kirti brought him decorative woodwork or a figurine, he would try to pick holes in it. He would tell her that such pieces were hard to sell. On hearing this, Kirti would pull a long face. By deprecating her handiwork, Magan would trick her into selling it for ten rupees, what was worth a hundred. Then he would 'season' the piece as an antique and sell it for an inflated price of something like 500 rupees.

Kirti had not attended an art school. She had learned her work from her father Narain, who was an accomplished craftsman. He had accompanied Bhavji, James Bergs and others on their excursions to Nepal and traditional art centres of India, searching for antiques that ultimately found their way into foreign museums and the antique shops of New York, Chicago and elsewhere. Tired of his unremitting peregrinations, Narain had, at last, called it a day and had settled down to create genuine art. Kirti would watch her father at work, lending him a hand when needed. To his great chagrin, Narain learned that old images fetched much more money than the new ones that he carved and chiselled with care within the confines of his room. He made little money and died living like a pauper.

One day while working on the image of Goddess Jagdamba, he injured himself with his chisel and died of tetanus, while getting treatment in a nearby cantonment hospital. They say he died a dog's death; deservedly so. While making the goddess's image, his hands would have lingered for days over her bosom, hips and thighs. Narain had also made Goddess Durga's image, said to be the most powerful in the Hindu pantheon. Undoubtedly, her wrath had fallen on him for taking liberties with her body.

'What have you brought?' Magan Takley asked Kirti. She took out a carved piece of wood from under the pallu of her sari and gingerly placed it on the desk for Magan's examination. He pushed a chair towards her, but she kept standing.

'How is your mother?'

Kirti didn't reply. Averting her face, she looked out at the road where it suddenly dipped. When she turned to look at Magan, her eyes were wet. Kirti's mother was in the cantonment hospital—the same one where her father Narain had died. The mother had stomach cancer. They had made a hole in her stomach by passing a tube through it and connected it to a large bottle which drained out the pus from her festering intestines.

'Again, the same thing,' Magan said, shaking his head. 'I've told you so many times that people are not interested anymore in such things. What have you got here? A recumbent Vishnu, a royal cobra, swaying its hood over the god and Goddess Lakshmi massaging his feet . . .'

Kirti turned her sorrowful gaze on Magan as if she had asked him about the object that would please him.

'The same that people openly do these days.'

'What do people do these days?' Kirti's lips moved, but her voice was hardly audible like a canary whose beak is seen moving, but no voice comes out of it.

Magan hesitated, fumbling for words. 'Make a Gandhi, make a Nehru.' And then suddenly realizing that he had blundered, he quickly corrected himself.

'A nude, for instance,' he said exhibiting his brighter side.

'A nude?'

'Yes, a nude. People like nudes.'

Kirti fell silent. She was a naive and simple girl and her mind failed to grasp the implications of such a request. At that moment, she wondered whether Magan would buy her wooden piece and if he did, how much he would pay for it.

She became thoughtful and then said haltingly, 'I don't know how to make a nude.'

'Come on, don't tell me that. Your father made them by the score.'

'Oh, those? But they were images of goddesses.'

'What difference does it make?' Magan said. 'A goddess is a woman too. All you must do is to avoid putting that sacred garland round her neck. For God's sake don't do that. Your father did it and paid the price for it. He died a horrible death.'

Kirti's body shook with an unknown fear. She felt that she would not be able to stand, and yet she refused to sit. As she stood there leaning against the chair, Magan watched her body. Like the other female statues, he realized that Narain had carved her body like that of a goddess. Magan's mind was in turmoil at his helplessness in not being able to communicate with her. Little did he know that the girl standing before him was also struggling because of her helplessness. Her throat felt parched.

'I . . . I don't have a model,' she said.

'Model?' Magan drew closer to her. 'You can have them by the hundred. Show any young, beautiful girl a glittering coin and she is game.' Kirti did not say anything.

'To earn money, one must be prepared to spend,' he said. Magan's remark deepened the sadness on Kirti's face. Tears came to her eyes.

It always happens with a woman. She evokes reactions of either the husband or the father in a man. Magan stretched out his hands to embrace her, saying, 'Kirti, you've got nothing to worry about as long as I'm there.' But Kirti pushed his hands away. Magan felt slighted but he kept a straight face as if nothing had happened. He still held the trump card. He picked up the woodwork from the desktop. 'Here, take it away,' he said giving it to her. 'I'm afraid it's of no use to me.'

Kirti looked down gloomily and then raised her head. 'Next time I'll bring a nude,' she said. 'Keep this one as my gift for you.'

Magan smiled in satisfaction. There was a grave look on Kirti's face. He lifted the top of his table and took out a crumpled ten-rupee note.

'Here, take it,' he said.

'Only ten rupees?'

'That's all I can give you. I told you I've no use for it.'

'With this money . . .' She didn't complete the sentence. Her voice sounded very tired.

'I know what you wanted to say,' Magan said. 'This money won't pay for even one bottle of medicine. Just get me that nude. I'll pay you handsomely.'

As Kirti left the shop, her lips were dry and she was breathing heavily. She passed in front of Saraj's store, with her head held high, nostrils flaring, and rebellion brewing in her heart. Michael had joined Saraj, and standing outside the shop, they were drinking together. As Kirti passed by, Saraj said something that Magan failed to understand, but he knew it must have been a raunchy joke. Kirti ignored Saraj out of sheer defiance.

Magan had already pulled down the shutters of his shop. He was closely examining the woodwork he had bought from Kirti. It was a beautiful piece of art. The cobra's hood took his breath away. Kirti had deftly injected different colours into it, which gently rippled into each other. Vishnu had everything that a devout woman looks for. Lakshmi, however, sat huddled and had been hazily delineated. It appeared that Kirti was not fully acquainted with the female form.

Firmly holding Kirti's woodwork in his hand, Magan picked up a knife and engraved the words, '*Sad Ham Nama*' on the image. Then he took it to the back room and, digging into the loose earth, pulled out an idol, one of Kirti's earlier creations. Depositing the new piece in the hole, he sprinkled *katha* water and covered it with the earth. Then he turned his attention to the image that he had just taken out. He rubbed off the dirt around it and examined it minutely. Numerous fissures were running down the figurine, making it look centuries old. The next day, when he showed it to some tourists, they were delighted. He told them that there was a mention of the image in Kalidasa's Raghuvaṃśa. Raghu had founded a city called Trikut in the Konkan region where this type of image had originally been discovered. Many of them had found their way to the private collection of the Wadiar Raja of Mysore. Sheer luck had brought this image Magan's way. Magan Takley was able to sell the image to a tourist for 500 rupees. He recalled he had paid Kirti only five rupees for it.

Within a week, Kirti came back with a nude. She looked somewhat troubled. She was coughing wheezily as if she had caught a chill. Time and again, her hand went to her throat covered with a thick wad of cotton wool around which she had wrapped a filthy rag.

As was her habit, she placed the piece before Magan for his inspection without saying a word. This time she had not carved it in wood but had shaped it from stone. She looked expectantly at Magan. He went into raptures over it. His only objection was that it was relatively small. If she had made it life-size, both would have gained immensely.

Magan lifted the Yakshi and studied it closely. Despite her best efforts, Kirti had not succeeded in making a real nude. The figure was covered with a fine piece of wet cloth. In some places, the fabric clung tightly against the body, and in others, it hung loosely, exposing the Yakshi's body despite the best efforts to hide her nudity.

Taking his eyes off the Yakshi (female version of Yaksha, the Goddess of Wealth), Magan looked at Kirti. 'Wah, you have done wonders!' he exclaimed. Kirti looked at him abashed and pulled the magenta sari tightly over her body.

Magan found her secret. Standing naked before a mirror, she had worked on the idol by watching her reflection. Once in a while, she had thrown a wet piece of cloth over her body and that was how she had caught a chill.

'How is your mother?" he asked.

Kirti's face turned dark with anger. It took her some time to regain her composure.

'So, you managed to find a model?' Magan said, swaying his head. Kirti lowered her eyes and then looked out of the shop at the road where it abruptly dipped. Now was the time for him to take advantage of the situation. He would hug her and praise her for her handiwork. But even as these thoughts arose in his mind, Magan was thinking about money. If he hugged her, it might induce her to raise her price. He decided that he would pay her a hundred rupees for the nude. The bottle of medicine and all the other things would cost much less. But what if Kirti demanded a higher figure? He started getting apprehensive.

'How much should I pay you for it?' He casually tossed the question at her.

Kirti cast a fleeting glance at him. 'I must have fifty rupees for it,' she said.

'Fifty rupees?'

'Yes, not a paisa less.

Magan lifted the roll-top, and taking out forty rupees, he placed them before Kirti.

'I agree to your price,' he said. 'But I've only forty rupees at the moment. Come for the balance sometime later.'

'All right,' Kirti said and quietly picked up her money.

She was starting to go when Magan stopped her.

'Listen,' he said. Kirti stopped and looked back at him with an air of helpless surrender. I depend on you, she seemed to say.

'I hope this money will suffice for your needs,' Magan added.

Kirti nodded and made a gesture that seemed to say that she had no alternative but to resign herself to her fate. Then she told him that her mother would soon have surgery. She would require a couple of hundred rupees for that operation.

'I say . . .' she halted and then added in a listless tone. 'I wish my mother dies. The sooner she dies, the better for her.' She stood there, raking the earth with her toe. 'Death is surely preferable to such a miserable existence.'

Magan looked into her eyes. Instead of a girl of eighteen, there was a mature woman of forty standing before him.

'May I suggest?' Magan said, stepping closer to her. 'Make a maithuna for me. Then, I'll bear all the expenses of your mother's operation.'

'Maithuna?' Kirti's voice shook, and she looked wide-eyed at Magan.

'Yes, this type of image is in great demand.'

'But . . .'

I know your difficulty,' Magan swayed his head, evincing sympathy.

'Since you are innocent of sex, you will do well to make a trip to Khajuraho and have a good look at the images on the temple walls. I'm prepared to give you some money in advance for the trip.'

'You?' Kirti gave Magan a contemptuous look. 'Just now, you said that you were short of money.'

Magan was not someone who someone could be caught on the wrong foot. 'It's true that I have no money to spare. I have reserved some cash to pay the rent.' He tried to give her money, but she went away without accepting it.

As soon as Kirti left, Magan retired to the back room with the Yakshi and examined it closely. He took a small mallet and chipped off a part of the Yakshi's nose with a measured stroke. And after that, a leg. He also damaged some embellishments around the idol's neck. Then tying a thick string around the idol, he lowered it into a cauldron for an acid bath. As the fumes rose, he pulled out the idol and dipped it in freshwater. Yakshi's features had become hazy, and its body had become corroded. The acid had even eaten into it in some places, making tiny holes. Now the idol could easily fetch Magan a thousand rupees as an antique.

After a month, Kirti came back to Magan with another piece of art. And most unexpectedly, it was a maithuna, a life-size piece carefully packaged in a gunny bag and carried on a handcart. The cartman deposited it in Magan's store and departed after taking his carting charges.

With bated breath, Magan Takley cut the strings from the mouth of the bag and quickly removed the tarpaulin in which the piece had been wrapped.

It was the last word in perfection. Magan's mouth dried up. He thought that Kirti would be too embarrassed to look at the piece in his presence. But she stood before him, her face devoid of any feeling or any trace of excitement. The woman in the stone lay prone in a state of frenzy while the man, supine, held her by her shoulders. Magan's eyes perfunctorily surveyed the piece. He was certain that he would savour its sensuous beauty once he was alone in the shop.

'How much money do you require for your mother's surgery?' he asked Kirti.

'I don't want any money for the operation. I want it for myself.'

'For yourself? What about your mother?'

'She's dead. She died last week.'

Magan tried to show an expression of grief. But Kirti paid no attention.

'I want a thousand rupees for it,' she said.

'A thousand rupees?' Magan was astounded. 'Would anybody ever pay a thousand rupees for it?'

'Yes,' Kirti said in a firm voice. 'I've already talked to someone. Maybe I could even get more. But I had given you my word.'

'I . . . I can only give you 500 rupees.'

"No.' Her gaze wandered out of the shop as if she were looking for a cartman.

'I'll add 200 rupees more,' Magan said trying to regain her notice.

'No, nothing less than a thousand rupees.

Magan was surprised. She looked so self-assured. Had she made a trip to Khajuraho? Did she meet some tourists over there? One must keep an artisan away from his market.

He lifted the roll-top and counted 800 rupees. He placed them before Kirti. She counted the notes and flung them back at Magan.

'Haven't I told you not a rupee less than a thousand rupees?'

'All right, I'll make it 900 rupees."

'No.'

'Nine hundred and fifty? Nine hundred and seventy-five?'

Seeing the grim determination in Kirti's eyes, he handed her ten 100-rupee notes and lurched towards the image as if in a state of intoxication.

Magan looked closely at the woman in the maithuna, and it suddenly dawned upon him that it was Kirti herself. But why were there tears in her eyes? Was she overwhelmed by the bliss of union? Or was it the pain of forcible possession? Or again, was it that blend of pleasure and pain that encompasses all humanity? Magan's eyes turned to the man. He looked outwardly gentle, but something seemed to show a brute underneath. Why had Kirti so transparently brought out the animal in that man? It was undoubtedly a sexual union. But it was not a union between humans in the lap of nature. It was bewildering. Perhaps it was for the best. This piece of art would fetch him a lot of money.

Magan Takley raised the wick of his lamp to have a better look at the man. 'I've seen this man somewhere!' he suddenly exclaimed.

Kirti made no reply.

'You?' Magan said as the full force of recognition hit him. 'Did you go out with Saraj?'

Stepping up to him, Kirti slapped Magan. And then, holding the notes in her hand, she walked out of the shop.

14

The Trauma of a Lost Child

Ghamandi loudly banged on the door. His mother was lying tensely awake, waiting for him. She was painfully aware that having missed the first hour's sleep, she would stay awake the whole winter night that would drag on drearily, without an end. Apart from counting the reeds of which the ceiling was made, she would listen to the ceaseless chirping of crickets that made her sink into despair. Although the banging was persistent, she was in no hurry to get up from her bed. Not because she wanted to register her protest by keeping Ghamandi standing in the cold as a punishment for coming late, but because he had arrived and, therefore, he should be patient.

Being a little decrepit and experiencing a pleasant lethargy, a sweet droopiness akin to a twilight state between sleep and wakefulness, her mind was filled with thoughts. After a while, she sat up in her cot, and lying on her stomach, she dangled her feet on the other side of the cot and heaved a sigh of relief. Dragging her feet, she came to the candle stand, and after raising its wick, she went back and searched for her snuffbox from between the strings of the cot. Taking two pinches of snuff and inhaling them contentedly, she proceeded towards the door. At the third round of banging, she felt as if the door was going to crash and fall to the ground.

'Stop! You ruined one!' she said, thoroughly peeved. 'You keep me waiting endlessly, and you can't wait for a moment!'

Standing on the other side of the door, his mother's rebuke, piercing through his muffler, ravaged Ghamandi's ears. 'You ruined one!' Ghamandi was fond of this rebuke. His mother would eagerly bring up the subject of his marriage, and he would draw a mask over it by expressing his indifference. To his great amusement, his mother had the unique knack of cursing a ruin and blessing his life as a householder in the same breath. Ghamandi felt remorseful at showing his temper to the poor older woman. He tightly wound his muffler around his ears and took out a half-smoked stolen Marco Polo from his pocket and lit it while leisurely looking around. Thinking that proximity to fire might lessen the rigour of intense cold, he waved the cigarette in the air, forming an arc of light. This was Ghamandi's favourite trick, very annoying to his mother. She described it as sinful. At that moment, it was not Ghamandi's intention to draw comfort from the imaginary circle of fire as to express his lingering displeasure at his mother's sweet words.

The wayward glow like a moth circling formed in the air fascinated him. Ghamandi wanted to knock on the door, but he smiled at his foolishness. He knew of many half-witted people who squandered away their precious time in odd places, but when they were required to reach a particular spot on time, they wasted their breath by trying hard to push their bikes or walking at a breathless stride. To savour the thought to the full, Ghamandi took a long puff at his cigarette and moved closer to the drain, running by the side of the door.

In the washerman's yard, the berry tree had bent to one side under the westerly breeze. A thin sliver of the crescent moon looked entangled in its branches. Tonight, his mother must have wrapped her dupatta around her neck and cast some of its fibrous threads towards the first night of the moon. The breeze ruffled through the leaves of the berry tree, and its branches and the sliver of the crescent moon got mishmashed into each other. Ghamandi panicked when his mother flung open the door.

'Ma!' Ghamandi fell back a step. Only a moment ago, he was clenching his teeth.

'Come in,' his mother said in an irritating tone.

'Why don't you come in? What are you afraid of? You think I know nothing about it?'

Ghamandi saw that there were no teeth left in his mother's mouth. It had come to him almost as a discovery, but he kept the thought to himself.

'What's it you know about?' he asked.

'Hm!' His mother shook her head. He saw her swaying her head in the dim candlelight.

'Yes, what about?' she said, teasing him.

Ghamandi realized there was no point in hiding anything from his mother. His mother had been a wife to a drunkard husband for twenty-four years. Whenever Ghamandi's father came home drunk and knocked on the door, his mother instantly knew that he had come dazed with a drink. From the sound of the knock on the door, she could even make out the quantity of liquor that he must have downed. Ghamandi was doing what his father did. Trying to drown his drunken sound in the sound of the westerly breeze, he would try to reach his cot and fall asleep, hoping that the wife would not know about it. There was a tacit understanding between Ghamandi's father and mother over his drinking bouts. Only their eyes did all the talking. Ghamandi's father, when he was drunk, would not utter a single vulgar word, and in return, his mother would refrain from squabbling with him. She would place his food near the head of the cot. Before going to bed, much against her wishes, she would put a bowl of water under his cot and carefully cover it up with a piece of cloth.

As the morning arrived, she would untie a coin knotted at the end of her pallu and fling it toward Ghamandi.

'Go and fetch churned curds,' she would tell him.

Ghamandi would hurry away to the bazaar to buy half-churned curd sweetened with jaggery for his father. While drinking it, his father would laugh and cry by turns and promise to mend his ways but showed no intention of giving up the heavenly pleasure of the bottle. Hearing this from his mother's mouth for the umpteenth time, Ghamandi gave a sarcastic laugh. 'Ma, how good you are, Ma!' he said.

His head reeled. In the westerly breeze, the liquor seemed to have become more potent. The glowing moth of the cigarette smoke seemed to have spent up to its phosphorous. Throwing away the cigarette, Ghamandi caught the edge of his mother's dupatta and said, 'Other people's mothers are also their spouses, but you're just a mother to me.' They giggled together at this idiotic remark.

The boy was harbouring a very different image of a wife in his mind. He thought a wife was a woman who greeted her husband with shoe-beating when he came home late in the night, fully drunk. He had a living example of this in the wife of the rolling mill's mechanic to whom Ghamandi was apprenticed. This saga of shoe-beating at the hands of his wife came within Ghamandi's hearing with regular frequency. For that matter, even a mother would not spare a wayward son for such disreputable behaviour. But Ghamandi's mother was made of different mettle. She was a birth mother to Ghamandi. All her son's sins sank into oblivion in her vast and fathomless heart. If one were to accept the implication of Ghamandi's idiotic remark, then Ghamandi's mother would have also been a mother to her husband.

Dumping himself on the cot, Ghamandi took off his rubber shoes, which froze in the winter and were blazing hot in summer. But he was proud of these shoes. Without them, he would be called a poor man. As was his daily practice, after taking off his shoes, Ghamandi would place them near the hearth to warm them up.

His mother would curse him. 'May your mother die, what indiscretion! May your grave swallow you up!'

Shoes near the hearth! What blasphemy! With the shoes still resting near the hearth, the Hindu dharma continued to be defiled. At last, Mother would fling the shoes into a corner. Muttering to herself, she would untie a four-anna coin from the end of her dupatta and put it under Ghamandi's pillow. After placing a bowl of water under his cot, she would get lost within the bowels of her bed.

How nice! The gladdening thought crossed her mind again and again. So Ghamandi had stopped associating with Banwari and Rasheed. His mother did not object to his drinking or keeping company with people of questionable character. She thought this was the result of her being soft and indulgent to him. But she had her fear all the same and tried to dispel it by putting some snuff to her nostrils and inhaling it vigorously. She knew of only one way of eradicating herself—to riddle her lungs with snuff. But now even snuff had stopped working on her. By being soft she had even subdued her husband and smoothened out all the angularities of his personality so much that a time came when he could not look straight in his wife's eyes. In the same way, Ghamandi was reluctant to toss around words with his mother.

She was conscious of this and put it to fair use. 'May your mother die, and may Bhagwan make her rot in hell!' But still, she knew of no practical way of curbing her son's evil ways.

Today Ghamandi had once again returned from the workshop at six, although it was his standard practice to come much later and enter the lane when Nathu, the watchman, made his evening call proclaiming that he was now on his nightly beat. Ghamandi would utilize the intervening time by watching some old movies. He would sing songs from Wadia's film Miss Nadia, and for the last two years he had been marveling at how she mysteriously disappeared into her character. His return earlier than usual, put his mother on her guard.

'Son, run up and fetch me some cumin seeds,' she said, wantonly creating some work for him.

'Cumin seeds, Ma?' he said. 'For the curds?'

'You think I want to put them in your hair?' his mother said in a loving tone. She held some money before him. It was a sizeable amount.

'It's for you,' she said. 'To go to the theatre.'

'No, Ma, I won't go to the cinema.' Ghamandi shook his head. 'No more shows for me. They lead me astray.'

The older woman gave Ghamandi a surprised look. Still an immature youth, but how wisely he talked. He may even catch the evil eye for being a wise man beyond his years. Not that she wanted her son to be a boozer. Only a rung or two below the addiction stage so that he did not go to utter dilapidation. For that matter, she did not like his being a self-righteous type either. She had seen intelligent children, and God had sent for them.

Ghamandi took the money from his mother to buy cumin seeds. Going to the door, he looked outside, casting furtive glances on all sides. He took one step and immediately pulled back his leg.

'Chachi is standing outside,' he said, 'and Munshi too!'

'So what?' she said, her knitted brows looking like a trident.

'Yes, there is a reason,' Ghamandi said. 'I refuse to step out as long as they are there.'

His mother tried to reason with him.

'Have you stolen Munshi's necklace that you are afraid of facing him?'

But Ghamandi was adamant. His mother covered her mouth with her dupatta. She did so only when she was faced with a severe predicament and when in total despair. She would also beat her breast to give vent to her feelings.

Before this, Ghamandi never avoided girls who lived in the lane. Instead, he strutted before them like a cock. He would playfully snatch away their children from their laps and walk around carrying them in his arms. The women blessed Ghamandi for this because it enabled them to finish their chores undisturbed. And today, the same Ghamandi was fighting shy of Munshi and Chachi.

Coming back, he spread an old rubber cloth, dating back to his father's time, on the floor and placed a cracked mirror and a small jar of ointment by his side. He stretched out his legs and applied the lotion on some sores. Then looking into the mirror, he squeezed some festering sores and tenderly applied the ointment on them. With her dim eyes, his mother assessed the condition of his sores.

'Oh, your blood has turned foul!' she exclaimed and reeled out the names of many nostrums made from neem leaves and herbs.

The night had reasonably advanced. After attending to his sores, Ghamandi stretched himself out on the rubber cloth and closed his eyes. There was an opportunity for his mother to get into her bed, but she kept sitting on the wicker stool. She knew she would feel more comfortable in her bed, but a pleasant thought kept her glued to her seat. She sat huddled in it. Her old age was like sweet sleep in which, when feeling cold, a person curls up his legs against his chest without pulling up the blanket resting under the feet.

His mother suddenly wanted to say something. She had known the secret of her son's silence. In a state of drowsiness, deep-rooted secrets often rise to the surface. Tightening her fist, she raised it to beat her breast, but her fist remained static in the air. Once again, she was wallowing in a pleasant state of semi-wakefulness where Ghamandi and his father floated before her eyes.

A strong gust of wind flung the door open. Like a whirlwind, the cold wind blew into the room, carrying leaves and wild berries. In the current, scraps of paper went flying into the lane and invaded the space through the open door. A dry leaf came rolling and struck against the threshold. Ghamandi got up to close the door, but the leaf wedged against the entry obstructed his effort.

The wind, sizzling through the wild berry tree and the noise of the crickets, froze his mother's blood. The wick of the clay lamp in the candlestand was dying.

'Won't you lie down, Ma?' Ghamandi asked. His mother shook her head. Lifting her in his arms, Ghamandi laid his mother in her bed and covered her body with a blanket. Little did she realize that if she had kept sitting like that during the night, her body would have gone stiff with cold, and she would not be able to straighten her back, and that would be the end of her.

Ghamandi felt her weightlessness as he lifted her. The older woman found her body tingling with a pleasant sensation as she slipped into the bed, and the soft coziness of the quilt changed the feeling into bliss. There was a time when she had lifted her son. Now he was lifting her. Recalling those happy times, she held a pinch of snuff against her nostrils and inhaled deeply. She had reached a state of bliss where a person wants to make it permanent.

Today, her son had lifted her in his arms and put her in the bed that had the grave's eternal peace, but the bed could never be the grave. A woman is nothing if not a mother. A wife also becomes a mother, and then a daughter becomes a wife and a mother. Every time, it is mother and son. The woman is the mother and the man the son: the mother feeds, and the son benefits. The mother is the creator, and the son the created. At that time, they were mother and son—just mother and son and nothing else in the whole wide world.

The mother was hovering between sleep and wakefulness. She lay there thinking, but the images were distorted, and they sank into a dark abyss. The village had expanded, but the same washermen's lane behind those houses, the same leafy plants and the same wild berry tree, the wind rushing through them. The moonless night had turned opaque like dark kajal in one's eyes and the moonlike glow on her son's face was shattering that darkness. She had mistakenly taken him as dead; her husband was very much alive and was asking for his morning bowl of half-churned curds. He was thirsty. Due to the liquor that he had drunk, his body was going to pieces. But her husband was dead, and to offer something to a dead man was not auspicious. But how could she refuse him? She was a wife and a mother. She snatched away the bowl before her husband could put it to his lips. But why? Because her husband was not dead. He was standing right in front of her. The same lips through which one could see his gold tooth—the same mustache despite being bushy, could not hide his tooth.

There was a knock on the door, jolting Ghamandi's mother. A pall of illusion seemed to have fallen before her eyes.

She kept lying on her bed. Her feet which had gone cold and stiff like wood, had gradually recovered their warmth. Perhaps Ghamandi had rubbed them to restore their warmth. Mother laughed in her imagination. Ghamandi did not want to see her dead. Only if he had a wife. His mother's frail, moth-eaten body, how long would it last? Her snuffbox— where was her snuffbox?

Mother dozed off, but the sound of banging on the door continued. Perhaps Banwari and Rasheed had come to see Ghamandi. The older woman had felt reassured that her son was going to mend his ways at long last. But of late, she had started worrying even more, fearing that his bad company was going to spoil him beyond redemption.

Soon the older woman was awake. She was looking so satisfied and at peace with herself. She had allowed Ghamandi's father to put his lips to the bowl of half-churned curd. He was indeed thirsty. His body was going to pieces, and he was looking at her with eyes full of entreaty. He had managed to take a sip from the bowl, but the older woman wanted to believe that he was not drunk.

She turned to look at her son, who was standing in the door. 'Son, may you be blessed,' she said in a faint voice that he failed to hear. She seemed to have cast a soundless kiss on the wind.

Finding his mother asleep, Ghamandi went out of the house.

'I tell you, I'll not go anywhere else. Only to the cinema.'

'First come out, *salay*!' Rasheed said. 'Are you coming out or not?'

The chirping of crickets was ceaselessly breaking into his mother's mind along with other sounds, although she seemed to be asleep. Ghamandi locked the door from outside and departed with his friends.

His mother suddenly sat up in her bed. Perhaps she had again remembered her husband—and her son, who from his appearance and habits had become his father, although he was still hovering between adolescence and adulthood. But he would soon attain majority and need a wife, his mother thought to herself. A mother's heart. 'I know why Ghamandi has stopped going out on his escapades these days,' she said to herself.

She knew Ghamandi was more sensitive than his father. There could be no greater calamity than reminding him that he was a drunk. And offering him a four-anna coin was like a slap in his face—a soundless slap. To have a row with a husband or a son who came home drunk, or to offer him a four-anna coin, or to place a bowl of water under his cot as drinking causes dehydration—they were all unkind cuts, each one no different from the other. Perhaps these were more heart-chilling than open fights. Maybe that was the reason why Ghamandi's father had not dared to look her in the eye. She was the one responsible for trampling over his ego and reducing him to a cipher. And now she was doing it to her son. She firmly resolved that henceforth she would not tie a four-anna coin in her pallu, to keep it handy to buy curd. Nor would she place a bowl of water under his cot. She would squirm, suffer, eat her heart out but leave her son alone. He should not know that his mother knew everything. Even Ghamandi's father had thought that if she had raised a howl at that time at his misdemeanours, he would have felt bad about it at that time, but in the end, the result would have been good. He would have given up a bad habit in the first place, and if he had persisted with it, his remorse would have taken the bitter edge off it.

Now when she quietly placed a bowl of water under his cot and moved away, putting some snuff in her nostrils, Ghamandi's inebriation would swiftly ebb away. Maybe Ghamandi could not stand his mother's scolding anymore. He gave up boozing and came home on time. His mother decided if Ghamandi came home drunk tonight, she would not utter a single word of rebuke.

Ghamandi returned around eleven and entered the house to the accompaniment of a guest and gusts of wind and swirls of berry leaves. Tonight, the wind was more boisterous than Ghamandi himself. His mother, as was her habit, lay there counting the beams under the roof and singing a long-forgotten dirge to drive her away from sleep. Ghamandi, as he entered, blew on his hands, rubbed them together, and holding the old woman's feet, said, 'Ma!'

Finding her awake, he said, '*Arre*, still awake? Why haven't you gone to sleep, Ma?'

Ghamandi's mother's answer was brief, 'Ghamandi, there's no sleep in these eyes.'

She could not say more. Ghamandi was completely in his senses. He hadn't taken a drop of liquor. But he couldn't help it if his mother had willfully resolved not to grasp the situation?

The trees had shed their autumn leaves. This time the easterly wind did not bring any benediction except a guest.

'Ghamandi,' the old woman said, 'go and change this *chapni*.'

Chapni, the ritual of exchanging cooked dishes among neighbours, was very much in vogue in the neighbourhood. His mother would send a dish of cooked vegetables to Chachi, and in return, she would get cooked meat or some other item of food in the same utensil. This exchange meant a lot of saving, and one was saved the drudgery of cooking an extra dish. This way, one could have a hearty meal consisting of a variety of items.

Ghamandi shook his head, casually tossing aside his mother's request.

'Ma, I'm a grown-up now,' he said. 'I'm not going anywhere.'

'Lo and behold, you bring more trouble for me,' his mother said happily. 'So, you've grown up, have you?'

The guest had gone out at that time. Lying on the oilcloth (a kind of cloth) under the hanging wire food basket, Ghamandi applied the same ointment over his sores. The sores had shown no signs of healing. Fanning with the end of her dupatta, his mother was trying to drive away the flies.

'Your blood has gone bad.' This was a statement of fact. He had inherited blood that was unpolluted, but he had poured acid over it by his actions, and as a result, what was whole had fragmented. Even his body was splintering. Ghamandi looked at his mother with an offending gaze and said, 'Ma, I have too much heat within.'

Millions of questions arose in the mother's mind, but she replied, 'How come?'

Ghamandi got hold of the bed's falling ropes and told her that it was all Rasheed's doing. Crying, he added, 'I'm blameless in this matter.' The mother repeated her question, 'How come?' This enraged Ghamandi. He wanted to hurl abuse at his mother but restrained himself. He wanted his mother to know the cause of his suffering. The mother could not bear to see her son's tears. Disease is a part of life, but no one must have experienced this much bad blood. In her sleepy state, she made her dead husband drink some curd.

In frustration, Ghamandi started to recite the story of rotten fruit. Fifty years ago, the fruit was not allowed to excessively ripe, so that it fell on the ground in an awful state. The mother, who was married at the age of ten, could not understand this. Like those ignorant of human physiology, the human back was nothing but a backbone; for the clueless mother terrible blood was the sign of leprosy and other horrific diseases. These diseases could not be cured with home remedies.

She didn't want to say anything more, although she was still confused. She knew one thing: since Ghamandi's blood had gone bad, he had lost his balance of mind. He was breaking things. If he showed strong reaction to something, he hit the floor with his head.

Mother left for chapni. Chachi gave her a curry dish, she did not accept mother's offering. This rankled the mother. She had been widowed ten years ago, but she had not taken anyone's insult. There was no reason for her to bow down now. She picked up a fight with her sister-in-law, who was equally belligerent in her response, 'I have seen it. Don't be too arrogant. If you had taken care of your son, he would not have wandered in the street looking for other women.'

Mother was right. Ghamandi had nothing to do with chapni. If the sister-in-law wanted to cut off her relations, then she should say it clearly. But Mother could not get things quickly. Ghamandi blames Rasheed and Banwari for his afflictions. Sister-in-law does not want to deal with her, and she is bringing in Ghamandi for nothing.

Other women confronted Mother but she refused to flinch. At her wit's end, she fought with Mushiji, who warned her that Ghamandi would face serious consequences if he was found urinating near his house.

At the end, when her guest made the older woman aware of the whole thing, she beat her head in despair and gave two mighty blows to her son. 'Oh, God, you have brought a bad name to your father and grandfather,' she wailed.

She again fell out with her neighbour, hitting her in her raw spot. 'Don't you remember the days when your sister was having an affair with everyone. She went after everyone, the blind and the one-eyed. And one day came back to her father's house holding her swollen belly.'

Coming home, the old woman cursed Ghamandi. When all doctors failed to cure him, he tried to seek solace in his mother's nostrums. But she would only say, 'May the grave devour you!'

In Ghamandi's eyes, the world had been reduced to a big boil, stretching from north to south and east to west where rivers of pus flowed.

It was night. Lying in her swing, the old woman was whimpering. 'My enemy, where did you pick up this disease? Your whole body is covered with sores. This disease is nothing but hell fire. It is the rich people who indulge in it. It's the largesse of the rich. Does a poor woman like me have the means to extinguish this fire? How can I explain it to the medicine man? I'm your mother, Ghamandi. My neighbours taunt me. They stop me on the way and ask me funny questions.'

Ghamandi was lying near her cot looking the least remorseful. He stared at the ceiling with a deadpan expression. The nails in the ceiling had descended into his eyes, and the chirping of the crickets was driving him crazy. The last gasp of chill in the air had stoked the dying heat of his body. The door was ajar. The berry tree seemed to be whining. The moon tainted with a sulfurous blot on its face in the sky was palely looking down on the world. Ghamandi's bloated stomach, letting out a miasma, had made his eyes misty. His eyelids started becoming heavy. The nails returned to the ceiling where they belonged. The crickets stopped chirping. Ghamandi's sores stopped festering.

The world was asleep, but Ghamandi's mother was still awake. Stuffing her nostrils with a heavy dose of snuff, she inhaled twenty times and rose to her feet.

Picking up the lamp with her right hand, she got closer to her son, dragging her feet, and fondly ran her fingers through his hair. Ghamandi was asleep, but even in his sleep, his mother's affection was giving solace to every fibre of his body. She looked at her son, smiled, and said, 'My son, may God bless you! Son, you have matured into manhood. Let people grow green with jealousy. The flesh of my flesh, may God let me die in your place!'

15

The Tall Girl

At last, when Munni Sohi shot up to five feet eight inches, Grandmother Rukman beat her head in despair. 'Wretch, where will I find a husband for you?' she cried, tugging at the few hairs that remained on her scalp. Wailing, she fell back and sank into her old, sagging cot, like water seeping into the soft earth.

Munni Sohi stood before Granny, speechless. She looked helplessly first at herself and then at Granny Rukman. 'How am I to blame for it?' She seemed to say. Like every growing girl who feels uneasy at the first stirrings of puberty, Munni was ashamed of her ungainly height. There was no reason for it, though. Does a tree ever feel ashamed of itself when it starts to bear fruit?

By the side of Granny's bed was a small walnut table, covered with a colourful tablecloth, knitted by diligent hands. On it lay the Gita, dog-eared and musty, printed in antique type, as if hailing back to the days of the Mahabharata. It was always there, resting on its spine, its pages fluttering in the breeze. Who knew? Granny might depart any moment.

Granny was eighty-two years old. People despaired over her senility, but her hopes grew younger as her years advanced. She wished to live another eighty-two years (if not more), as if she had not savoured life to its fullest. Her dull eyes revolved restlessly in their sockets as if searching for a miracle and her jaws constantly worked as if trying to squeeze more taste from her mouth. Her face was dainty like a leaf fallen from a peepul tree. It was covered with a web of veins, with not a hint of green. The relic of her ancient youth seemed to have got stuck somewhere inside her. When the fit appeared, she would cough wheezily and, puffing out her cheeks, spray a bagful of wind around her. Failing to catch her breath, she would tumble in a heap on the bed, the whites of her eyes disappearing behind their sockets as if they were fixed on the tenth gate of heaven. Escaping the five circles, her life seemed to have entered the sixth one, and her throat would start making a rattling sound. Sheela Bhabhi would come running in her petticoat, her eyes wide with fright at Granny's belaboured breathing.

'*Haaye!*' she would cry. 'Quick! Call someone, call my husband.'

Munni Sohi would burst into the room. 'Father, where are you? We are about to lose Granny!' Then she would fall upon Granny, and cling to her saying, 'Granny, look at me. I'm motherless. Granny, don't leave me behind.'

Sheela Bhabhi would quickly pick up the Gita from the table, and she and Munni Sohi would recite its seventeenth chapter in a hurried, desperate voice. After finishing the chapter, they would look hopefully at Granny, wishing her an easy exit. The presence of death coupled with their fear-stricken intonation would fill the air with eerie vibrations.

'Granny!' Munni would wail as if overwhelmed by the sinister void, and her voice would keep reverberating in the room.

Sheela Bhabhi would run her hand over Granny's cold forehead, idle hands and stiff body. 'Help me remove her from her cot,' she would cry. 'Pity, O God! If she dies without proper rites, who'd bear the penalty for it? Who'll give money to the priests? The railway fare alone to Hardwar costs seventeen rupees and nine annas!'

They would drag Granny down from the bed like a cover being pulled off the pillow for washing and leave her resting on the floor. Then Munni Sohi would rush into the kitchen and return with a lamp made of flour dough and its wick dipped in ghee. She wildly struck matches, one after another, until one of them lit the wick, and she held the lamp before Granny's eyes to brighten her way to heaven in the midst of eternal darkness. Then placing the lamp on her outstretched palm, she stood aside, intoning *Hari Om! Hari Om!* along with Sheela Bhabhi, and then both recited the sacred Gayatri Mantra: *'Om Bhuur Bhuva Swaaha . . .'*

Certain that Granny's life was extinct, Sheela Bhabhi stood above her, forcing tears from her eyes. But Munni Sohi's grief was genuine; she shed pearls from her eyes. What other support she had except Granny? And now Granny too was gone, leaving her derelict and forlorn. Inordinately tall and athletic, who would accept her in marriage? Even if someone did, he would not take long to desert her. The world was like a bottomless ocean, and its other end could not be seen. A motherless girl, which member of her family would care to hold her finger and chaperone her through life?

Not her brother Davendra, anyway, who lived only for himself. She had heard that he was having an affair with a nurse at the TB Hospital, a few streets away, and was missing from home most nights. When he came, which was not often, he reeked liquor and the nurse's body odours. He believed that he could tolerate the level of his drink. He would walk with an exaggerated swagger to prove the point, but that gave away the game. A man is a man, not a peacock. He should not try to strut like one. He would neither smile nor frown but put on a fixed stare.

At last, Sheela Bhabhi would have a terrible row with him and go at him hammer and tongs. While he tried to push her to the water storage, she would pick up a bell-metal pot, the heaviest of the kitchen utensils, and try to break it over his head. In reply, he would pummel her with masterly blows. Not to be outdone, she would, in the end, crush him, scratch his face or plunge her teeth into his arm. To look at them, it would appear that the natural conjugal relations between husband and wife were confined to the endearing give-and-take of powerful blows.

Not satisfied with the encounter, they would send the utensils crashing into the street. This was a signal for the neighbours to step into the house and intercede. Big and small, they swarmed over the house, pontificated and mouthed big sermons—all of which brought about another round of fighting to its conclusion. Does one roll up one's sleeves to patch up a quarrel? They came just to prolong the fight and watch the fun. In the beginning, when Sheela Bhabhi was a novice at the game, she quickly threw down the gauntlet and hid inside for fear of being seen in her torn clothes. But a day came when she stood defiantly naked, her hands on her bare hips. Hey Ram! God provides one covering to the woman and the man another. If one must live among men, one must perforce protect oneself as men do. But Bhabhi would stand among men in God's attire!

And then there was the father. When he served as Deputy Superintendent of Police, he was a terror in the family. A slight lapse and he came down upon them like a ton of bricks. A slight delay in turning on the lights as night fell, and you had it. A little more salt in the food than what was to his liking had consequences. The plates, bowl, et cetera went flying like a hunting weapon. This act was accompanied by choicest swear words, the likes of which even the violent troublemakers in the bazaar would not choose to deliver.

Then his wife died, and the world seemed to have crashed around him. He was so overcast with gloom that they feared that he might die too. He would leave early in the morning for the canal banks where he spent the day with a phony Mahatma, listening to him recite couplets of Sant Tulsidas. Either the Mahatma garbled his interpretations, or the father read his meanings into the verses: his gloom gradually deepened. He stole into the house late at night and sometimes went to his bed without eating his dinner. No one dared to question his ways. They were afraid that if he took it into his head to turn a sannyasi, the family would be deprived of the benefit of his pension. As it was, Davendra's cycle business had already folded up. Because of his scandal with the nurse, the cycle company had terminated his agency.

Suddenly Granny stirred. Sheela Bhabhi felt her forehead. 'She's alive!' she cried in despair.

As if galvanized, Munni Sohi rushed forward in ungainly strides and put her hand on Granny's forehead. Compared to the warmth of her youthful blood, Granny's forehead was cold, but it still had a faint touch of warmth. Munni's hopes revived, Sheela's hopes faded.

'Sheela Bhabhi, let's put Granny back on the cot!' Munni cried. 'Quick! She's alive.'

'I can't, I can't,' Sheela Bhabhi snorted. 'I can't lift this log of damp wood.'

Munni lifted Granny in her lengthy, powerful arms and deposited her on the cot. Soon Granny regained her power of speech.

'Munni!' she mumbled.

'Yes, Granny.' Munni looked at her with a new surge of hope. It seemed that they had switched places; Munni had become Granny, and Granny was the new Munni. Walking towards each other, they stood at a point where Munni had taken up Granny's place. Young or old, the maternal instinct never dies in a woman. She lives in the filth of her children and dies in it. And when she is dead, men casually dismiss her by saying that her time was up.

'Did you call me?' Granny asked Munni.

'No, Granny, I didn't call you.'

Granny raised a warning finger at Munni. 'Girl don't forget,' she said. 'I gave birth to your father and then . . . Are you trying to be clever with me? I know your cunning intelligence. They say women know 404 stratagems. But you go one better. You know 405.'

This loving reproof had brought Munni closer to Granny, 'Believe me, Granny . . .' Then Munni's face suddenly brightened. Oh yes, she must have called out for Granny when she was teetering between hope and despair. Maybe her voice had penetrated through the celestial spheres and brought Granny back to this world, where she had left many tasks unfinished.

'Yes, Granny, I called you back,' Munni replied wholeheartedly. 'You're the only one who cares for me.'

Women of the neighbourhood came to enquire after Granny's health. Sheela Bhabhi stood there for a while, listening to the 'love talk' between Granny and her granddaughter and then curling up her nose and knitting her eyebrows she made for the kitchen.

Granny tried to sit up in bed. Old age can bear everything except its weight. The weight is not of the body but the heart. On the verge of death only a short while ago, she brushed aside Munni's helping hand.

'Gullu's mummy,' she said, 'this girl is my arch enemy if there's one.'

'What makes you say so, Granny?' Gullu's mother bent closer to Granny.

'I was going away for good,' Granny replied. 'But this wretch blocked my way.'

The loving taunt dried up Munni's tears. But Granny was still living those visions which she had seen in the moments of her very short death.

'Jamuna,' she turned to one of the other visitors. 'It was a beautiful garden. There were lush green creepers all around, laden with flowers. And what lovely flowers! Refulgent like the divine light itself. Rishis sat under the creepers, some singing, others meditating.'

Gullu's mother Jamuna and Munni were listening to Granny in rapt attention. Granny's voice floated from a low drawl to an animated voice later.

'The place was resplendent as if a thousand suns were shining upon it' she said. 'But there was no trace of heat. Only a strange coolness where even a stony heart would turn rich with a profusion of blossoms. There was only one flame which kept leaping towards me.'

'Flame? What kind of flame, Granny?' Granny looked at Munni. 'This barren girl's sound, what else?'

'But Mother, a sound consists of words, not flames.'

'You're a fool!' Granny was annoyed. 'Don't you know that in the eternal world, there's no distinction between light and sound? They are the same.'

There was no stopping Granny. Like a fully wound-up mechanical toy, she went on and on, making amends for past silences. And then to have an eager audience like Jamuna and Gullu's mother—she couldn't have asked for more. They had elevated her to the pedestal of a goddess.

'By any chance did you happen to meet Grandfather in heaven?' Munni of the 405 cunnings asked.

A hint of greenery suddenly surged through the withered and fallen leaf.

'Of course, I met him, Munni.' Like a newly wed, Granny spoke in a bashful voice. The talk had taken a new turn. The women nudged each other.

'Did he speak to you?' Munni asked.

'Yes, he asked me for lassi made of *peda*.'

'But Granny don't they have peda in heaven?' Munni looked at Gullu's mother, hinting that she had finally trapped Granny.

'No, neither pedas nor sour *kadhi*,' Granny snapped back. She was very fond of sour kadhi.

'Then what good is heaven?' Munni said. 'Why go there at all?'

'That's what I want to know, too,' Granny said, turning her innocent face on her audience.

'Tomorrow, you must invite the priest and regale him with peda. Let him have them to his fill. Invite Pandit Ralliaram also.'

Jamuna and the other woman suppressed their laughter. But Granny took no notice of them and continued, 'He just came up and stood before me on the threshold of a temple, studded with diamonds and rubies. Young and strong. Broad chest. A glowing face, big mustache, thick and jet black.'

'Black, did you say?' Munni asked. 'Was his mustache still black?'

Granny pouted her loosely hanging lips, and a faint smile rippled across her hollow cheeks. 'Stupid girl, don't you know?' she said. 'Death has no sway over heaven. No one grows old. I saw a girl standing with your grandpa—a gorgeous girl!'

'How do you talk, Granny?' Munni said. 'You mean Grandpa in heaven also?'

'Why don't you ask me who that girl was?' Granny cut Munni short.

'Who was she?'

'It was me—me when I came to this house as a bride.'

The women rolled with laughter, but Granny went on, unmindful of it.

'You know, he caught hold of my hand,' Granny continued. 'He said, "I can't do without you," but I jerked away his hand. "Jagan's father," I said, "I can't come to you just now. I've still had many things to attend to in the world. You must wait for me."'

Tears rolled down like a stream over Granny's withered, leathery face. The women became quiet. Granny's one hand suddenly fell on the Gita lying on the table and holding the end of her sari with the other, she wiped away her tears and then focused her eyes on Munni.

'Oh Munni!' she wailed. 'Will any man ever accept you?'

Retired Deputy Superintendent Jagannath Tyagi's house, known as Deputy Bhawan, attracted all young and older people, dark and fair. But to everyone's annoyance, they all fell short of Munni's complexion and her height.

Not only was she tall; Munni was hefty and loose-limbed too. The warm blood pulsating through her youthful body had turned her complexion coppery, and she looked like a *yakshi*, the female earth spirit, formed by the deft hands of the sculptors of Konarak.

While on the street, she walked a step ahead of herself. 'Watch out, here I come!' she seemed to convey. 'Get out of my way.' And people would hastily step aside to let her pass.

All girls of the Tyagi family were like her—tall and stately. And the men, stunted, mean-looking and devoid of personality. Grandfather was the first man in many generations who had broken the pattern by marrying a short-statured girl and that was Munni's grandmother. Munni's mother was of medium height, and Davendra's wife Sheela almost a dwarf in comparison. Grandfather had hoped that in coming generations the height of the boys and girls would average out. But Munni had belied the expectations of the family. She had now shot up to five feet and nine inches.

Many summers came. Then autumns followed by winters and springs. The kachnar (orchid) tree in the front yard of Shahid Mian's house revealed many coats of green and grey and then cast them off. The wooden projection in front of Deputy Bhawan became furrowed with age, and the rains beat down on its top, season after season, covering it with moss. Everything changed. But not Munni. She was still in the house as if she had been born to stay there forever.

That was one of the hottest summers. Jamuna's two cows stopped yielding any milk. It seemed everything had dried up. Because Gullu's mother had gone to the hills, her house in its desertion and no one to take care of it or clean it gave the appearance of a nursery for the owls. The earth was emitting so much heat that it rose upwards and got into people's brains, and it covered the sky, but these clouds made up of empty fumes drifted away, just like someone coming to the garden to linger for a while. Everything was covered with a layer of grime, including people's thought processes. The dry earth was leaping towards the sky and the sky was vaulting over the earth and this tension revealed an inner conflict among the forces of nature.

Even Apa Firdaus, Shahid Miyan's sister, who her husband deserted, was claimed by him after two years' patient wait. The husband apologized profusely and promised never to misbehave in the future. He even brought with him the qazi who had initially performed the Nikah ceremony. While bidding farewell to Apa, Munni wept so much that containers could have been filled with her tears.

'Don't cry,' Apa hugged her. She assured Munni of an early visit. Allah willing, I'll come to attend your wedding.

'Then you'll wait in vain,' Munni gave Apa a sad look. 'That day will never come.'

'Does one ever cry so much on parting with a friend?' Trambika Bai, a woman of the Digambar Jain family, said. While Munni gulped down her sorrowful tears, Granny transformed her blood into watery tears. Sheela Bhabhi was fed up with her. More so because Granny often wetted her bed. But it was Munni who washed the sheets. Sheela would go into her room, covering her nose with a thick handkerchief. As usual, Davendra was annoyed with his wife.

'Do you want to pack off Granny for good?' he barked at her.

'Yes,' Sheela snapped back.

'Then do one thing.'

'What?'

'Marry off Munni.'

'I say good riddance to both Granny and her granddaughter,' Sheela Bhabhi sputtered with rage.

'They have completely worn me out. Do you know, yesterday that darling sister of yours was looking at a pair of sandals with high heels? Let her wear them. Let her head make a hole in the sky and disappear forever.'

Davendra was in no mood for another fight, but Sheela was not willing to stop.

'Not that I'm concerned in any way,' she said. 'It's not for me to find Yamraj to carry them off.'

Davendra caught the hint. He was entrusted to find Yamraj for Munni Sohi. But being a shirker, he never came to grips with the family's problems. He just let matters drift, hoping that they would sort themselves out sooner or later. Like his father, Jagannath, he also took refuge behind the shastras. Didn't the holy books admonish humans to leave the results to God?

From the veranda, Davendra moved into the courtyard. The sky was overcast with rain-laden clouds. As the first drop of rain fell, he found his childhood friend, Gautam, standing at the door. Gautam had a cycle agency in Calcutta and had come to fix up a subagency in Dimapur.

Though only five feet two, he was stockily built and resourceful and seemed to have ripe, red tomatoes hidden behind his cheeks. He would break into a jig on the slightest pretext as if he did not know how to keep his energy on a leash. Davendra asked him to stay for tea.

Sheela Bhabhi had heard a lot about Gautam, although she had never set her eyes upon him. Davendra whispered something in her ear.

While making tea, she made just one mistake. She warned Munni not to peep into the sitting room.

'Why?' Munni asked. 'Has he come? I mean Bhaiyya's friend.'

'Yes.'

But for Sheela's warning, nothing would have gone wrong. Munni was eager to know what was going on in the sitting room. As soon as Sheela left the kitchen, Munni made to the mezzanine from where a skylight opened into the sitting room.

As Sheela came into the sitting room, carrying the tea-tray that contained besides tea some salty snack, Davendra jumped up.

'Wait, I'll get some peda for you.'

'There's no need for them, really.' Gautam barred his way.

'I'll be back in a minute,' Davendra insisted. 'I know you are fond of peda.' Before Gautam could stop him, he was gone.

Munni's eyes were glued to the skylight. Gautam was gaily chatting with Sheela Bhabhi and cracking jokes with her, which though within the bounds of decency just fell short of obscenity. He took liberty with his friend's wife, calling her Bhabhi as if the bhabhi–devar informal and sexually suggestive relationship existed between two of them.

'Bhabhi,' Gautam said. 'You must bear Davendra a son. And be quick about it. Otherwise, he'll go for a second wife.'

Davendra had not yet returned. Sheela filled a cup with tea and forwarded the snack towards Gautum, while saying laughingly, 'Yes, I know. Once he had dropped a hint.'

'What did he say?'

'He said if I did not produce some result by the next Baisakhi, he would take another woman.' Sheela intentionally turned her face around as if she was going to cry.

'Did he say that?' Gautam leapt up from his chair and his hands went to his sleeves. Then he found that Bhabhi was laughing.

'Oh, Bhabhi, you took my breath away,' Gautam heaved a sigh of relief and sank down on the cot which served the purpose of a sofa. Bhabhi had indeed fooled him. He had really taken her seriously while she was joking. Holding the cup of tea, Gautam edged closer to Sheela and brought his mouth near her ear. 'I'm not joking. Davendra Bhaiyya is having an affair with a nurse,' he whispered.

A flame of anger leapt in Sheela's heart. Her ego was hurt. She wanted to hit Gautam hard.

'Yes, he can keep another woman.' Her nostrils flared. 'He's a man. He can do it. Only a man can have a mistress, not a mouse like you.'

Davendra came in with the sweets and looked at Gautam, who was wiping his forehead with his handkerchief.

Searching for Munni, when Granny came to the mezzanine, she found her lying on the floor as if she had fainted. Granny beat her head and shrieked for help. Sheela came running, followed by Gullu's mother. They pushed a spoon between her teeth and forced open her locked jaws. They pressed her hands and massaged her body. The situation was however saved. Gautam had departed by then.

Some said Munni had slipped on the rough floor, others that she was under a spell. But in their hearts, they knew the reason. When Munni recovered, she felt abashed at her condition, and hiding her head in Granny's lap, she broke into tears.

By the evening, Munni was well again, and the house had fallen into its routine. By mistake, Sheela Bhabhi had added salt a second time in dal and vegetable curry cooked for father. What would he say? A man of volatile temper, he might fling the food into the courtyard.

When father came, Munni served him the food with trembling hands, and he sat down to eat. Sheela's eyes were riveted to his face. Father took a bite, rolled the food on his tongue, and then swallowed it quickly as if it was dessert.

'Father, I'm sorry,' Sheela said. 'By mistake, I put too much salt in the curry.'

Father feigned ignorance.

'No child,' he said in a gracious tone. 'The salt is just to my taste.' He ate a few morsels and then pushed away the thali.

'I'm not hungry,' he said. 'The Mahatma gave me two helpings of prasad.'

Tears came to Munni's eyes. She brought a bowl of dal from Jamuna's house, but her father was not interested. Sheela went inside to make his bed.

'You must eat, Father,' Munni insisted.

Father was indeed hungry. He broke a piece of the chapati and dipped it in dal. 'Sheela will feel offended,' he said.

An agreement was reached with Gautam that he would return the next day to meet the girl. Munni, of course, had no illusions about the outcome. Bhabhi Sheela had been so rude to him that if he had any iota of self-respect, he would not step into their house another time. But Sheela's taunt seemed to have worked the other way. It was a challenge to his manhood. He would try to prove that he was a man, not a mouse.

Father was waiting with Granny and Davendra to receive him in the sitting room. They had decked up Munni in elegant but simple clothes and made her sit in a corner. She had strict instructions not to get up in his presence, or the game would be over.

Gautam came wearing a stiffly starched turban, rising a foot high over his head, like a plume, making him look taller than he was. As he stepped in, he cast a swift glance towards Munni and saw her sitting in a corner, her eyes fixed on the floor. She was feeling jittery, and her hands had gone limp with fear.

But Gautam was feeling quite at home. He reeled off a few inanities and cast another glance at Munni.

'Davendra Bhaiyya, do you ever drink water?' He put on a smile as if he had made a big joke.

'Why water?' Davendra said with enthusiasm. 'We'll serve you sherbet.' And he called Sheela.

Accustomed to doing chores, Munni tried to get up. Granny forced her hand on her. 'Keep sitting. Where are you going?' she commanded. Munni, who had only half risen, quickly sank back. But even then, she looked double her size.

That evening they distributed sweets among the neighbours. They were deluged with a spate of congratulations. Gautam had approved of Munni.

Everyone believed that Munni Sohi was finally getting married, but Granny Rukmani doubted it. 'I will believe it when this purest of the pure would depart from the threshold of the Deputy Bhawan, sitting in a *doli*, while sprinkling a handful of rice from over her head.' She was imagining things that go wrong in a wedding. 'Look Bahu, even if Gautum's father throws junked coins over the doli, treat them as gold coins.' She was afraid that her fears would come out true and something would go wrong. She promised a new set of clothes for the family deity if all went well. To that promise was added a cauldron of halwa for the shrine of saint Buddhan Shah. She went to the priest, taking Shahid Mian's mother along with her to act as a go-between, to make sure that her wishes were fulfilled.

Women, those seasoned in the wedding game and the novices alike, were lavish with their advice as to how a woman should keep her husband under her thumb. Granny, whose husband had departed fifty years back and whose memory was as faded as her eyes, was foremost among them. 'Look, Daughter,' she said, 'I'll be by your side and yet not by your side, for a widow must not cast her evil shadow upon a bride. This is how things have always been, and this is what the shastras require, for they can never be wrong.'

She heaved a deep sigh of relief and wiped away a tear from her eye. 'Listen, when he goes around the sacred fire with you, you must stoop low—as low as you can. Otherwise, everything will come to naught in a second. Look, I'll show you how to do it.'

She placed her son Jagan's turban over her head and held a wooden washing rod in one hand in place of a sword. Posing as a bridegroom she walked stiffly with an exaggerated swagger, asking Munni to follow in step behind her.

She turned to look back at Munni. She was not walking stooped down.

'Wretch!' Granny admonished her how a woman must learn to bend before her man. 'If she doesn't do so, the world will come to a stop. One who learns to bend rises high in the end.' Granny didn't realize that this smart girl would learn not only to bend but how to crawl before her husband, if the circumstances so required.

Suddenly, the Shyam Gali discovered a whole crop of young girls. They were not born yesterday. They were there all this time. No one noticed them before, but as soon as the wedding was announced they started to appear like flies in the mango season. Someone was trying her hand on the dholak, and another one was practicing her singing. They talked about the groom and how to cheat him with their tricks. During the wedding itself, the girls thought, they had the freedom to do things that were taboo otherwise. These make-believe sisters-in-laws would act like apsaras, manekas or houris in mythical stories who befouled the vows of abstinence of yogis, peers, and sufis.

This world is a wonderful place. God created human beings and then asked the angels to bow before them. When all the sisters-in-law leave, and there is the wedding night, then the bride is the only one left, sitting alone on the bed, waiting for the farmer to come to plough the virgin land. With a turban on his head, he would often look like Raja Janak. With his plough, which is sharp and forged with high heat, he would dig deep into layers of the soil to produce someone like Sita.

The groom carries a sacred book in one hand, and a goblet in another. He has played and danced with countless *gopis* in the dark pages of human history. He has love as well as fear in his eyes. He thinks that this time he will conquer the beautiful maiden and then he will lose consciousness in the act of loving her. But he doesn't realize that he is a small particle in the flow of life. He is a device through which to create, to bring into life that which is inert. After he has done his part, he is forgotten like a kernel of wheat in storage that has served its purpose. Wish men understood this so they didn't grab women like one obssessed by hunger. If that happened, then a woman would not be required to try to protect her purity and self-respect. And she doesn't have to embellish herself with silver and gold to make herself attractive.

The marriage was only a few days away when they learned that Gautam had given up his bicycle business and taken a forest contract in Assam, about fifty miles from Dimapur. The place was inaccessible, and letters were carried there only once a month by special couriers. Therefore, the marriage was postponed for an indefinite period, which came as a great blow to Granny. A cold sweat broke out on her body which had no relation to the season. Previously, whenever a letter came from Gautum, she called Munni to her side and planted a kiss on her head. But this time she hit her head in desperation.

'You were born at an ominous moment!' she cried. 'You're a curse to the family. Disaster will trail you wherever you go, whether in Assam, Bengal or Bihar. Nay, the whole land will reel under your curse.' Granny feared that Gautam must have seen Munni standing in an unguarded moment and that he was now trying to find an excuse to back out of the marriage.

The Gita was opened forthwith, and its seventeenth chapter recited with all solemnity. The recitation had a magical effect because another letter came from Gautam announcing that the Brahmins, who had studied his horoscope, had declared the twentieth day of May next year as an auspicious day for marriage. The fact was that Gautam was so fascinated by Munni's height and sturdy dimensions that he had fallen head over heels in love with her. The postponement was solely due to extraneous factors and had nothing to do with her person.

Granny's hopes revived. She started counting the days and months, as the widow counts the wooden planks in the ceiling and the widower counts the stars. Then in a fit, she showered abuses on gods and men, water and sky. She had endurance but no gratitude. By then, Munni had shot up to five feet ten. Her story had become the mythic tale in which the storyteller goes on telling the story to the emperor only to save his life. A small sparrow comes out of the hole to steal a grain of wheat. She comes again and again. There was much wheat in the storeroom. There were one too many stars in the sky. The kachnar tree in Shahid Mian's home had millions of shoots and branches. It seemed that marriage, only marriage could stop this turbulent action. Otherwise, one day Munni's height would reach the sky and she would fly away just as Mahamaya did to save herself from Kansa. She turned herself into lightening and leapt toward the sky.

Thinking of the wedding date, Granny mumbled, 'By then Gotu will also add an inch or two to his height.'

'One can never be sure, O mother of mothers,' Jamuna responded.

'For all we know he can shrink too,' Trambika Bai said, nudging Jamuna in the ribs.

'*Arre,*' Granny rebuked Trambika. 'You can't fool me like that. Sonless woman, does a man ever shrink once he has grown? Trambika, I've grown old but I'm still one up on you in terms of wisdom, twenty times out of twenty.'

Gullu's mother did some math. 'If the boy's height remained the same, but the girl gained height equal to two or three fingers, then he would look shrunk. Isn't it?'

Granny didn't know any math. The very thought of Munni gaining height equal to two or three fingers made her blood run cold. It was like a fallen peepul leaf had arisen and joined the other leaves of the tree and was making a hell of a noise and was showering choicest abuses on Trambika and Gullu's mother. 'Let your father shrink, let your brother shrink, let your husband shrink . . .' 'The women gathered those abuses and hid them in the pockets of their clothing and marched to their homes jesting about Granny, and when they reached their homes, the men present in their homes looked shrunk!

Munni Sohi had begun to hate every vein and fibre of her body. The very thought of marriage had become abhorrent to her. Was marriage the be-all and end-all of life? There were so many other ways of achieving salvation in life. Indeed, marriage was not the only one. If you're determined to reach someplace, you have many options. There are roads, and there are many pathways. There is no one ceremonial, decorative road going to a place called 'marriage.' Tired and frustrated, she would lie down to snatch some sleep, only to see bridegrooms galore in her dreams.

One day, Davendra saw a French film *Moulin Rouge!* He was so impressed by an actor's work that he generously abused India for lacking in industrial progress. Even bicycle parts are imported from England. India's make-up artistry was so poor that they can't make a tall person look trim and a small person look tall. He forgot the natural principle that a short person would always stay short. He was so obsessed with the idea that he asked Munni to tie a small rope around her two feet and then learn to walk. 'If you can do this, you will look shorter while you do your sacred rounds with Gautam.'

'If the rope becomes loose . . .' Munni's friend Gauran asked an innocent question.

'Stay quiet,' Davendra admonished her. 'Munni will finally get married, but you . . . two-and-a-half footer. No one will marry you.'

Gauran showed her teeth to Davendra in anger. She cried and then silently approached Munni, 'Munna, can't we do an exchange. I need height. Give me some of yours, and you can take anything from me.'

'If we could do this, then there would be peace in this world. We shall have a new kind of world.'

Meanwhile, Davendra was teaching Munni how to walk and failing.

At last, the wedding day arrived. The wedding party came, and the marriage rites were performed around the sacred fire. Munni stooped low as she walked around the fire, but even then, she looked taller than Gautam. 'Lower, still lower!' Granny kept whispering into her ear.

In place of benedictions, Granny hit Munni's head with a fist. 'Wretch, you'll never find a home unless you keep your head low!' Granny muttered again and again.

Pandits recited mantras and offered their teachings, 'Don't behave like animals. Don't do things that are out of place. Don't produce sick and disabled kids that are not needed.' The sick and disabled who watched the ceremony didn't react because they couldn't grasp Sanskrit's words.

After the marriage ceremony, when Gautam came to the house, he found Munni Sohi sitting inconspicuously in a corner. She had gone stiff with constant sitting as if she was still curled up in her mother's womb, waiting to see the light of day. In the evening, Gautam wanted to go to the cinema with Munni, but Granny put her foot down. Taking a cue from her, Jagannath said, 'Son, we Tyagis are rather conservative in such matters. When you take Munni under your wing you're at liberty to do what you like.' Gautam kept his silence.

The wedding party departed the following morning. Granny had opened a rice bag. Davendra was supposed to lift Munni and put her in the palanquin, but he could not lift her. Munni embraced him, clung to him and they walked together while Granny sprinkled rice over their heads. She must have have emptied a bagful. As the palanquin bearers placed it on their shoulders, Munni's father-in-law showered one paisa coins worth ten rupees that he had drawn from the bank the same day. Children gathered them as they looked like gold coins in the sun's light. Granny was crying and at the same scolding the kids, 'You scoundrels. Let the palanquin leave.' She was afraid of its return.

Davendra, taking the cue from Granny, started hitting the kids, although he was feeling like a child, wanting to pick up a coin or two in his heart.

Sheela Bhabhi, as was expected, shed a few crocodile tears, although in her heart, she was feeling immensely relieved at having washed her hands of a huge responsibility. Granny stood there, her eyes shaded with her hands, watching the receding palanquin. Sheela scowled at Granny. 'It's time for this hag also to depart,' she muttered under her breath and stepped back. Other women, Gullu's mummy, Jamuna,

Trambika shed tears, while they were thinking of their own separations from their family members when they got married.

Davendra looked at Granny, and in that emotionally charged moment, he embraced her and loudly wailed, 'Mother'. Granny clung to him, and she was about to fall; Davendra lifted her and walked towards an imaginary palanquin.

Munni was gone, and along with her the glory of the Shyam Gali and Tayli Mohalla also seemed to have departed.

'Any letter from Munni?' Young and old neighbours would often enquire. It takes a month for a letter from Dimapur. But we are expecting one, any day, said everyone with superficial confidence.

But deep inside, Granny Rukman was worried that Gautam must have quarrelled with Munni and turned her out of his house. For all she knew, Munni might be rotting somewhere in the jungles of Assam, infested with leeches the size of snakes that sucked a man dry of his blood before he knew it. Or a cheetah might have made short work of her. Surely, something was the matter with her, for she was not the one to observe such a long spell of silence.

When a letter came from Munni, she would ask Davendra to read it aloud to her. Then she took it to Shahid Mian, and a third time had it read by a Jain priest. If the letter was long, she suspected that Munni had spun out unnecessary verbiage to gloss over the actual situation. If the letter were brief, she would complain that Munni was hiding something from her.

'Look hadn't I told you? Her husband was sure to disown her!'

She would say. 'Hey Ram! What's in store for this poor girl? I wish I had wings to fly over to Dimapur.'

Oh, no, it was too good to be true. How could a five-foot tall husband put up with a six-foot tall wife? Sooner or later, she was sure to come to a sad end. Granny would close her eyes and start mumbling a prayer.

One evening the religious discourse lasted longer than usual, and Jagannath came home very late. Sheela had gone to sleep. For fear of waking her, he tiptoed into the kitchen and in the darkness searched for the food which was kept covered for him whenever he was late for his meal. He hit his head against a hanging wire basket and started bleeding. But there was no food. Only a glass of water was lying in the alcove. He blessed God for it and drank the water in quick gulps. He had gone without food since morning, for he had remained too busy listening to religious discourses. Although the shastras required humans to respect and care for the body (it being the abode of God), Jagannath had lost interest in mundane things, and nothing ever brought a smile to his face. He believed that he was meditating upon God, whereas God thought he was in love with humans, especially his departed wife, whom he often beat because he was so much in love with her.

The water hit Jagannath on an empty stomach and, although he was in pain, he went into his room and sat down to meditate.

'Son!' he heard Granny calling him. He turned his face in the direction from which the sound had come. 'Son, have you eaten your meal?'

'Yes, Mother, to the fill. Now I'm so busy digesting it that even my sleep has vanished.'

'Would you like me to get you some digestive supplement? May I wake up Sheela?'

'No, Mother, I can do without medicine.'

Soon Jagannath fell into a deep slumber from which he never woke up.

In the morning the house was in an uproar. Sheela wailed the loudest. She was feeling guilty at having sent her father-in-law on his last journey on a hungry stomach. She had not realized that he would take her neglect so much to heart. What heavy punishment for such a small lapse! Above all, to the family's utter loss, his pension would also stop. And the one person whom Sheela wished to see dead was still alive.

Granny was heartbroken.

'Jagan, my son,' she wailed. 'How cruel that you're going to ride your last journey over my shoulders!' When they lifted his bier, she fainted.

Someone who listened to Granny's words whispered in Shahid's ears, 'What a memorable statement. If you write it down, people will go crazy reading it and shedding tears.'

Sheela hoped that Jagannath's death would be a cue for Granny to depart. She lay in a stupor for many days, like a dead weight on Sheela, who had to attend upon her just to show-off to her husband. At last, she arranged a recitation of the Gita to hasten Granny's exit, but the older woman still lingered. Perhaps, she had reached a stage where one becomes immune to Gita's recitations.

The first question Granny asked on regaining consciousness was whether there had been any letter from Munni. She had her misgivings. Davendra assured her that there was no reason for any concern.

Munni Sohi learnt about her father's death a month and a half after the event. By then, his ashes had been consigned to the Ganges. There was no point in hurrying down from

Dimapur and infesting the house with the leeches of Assam. But when months passed, and still Munni did not come, Granny growled, 'How can a dead person come? Her husband must have strangled her to death in the jungles of Assam!' In her heart, Granny was convinced that a mismatched couple never came to any good.

The rains were over, washing the sky clean of all particles of dust. The kachnar tree, being in the shade of the house in front, had escaped the ravages of the sun. Its buds had opened to receive the season's showers' benediction, and the tree stood resplendent in all its purple glory. One branch had invaded the opposite house window, where a new bride, who had recently come from Lucknow, stood framed in the windows, looking like a ladybird in her red velvet clothes.

Shahid Mian's sister, Firdaus, had returned home. She had not attended Munni's marriage, which had driven her family crazy with her persistent enquiries about Munni. She was sitting with Granny when Gauran came in running. 'Granny, Munni has come!' she cried.

The news of Munni's unexpected arrival created a stir. Everyone ran out to meet her. Munni got down from the tonga—all six feet of her hulking body. Gautam looked like a dwarf beside her. As she came to the door, a heavy hand fell upon her head.

'Bend low, wretch!'

Munni turned around to look. Granny was standing on the threshold, her body quivering with joy.

'Granny!' Munni cried and clung to her. But Granny didn't seem to hear her. 'Where's Gautam?' she asked. 'Has he come?'

The family had accepted Gautam as one of its own. Granny laughed and joked with him and never alluded to his height. Munni was seven months pregnant. After a few days' stay, Gautam touched Granny's feet and departed, leaving Munni behind for her delivery.

Granny's illness returned. This time she seemed to be dying of a surfeit of happiness. One night at about two, she had a paroxysm of coughing and failed to catch her breath. Sheela and Munni ran to her bedside in panic. Sheela thought that her end had come. With Gauran's help, she removed Granny from her bed and laid her down on the floor. A lamp was lighted, and then they started reciting the seventeenth chapter of the Gita, dedicating the fruit to God on Granny's behalf. But Granny was still alive. Her face was lit with a divine smile. Suddenly, it became animated like a naughty child's, and she looked to her right where Munni was sitting. She had put the Gita back on the table and was tensely waiting for Granny's life to fly away.

'Munni!' Granny said in a weak, faltering voice. Munni brought her ear close to her mouth.

Granny mumbled something in her ear in a faint voice. Munni's face reddened and she hurriedly stepped back.

'What did Granny tell you?' Gauran asked.

'Nothing!' Munni's face was still reddish with shame.

At last, when Gauran persisted, Munni looked bashfully at her and said, 'Granny asked me, "*Hey* Munni, how does he make love to you?"' They looked at Granny, startled. She was still smiling.

After this, the whole atmosphere was charged with magical energy, and the pages of the Gita, kept on a small table nearby, started to flutter. And while quivering, they stopped at a page that is generally reserved for THE END.